AF411815

Red Planet Blues

Red Planet Blues

Kerry Lou

Mothership Press

Manufactured in the United States of America

Library of Congress Catalog Card Number: 98-65198

ISBN: 0-9662604-0-6

Cover art: Kerry Stiles

Cover design: Pearl & Associates

Produced in association with Tabby House

The following terms, found in the book, are acknowledged as registered trademarks or copyrights: Beanie Babies, Neet, CNN, Prize Patrol, Mustang, Magic Kingdom, Xerox, Barbie, Budweiser, Bacardí, "Star Trek," Frederick's of Hollywood, Toyota, Memorex, Impala, "X-Files," *Rolling Stone*, McDonald's, Tampax, Zorro, Vegematic, Thorazine, Victoria's Secret, Epcot, Kmart, Technicolor, Camero, Dom Perignon, Disney and Zippo

Mothership Press
3310 Dartmouth Lane
Sarasota, FL 34239

Dedication

to Fran

Earth Angel

Contents

1

Blown to Smithereens

Moonrise over the Superstition Mountains was unusually spectacular that fateful evening. The crimson lunar orb, peeking over the distant crags, made the desert landscape resemble an alien galaxy. Amber saw the red light reflected in her car's hubcap, but was more concerned about the flat tire surrounding it. Still standing in stunned disbelief, her mind racing for a solution to this unexpected predicament, she failed to notice the otherworldly quality of the sky. Even if she had looked up at the moonglow turning her auburn curls to soft flame, it could never have prepared her for the radical change that was about to explode in her life.

"Damn yuppie clothes, too," she muttered, looking down at her powder blue suit with the tight skirt. "Not that it matters, since the spare is flat." She felt like kicking the tire with the toe of her powder blue high-heel, but that would only compound the stupidity of driving around for more than two months with the crippled spare in her trunk.

Amber sighed and scanned the parking lot of Superstition Press, the huge concrete-and-glass building that she had just exited. The asphalt expanse was deserted except for three scattered cars; most everyone had left by four-thirty, and now it was almost eight.

A white pickup truck pulled in from the street entrance on the other side of the parking lot. "Hey, maybe this is our knight in shining armor," she said, patting her Toyota's fender. "On a white charger, too."

The pickup slowed and came directly toward her; it looked brand-new—shiny and flawlessly clean. As it rolled to a stop, Amber could clearly see by the glare of the streetlights that she had never met the man with the long ponytail who now leaned out the window and grinned.

"Hi. I saw your flat when I went out for dinner break; wondered who was going to get that surprise," he said cheerfully.

"Dinner break?" she echoed. "What do you do, live here?" Suddenly, fixing the car was not the only thing interesting her.

"Practically. I'm the new systems manager, so I've been hanging around at night, reading manuals and getting familiar with the setup. It's slightly different than the computers I'm used to working on."

"Well, are you any good at working on tires?" This handsome stranger with his muscular arm draped over the door was beginning to make disaster look like opportunity. His face was classically proportioned—straight nose, strong jaw, piercing blue eyes. And probably ten years younger, Amber reminded herself. *Girl, you have been without a boyfriend too long!*

"Hey, at least give me a challenge," the man said, climbing out of the truck.

For a moment Amber was startled, then realized he was talking about the tire, not reading her thoughts. "Okay, how about the spare's flat, too?"

"That could prove to be more time-consuming," he admitted with a chuckle. "But it's not a problem." Her eyes couldn't help devouring him as he walked toward her in a plain white T-shirt and jeans that fit just right. Suddenly she felt like a teenybopper meeting a blind date.

"I'm Amber Voss," she said, extending her hand. He grasped it and she felt a warm thrill at the touch of his flesh.

"Bradley Robinson," he returned. "But my nickname is Blue."

"Really? That's wild!"

"It is? I thought it was common to base nicknames on eye color."

"See, in my family all the kids have color names," she explained. "First Violet and Rose, then Amber. Even the cat, Emmy, her real name is Emerald. That's because of her eyes, too."

"Invite me to your next family reunion and we'll make a rainbow," he said.

Amber laughed, impressed with his wit. "That might be fun." This guy was just too good to be true! Next she'd find out he already had a wife and six kids. She tried to remember if she'd seen a ring.

"Well, is the spare in the trunk?" he asked, casually raising his left hand and wiggling his bare fingers.

"Oh! Yeah, it is." She whirled and hurried to open it, wondering if he'd really just tapped into her mind or if he'd simply been swatting at a mosquito.

He strode over, hauled out the tire and studied it critically.

"You'd think by the end of the nineties they could come up with a tire that wouldn't go flat," Amber observed.

"Twentieth century technology is pretty primitive when you think about it," he agreed, looking up with another charming smile. "This one's got a nail in it; should be easy to repair."

"So, what are we going to do?"

"Fix your tire and take you home. Not necessarily in that order." As he loaded the spare in the back of the truck, Amber's attention was drawn to his long, thick hair. The strands were various shades of tans, golds and browns, restrained in a cord of black leather; they seemed to move and shimmer on their own like a bundle of snakes. *Who was this guy?*

"I have a friend who owns a garage," Blue continued. "We'll fix it tonight and I'll put it on your car in the morning. In the meantime, I'll drive you home."

Mmm, I'll bet you could.... Out loud she said, "Do you think it'll be safe here?"

"There's a night guard, and I'll be here most of the time, too. It'll be fine."

"Don't you ever sleep?"

"Not much," he answered. "I've got a lot to do. Come on, get in." He indicated the white truck, which stood gleaming like Cinderella's coach.

Amber looked at the height of the truck's step and then down at the tightness of her dress. She'd have to hike it to her waist to climb up there!

Without a word, Blue whisked her up in his arms and lifted her into the seat. "Such impractical clothing," he commented, once again reading her mind.

"You really are carrying this white knight shit to extreme lengths," Amber accused, but she was laughing as she scooted across to the passenger side. "And believe me, I don't dress so impractically all the time. Usually it's impossible to get me out of shorts and a tank top."

"I'm not saying you don't look good in it," he insisted, as he climbed in behind the wheel and fired the engine.

In any logical state of mind, Amber knew she would question the intelligence of hopping in a car with a man she'd known for a few minutes, especially after a comment like that. But instead of panicked, she was pleased by his compliment.

"Where do you live?" he asked, as they approached the parking lot's exit.

"In Tempe, not too far from here. Near the university. You go down Apache Boulevard and then turn on Juniper Street. I'll show you."

"Good. I don't know the town too well yet. It's all new to me."

"Oh, you just got here?" she asked. No wonder she couldn't remember seeing him before.

"Yes. I've only been in Phoenix for ten days. Got transferred out here, so to speak. So far it's pretty amazing...and what do you do at Superstition Press?"

"I'm a freelance graphic artist, so it's not like I'm on their payroll," Amber answered. "I'm just doing some illustrations for one of their books. Actually, right now I'm trying to land a contract. That's why I was there late, working up several different samples for them. It's a nutty book about UFO landings and aliens, but I guess that's mainly the kind of stuff they produce."

"You don't believe in alien life forms?" Blue looked over at her and his ponytail snapped like a switch.

"I believe in the possibility, but what I'm saying is I've never seen a UFO. I'd love to see one! In fact, I'm a little irked that I haven't seen one, living out here in the desert where there's nothing to hide behind. Maybe they just think I'm not ready," she laughed.

"But you do think you're ready to view an extraterrestrial craft?" He looked over, smiling and clearly enjoying their banter.

"Absolutely," Amber affirmed. "Bring them on!"

They were zooming down the interstate now, through vast, flat pastureland that was devoid of buildings and lights.

"Your sisters are named Rose, and Violet," Blue said, amazing her with his recall. "Those are both colors that are also flowers. But your name is a color and also fossilized tree resin."

"Well, that's one way to phrase it," Amber countered, "but it's actually considered a gemstone. They make beautiful jewelry with it."

"Yes, because of its high polish, hardness and translucent quality," he added. "And did you know one of its very interesting properties is its ability to quickly become electrified on application of friction?"

Amber shot him a sidelong glance to see if he was joking, but couldn't detect a smirk.

"Really," he protested, looking over and laughing at her dubious expression. As they rounded a curve the moon again became visible directly ahead, still low on the horizon and gigantic. Blue braked the truck abruptly and turned into a dirt road that bisected the field to their right.

Adrenaline jolted Amber's nervous system. This detour wasn't in the program! Suddenly she felt like a complete idiot for trusting anything when it came to men—especially her own instincts. "Uh, where are we going?" she ventured.

"Not far." Then he seemed to realize he was scaring her. "Oh, Amber, don't be afraid of me. I just want to see the moon." He slowed and stopped the truck, killed the engine and turned off the lights.

Just wanted to see the moon, yeah, that's a good one. While he stared out the windshield, she waited in the dark to see what he would do next.

"It's my first full moon!" he said excitedly. "I mean, since I've been here...I'll be right back!" Before she could protest he was out the door.

The moon flooded the Earth with a surreal radiance, softly illuminating the field, the barbed-wire fence, and the man standing in the road with his arms outstretched to the heavens. Amber's heart rate dropped as she watched him, holding his position as if in an attitude of worship. Maybe he wasn't a rapist after all.

In a few minutes he came back and threw open the car door on her side, pumped as a kid at the circus. "It's so incredible! It's as if I'm viewing it through a telescope, but I'm just out there seeing with my own eyes! Look, you can clearly identify the Sea of Tranquillity, above that the Sea of Serenity, and next to that the Sea of Rains. And see, right below, at the end of the Apennine Mountains, that thing that looks like the scar from a human umbilicus, that's the Copernicus Crater. It's so beautiful!"

Amber could see he was truly in awe. "What, they didn't have the moon where you came from?" This guy had definitely been behind the monitor too long!

"Not like this," he answered. "The sky seems so open and gigantic in Arizona; I'm used to being closed in."

"A city boy, huh?"

"Something like that." He walked around and bounced into the driver's seat. "Sure feels good to be out in the wide-open spaces." He turned neatly and maneuvered them back onto the highway.

"Man! I've never seen anybody freak out so much over the moon," Amber said. "You computer geeks need to get out more often. Looks like the sun hasn't hit that skin in eons!"

"So take me."

"Take you where?"

"Out. You know, like for a date." He glanced over and smiled.

Amber burst out laughing. "Do you get all your dialogue from TV?"

"Most of it," he chuckled.

Amber paused, debating with herself. The systems manager for Superstition Press had to be harmless, even if a bit young and eccentric, and the attraction she felt for him was already beginning to itch.

"Okay," she decided. "I'll take you out and show you the town. It's the least I can do for your rescuing a damsel in distress."

"Saturday night?" he replied quickly.

Amber gawked at him, wondering which one of them was the more aggressive. "Well, amazingly enough, I am free on Saturday."

"Great! Guess the full moon does bring good luck."

They turned on Juniper and Amber gave directions to her house. Blue pulled into her driveway and stopped the truck. "Wait," he ordered.

In a flash he was out of his door and around opening hers.

"I told you not to overdo it," she said, but allowed him to lift her to the ground.

He steadied her on her wobbly shoes, then stepped back to obviously check out her figure. "Women certainly put themselves in crazy footwear," he said. "Though I can understand why a man would admire your contracted gastrocnemius muscles."

Amber had no idea what to make of his strange comments. "Well, thanks," she said lamely. "I mean, for the ride."

"What time should I pick you up in the morning?"

"Oh, that's okay." She rummaged in her purse for her house keys. "I can get one of my friends to drive me."

"I really don't mind," he insisted, "and I have to go there anyway."

He was enthusiastic about her. That showed considerable intelligence. "Pick me up at seven-thirty?" she said.

"Cool!" He broke into a grin but didn't make a move to leave, instead snaring her in his sparkling, cobalt stare. Their eyes drilled into each other for a long moment. "I'll wait to make sure you're safe," he offered at last.

"Oh, okay...thanks again," she stammered, yanking her vision from his face. She strode up the walk, ultra-aware of how her shoes and her tube of a skirt were making her ass twitch. After opening the front door, she turned on the outdoor lights and waved to him. "See you in the morning," she called.

Blue saluted, hopped in the truck, and rolled out of sight.

"What a weirdo," Amber muttered as she locked the door behind her and threw her purse on a chair. That bizarre hair, that pale but beautiful body, and those insane eyes. Nobody has eyes that blue! "What a *fine* weirdo!" she yelled.

Amber kicked off her shoes, crossed the living room to her aquarium, and tapped in some flakes from a tiny cannister. "I gotta call my girlfriends, Oro!" she said to her goldfish.

From the kitchen she could dial and raid the fridge at the same time. She pulled out cheese, tomatoes and a jar of pickles while she listened to the line ring. Krystalee Collins was a childhood buddy from elementary school through high school, before Amber had left Arizona to explore the big, wide world. Then, when she had returned to be near her parents, she and Krystalee had slipped right back into being best friends, even though twenty years had passed. Amber thought of her as a sister in every sense of the word.

She heard the answering machine pick up. "Hi. You've reached 837-1188. Leave a message and be quick about it, okay? Y'all have a nice day."

"Hey, this is Amber, calling to report an all-alarm man alert. Meet me tomorrow after work—that's Friday, for all you informationally impaired—at the Broadway, and I will brief you. Also trying to contact Quinn, so if you see her or talk to her before I do, pass the word. Y'all have a nice day, too. Bye."

Krystalee was single again, after having been married three times, and she liked to go out "celebrating her freedom" often. Amber didn't expect her to return a call on Thursday night.

Next she punched up the number of Quinnsetta Sheppard, and after one ring heard her friend's impatient voice. "Talk to me."

"Hi, it's Amber. What's happening?"

"Oh hi, sugar. I'm just running off to an appointment."

"This late?"

"Honey, in the fast lane they work 'til late and then train." Quinn was a former competitive bodybuilder turned personal trainer. She was paid well to sacrifice her evenings.

"How about tomorrow at five? Can you meet me and Krystal at the Broadway?"

"Yeah, that'll work," Quinn said after consulting her calendar. "What's up? New man?"

"What are you, psychic?" Amber demanded.

Quinn's deep laughter filled her ear. "No, you're just transparent as hell."

"I'm translucent," Amber corrected.

"Yeah, right. Gotta go. See you *mañana*," Quinn said, still laughing, then hung up.

Amber got crackers from the pantry and ate her picnic supper in front of the television, washed down by a stray beer she found in back of the mayonnaise jar. Nothing on the screen was penetrating her consciousness at all; she could only think about the long-dormant desire that this strange, mesmerizing man had fanned to a full blaze. She had always been accused of having an overactive fantasy, and knew to be wary of the urge to give her heart—and her body—before letting her intellect assess the situation. But tonight, alone and safe at home, she allowed her imagination to soar, letting endless possibilities take her down pathways to ecstasy. When she slept her dreams were vivid and erotic; she woke at dawn, full of energy.

After showering and styling her hair as much as the natural curl would allow, Amber made sure to put on a more practical outfit—khaki pants, an olive-green top, and a tropical print overshirt. She sipped coffee and paced by the front window, nervously anticipating the appearance of a Blue man in a white truck.

2

Like a Landslide

When she saw the truck pull up to the curb, Amber rushed to the bathroom for a last swig off the mouthwash bottle. She glanced in the mirror to check her hair and makeup, such as it was; even though she was an artist, she never seemed to get the hang of painting her own face.

Dashing back to the window, she saw him walking up the driveway, this time in a pin-striped shirt and tie to go with his blue jeans. One look told her that last night had not just been idle fantasy. The morning sun sparkling in his crazy hair and bouncing off his alabaster skin let her see him in blinding detail, and she still liked what she saw. This was serious fantasy! With every cell tingling, she went to open the door.

"Good morning! Your chariot awaits," he said, beaming.

Amber tried to resist acting like a perky cheerleader. "Hi. How're you doing?"

"Excellent," he answered. "Ready to go?"

Amber grabbed her purse, locked the house and followed Blue out to his truck. He held the door open for her, but this time she had no trouble climbing in by herself. When he had closed her door and slid into the driver's seat, she said, "You know, opening car doors for women is kind of old-fashioned, in case they didn't teach you that back in the old country where you come from."

"Really?" He sounded truly surprised. "The heroes all do it in the movies."

Amber laughed. "Hey, I'm not complaining! Personally, I'm rather fond of chivalry. I just want to hip you to the fact that you're acting like a dinosaur."

"I don't mind following in the footsteps of the lizard kings," he said, smiling as he buckled his seat belt and started the truck. Then he fell silent as he steered into the flow of morning rush-hour traffic. Amber felt no pressure to make conversation, simply basked in being two feet away from him. There was no denying that, overnight, her attraction to him had already grown more intense.

"How long are you going to be working at Superstition Press?" said Blue, interrupting her thoughts.

"Well, I have a meeting with the big boss this morning. If they like my work, I'll be around for a little while."

"Great! Then what?"

"Then I look for other work," Amber said. "I've got a few irons in the fire, so we'll see what pans out."

"Irons in the fire? Pans?" Blue looked over, wrinkling his brow. "Does it have something to do with cooking?"

"No, Tarzan, I'm talking about art jobs that may or may not materialize," she said, returning his puzzled look. "Man, are you from outer space or just pretending?"

"Oh, I'm really from outer space," he answered, turning into the parking lot of Superstition Press. "But wait til you see how I fixed your flying saucer."

They stopped where Amber's car was parked and she could see that it now rested on four fully inflated tires. "It looks like new," she enthused. "Thanks a ton!"

"I fixed both tires, so you won't have to risk having this happen again."

She stared at him incredulously. "If I can get somebody as sweet as you to help me, I don't care if I break down again."

"Anytime," he replied, eyes sparking.

They walked up to the door together, and Amber was having a hard time ripping her eyes from the strange, handsome hunk beside her. She did not want to wait all the way until tomorrow night to see him again.

"What do you want to do on our date tomorrow?" he asked.

Apparently his mind-reading capacity isn't an illusion. "It may not seem original, but I was thinking about an early movie and a late pizza or something," Amber answered. "Aim for the seven o'clock show."

"Everything around here's pretty original to me; that sounds great. I'll come get you at 6:30."

When they reached the building, Blue held the door for her; then they were standing in the foyer, each unwilling to leave the other.

"Gotta go," she said. "Don't want to be late to my meeting. Listen, thanks again. I really appreciate it."

"My pleasure," he replied, watching her turn and walk down the hall. "Amber!"

She stopped and looked back.

"Come see me before you leave today?" It was more a question than a request. "Second floor, far west corner."

Amber restrained herself from bursting out laughing. This guy was just too much! As if reading a script of her own design, he kept saying and doing exactly the right thing! "Okay, I'll come visit," she assured him. "See you later."

Amber's meeting went perfectly; they liked her sketches and signed her up for the project. She spent the next two hours in the company's archives, going through mountains of UFO reports and drawings. One thing was sure, *something* was going on out there.

As fascinating as the material was, the image of Blue kept breaking through her concentration. Still she kept at her task, wanting to let a proper amount of time expire before she raced up to his office to drool over him again.

At last she looked at her watch and it was two o'clock, time enough to go see him. Her heart thumped at the thought.

"Forty-one going on fourteen," she muttered as she sighed and grabbed a stack of papers. If anybody asked, she was going to the Xerox room. She went up the back stairs to the second floor, which housed the computer mainframe and its many terminals, and wandered down a narrow corridor, lined with doors.

Radio music blared from the open door of Blue's office. His back was to it, hunched over his keyboard, fingers flying.

This is not my imagination, Amber thought as she watched the way his serpentine hair lolled between his broad shoulders. Absorbed in his work, he didn't seem to notice her presence. She sneaked up behind him and slowly stretched out her hand toward his ponytail. Just as she was ready to grab and tug, it whisked out of her fingers as Blue suddenly jerked around in his chair. Amber yelped and jumped back in surprise.

"I'm supposed to be scaring you!" she squeaked.

Blue grinned. "Won't work. I can feel your aura a mile away."

"You can feel my aura?" she repeated.

"Yeah. I can see it, too." He leaned back and observed her; she returned his stare. He had taken off the tie and undone the top button of his shirt; automatically she scanned the row of buttons below and thought about popping them one by one.

"It's extending out about three feet," he continued, "and glowing the most beautiful shade of pink."

Amber could feel her face flushing pink, too.

"Come here," he said, holding out his hands. She floated forward, slipping her hands against his extended palms.

"Close your eyes," he whispered, and she obeyed. Instantly she was aware of a warm tingling filling her hands. Soon it intensified and began moving up her forearms. Then it simultaneously invaded her head and shot down her legs. Within another minute she could feel the energy cascading off the soles of her feet and pouring out the top of her head like a gushing fire hydrant. Astonished, she opened her eyes.

Blue was still sitting in his chair, eyes shut, and a serene Mona Lisa smile played on his lips. Amber stared shamelessly, relishing the liberty of watching him unobserved. His face was smooth and perfect like a white marble statue, and she felt her body-rush intensify as she drank in his features. The pleasurable, buzzing sensation which flowed from his hands had her rooted to the spot, hypnotized, unable and unwilling to move. Trapped like a bug in amber.

Suddenly his eyes flew open. "Quickly electrified," he said in a low, throaty voice. Amber gasped as his words sent another lightning surge through her body. This time it sizzled down her spine and burst into pinwheels of fire between her legs. "What is this?" she hissed, still gripping his hands.

He laughed easily, never breaking eye contact. "No magic power," he assured her. "It's just life-force, my field pouring into yours. And vice versa—now I'm pink, too."

"I don't know, I've never felt a force quite like this in my life," Amber protested. She felt as if she were hanging on to a live wire.

"Well, I am juicing up the frequency a little bit," he admitted. Gently he pulled her toward him; Amber took a step, unable to tear her eyes from his. She had the unmistakable feeling that he was going to try to kiss her, and she was very afraid that she was going to kiss right back.

A voice behind her shocked them out of their trance. "Uh, excuse me...."

Blue dropped Amber's hands and she whirled to see a young man with rumpled hair standing in the doorway. "Sorry to interrupt," he said nervously, "but I need some help with this new formatting sequence. I'm totally clueless...I mean, when you get a minute."

"Come on in," Blue said expansively. "Amber has to go anyway." He turned to her, melting her again with his smile. "But I'll see you tomorrow."

"Thanks again," she said, turning to leave.

"Thank you," he replied, not saying what for.

Amber hurried down the stairs and into the heat of the afternoon, eager to be out of the building and attempt to make some sense of what had just happened.

Her inner dialogue was going off like Roman candles on the fourth of July. *Oh, now you've really gone over the top, Miss Fossilized Tree Sap. Sap is right! Do you really think this young thang has any interest in you, a woman on the cusp of old baghood? Pink auras and blue eyes, indeed!*

Then why was he bothering to shower all this attention on her? Why not just fix her tires to be a good Samaritan and then bolt? And what was with the hand-holding and the "field" that made her body vibrate like lips on a kazoo?

Cheap thrills, said her cynical side.

"Goddamit," she said out loud, as she reached her car and slid inside, "I'm going to nurse this romantic fantasy for at least the next twenty-four hours, so all you cynical thoughts can go to hell. This stuff is too rare; you have to enjoy it while you can." So saying, she put the car in gear and banished the chorus of doubts.

* * *

Amber perched on a stool at the bar of the Broadway Restaurant and waited impatiently for Quinn and Krystalee to show up. She had spent the rest of the afternoon killing time doing laundry and assorted mindless household tasks, imagination racing all the while; now she was anxious to start this important meeting, a reality check with the girls over her new heartthrob.

"Hey, girlfriend," Quinn's voice sang out as she and Krystalee entered the bar. They made a striking pair, the tall, athletic black woman with high cheekbones and queenly demeanor, and the petite southern belle with the chestnut mane, as always, dressed in the latest trendy fashions. The three hugged each other.

"Let's get a table in the corner," suggested Krystalee with her drawl. "We need privacy to dish this dirt." She was known for giggling like an airhead but was quite the brain, working in the geology department at Arizona State as a research scientist. Now that she was single again, she saw a select group of men which she referred to as her "stable," only half-jokingly. She still had a horrendous appetite for males of the species, but her latest vow was to keep her heart safely out of the picture.

Quinn, on the other hand, had been with the same boyfriend for seven years. They still kept separate residences; with the frequent visits of his kids and her erratic work schedule, it was just easier that way. They each got plenty of solitude, and when they were together, they truly appreciated and savored each other. Quinn had a hard time understanding why a woman would give up pieces of herself just to have a man.

"T-G-I-fuckin'-F!" Krystalee declared as she plopped into the thick chair cushions. "It's been a hellacious week." A waitress appeared. "I'd like a draft, and what do y'all want?" After Amber and Quinn both ordered white wine, the burning subject of Blue was addressed.

"So, girlfriend," Quinn boomed. "Who is this man who's got your panties all in a bunch?"

"I don't know!" Amber yelped, laughing. "I swear he dropped from heaven. I mean, he fixed both my flat tires and had the car ready to roll by the time we got there at eight o'clock in the morning!"

"*What*?" Krystalee exploded. "He stayed up all night to fix your car? This dude sounds demented."

"When I asked him about it, he just said he doesn't need much sleep...which must be true because he looked gorgeous as ever this morning," Amber reported.

"Ooh, the girl is hungry!" Quinn cackled.

"Ravenous is more like it," Amber said under her breath as the waitress returned with their drinks.

"Well, hallelujah!" Krystalee raised her mug high. "I thought you had entered the convent a long time ago. Welcome back." She took a hearty swallow.

"It's not that I've been trying to be a puritan, it's just that nobody has even remotely flipped my switch in an eon." Amber sipped her wine. "This guy not only flipped the switch, he about burned out the circuits."

"That's what I'm worried about, sweetheart," Quinn said in a maternal tone. "We know how desperate you get when you get desperate. If you're stuck in the desert, you'll drink piss thinkin' it's champagne."

"Dammit, Quinn," Krystalee barked. "Save the moralizing until after we determine whether she's fucking up or not! I want to hear the juicy details."

"The trouble with you is, you get your idea of morality from Prince songs," Quinn retorted.

Krystalee bristled. "Well, what's wrong with that? Prince is one of the most moral people in the universe! Doesn't drink, doesn't do drugs, totally into God—"

"And sex," sniffed Quinn.

"So? Isn't that a God-given drive?" Krystalee insisted.

"It was until people turned it into a marketing ploy. But you're right, this is Amber's trip. Tell us, what does the mystery man look like?"

"Well, he's...white," Amber began.

"Thank God! Now your parents will approve!" said Quinn. "Go on."

"No, I mean really white! Like from Sweden, some kind of mole, somebody who never goes outside. But I don't know, on him it looks good. And he has the most incredible blue eyes...."

"Sounds like the beginnings of your very own Aryan nation," Quinn commented, rolling her eyes. Her skin was the color of dark chocolate, and she failed to see the appeal of something that looked like it had crawled from under a rock.

"Shut up and let her emote," Krystalee snapped. "I'm getting such a good vicarious thrill."

"And his hair is really weird, too," Amber continued. "It's long and all different colors and it's like it moves, like it's alive...."

"Oh, this is too much, Quinn!" Krystalee hooted. "His hair is alive! Oh my God, girl, you are gone, gone, gone!"

"Stop laughing! This is serious!" Amber protested, but she was laughing, too.

"And his hair is different colors? Like what? Yellow, purple and green?" Krystalee tossed her head back and giggled loudly.

"No! I mean like one minute it'll be brown, and then parts of it are kind of coppery, and when you look closely, the strands kind of dance around each other...." Amber looked up at her two friends. They were staring, wide-eyed, then they both burst out laughing.

"Oh no! I'm dying!" Krystalee was melting down into her chair, shaking with glee. "Quinn, now his hair is not only alive, it's doing dances. Was it the Bump or the Funky Chicken?"

Quinn got her laughter under control. "No, K-lee, this is serious. If only for the simple reason that Ms. My-Career-Is-Everything thinks it's serious. And whether this guy is a magician or a bullshit artist—"

"Or the real thing," Amber interrupted.

"Yeah, well, the jury's still out on that one. How about presenting more evidence?"

Amber told them everything she could think of—their initial meeting, the detour in the pasture to watch the full moon, the strange things he said, and the wild sensations she'd felt when he held her hands in his office this afternoon.

"It was like an electric current," she said, "only not an uncomfortable feeling at all."

"Lust will do that," Krystalee commented. "You should have grabbed him by the ponytail and stuck your tongue down his throat."

"Oh, please!" Quinn wailed, wrinkling her nose.

"Don't think it didn't occur to me," Amber said, and they all laughed.

"So the big date is Saturday? Got an attack plan?" Krystalee asked with a leer.

"Would you two please think with your brains for a minute?" Quinn pleaded. "Don't you know nobody goes to bed on the first date anymore? Sex can get you killed these days!"

"Yeah, but what a way to go," said Krystalee, draining her beer mug.

Amber was too giddy to heed any warnings or advice, no matter how logical and levelheaded. "And get this," she added, lowering her voice. "He's really young."

"Ooh, a sweet young thing!" Krystalee enthused. "How young? Way young?"

"Krystalee, get a grip," Quinn admonished. "Chronological age doesn't matter nearly as much as attitude. Besides, you're a very youthful forty-one, Amber, even though it's slightly undignified to be acting like you're sixteen...so, how young is he?"

Amber paused and sipped the rest of her wine. "Well, I don't know exactly; it's kind of hard to tell..."

"Ten years younger?" Krystalee prompted.

"Maybe..."

"Fifteen years younger?" Krystalee's eyebrows shot up.

"I don't see how that's possible. Systems manager at age twenty-five?"

"Ha! You should see my seven-year-old niece run a computer," Quinn said. "Kids grow up on a keyboard these days. And I hate to point it out, but if he's that young, he's of a different generation than you, my dear."

"Well, I'll just have to ask him on Saturday," Amber declared.

"Okay, but ask him after he takes you for a ride on his magic carpet," Krystalee suggested.

Quinn pointed a manicured index finger at Amber and the muscles jumped in her forearm. "Do *not* listen to Hot Pants over here! When you are with this cat tomorrow, please think with what's between your ears and not what's between your legs."

"Yes, ma'am," Amber promised, smirking.

"That's better. Because I don't want to be sitting here, down the road, listening to you cry over Mister Dancing Hair."

"Okay! Okay!" Amber said as she cracked up.

"And do not say a word, Miss Dick-On-The-Brain," Quinn continued.

Krystalee clapped her hand over her mouth, then lifted it slightly and whispered loudly, "But just in case, put the satin sheets on the bed!"

3

Crush and Burn

Huge, black, slanted eyes stared up at Amber from the bulbous head in her sketch. This was the creature that thousands of people had identified as the being who had kidnapped them, examined them, and then scrambled their memory of the event. Under hypnosis, the victims had all described the same ET, with only slight variations in details—gray skin, giant eyes and a mouth and nose that were barely openings.

Her glance fell to another sketch, beside her on the couch, of an attractive man with long hair and a tight white T-shirt—tighter than the one he had actually worn, but what was wrong with a little artistic license? Amber took a deep breath and sighed. She was never going to get any work done at this rate! Even an outer space invasion couldn't wrench her attention away from her impending rendezvous with Blue.

The phone rang and Amber scrambled to get it before the machine picked up, anxious to be distracted. "Hello?"

"Hi, sweetie," said a familiar voice.

"Hi, Mom. How're you doing?"

"I'm just fine, how are you?"

"Great," Amber sang.

"That's what I heard," her mother replied. "I ran into Krystalee at the grocery store."

"That little big mouth. So what did she say?"

"Well, the wild rumor is that you're in love."

"Oh, right! Mom, we're just having our first date tonight!" Amber protested.

"She said she hadn't seen you this excited about a man since the Jurassic. I just thought he might be something special."

Amber laughed. "Well, he is. At least I think so. I only met him two days ago."

"So where's he from?"

"You know, I never did get that out of him. He said he'd been in Phoenix for ten days, something about being transferred, but he never did say where from."

"In that case it would only be neighborly to show him around." Good old Mom. No dire warnings and worst-case scenarios; she always looked at the positive.

"That's what I figured," Amber agreed. "And I got the illustration job with Superstition Press, which is where he works as the local computer whiz, so I'll be around there at least another week."

"That's wonderful, honey!"

"Yeah, it's a pretty cool assignment. All about alien abductions and UFOs."

"So you can let your imagination run wild."

"Not really," Amber said. "The people that have been hijacked all talk about the same kinds of experiences. It's pretty easy to draw because their descriptions are detailed, and real similar."

"Do they have big, round heads and huge eyes?"

"Yeah! Don't tell me they grabbed you, too!"

"No, but I saw them on TV the other night," Mom reported. "It was a show about a UFO crash back in the forties."

"Must've been the one in Roswell, New Mexico," Amber said. "In 1947. The government denies it ever happened, but lots of the information about it is still classified. I'm learning tons on this assignment."

"Well, I'm very proud of you, honey, keep up the good work. Let me ask your father if he wants to say something." There was a pause, then muffled voices in the background. "He says, in regard to your new boyfriend—"

"He's not my boyfriend, Ma, just my date," Amber corrected.

"'New brooms sweep clean,'" her mother recited. "No editorial comment necessary, I'm just passing that along."

"Thanks a bunch. But I'll keep that in mind," Amber replied, unable to keep from smiling. Her father's homespun maxims were something she had come to cherish.

"Call us on Sunday and let us know how it went."

"Geez, Mom, it's a date, okay? No big deal. But I'll call if there's anything to report."

"Okay, dollbaby, talk to you tomorrow. Have fun; I love you."

"Love you, too. Bye."

Amber hung up, thinking about what her Dad had said. What was the message? New brooms only cleaned well in the beginning, then quickly became old brooms? What if your house was full of dustballs and cobwebs, simply because there had been no broom whatsoever near the premises for ages? Wouldn't any broom, new or otherwise, seem like a gift from the gods?

Amber looked at the clock. "Oh, shit!" she wailed. "It's barely noon and I'm going to go through another trillion of these head trips before I see him again!"

She went back to the couch, pushed the alien face aside and picked up her drawing of the man. Using different shades of colored pencils, she tried to recreate the exotic texture of his hair. Then she picked out cornflower blue and filled in the eyes. *Nope, not luminous enough; should've tried indigo.* She wanted to enhance the mouth, but outlining it in pink wouldn't work. His lips were almost the same white as his face; if anything, they were slightly purplish, as if he'd been snacking on blueberries. Concentrating on recalling his lips made her think about what she wanted to do with them, and butterflies swooped through her stomach. With pleasure she remembered the zinging current created by their joined hands, the intense excitement when he pulled her closer and the realization surged through her like a wave: *Kiss!* If only that little nerd hadn't interrupted them, she was sure he would have drawn her into a sweet caress. When she thought about the months that had passed since she'd been wrapped in strong arms having her tongue sucked, another shiver of desire tickled her deep inside.

The phone shrilled again and Amber jerked out of her daydream. She threw the drawing aside and answered breathlessly. "Hello?"

"Hey, gal, what's shakin'?" It was Krystalee.

"Me! I'm sitting here going out of my mind!" Amber whined.

Krystalee giggled. "All shook up, huh? So go out to lunch with me. Just finished running some samples at ASU, so I'm done with work for the weekend and ready to celebrate."

"You're always ready to celebrate."

"Well, darlin', ain't that what life is for? Live fast, die laughing?"

"Anyway, I don't think I can eat," Amber said. "I'm too much of a nervous wreck."

"You crack me up, I swear! Act like you never been on a date before. Besides, you have to eat!" Krystalee's twang was intensifying, always a signal that she was about to dispense some motherly advice. "Otherwise you'll go out, drink three quick glasses of wine to get over the jitters, and be *on your lips*...is any of this sinkin' in through the cloud you're on?"

Now Amber was giggling, too. "Okay, okay! I'll go with you. It'll be a good way to kill time, and maybe I can pick up something new to wear while we're out."

"We'll go to the mall! You gotta have new threads; it's good luck."

"Yeah, where does it say that?"

"In my book. Be over to get you in ten minutes."

Not surprisingly, a good girlfriend, lunch and shopping made the afternoon slip away. Amber bought a snug-fitting, long-sleeved crop top with teal and lavender stripes. The plunging neckline wasn't really her style, but Krystalee insisted it wasn't too slutty at all for the first date. Then they picked out a pair of teal-colored jeans that were almost hip-huggers.

"I don't know," Amber said, frowning. "I'm going to look like a Barbie doll in this outfit. All I need now is the five-inch, black patent leather heels."

"That can be arranged," Krystalee responded with a wave of her hand. "You look great in it with that hardbody, and most importantly, he's gonna get hard as soon as he sees you."

"Would you stop!" Amber pleaded. "I'm trying not to think about sex, I'm trying to keep my mind on higher principles."

"And failing dismally," Krystalee replied. "I'm all a-flutter just from the contact high! Anyway, there's no turning back now, it's past four and you're barely gonna have two hours to get ready for Prince Charming. I'm taking you home."

Two hours later, Amber was doing her final check in front of the full-length mirror. *Not bad for an old bag, even if there is a little essence of Barbie in there.* She had opted for white sneakers instead of spiked heels, remembering the ascent into Blue's truck. As soon as the thought of his truck flashed through her mind, she turned to see it pulling up to the curb. Ten minutes early! A good sign; he was eager, too.

She watched through the screen door as he strode up the driveway, her heart boosting into warp speed. After the eternity of the last twenty-four hours, laying eyes on him made her giddy as a pup greeting its long-lost master.

"Hi, Amber," he said when he looked up and saw her standing in the doorway.

"Hi, Blue." She held open the screen for him and he came in, never swerving his attention from her face. Then he noticed her clingy outfit.

"Wow," he said, then paused to scrutinize her. "It sure is nice to see you again."

"I know. Yesterday seems like a long time ago." This was not the kind of witty conversation Amber had been planning to make, but she was too thunderstruck by his presence and the swirling emotions it caused. She imagined how natural it would be to glide into his arms.

But instead of grabbing her, he asked, "So...are we going to see a movie?"

"Sure," she replied, thinking about sitting next to him in the dark for two hours, "What do you want to see?"

"Oh, I don't have a preference. You decide."

"Okay, let's go see *Death Do Us Part*. It's supposed to be some kind of thriller."

"Sounds like it's about marriage," he commented.

Amber arched her eyebrows. "Or murder!"

As it turned out, they were both right; the story involved a woman who was married to one man while having an affair. She plotted with each to kill the other, meanwhile taking advantage of both men's passion. Eventually she took the fatal bullet during their cross fire. To be sure, a cheesy plot, but Amber didn't care what was on the screen after Blue leaned over and whispered, "Can I hold your hand again? That was nice."

Nice was not really how Amber would have described the cosmic churning and yearning whipped up yesterday by the touch of his hand, but she was not going to argue. Wordlessly she offered her hand, he snagged it gently, entwined their fingers and let them land like love-locked starfish on his thigh. A deep current of satisfied contentment suffused Amber's body. It was less intense than yesterday in Blue's office, but she could definitely feel her aura warming, pulsing, expanding. Occasionally he caressed the back of her hand with his thumb, or stretched his fingers to reach other areas of untouched skin. Then she could feel the energy flaring, the exquisite, almost painful longing between her thighs, and her brain, still in junior high, scream-ing, "He likes me!"

That led to another, more adult thought: *What's going to happen later? We both dig each other and we both know it. If he puts the move on me, how could I ever say no?* Quinn's lecture popped up in her mind, but this was no time to listen to reason. Too young, too fast—too bad! At least for the duration of the movie, she vowed to indulge her fan-tasy.

When the house lights came up, Amber looked over at Blue and realized that the night was young and this fantasy was going to con-tinue. She directed him to Jackson's, her favorite pizza place near her house in Tempe. It was fairly crowded but there was an empty table for two.

"What do you want to drink?" Amber asked as the waitress ar-rived.

"Whatever you recommend," Blue answered.

"Okay, bring us a carafe of red wine." Krystalee's voice piped into her consciousness: *three glasses of wine and you're on your lips.* Now it looked more likely to be three glasses of wine and she would be on *his* lips.

The waitress left to get the wine and they picked up their menus. "So, should we split a pizza, or do you want something else?"

"Whatever you want is fine with me," he said amiably.

"Okay, let's do pizza, then. What do you like on yours?"

"I...really don't have an opinion. You decide."

Amber looked at him quizzically over the top of her menu. "Well, you must have a preference," she insisted. "How about pepperoni?"

"Pepperoni," he repeated slowly, as if saying a mantra. "Is that made from peppers, or is it meat?"

Amber frowned. He seemed sincere, but was this a joke? "Uh...don't tell me they didn't have pepperoni in Wonderland, your hometown. Okay, for all of you just joining us here on planet Earth, pepperoni is made of meat."

"Trust Earthlings to name a meat product after a vegetable," he replied, laughing. "No pepperoni. Muscle tissue is not my nourish-ment of choice."

"You're a vegetarian then? Maybe that explains why you're so...different."

"It's true I don't eat meat, but it doesn't really have anything to do with philosophy," he explained. "I'm not against consumption of animals, I just want my food to enhance the life force. And the way meat is produced here, its vibrational content could be downright detrimental."

Amber wasn't about to let his dietary quirks distract her. "Well, you're lucky, because one of Jackson's specialties is the Vegomatic, and I know from personal experience that it has no meat on it."

The carafe arrived and Amber ordered the pizza. She smiled as she poured the fragrant, dark red wine into their glasses. "Cheers." *Here's hoping you're not gonna be too weird for me,* she thought as she took an unladylike swallow.

Blue sipped the wine and swished it around in his mouth. "Amazing taste!" he declared. "I was expecting it to be sweeter, not so pungent." He took another taste.

"This can't be your first time drinking red wine! Where have you been?"

"Underground," Blue answered with a grin.

"Well, thank God you finally emerged into the light! This is a good start, Jackson's Pizza. There's a lot more I'd like to show you when you have the time." The sentence was out before Amber realized how potentially lewd it sounded.

Blue didn't bat an eye. "I want everything you have to give," he said earnestly.

Amber was momentarily speechless until she realized he was repeating a phrase that the woman in the movie had spoken to both men. She laughed, relieved, and took another fortifying swig from her wineglass. "So, how'd you like the film?"

"It was very interesting, but there were some things I didn't understand."

"Like what?" she prompted.

"Like why was the woman made out to be the evil one who had to be punished? She only went looking for another man because her husband ignored her."

"Yes, but that's usually not an excuse."

"Nobody was hurt by it. Until the husband found out, both men were happy and so was she."

"You're right," Amber agreed. "She was happy in the beginning, getting off on her secret little life, then jealousy entered the picture and everyone went haywire."

"It makes no sense; human society has many traditions where men have multiple wives, but none where women have multiple husbands. It seems to me a queen with a male harem would be the more logical arrangement."

"That certainly fires the imagination," Amber laughed. "I'm glad you've at least heard of feminism before."

"Essence of the female, integration of goddess energy," he said, "that's the hope for the planet."

"Amen." Amber lifted her glass and drained it.

"So why didn't that woman seize her power and simply leave?" Blue pursued. " She didn't really love either man, and she wasn't so bad-looking that she couldn't find somebody else."

"Not so bad-looking?" Amber echoed incredulously. "That's Surya Seylon, the super-model! She gets like ten grand an hour just to have her picture taken!"

"She's considered beautiful? But she's so thin and frail, no shape or muscle tone. I prefer your body."

Amber was happy to see the waitress approaching with their pizza. *Is this guy really from Duhsville or was that a major move on me?* she wondered. In any case, things seemed to be steaming along just as she'd planned. The pizza looked gargantuan, and she suddenly realized she had no appetite at all—at least not for food.

Blue, on the other hand, scooped up a piece and aimed it at his open mouth.

"Whoa!" Amber yelled, grabbing his wrist. "That thing's thermo-nuclear! Give it some time to cool!"

He lowered the slice to his plate. "Thanks, Mom," he said with an impish smile. "It's nice to know you care."

She poured more wine into both glasses. "I wouldn't want your tongue to get burned," she said with a boldness that tingled her spine like bubbles in champagne, uncorking several shameless, oral-oriented fantasies.

"Is it ready?" he asked.

Amber almost moaned, then quickly realized he was talking about their dinner. "Yeah..." she stammered. "I think we can try it now." She picked up a piece and gave the tip of it a ginger nibble.

"What an incredible texture!" Blue sputtered, as a long string of mozzarella looped from his front teeth.

"I guess they didn't have pizza in the outer outback where you hail from, either," Amber observed. "When are you going to break down and tell me more about you?"

"Soon, I promise," he said, taking another big bite and smiling as he chewed.

By the time the pizza was gone, so was the wine. A smooth, sweet glow had already taken the edge off any misgivings Amber might have had; Blue was looking better and better by the minute. He reached across the table, laid his hand on top of hers, and said, "I do want to tell you about me, Amber. I just needed to make sure you were the one. And you are. Let's get another flask of this wine and go to your house."

Once again Amber was startled by his brazenly honest statements, but there was no denying that his words thrilled her. Soon they were alone in her living room, sipping more red wine. Soft jazz played on the stereo and scented candles were burning. She couldn't imagine a more perfect seduction scene.

She set her wineglass on the coffee table and inched a little closer to him on the couch. He took another drink, set his glass down, too, and reached to take her hand.

"Amber," he pronounced, then paused. "This is going so fast, I never realized...the way you make me feel, there are chemicals coursing through me that are so new...."

Oh man, the melodramatic stuff guys will dream up to get laid! "It's okay," she said in a low voice. "Come here." Might as well get down to it.

He turned to her, let her slide her arm around his torso. Then with an audible groan he wrapped her in his arms and pulled her tight. Amber hugged back, flooded with the urgent desire to kiss him for about the next billion years. She brought her head up, searching. Then her hand came up, located the back of his head, and steered it forcefully toward her puckering lips.

And then, finally, her lipsticked red ones met his quivering bluish ones, and her tongue slid against them like the wanton waves licking the cliffs of Dover. And he pulled immediately away.

"No!" he exclaimed, rising and pacing to the center of the room. "We can't exchange intimacies like this with no discussion, no commitment."

The wine buzz intensified in her brain. Amber couldn't believe she was hearing this. It sounded like soap opera dialogue from the fifties! "Blue," she said calmly, "all I want is a kiss."

"You just don't understand," he said, shaking his head so that his ponytail flipped crazily. "Where I come from nobody does those things unless they plan to create a family unit. Otherwise the mating dance has no purpose."

"What is it? I'm too old for you?" Amber snapped. "Cut the bizarre language and tell me the truth!"

"Too old? Is that what you think?" He began to chuckle, the ponytail jerking.

"Yeah," she replied. "How old are you anyway? Twenty-five?"

"What does that matter? You know we match." He turned to pierce her with his awesome indigo eyes.

"Then kiss me," she insisted.

Blue hung his head, breaking their gaze. "It's not that I don't want to," he said slowly, "it's just that I...don't know how."

Amber burst out laughing, almost spritzing her wine over the carpet. "Oh, sure! Now, on top of all this other weird shit, I'm supposed to believe you never kissed. I guess you've never had sex in your life either?"

"No." He turned and walked over to Amber's fish tank, staring into it and refusing to say more.

She sat for a minute, taking another sip of wine and wondering what sort of twilight zone she had wandered into.

"This is like me," he said finally, still watching the fish. "Trapped in a tiny world, but situated in a big world, trying to reconcile the two."

"You are confounding me again, oh annoyingly inscrutable one. Where in the bloody motherfucking hell did you come from? The *Vatican*?" Amber had lost her patience along with her dignity.

"No," he replied, turning to face her again. "It's time you knew. I came from Mars."

4

Stranger Than Science Fiction

"*M*ars?" Amber squeaked. "As in Mars, Ohio, or Mars, the planet named after the god of war?"

"As in Mars, the fourth rock from the sun. Your people named it that, not mine." He stood before her, tall and proud, proclaiming himself an emissary of a distant world.

Amber's heart was sinking in a maelstrom of disappointment and disbelief. He was serious! *I can't believe I picked another nutcase!*

"So, how are things on the Red Planet?" She made no attempt to hide her sarcastic tone.

"Dusty and deserted," he answered. "There isn't much atmosphere anymore."

"I suppose that's why you left in your spaceship and came down to Earth?"

"Exactly. Except it was my parents who were refugees from the Mars disaster. I was actually born here."

"Oh! So you've never been on Mars yourself?"

"Not in this physical form. But I've been there many times in my mind."

"I'll bet," Amber said curtly, getting up to retrieve the wine from the kitchen. When she came back, Blue was sitting in an armchair, watching her expectantly. She set the bottle down on the coffee table, after filling her glass. *I'll need every drop of that puppy before this conversation is over.*

"Okay," she began, as if calling an end to the joke. "Do you really want me to believe you're a Martian?"

"I know this is difficult for many humans, but the truth is Martians have been living on your planet for more than a hundred years.

We built vast underground complexes in different locations around the globe when our home planet was no longer able to sustain life. I grew up in one under the Superstition range."

"I swear, this wine has gone to your head!" Amber's own head was whirling, trying to find some way to process what he was saying. "You're telling me you've lived in tunnels your whole life?"

"Well, I've been on the surface now for twelve days," he said. "And it's not really like a dirty tunnel; some of it is pretty magnificent. You'll see."

"I highly doubt that," she shot back.

"You don't believe me, do you?"

"Don't look so hurt! Did you really expect me to?"

"But Amber," he protested softly. "It's all the truth."

She looked over dubiously. He sat perched on the edge of his chair, wide-eyed and earnest, like a darling little boy telling the biggest lie in the world. "Well, how about some proof? You know, like a picture ID showing you're a Martian citizen, or an outer space passport."

"I am a diplomat in the Galactic Federation, but we don't use anything so primitive as written credentials."

"How do you say this shit with a straight face? The Galactic Federation is directly from Star Trek!"

He flashed her a cryptic smile. "Did it ever occur to you that Star Trek may simply be reflecting reality?"

"No, it didn't! Next you're going to tell me the aliens abducted the show's writer and stuck a probe up their nose to implant the ideas."

"Actually, they inserted it through the ear," Blue said matter-of-factly. "And they didn't abduct him; they did it right in his bedroom."

"Jesus Christ," she mumbled, shaking her head. This was getting increasingly insane. "How are you gonna be a diplomat? You're barely more than a kid!"

"Why do you keep saying that? In Earth years I'm seventy-three, although Martians average a life span of more than two hundred."

Amber collapsed on the couch's pillows, shaking with laughter. "Oh, now I am really sure! I've got the hots for a seventy-three-year-old? What do you old farts do at the Federation meetings, check for Klingons around Uranus?"

Blue eyed her soberly. "For some time now we have been working on a way to save your planet. In case you haven't noticed, Earth is irrevocably headed toward its own global disaster."

Amber's giggling dried up. Apparently he wasn't going to break character and admit this was all a game. Even if it was a game, what was the point? He was using this charade to avoid kissing her, not to lure her into the sack. "Why are you telling me all this? If you're the galactic diplomat, go complete your mission. Why involve me?"

"Because this *is* my mission," he said, rising and beginning to pace around the living room. "For a hundred and fifty years we Martians have remained hidden, even though involvement with Earthlings would have been mutually beneficial. We've been waiting for your race to become less warlike and more spiritually advanced. Now it is time for us to emerge and help awaken your people to the dire consequences of mistreating your planet. I was chosen as one of the first to come to the surface and make direct, personal contact."

Amber's arms were peppered with goosebumps. He sounded so convincing, for a split second she entertained the notion that it might be true.

"My birth was an experiment in genetic alteration," he continued. "That's why I'm able to breathe your rich air, eat Earth food, and pass among you without too much awareness that I am different. In the galactic community they call my species 'The Blues,' for our blue pallor, and our blue blood. Amber, you can see that at least that part is true!"

She looked at him standing there and it was undeniable, he was definitely different. And in spite of his off-the-wall ramblings, her body still yearned to press him tight. "I...I don't know what to think, Blue," she stammered. "I want to believe you, but it's all just so crazy...."

He stopped pacing and turned to face her. Without a word he lifted his hands and undid the top button of his shirt. Amber's mind cartwheeled. *After all this buildup, it's going to end in a striptease?*

The second button yielded, then the third. Amber couldn't even breathe, let alone say anything. Her undivided attention was focused on the emerging expanse of his pectoralis. She could clearly see the etched canyon that divided the twin slabs of chest muscle, taut and completely hairless. Then he pulled the fabric aside to expose his nipple, round and puckered like a royal blue poker chip. Amber leaned forward to verify the color, but there was no mistaking it, even five feet away. "Wow," was all she could think of to say.

"The genetic manipulation allowed me to survive on Earth and withstand its stronger gravity," he went on, "but it also gave me glands that produce chemicals, and the emotions to go with them. Except I never understood exactly what that meant, until I met you."

He paused, and Amber remained speechless. If this was horseshit, it was some of the best she'd ever heard.

"Amber, since the first time I entered your etheric field, my vibrational level has been altered," he persisted. "Something has come alive inside me, something I've never felt before."

"Yeah, it's hell going through puberty at seventy-three," she said, but she could feel her own aura swell with a pleasant tingle.

He laughed, finally breaking the solemn atmosphere, and sat on the couch beside her. "It's not hell at all," he said. "It feels more like heaven."

"You've got more lines than the Cali Cartel," she accused, though his words were melting her. "And as long as you're into confession, how about explaining why I feel like I'm having an LSD flashback every time I look at your hair?"

Blue chuckled. "It's not that good an illusion, is it?"

"Illusion? What are you talking about?"

"Martians don't grow hair. So, I use a method whereby a section of my overconscious mind assembles the necessary molecules to make hair, then binds them in a pattern and orchestrates their movement."

"Needs a little work," she commented.

"Want me to turn it off?" he asked.

"No! No, I don't think I could handle that right now."

"Yes, I intuit that bald men have a negative attraction for you."

His shirt still flapped open and his chest drew her gaze like a magnet. This certainly did not feel like negative attraction! The twin blue nipples glared like a pair of eyes, shamelessly challenging her.

"Go ahead," Blue said suddenly. "Touch me."

She looked into his face like a deer caught in headlights.

"I'm telepathic," he whispered, as if that explained everything. "I know what you want. And I want the same thing."

Amber's heart drummed rapidly as she body-rushed from head to toe. There was no time to analyze, there was only this moment, this wide-open window of opportunity, and her hand soaring toward it like a lusty dove. Her fingers landed at the base of his throat, and they both shivered at the meeting of skin.

"You Martians sure are purty," she sighed, stroking up and down his sternum. He let his head loll back against the couch, eyes half-closed. By the time Amber finished unbuttoning his shirt, she was about to spontaneously combust.

Now for that incredible, extremely erotic nip! She sent her fingertips on a sensuous safari, up the ridges of his abdominals and across the wide plain of his chest. When they brushed over the blue circle on the left side, it puckered into a tight point. Her fingers surrounded it, tenderly pummeling and pulling.

Blue's eyes popped open, surprised but glazed with lust. "Amber...such acute sensations...."

"What about your Martian principles?" she asked, bringing up her other hand to caress both sides at once. "What about family values?" Maybe it was foolish to remind him of that, but by now she was fully convinced she would not sleep alone tonight.

"I'm on the surface of Earth now," he replied, panting slightly. "Perhaps I should conform to the local customs."

"Without a doubt!" Amber returned, laughing lasciviously as she continued to pet his torso. She watched her hands roam over his body, trying not to divert her stare to the obvious protrusion under his zipper. The open floodgates gushing in her underwear was a little more difficult to ignore.

"Show me how to kiss," he blurted out.

Is he real or Memorex? Right now, who gives a shit? she reasoned. "Okay...first you have to get close." She slid her hands under his shirt and around his back; he shifted toward her, encircling her waist. Their upper bodies pressed together, only the thin barrier of her low-cut blouse separating his nipples from hers. His breath was sweet and warm, like a pony after eating apples and hay.

"Now the lips have to touch...." She stretched her neck like a flower reaching for the sun.

He bumped his lips into hers and a fiery tremor singed her nerves.

"Uh-huh," she whispered, softly kissing his closed lips. She gave them a gentle lick, and he slackened his jaw. Without further fanfare, her tongue slithered in.

For a neophyte he certainly was a quick student! He tightened his hold on Amber and seemed to get right with the program, latching onto her mouth and filling it with his twisting tongue. Her heart pounding madly, she crushed herself against him and kissed with the gusto of a bear reaming out a honey jar.

Without warning a lightning bolt of lust spiked her between the legs and pushed her over the edge to a shattering orgasm. She wrenched her mouth from his and growled as each ecstatic contraction pulsed through her. At last the convulsions subsided and she clung to him like a wet towel, heart still hammering, mind blown, but alive and well in the sweet afterglow of satisfaction.

"Amber, I'm so sorry!" Blue wailed. "I knew I should have stepped down that frequency! Are you all right?" Gently he peeled her from his shoulder.

Amber was smiling woozily. "Have you lost your mind? That was incredible! I mean, I didn't really plan for it to happen so soon, we skipped a few of the good parts, but baby, I'm starting to believe you really are from outer space!"

Blue released her and stood up. "I didn't plan for this to happen at all!" He started pacing again, jamming his hands into his bogus hair. Then he stopped and turned to her again, his face a mask of confusion and pain. "That was your sexual climax!"

Amber nodded, grinning like a well-fed cat. "So? We're both over twenty-one. Why are you so upset?" She was about ready to add, *Come over here and get your climax, too.* Surely he'd feel better when he was in her condition.

"Because we're doing things that belong in the realm of spouses," he announced, resuming his pacing. "And we're not spouses! I had no idea that events would unfold like this, I wasn't briefed on this aspect of the plan!" He whirled before her, his hair following him like a comet's tail. "I didn't realize it was my mission to fall in love with a human!"

Amber was beyond being flabbergasted. As she reclined, her body purring, staring at the only man who'd ever gotten her off with a kiss, love with a Martian didn't seem like a bad idea at all. "So what should we do?" she finally asked.

His eyes were blue steel. "We should be married as soon as possible."

5

Freefalling

He's a *virgin*?" Krystalee shrieked, rattling the table with an acute fit of giggles and snorts. "That's even weirder than trying to make you believe he's a Martian!"

It was Sunday morning and the three friends had gathered on the patio of Krystalee's town house to brunch on baked eggs, whole wheat bagels and mimosas. Amber had just been filling them in on the amazing events of the previous evening.

"How did this guy find you?" Quinn asked. "Looked under 'gullible' in the dictionary and there was your picture and phone number?"

"Forget that!" Krystalee fanned her hand in the air. "Tell us what happened next!"

"Well, then he gave me a little Martian history lesson," Amber continued. "About how his parents had to leave when the planet became a dust world, and how the Martians have these underground places they live in, and how they're waiting to merge with the humans...."

"Yeah, I'm sure he's got the urge to merge," Quinn interrupted.

"That's not it at all!" Amber insisted. "It's almost like he's afraid of sex, but definitely interested in it. See, on Mars sex was just a way to reproduce; the people paired up according to law and there was zero passion involved! But because of the way Blue's genes have been altered, he's developing human emotions now."

"Excuse me, but you sound like you really believe him." Quinn said.

"He also told me," Amber went on, ignoring that comment, "that the genetic tinkering and the hormones...enlarged his genitalia."

Both women burst out laughing. "He *told* you?" Krystalee shrilled. "Didn't you want to see the proof?"

"Of course," Amber responded. "But it didn't get to that."

"Oh shit, this guy's kinkier than I thought," said Krystalee.

"But I did get off," Amber added with a sly smile.

"What?" Quinn exploded. "I thought I told you to think with your brain!"

"You mean you came? Without seeing his dick?" Krystalee cried. "Honey, you got some splainin' to do!"

"Well, this is the wildest part of all," Amber said slowly, her body buzzing at the memory. "The rest of it may be utter fantasy, but this I know is true because it happened to me. He made me come with a kiss."

There was a stunned silence, then Krystalee gasped, "Okay, he was kissing you, but what were the rest of his appendages doing?"

"I swear, Krystal!" Amber pledged, throwing up her right hand. "Believe me, I'm as shocked as you are! Even when I was a hot-to-trot teenager I never had that kind of experience. I mean, we were really getting into the kiss and everything, and then all of a sudden the energy just kind of built and exploded in about ten seconds—took me completely by surprise."

"And where were his hands? Quinn, my bullshit detector just pegged right off the scale!"

"I mean it! His hands were on my back!" Amber protested through giggles.

"You realize what you're saying contradicts all laws of physics, not to mention biology," Quinn interjected. "Nobody comes from a kiss. At least not on those lips."

"Let me tell you, this guy does violate all known laws! I'm really and truly tempted to believe he is from Mars." Amber proclaimed.

"So that was the upshot of the romantic encounter?" Krystalee pursued. "You came, he went? Didn't he ask for anything in return?"

"No. Not that I wasn't willing to give him anything he wanted. We talked a little bit more, then he left—without kissing me again."

"Oh, Lord help us!" Krystalee exclaimed, standing up from the table, "I've got to put more champagne in my orange juice on that one! Anyone else need something?"

"The Artist Formerly Known as Prince does not drink," Quinn reminded her brightly.

"Hey, I said he was my idol, not my role model," Krystalee shot over her shoulder as she went inside.

"Now, Amber," Quinn began in a somber tone, "All fun and joking aside, do you really know what you're getting yourself into here? To say the least, the man sounds unbalanced."

"I know it seems that way," said Amber uncertainly, "but when I'm with him it all makes a kind of weird sense. And what about the blue nipples?"

"Easily obtainable in a tattoo parlor. Where is your brain?" Quinn winced.

"And the orgasmic kisses?"

"Let's not put you through the humiliation of counting up the months it's been since you went to bed with a man. Your imagination alone could have brought you off; it's not so unheard of."

Krystalee returned to the patio and tossed a book onto the wrought iron table in front of Amber. "Read it and weep," she said. "I don't know what rock you were living under when this became a best-seller."

Amber picked up the hard-backed volume. It was entitled, *Men Are From Mars, Women Are From Venus.*

"He's not even an original con artist," Krystalee said.

"I guess I have heard of this book," Amber admitted, "but I've never read it."

"Let's just hope he has," Quinn said. "Maybe some of the ideas in there took root. Because I can see you ain't about to give up on him yet."

"Why should she? He sure beats television." Krystalee observed.

"Why?" Quinn snapped. "Because he's obviously certifiable. The only thing she has to look forward to with him is a padded room!"

"Well, as long as there were mirrors on the ceiling...." Krystalee mused.

"Listen, you guys," Amber said. "If you think what I've told you so far is crazy, wait til you hear this: He wants to get married."

"Oh, yeah, right!" Krystalee launched into peals of giggles. "That's insane, he hasn't even met us!"

"Did he really say that?" Quinn pressed. "In those words?"

"Well, yeah. He said he wanted to marry me as soon as possible. Believe me, I totally freaked."

"I don't get it," said Krystalee. "First he doesn't want to fuck you, and now he wants to *marry you*?"

"No, it's the other way around," Amber corrected. "He wants to marry me, then fuck me."

"So what did you tell him?" Krystalee asked breathlessly.

"Well...nothing, really. I said I'd think about it."

"Krystal, go get me the remote phone so I can call 911," Quinn growled. "Our girlfriend here is in need of the little men in white coats! Have you completely lost every brain cell that ever existed under that carrot top? Get away from this jerk, far away."

"Now wait a minute, let's not throw out the baby with the bathwater!" Krystalee cried. "Let's give the guy credit for recognizing quality when he sees it and wanting to commit to it. Besides, Quinn, you and I would look so hot in matching bridesmaid's dresses!"

No, that's not what he wants," Amber cut in. "It's supposed to be a Martian ceremony."

"A Martian ceremony, huh?" Quinn echoed sourly. "Does this by any chance involve you lashed to a rock altar while the painted dancers leap in the firelight? Sounds satanic."

"How should I know what's involved? Until yesterday I thought Mars was just a big ball of red dust!" Amber said.

"Here's how you do it." Krystalee grabbed a napkin. "Okay, so say this is the First Martian Church of Zot, or whoever it is they worship. Now, over in this section we seat the folks from the Milky Way, other star systems over here, and anyone with more than seven tentacles has to sit all the way in the back."

"It's not funny! She's seriously considering doing it!" Quinn barked.

"Well, it's not like it would be binding, in any sort of legal sense," Amber reasoned. "It's not like I would have to tell my parents or anything."

"And it's not like there would be any sort of ceremony to it except you getting bonked on the head!" Quinn yelled. "No, no, *no*—don't do it!"

"Wait a minute, he's already had plenty of opportunity to attack her," Krystalee pointed out. "Why would he go to all this trouble if that's what he wanted?"

"Why? Because he's a sicko! You can't figure out a twisted mind."

"Let's get back to the juice," Krystalee said eagerly. "Where and when are the happy nuptials supposed to take place?"

Amber felt her pulse jump. "He wants to take me to the Martian complex under the mountains..."

"Has a romantic ring to it," Krystalee trilled.

"...blindfolded."

Quinn erupted. "No way! Girl, don't you read the papers, don't you watch CNN? The whole country is an open-air insane asylum, and you want to run off blindfolded with somebody you don't even know! Get me that phone, K-lee, I'm calling the cops to put her in protective custody before she gets herself hurt!"

"You know, it reminds me of this pictorial I saw once," Krystalee said dreamily. "This guy was taking his girlfriend for a ride in a limo, and the only thing she was wearing was a blindfold, a corset, and stiletto heels. They go to the park and he tells her he's going to make her fuck the first guy they see. So then here comes this cat on a motor-cycle."

"Krystalee!" Quinn hissed.

"Okay, sorry!"

"If only you didn't get your notions of normal male-female relations from the pages of Hustler!" Quinn lamented. "But it won't be so sexy going to identify Amber's body at the morgue."

"Oh, you always think the worst's going to happen," Krystalee accused. "So, Amber, when's the big day? I gotta make an appointment to get my legs waxed beforehand."

"Uh...he wants to do it soon. Like tonight," she admitted with a grimace.

"Oh! Tonight! Okay, that's it, straitjacket time!" Quinn was getting truly perturbed. "Let me see—you meet him on Thursday, and marry him on Sunday. Hello in there! Does this sound rational to you?"

"You know, Romeo and Juliet got married the *day after* they met," Krystalee offered. "By that timetable, you guys are being downright cautious."

"And look what happened to *them*! Please, just stick to Prince and Larry Flynt and leave Shakespeare out of this."

"Well, Prince would just advise you to pretend you're married," said Krystalee smugly. "Then go crazy all night."

"That's exactly what's going on here, a whole lot of pretending. And I don't like it one bit."

"Oh, Quinn, take a chill pill," Amber pleaded. "No matter what, I'm going to be all right. I just feel it."

"In other words, you're going tonight, aren't you?"

"I didn't say that," she corrected.

"Can't wait to get the details tomorrow," said Krystalee.

* * *

When Amber got home at 2:30, there were three messages on her machine. The first was from her Mom: "Did you survive your big date? Give us a call when you get up. Bye, sweetie." Obviously her parents thought she was sleeping in after a vigorous night of disco dancing. She'd have to call soon and check in.

The second message was from Blue. Amber vibrated like a windchime at the sound of his voice: "Hello, Amber. Everything is arranged for tonight. I've been working on my hair all day; hope you like it better. I don't really have a phone, so I'll try calling back later. I love you."

Amber collapsed on the couch in a romantic swoon. *He loves me!* It didn't matter that he was a few cans shy of a six-pack, that he wanted to take her blindfolded to a secret cave in the desert, and that he claimed to be a Martian virgin. He had the unmitigated brilliance to see she was priceless, and if he wanted to shower attention on her, who was she to say no?

The third message was from her sister, Violet, who also lived in the Phoenix area: "Hey, sis, what's the four-one-one on your new main squeeze? I'm on pins and needles; call me after five today. Bye."

Amber grabbed the phone and dialed the number of her parents' Scottsdale home. "Oh, hi, sweetie," her mother said sunnily. "We've just been talking about you!"

"I'm sure. But I'm fine—no hangover—and I wasn't sleeping in, I was over at Krystalee's with her and Quinn."

"Oh, that's nice. So how was the date?"

"I think it went real well. I think we like each other."

"You think?" her Mom queried.

"Well, he kissed me, let's put it that way."

"And that's all?"

"Mom! It was our first date!"

"Since when has that ever stopped you?"

Amber had always been honest with her mother. Now she thought, maybe too honest. "Okay. You want the truth? I was ready to jump all over him but he claimed he was a virgin, kissed me, and went home." A neatly edited version, she realized, but not entirely untrue.

"That sounds awfully odd."

"Well, I thought so, too! Then just now I get a message from him and he says he wants to see me tonight and...he, uh...said he loves me."

"Doesn't waste time, does he? But that's not necessarily bad. So are you going to see him?"

"I don't know. Krystalee thinks I should go for it, but Quinn thinks Blue has a personality disorder."

"And what do you think?"

"I think he's a flame and I'm a moth. I can't *not* pursue it; I have to see what's going to happen."

"Then go ahead. Honey, you know what's right for you. Hold on a second, let me see if your father wants to talk to you...." Amber could hear her mom calling her dad. There was a pause, then she came back on the line. "He can't leave the hockey playoffs right now, but he wants you to remember that nobody buys the cow when they can get the milk for free."

"Oh, gee, thanks!" Amber said. "Would you please tell him I haven't dispensed any milk to this guy, free or otherwise?"

"He's only kidding you, anyway," Amber's mom assured. "You just go and have a good time tonight. But, you know, be careful."

"Don't worry, I got a brand-new case of condoms in the mail yesterday."

"I'm not just worried about that. Anybody his age claiming he's a virgin has got to have a few bats in his belfry. Just don't do anything crazy."

Without asking if her mother considered marriage to be in that category, Amber reassured her and said good-bye. She hung up and looked at the clock. Almost three. There wasn't much time until sundown, and she had no idea how she was supposed to prepare for her Martian wedding.

Rushing to her bedroom, she threw open the closet doors and inspected her wardrobe. If she was going to get married tonight, what to wear? What did the well-dressed bride on Mars look like these days? Certainly not this filmy white linen dress she ran around in during the sixties! *What am I keeping this thing around for anyway?* she wondered, holding it against her in front of the mirror. It seemed threadbare and shabby now, the hippie costume that had served as freak flag in her youth.

"Maybe I could get married in red," she said to herself as she pulled out the Frederick's of Hollywood spandex sheath. *Better do a few more crunches before you try that on!*

The phone rang and Amber threw the dress on the bed. She raced to the living room. "Hello?"

"Hi. You weren't expecting your alien, were you?"

"Hi, Quinn. Actually, I was."

"Amber, don't do it. Don't go with him tonight."

"If I don't, It'll always be could've been, should've been. I have to," Amber declared.

"Oh, shit! Could you at least leave a trail of bread crumbs for us to follow? I won't be able to rest until I know you're back here safe and sound."

"I will be," Amber promised. "Probably with the story of a lifetime."

"Huh!" Quinn snorted. "I only hope you're *not* right about that. And don't forget to take a bunch of rubbers."

"Yeah, yeah. I already discussed that with Mom."

"You did? You mean you're burdening that poor woman with this insanity! Did you tell her he's from Mars?"

"Of course not! I gotta make sure I believe it first."

After extracting a promise to be extremely careful and to call first thing in the morning, Quinn let her go. Amber hung up and slumped into the couch. This was all going just a little too fast.

The phone rang again and Amber jerked with a gasp. Couldn't they leave her alone for two seconds and let her collect her thoughts? "What?" she said crossly into the receiver.

"Hi. It's Blue. Did I call at a bad time?"

"No! No, not at all! I'm just...nervous, I guess...." Amber stammered. Here he was, on the phone. Was she really going to say she would marry him?

"Don't be. It's going to be beautiful. I have it all prepared." His voice was edged with the excitement of a sixteen-year-old anticipating his first screw.

"Are you...really sure we should do this?" she ventured.

"Absolutely," he answered without hesitation. "I'll come for you at sunset. Then get ready to see something no human has ever seen before."

Oh sure, that's what they all say. "And you promise I'll be perfectly safe?" she couldn't help asking.

"Of course, Amber. That's what this is all about—protecting you, taking care of you, giving you everything you need. I understand you're confused, but I also sense you have the ability to grasp and integrate the information I'm giving you."

"God, you talk weird sometimes," she said.

Blue laughed, and the easy happiness in the sound burned into her heart.

"Don't listen to anything else but your inner voice," he instructed. "Run this through your gut feeling, and see what it tells you. I'll respect your decision, and you can turn me away if you want to. But I will be there at sunset."

"Okay. But you are coming to get me in your truck, aren't you?"

"You mean, as opposed to my beamship? No, I don't think you're quite ready for that," he chuckled.

"I'm not sure I'm ready for any of this," she admitted.

"Amber. Get in a hot tub of bubbles," he commanded. "Breathe long and deep. When you're relaxed, ask your heart; it knows my love is sincere. See you at sunset." Then he hung up, without giving her time to reply.

"Damn!" she said as she replaced the receiver. "I didn't ask what I'm supposed to wear!" He hadn't given her a number, and what was she going to do, ask information to connect her to Martian underground headquarters?

However, maybe his advice wasn't so bad; a bath would at least rinse off the cold sweat. Amber went to the bathroom and started the water running. She rummaged in the cabinet, but couldn't find anything except an old envelope of gardenia bath salts. She poured the crystals in, followed by a squirt of shampoo, and the tub began to fill with fragrant bubbles.

Soon she was lying up to her chin in gardenia foam. It really did feel good, the warm water cradling her and the chance to think. Remembering what Blue had said, she focused on her breathing, gradually slowing it and drinking in larger draughts of air. Her eyes closed and her limbs seemed to float.

Okay heart, tell me, she thought as she drifted. Another deep breathful of flower perfume expanded her chest. Suddenly Amber heard a loud crackle, like a drop of water flung into a hot skillet. Her eyes flew open and she was astounded to see that she was no longer lying in the bath but standing in the middle of a manicured garden, surrounded by bushes covered with waxy, aromatic gardenia blooms.

Amber tried to look down at her body, but discovered that she couldn't really see it. There was just an intense light when she directed her attention to herself. Apparently she had become pure shine. Instead of disturbing her, this thought made her feel elated. She looked around; many other flowers of all shapes and hues swayed in the scented breeze. By willing to move, she found she could roam the garden's stone paths, admiring its beauty. She began to notice that all the plants were turning in one direction, reaching toward the sun. Following the straining petals' guidance, Amber ran out of the garden and entered a green meadow. There on the horizon, instead of the sun, was a glorious rainbow. She flew over the slopes of grass and wildflowers, chasing the shimmering arch, watching in ecstatic amazement as it drew closer. Then, cresting a large hill, she saw the spot where the rainbow was connected to the earth, feeding it bands of pulsing color. Without hesitation her light-self rushed into it like a kid jumping into a sprinkler. Immediately she sensed the electricity of the colors' rushing energies. With delight Amber marveled, *So this is what purple feels like, and red, and green!* The light of her being was merging completely with the sound, taste, and vibration of the colors.

Loud ringing pierced her vision, and Amber thrashed awake. She was back in the tub, water sloshing while the phone jangled. The bubbles were gone, the bath was lukewarm, and her skin was the texture of prunes. Where in the world had she been?

Still wrapping a towel around her, she hurried to the phone and picked it up.

"Amber?" said her sister, Violet. "You sound like you've been running a marathon."

"Oh, man, I must have fallen asleep in the bathtub; had the most bizarre dream."

"What are you doing sleeping right before your date with your new man? I was figuring I'd have to talk you down from the ceiling." Violet was married with two kids, a job, and a normal, regular life. Extraterrestrials, galactic missions, and out-of-body experiences were never going to fly with her.

"I don't know what I'm doing anymore, Violet. This guy is totally messing up my mind," Amber confessed. She provided a few of the particulars about how she and Blue had met, carefully leaving out references to Mars.

"So what are you guys going to do tonight?" Violet asked. "I mean, it's Sunday. Doesn't he have to go to work in the morning?"

Amber hadn't thought of coming up with a cover story. *It won't take long, sis, we're just going to have a little bitty Martian wedding.* "Uh...I don't know. Figured I'd let him decide."

"That sounds dangerous, men making decisions. Better for you to take the reins."

"Well, we won't be going anywhere if I don't quit jabbering with you and put some clothes on."

"I have a feeling he's just gonna want to take them off again."

"Hey listen, I already got the lecture about free milk from Dad. Don't worry, this one is very different from the last one and the one before."

"Amen to that," Violet said, laughing. "Okay, have fun chasing rainbows. Bye."

Amber stood, still dripping, looking at the phone in her hand. *Did she say chasing rainbows?* "I've reached the outer-fucking-limits now," she mumbled, throwing the phone down. She went back into the bathroom and showered, washing her hair while her mind tried to make some sense of what was happening. Her body still tingled from the intense feelings she'd experienced in her dream, and a strange, almost painful pressure radiated from her solar plexus, as if she had been punched in the stomach. Was that the answer her heart was supposed to be giving her?

Then she remembered the joy of flowing into the undulating rainbow, where there was no notion of self, no indecision, no fear.

"No fear," she said to herself in the mirror as she toweled her hair. That had a good sound. Weird as he was, she just couldn't believe he would ever hurt her. Once that was established, she could let her imagination blast off to all the exciting things yet to come this evening. If his kisses were that intense, lying naked in his arms would probably burn her to a cinder!

Two hours later, as the sun was sinking, Amber was still driving herself crazy. She was as ready as she was ever going to be, having finally selected a flowing skirt of bright batik print and a white top with lots of lace—more feminine than she usually wore, but after all, it was her wedding night!

Like a caged tigress she stalked around the house, never allowing the picture window to be out of sight for long. The sun seemed to stall on the horizon, still throwing long shadows. Then at last it disappeared, and Amber turned on the outside lights. She watched and paced as dusk slowly descended, her nerves snapping.

"I'm sure he's going to show up while I'm in the bathroom," she said out loud as she went in to brush her teeth for the third time.

When she came back to the living room and looked out again, she could barely believe her eyes. Not only had Blue arrived while the water was running, he was already halfway up the driveway, and she could instantly see why he had waited until it was this dark.

Here came the bridegroom, fully a month before Halloween, in a billowing purple caftan that made him look more like Gandalf the Wizard than a galactic diplomat. His hair was loose, spilling over his shoulders like a million electric filaments, and on top it was contained within a woven headpiece that glittered with colored stones.

"Hope the neighbors aren't watching," she whispered to herself, even as she felt her energy field growing and glowing at the sight. Heart in her throat, Amber turned from the window and hurried to the front door.

6

Goin' to the Chapel

Blue was a cosmic king striding grandly to the doorway, his features clenched in determined purpose, but when his eyes met Amber's, his face broke into a wide, boyish grin. He bounded into the house and swept her up in a whirling hug.

"I've been dreaming of this," he whispered, holding her tightly against his chest. Then he released his grip and bent to kiss her.

"Hey! Maybe we shouldn't start this up so soon!" Amber said, pulling away from him. At 7:45 P.M., it was just a little too early in the date for multiple orgasms.

Blue laughed softly, maintaining a firm grasp on her waist. "I've got the frequency fine-tuned now," he insisted, bending toward her again.

The masculine spice of his breath made her suddenly realize how hungry she was for his mouth. Her eyes stayed riveted on his lips as they sailed closer, then docked on hers in sweet, wet passion. Their tongues leaped and twirled like trained dolphins.

Finally he pulled his lips away and hugged her. "Guess it still has quite a bit of power," he rasped. Amber moaned agreement; his kiss hadn't lost any of its ability to fire up her nerve endings.

"But we'd better save this for after the wedding," he said as he released her and almost staggered back.

Now she took a good look at him and saw the outrageous complexity of his robe, the purple interwoven with strange, golden runes, and the headdress covered with hundreds of bright stones. Either the guy was a total freak or he sincerely wanted to marry her!

"What?" he asked, whether reading her face or her thoughts.

She hesitated, wondering how to put it. "You just seem so...serious about all this. I mean, getting married." She gestured to his wedding outfit. "I feel completely underdressed!" She tried a lighthearted laugh but it came out like a croak.

Blue's crestfallen expression let her know she'd hit his balloon head-on. "Of course I'm serious! I've never been more serious about anything in my life. What did you expect?"

"I don't know!" she wailed. "I guess I expected we'd go sit under the moon somewhere, light some candles and incense, repeat a few Martian phrases, and then...."

"And then what? Have casual sex?" he said curtly.

"Well, don't make it sound like a satanic ritual!"

"I'm not saying that, darling! But that way it's just biology! When emotions are brought to it, sex becomes so much more than the spilling of fluids. Together, we can elevate our energy into a higher realm; we can access dimensions neither one of us could ever attain alone!"

Amber sat down on the couch, speechless. She couldn't tell if she was stinging from his amazing words or his use of the term "darling."

"We live in third-dimensional reality," he continued, "but the universe is actually nine-dimensional. Not to demean it, but physical existence barely scratches the surface of what is truly possible. Still, we are here in 3-D precisely to search and explore and evolve. That's where the serpent energy comes in."

"I hate snakes," she broke in.

"No, you'll love this one! It's simply the coiled energy that lives at the base of the spine. Your Eastern traditions call it kundalini. When it can be controlled, channeled, and brought up to the higher chakras, there's no telling what powers will be awakened."

Amber couldn't help noticing how beautiful he looked, with his robe swirling and sparkling at every gesture, even though what he was saying was not exactly normal male conversation.

"When two people have sex, it's not just their bodies that intertwine, it's their energy fields, too. Your frequency holds the vibration of your partner, connecting you energetically—sometimes even years after the physical relationship is over."

"Gross!" Amber wrinkled her nose, thinking of the pollution her aura must surely be clogged with after all these years of Mr. Wrongs.

"That's why it's so important to find the proper mate, so that the sexual and the energetic coupling enhance instead of drain you," Blue explained.

"For somebody who never had any, you sure know a lot about sex," she observed.

He laughed. "I admit, it's always been just another teaching. I never fully understood what it meant until I met you."

"But why me? Out of all the billions of Earth girls! And don't tell me you Martians don't consider it 'casual' to marry somebody after knowing them four days!"

"Drastic times call for drastic action," he answered. "Besides, we've known each other much longer than that. Don't you feel it, too?" He pierced her with his blue stare, but before she could say anything he rushed to her and sank to his knees. He grabbed her hands and covered them with small kisses.

Amber sighed and burst into flames again.

"Amber, listen to me," he pleaded. "There just isn't time to explain and convince you, but this has been predicted and I know in my soul that you are the one—the one whose brain is wired slightly differently than most of humanity, whose heart is able to expand to accept the concept of extraterrestrial beings. You are destined to help lead your planet into the twenty-first century."

"Whoa, wait a second! The subject just went from fucking to the future of the world!" Amber tried to protest even as that familiar, warm tingle began to flow from his hands.

"Please don't phrase it like that!" Blue objected. "Our lovemaking is a sacred subject. And it does have a lot to do with the future of the world, but we don't have to think about that right now. Just know I love you," and as he said it she felt the tingle surge and intensify. "More than I've ever cared about any creature, more than my own physical vehicle. I swear I never knew emotion could feel like this! It's like plugging in to the power of Primary Creator."

"Well, gee, now that you put it that way...." Amber was completely blown away. What the hell, why not go through with whatever ceremony he had in mind and then treat herself to a huge helping of his ardor? Men with this kind of rap, Martian or otherwise, did not come down the pike every day.

"Just come with me to my place tonight. You won't be forced to do anything you don't want to do, I promise." The buzz coming from their joined hands was beginning to make her dizzy, but she nodded her assent.

"Yes!" he exulted, jumping to his feet and pulling her with him. "Kiss me again; I don't think I can live ten minutes without your lips!"

Amber clung to him, a demented hummingbird sucking his nectar, while white-hot desire sparked every cell in her body. His hands ran down her back and across her butt, pulling her hips close. *Forget the wedding,* she thought, *I want him right now!*

Once again he appeared to be reading her mind. "Let's get out of here before we do something unseemly," he said.

Soon they were on the Superstition Freeway in his truck, heading east out of the city. The moon had lost some of its girth in the past four days but none of its beauty, glowing in a thick field of stars.

"This looks like a good night for a close encounter with a UFO," Amber commented as she scrutinized the sky through the truck's windshield.

"Perfect night for viewing," he agreed. "Ships are going in and out of this area almost every night. Of course, not everyone is capable of seeing them."

"Why not?"

"Because of the limitations of the human brain. People build up a belief system and rigid boundaries on what they consider reality. Then when they pick up a signal that doesn't fit, one that would totally shatter their paradigm, it may not ever make it to the conscious area of the brain. It might get stuck in their subconscious memory."

"Is that why so many of the abducted people only remember it under hypnosis?"

"Exactly. The hypnotist helps them alter their brain-wave frequency so they can slip into another dimension where time doesn't exist and access their past, or even glimpse their future. Time only flows in a linear progression in the third dimension; everywhere else things happen simultaneously, strange as that sounds to all of us stuck in 3-D."

"So is that what you meant when you said this had been predicted? You've been to the future?" Amber asked, almost afraid to hear the answer.

"I've seen aspects of it occasionally, yes, but in this case it was told to me by someone else, a member of the Martian priesthood. And even though priests have acute powers to see both back and forward in time, there's always an element of probability with predictions in 3-D. Sometimes the things humans do surprise us."

"So what exactly did they say about you and me?" she persisted. "I want details."

"They said I would experience direct physical contact with an Earth female who would change my life," Blue answered as he turned off the freeway. "I guess we're making up the details as we go along."

He pulled to the side of the road and stopped. "Sorry I have to do this, but for now I think it's best if you don't know where we're going," he said as he produced a length of cloth from his pocket.

For a moment adrenaline pumped through her, then her mind screamed, *Oh right, the goddam blindfold!* This bizarre date was beginning to get unnerving!

"Well, if you insist," she said, allowing him to cover her eyes. "Although I swear I would never tell anyone where your hideout is." As he cinched the scarf tightly around her head, she couldn't help remembering Krystalee's lewd story of the blindfolded woman getting reamed by a stranger.

"It's just that it might be better for you if you can't tell," he replied. Amber wished she could see what expression he was attaching to that ominous statement.

The evening was balmy and they drove with the windows down. Deprived of her sight, Amber focused on the sounds and smells of the night. After one turn, an intense perfume began to fill the cab.

"Mmm...orange grove blossoming," she sighed.

"It almost smells as good as you," said Blue.

Amber giggled happily, "You are *so* outer space!" Then she remembered her bathtub trip to the gardenia garden. "Hey, I did what you suggested this afternoon, you know, meditating in a bubble bath, and the weirdest thing happened."

"Really? What?"

"Well, after I did some of the deep breathing stuff, I heard this strange snapping noise and it was like I woke up in a dream. I was in a garden, only I didn't have a body, I was more of a lightball, and I could fly around and go where I wanted. Then I jumped in the end of the rainbow and sort of tried on the feel of the different colors. It was a pretty wild dream."

"No dream," he asserted, smiling. "You're beginning to awaken to multidimensionality. I knew it! The same thing is happening to you that's happening to me!"

"What in the hell are you talking about this time?" she demanded.

"Rapid evolution—mutation, really—triggered by the interaction of our energetic frequencies. This is so exciting! I'm finally coming into the sun after seventy-three years in a cave!"

Amber felt Blue's hand on her leg just above the knee. *Please, God, let him cut this crazy crap and get to the part where he takes my clothes off,* she prayed silently.

"Who knows what skills and powers we'll discover together!" Blue went on. He rubbed her thigh, sending up another tingling tsunami.

"Well, I'm not so sure I'm ready to mutate," she said. "It sounds so radical."

"Ready or not," he sang happily.

The truck slowed and turned onto a dirt road, or so Amber judged by the bumpy ride. "Are we almost there?" she asked.

"Very close," he replied in a hushed tone. "Brace yourself, Amber. Expand your mind and don't let your belief systems limit your perception. You are about to become the first human to experience Martian civilization."

Amber's heart bounded faster. The blindfold was making her doubly anxious, and she struggled with the urge to rip it off her face. She bit her lip and Blue fell silent; the only sounds were the crunch of the tires on dirt and rocks, the chirping and buzzing of the desert insects, and the thundering in her temples of her own pulse.

As soon as he stopped and turned off the engine, she asked, "Can I take this off now?"

"Not yet," he said quickly. "Wait til we're inside." She heard his door open and shut, then his arms were around her, helping her down. "Walk slowly and hold my hand. The ground's a little uneven here." He guided her across the rocky terrain for several minutes, then let go of her hand and told her to stand motionless.

Suddenly a roar erupted in Amber's ears and her body jerked into a violent spin. After several seconds the sensation abruptly stopped, leaving her dizzy and reeling. Blue caught her and pulled off the blindfold.

"Are you all right?" he asked nervously.

"Yeah, I think so," she said, blinking in the soft light of the silver corridor she was standing in.

"Good! I was hoping human bodies could withstand molecular transfer."

"You were hoping?" she repeated. "What if they couldn't?"

"You did it, that's the important thing," he said. "Come on, we're late as it is." He took her hand and led her down the tunnel, a luminous tube that had no light fixtures but just seemed to glow from its walls. In spite of his warnings to expand her consciousness, Amber was finding the awesome proof of extraterrestrial intelligence a bit hard to take.

"Blue, please, let me stop a minute," she called. He turned and released her hand, setting her off balance. She stumbled to the side and threw her hand against the wall to steady herself. The silver surface under her fingers, which had looked like steel, now yielded under her touch. She yelped and jumped back, staring as her hand's clear imprint filled in and became smooth wall again.

"We don't build with metal, we use a material that is organic," Blue explained. "A type of bio-mechanic fusion that Earth scientists are far from discovering. It's remarkable stuff, don't you think?" He turned to her, smiling, then saw her shell-shocked expression. "You're having trouble integrating all this, aren't you?"

"That's the understatement of the millenium!" Amber cried. "You're really a Martian!"

Blue chuckled. "That's what I've been trying to tell you."

"I know, but...there was at least a chance you were a lunatic."

"No, that would be someone from the moon. I'm from Mars," he corrected. "Now come on, we're going to be late to our own wedding." He put his arm around her shoulder and propelled her down the corridor.

"Oh my God, if Mom and Dad could see me now...."

"They'll know, too, soon enough," Blue declared. The tube bent into a long descent and they bounced down it together on the spongy floor. Then it evened out and led to a small, domed chamber, also silver, smooth and devoid of any markings.

"How's your crumbling belief system?" Blue asked, turning to embrace her.

"Put it this way, it's crumbling but I haven't flipped out yet."

"Okay, great. I have to leave you for a little while but I'll rejoin you soon. Wait here, my love." He kissed her quickly on the lips, then whirled and vanished through an opening on the other side of the room.

Amber looked around the chamber, stunned, amazed, and terrified. What in the world had she gotten herself into? Even more urgent, how would she get herself out? She was inside an underground maze where the walls were alive! "Lord, just let me get out of this in one piece, maybe even sane, and I swear I'll never let my pussy lead me around again!"

"What cat have to do with it?" said a voice seemingly from nowhere. Then a large, Martian woman, with skin as white as Blue's, barreled through the doorway where he'd exited. Her plump figure was loosely wrapped in a peach-and-black sarong, with a matching turban covering her head. There wasn't a visible hair on her body.

"Excuse me?" Amber said politely, feeling more than ever like Alice in Wonderland.

"I, Rana," the woman said, stopping to bow while gesturing to herself. "Welcome to Amber!" She rushed up, embraced Amber and gave her a powerful squeeze. Clusters of metallic, geometric shapes that hung from her ears chimed with a strangely alluring music.

"Rana?" Amber echoed, and the woman nodded excitedly, sending out another loud shower of notes. "I guess Blue told you about me."

"Rana know all," she replied, winking. "Rana very happy this day arrive!" She smiled broadly as she studied Amber's less than ecstatic face. "Amber just nervous. Blue make delicious husband. No fear! Come, follow Rana," she recited, turning abruptly and hurrying to the tunnel.

No fear, wasn't I just thinking that not too long ago? Amber scrambled after her guide, whose rotund limbs were moving her bulk at an incredible speed.

"Rana sorry the English poor," she said chattily over her shoulder while she power-walked up the corridor. "Rana have interest in Earth food, no Earth language!" She cackled and slapped her solid haunch. "Not like Blue, he brainful scholar; all times study."

They came to a branch in the tunnel and Rana sailed into the left fork, which seemed to lead downward into darkness. Amber panted behind. "Wait for me!"

"No fear, we here," Rana sang as they emerged into a grotto full of pools and waterfalls, lush foliage and orchids, illuminated by hundreds of hidden, colored lights.

"Wow," Amber whispered. "What is this?"

"Goddess garden," Rana whispered back, fairly dancing on her toes with excitement. "Energy of female in form. Understand? Follow!" She hurried across a stone bridge which spanned the nearest pool.

Amber trailed behind her, not bothering to say that no, she did not understand, and was in fact beginning to hope this was just another one of those quirky dreams. She paused on the bridge to watch a group of brightly-striped fish in the crystal water, their long fins swishing like prom dresses. "Martian fish, too?" she wondered.

"Certain!" Rana laughed. She was perched on moss-covered steps, already halfway up a small cliff. "Mars have big biology before disaster. Now here preserve. Follow!" She leaped up the remaining steps with mountain-goat grace.

When Amber climbed the last stair, she saw they were standing on the top of a cone, the center of which was a bubbling, steaming pond, perhaps ten feet across.

"A hot spring!" she cried.

"Special spring," Rana corrected. "Bath of bride."

"But I bathed before I left home, and Blue said we were already late! Are you sure he's not waiting for me somewhere?"

Rana's laughter shook her like Santa Claus. "Amber much eager beagle bride! That good! But no hurry; time not matter. Blue wait entire lifetime!" She giggled under her breath as she pulled a pouch from under her garment. "Rana prepare waters. Amber extinguish clothing."

Amber watched in amazement as Rana took a stone from the pouch, then crumbled it in her hand and cast it into the water, all the while mumbling an unintelligible chant. She repeated this procedure with other powders and potions, her demeanor becoming more serious and reverent as she worked. At last she turned the tiny bag upside down and a cascade of white flower petals snowed down to the water's surface.

"Gardenia," Amber said softly, recognizing the scent. "Can't I keep any secrets from you Martians?"

"Special for Amber," Rana said, beaming happily. "Bride bath no clean body, clean energy." She looked over expectantly.

"I was kind of hoping Blue would be doing this," Amber muttered, unbuttoning her blouse. When she was standing nude, Rana held out her hand and helped her into the water.

"Blue tell truth; Amber beautiful Earthling," she said approvingly.

"Yeah, how would he know? He's never seen me like this," Amber commented, slipping into the percolating warmth. Marriage did seem insane for two people who had never seen each other naked. You didn't know what you were going to find under those clothes! Stretch marks, flab pockets, weird scars—not to mention the unknown, possibly scary territory called the Martian cock.

"What pussy?" Rana asked, neatly complementing Amber's thought.

"What did you say?" she exclaimed.

"Pussy," Rana repeated. "Amber say pussy lead her. Rana think of feline mammal."

"Oh!" Amber laughed, remembering her outburst. "Well, see, that word is like a nickname for the, uh, female sex organs. I really have no idea who started it; doesn't look like a cat at all to me."

"Ah," Rana said sagely, nodding.

"By the way, just to give you a little tip on expressions in English, it's *eager beaver*, which come to think of it is also a mammal that means women's genitals. Hmm, I suppose men made up those names."

"This why English confound poor Rana!" They both laughed, then were quiet for a moment, listening to the gurgling of the spring. "Conclusion, Amber think only body want Blue. Not heart."

"Well...that's partly true, because I know for sure my body wants him. And my heart wants him, too, but it's scared. We barely know each other, and I mean, come on, he *is* from a different planet!"

"That advantage over Earth males!" Rana's ear-chimes rang as she shook her head.

Amber had to snicker. "Okay, good point there," she agreed. "So far he's been wonderful. It's me I'm worried about. He's so serious, and I'm not sure I can pledge forever without lying. And I'm gonna be in front of a friggin' Martian priest, and you know *that* guy doesn't take this stuff lightly."

"Certain." Rana's blue eyes narrowed. "Amber no love?"

"I didn't say that; I think I could love him. It's just hard to be sure enough to get married! I mean, I don't even know if Martian divorce exists."

"If match correct, no need divorce," Rana countered.

"Well, duh! But *is* this a correct match? My God, I haven't even seen him with his shirt off, let alone sleep with him! I mean, I've test-driven so many of them over the years and never bought, and now I'm buying without even taking it for a spin!"

Rana dismissed this argument with a wave of her hand. "Amber think life have purpose?"

"Sure, I guess so," Amber replied, splashing her hand through the flower petals.

"*This* Amber purpose," Rana declared, rising, as if the matter were settled. "No fear—joy!" She opened her arms wide, round face beaming. Then she added, "Amber cleanse, Rana prepare gown," and bounded down the slippery steps without waiting for an answer.

Now Amber was alone, adrift in her own private volcano crater. She could see what Blue meant about the brain rejecting strange images; her cerebrum struggled like a mean stallion on the verge of mutiny. *I keep thinking I'll wake up, or the drug's going to wear off!*

Yet here she was, still in this otherworldly cave, surrounded by exotic ferns and flowers. And taking marriage advice from a Martian handmaiden! Still, there didn't seem to be any backtracking this adventure, so she might as well go for the ride. What else could she do, molecularly transfer herself back out?

When Rana returned, Amber greeted her with a calm smile. The warm bath had helped reconcile her mind with her reality, and she felt more confident, less on the edge of freak-out. Whatever looking glass she had gone through, they were certainly treating her like royalty!

"More relax?" Rana said, holding out a large swath of white material. "Come now."

Amber rose from the spring and let herself be wrapped up. "I'm going to get married in a toga?" she asked.

"This towel!" Rana exclaimed, tittering merrily. "Follow Rana." They descended the stone stairs, then turned and entered a vaulted doorway at the tiny volcano's base. Amber gasped as they entered the room it led to; the walls were completely encrusted with shiny gems that reflected their image like a million mirrors. In the center of the chamber stood an intricately-carved rack draped with Amber's wedding raiment. It was covered with fantastic golden shapes, just like Blue's dress, and endless yards of ethereal, flowing fabric. The color was bright, blood-red.

"Where I come from you wear white when you marry," Amber said dubiously.

"Martian bride wear red," Rana responded, shrugging her broad shoulders.

There was no recourse but to allow herself to be decorated, wound in layers of soft, caressing crimson. Rana brushed her hair, making her eyes close and her scalp tingle with the sensuous stroke of the bristles. Amber felt her energy field begin to pulsate and hum. Then the Martian put the brush aside, covered Amber's forehead with her right hand, and placed the left in the center of her back. Presently Amber felt Rana's palms warm up against her skin, and soon they were burning. Electricity churned across her skull, but instead of pain the sensation was ecstatic. Suddenly her chest seemed to jerk forward, and she felt pure love energy pouring from her heart.

Rana released her, grabbed her face in both hands and kissed her loudly on the cheek. "Amber ready!" she announced. She led Amber by the hand, out of the dressing chamber and back into the silver corridor. After a few twists and turns they entered a vestibule that contained a gigantic, arched double door.

"Door open, Amber enter," Rana instructed, then turned to go.

"You're not leaving me!" Amber hissed. "Please, Rana, I'm nervous! I want you to be with me when I go in front of the priest!"

"Amber humorous," Rana replied. "*Rana* Martian priest!" She ran off, disappearing into the darkness so quickly that her laughter echoed even after she was gone.

7

Two to One

Amber had no time to process anything; the huge doors began to retract, and she stepped tentatively through the portal. But she was not prepared for what she encountered—a monumental, four-sided structure, the pyramid walls so vast that their intersection at the apex was too far up to see. Walls, floors, and every other surface were emblazoned with hieroglyphics and geometric images, throwing iridescent colors that glittered as she slowly and cautiously moved into the cathedral.

"Amber!" The voice pierced her eardrums, though when she whirled and spotted Blue, he was a speck in the distant luminescence. They rushed toward each other across the polished floor, red and purple flames intent on ignition. Footsteps rang out and ricocheted under their billowing robes. When they impacted and embraced, she reveled in the pleasure of holding his firm torso again. *It may not be love yet,* she said to herself, *but it's a reasonable enough facsimile.*

"You're the most beautiful bride in the Milky Way," he breathed as he pulled her into a kiss. Just as suddenly, he dropped to one knee, yanking her down beside him. Amber looked up to see Rana gliding toward them in a ball of pure golden light.

Blue bowed low, uttering words in a language Amber couldn't comprehend. She watched in amazement as Rana approached her, holding something in her outstretched hands. Soon she could see that the glow was actually coming from the golden cloak Rana was wearing, the details of which were hidden in the emanating light rays. Only Rana's sweet, motherly face was sharply in focus. As she drew close, Amber could see that the object she carried was a web of some sort, a woven network of glowing fibers all radiating from one blue stone. Wordlessly she spread it over Amber's head, adjusting the stone so that it rested just above and between her eyebrows.

"Thank the Creator!" a voice spoke inside her head. "Interaction is so much more enjoyable when we vibrate on the same frequency."

Amber's eyes shot to Rana's face. She recognized the voice, but now it was manifesting in her brain in impeccable English. Not only that, the Martian woman's energy field was now visible; layers of shimmering light outlined her in many colors, her upper shoulders and head were ringed in a thick band of lavender, and on top of her head a spinning funnel of deep violet formed a huge, inverted hat.

"The control stone increases your vibration, nudging you into the realm where energies can be perceived and thoughts interpreted," Rana's voice explained. "Language is such a primitive way to communicate! I apologize again for my lack of expertise in your tongue."

Rana really is the priest! Amber only thought it, but the answer echoed in her head: "Do not let one's ignorance of a subject convince you they are of lesser intelligence."

Rana smiled in amusement at her thunderstruck expression. Amber turned to look at Blue and discovered him staring at her intently, his aura also glowing in hallucinogenic splendor. From his chest a whirling emerald twister of energy pulsed out of the purple wedding cloak. Then she noticed a twin vortex, of identical color, sprouting from between her breasts.

"Face him and feel the power of love," Rana's voice instructed.

Still kneeling, they turned to each other and the green whirlwinds surged and connected. Amber watched transfixed as both of their energy fields leaped out several feet and brightened. Blue closed his eyes in mute ecstasy. Amber trembled as her heart was filled with a bounding joy.

Whoa! This is such a trip! No sooner had she thought it than her brain reverberated with of the voice of her groom.

"This is nothing compared to the trip we're about to embark on!"

She stared at his sparkling eyes and motionless mouth. Thinking at each other was so disorienting!

"Come quickly," Rana's voice intruded. "This shall be brief. It is clear you two should not stay apart." She took them each by the hand and pulled them to their feet, then sailed off into the chamber's vastness, Blue and Amber flanking her like neon pontoons.

In the center, Rana stretched her arms skyward and a golden light poured from the tip of the pyramid, high above in the darkness. She motioned for the couple to move into its rays, then had them sit opposite each other, cross-legged. Laying a palm on each of their heads, she began to speak aloud, musical words in a rhythmic cadence that Amber assumed must be native Martian. Rana's violet energy crown whipped and enlarged, throwing sparks of electricity. This seemed to have an effect on the golden light tube they were in; it began to shimmer and vibrate, emitting a low toning hum.

Amber felt a tingle starting under Rana's hand on her scalp. Within minutes she was pressed to the floor by the strength of it, a faucet of golden energy opened to the max.

"Mars and Earth, your time for integration is obviously at hand!" Rana smiled and nodded. She had them hold their hands up, then press them together, palm to palm. Both auras jumped at the touch of their flesh.

"We are here on this most auspicious day," Rana continued telepathically, "to bond two entities in the search for higher consciousness through sexual union."

Amber gasped in spite of herself. They certainly weren't getting their wedding text from American television!

"Merging of the sexual organs, inclusive of the emotional bonds thereby engendered, are not to be entered into lightly," Rana continued. "In honoring the corporeal vehicle, honoring of the soul contained therein is essential."

Amber tried to decipher Blue's expression, but his eyes were reverently downcast. "Promises are made to be kept," Rana proceeded. "Love is meant to be nurtured. Physical ecstasy is meant to be shared and used as a means to enlightenment."

She tapped them simultaneously on the head and a band of light arced between them like a purple rainbow. "Remember your mother and father, Primary Creator."

"See in all dimensions." Their foreheads were linked by a snaking blue light-band. "Seek contact and understanding." A turquoise light stream united their throats.

"The heart energy needs no encouragement today," she said, smiling. "Endeavor to keep it so." The green band was by now a solidly spinning tube.

"Develop and use the power of the mind, while denying it tyranny." Yellow light connected them at the solar plexus. "Honor and explore all emotions." An orange streak shot out from each of their abdomens.

"Pay homage to your incarnate bodies, and do not denigrate the secrets of pleasure they contain." Red erupted from between their legs like illuminated smoke and swirled together. For several minutes they sat connected, Amber almost swooning from the over-amping charge. She couldn't really tell where her hands ended and his started anymore, there was only the overwhelming tingle and an escalating hum in her ears. His eyes were closed and no thoughts were coming through.

When their energy fields were thoroughly merged, Rana raised her arms to the ceiling again and the golden beam vanished. "My work here is done," she announced happily. "Blue and Amber, you are now joined in a unique partnership, the first interplanetary marriage." Gently grasping their wrists, she urged them to stand. "I surround you with blessings," she said with a last squeeze of their hands. Then she pivoted and marched off across the floor's gleaming acreage.

Amber stared after her, feeling as if she could be knocked over by the blast from a butterfly's wing. Then the retreating priest's voice sounded again in her brain: "Blue is like a son to me, Amber. I advise you to cherish him."

"I will!" Amber yelled out loud, setting off a chain of echoes in the enormous structure.

"Something else it may be useful to know," Rana's voice intoned. "Martians mate for life."

A pinprick of fear poked Amber's heart. What had she just done? She didn't know how it would be to mate with him one time, let alone for life!

"One more thing," Rana's voice interrupted, even as she disappeared into the distance. "You may kiss the bride!"

Amber turned to Blue and all fear vanished. He looked so eager and excited as he drew her against him and lovingly assaulted her lips. For a moment she thought she was going to rocket into orgasm again right on the temple floor.

"Come on, we can't stay in church all night," he said, tugging her by the hand.

"Where are we going?" She began to trot to keep up with him.

"Home." He flashed her a seductive smile, then quickly led her out of the temple and into the maze of tunnels.

Amber pattered behind him, bare feet sinking into the yielding floor and brain focused on exactly what was to come next. It was entirely possible she'd have to jump through more social hoops before getting to the evening's featured business. Surely Mr. and Mrs. Martian would make an appearance on their son's wedding day!

Blue finally stopped in front of a large silver porthole in the tunnel wall. "I think your culture calls this the honeymoon suite," he said with a flourish, and the door slid soundlessly up.

Amber knew this was no time to be shy, yet she hesitated and peered into the opening. Obviously a reception was not part of the tradition, and now that she was about to get what she wanted, her heart skipped and her stomach fluttered nervously.

"Don't I pick you up now?" he asked, scooping her easily into his arms.

Amber giggled and wound her arms around his neck. "I guess you watched a lot of those old, romantic movies on TV?"

"My favorites," he replied, stepping over the threshold.

The room was a small cave of several chambers, divided by curtains of stalactites and stalagmites, and lit with many fist-sized, glowing crystalline balls. The walls were desert tan, but the floor and other flat surfaces were sifted with white sand, fine-grained and soft. Blue lowered her gently to the floor.

"Wow," Amber whispered, stepping into the first white sand-drift. Seashells, crystals, and glittering geodes were strewn everywhere, and a subtle fragrance permeated the air, though flowers or incense were not in evidence.

The sand felt like cake flour underfoot as Amber ventured into the main chamber, a long room with two high windows at its far end. A moonlit landscape was visible through their irregular edges. Then she looked down and realized that all she had seen so far had been mere decoration. Practically encompassing the entire end of the room was a platform covered with soft cloth, and her heartbeat galloped at the sight of the marriage bed.

"Oh my God, blue satin...." she sighed, moving toward it.

"You were thinking about satin sheets one time. The color was my idea," Blue explained. "Do you like it?"

She floated down on top of it like a red parachute and patted the empty space beside her. He grinned and rushed into her arms. As they toppled into the sea of satin, Amber threw the headpiece aside. Auras were fun, but she was more interested in his physical vehicle right now.

"Okay, that was cool," she said, leaning over him, "but let me show you how we do it here on Earth."

8

Wedding Cake

Amber was melting in his mouth, kissing him as if that were the only nourishment she needed to survive. Indeed she felt stronger, more charged and alive, as they sucked, nibbled and licked each other's lips. The soft light of the glowing crystal spheres darkened Blue's features; except for the gold sparks tossed off by his conjured hair, he looked exactly like a human.

She slid from his mouth to kiss him along the jaw, then on the neck below his ear. "Would you do something for me?" she whispered.

"Anything you want," he replied immediately.

"Could you...turn off your hair?"

He sat up, laughing softly. "Are you sure you're ready? I thought you liked me this way."

She looked at him sitting there in the purple tangle of his groom outfit, his shoulders rising and falling with the exertion of desire, and couldn't imagine not wanting to eat him up.

"I like you this way just fine, but it's not the real you," she said. "You don't have to pretend anything just to please me."

"I'm glad you feel that way." He was instantly shorn to the scalp.

"Whoa," she giggled, "that was quick!" It wasn't that scary, just a little startling for it to happen so suddenly. Amber had seen so many impossible things tonight, it barely fazed her to watch her new husband's hair, eyebrows, and lashes vanish into thin air.

"It's actually a concentrated effort to keep it in place," he explained. "This is such a relief!"

Amber discovered she'd been exactly right; the sight of him was still raising her temperature. In fact, in some exotic way his naked head, pale and smooth except for the bulging blue veins, was driving her lust to a dizzying altitude. She ran her hand over the contours of his cranium.

"Relief? You ain't seen nothin' yet," she promised, swooping down on his mouth again. She closed her eyes, letting her fingers do the talking as they slid over his muscular back. The anticipation of seeing him in his birthday suit was sweet agony.

"Yes, we should dispense with at least a few yards of fabric," Blue said.

Amber laughed; they did look like two huge poppies of purple and red spread over the royal blue satin. "Are you reading my mind again?"

"I'll need to if I'm going to please you." He reached behind her to unclasp her garment. "I want this to be like your first time, too."

A flashed memory of that first time bolted unbidden into her mind. She'd sneaked into her boyfriend's bedroom, and it had been rushed and marred by the terror of discovery. Now here she was, not only married but sealed in an underground chamber in a place nobody knew existed, about to taste a young, beautiful, extraterrestrial virgin. *You've come a long way, baby!*

However, Blue was beginning to seem less virginal as he worked to free her from her dress. She gasped, trembling, as it floated to her waist, exposing her breasts.

"Incredible...." He didn't hesitate to reach out with both hands, brushing their outer curves with his fingertips. The nipples hardened and Amber groaned. She was burning up, the throbbing between her legs almost painful.

"I knew there were chakras in the female areola, but it's amazing to see it. Here, take a look." He retrieved the webbing with the blue stone and a plump pillow for her to lean against.

As soon as the stone was in place, the room erupted in swirling color, illuminated by their energy fields. They radiated out to the walls in various-hued strata, pulsing like a frenzied aurora borealis. The energy portals that lined the center of Blue's body were huge, whirling vortexes of light.

Amber noticed she was doing some glowing of her own. She looked down at her twin white tits glaring in her tanned torso, tips puckered and pink. An equally rosy energy plume danced like fire from each one, widening as they spiralled up to join the bioenergetic fiesta.

Blue lowered his face toward Amber's chest; the pink chakras pulsed and grew. She could feel her flesh follow its pull upward, her nipples straining like baby birds to his descending lips. He stopped inches from her skin, letting his head be bombarded by the cyclones of energy, eyes fluttering dreamily as they surrounded and merged with his own seething aura.

At last he dipped down and drew one tip into his mouth, lightly tonguing and suckling it. Animal noises gurgled from Amber's throat. Then she heard his voice in her mind say, "Am I doing this right?"

"Uh-huh," she panted. "Perfect."

He lavished her chest with more attention, crooning telepathic sonnets about her beauty with every stroke. Then he pulled more red fabric aside and rained kisses on her quivering abdomen. Finally uncovering her completely, she lay before him clad only in a skimpy thong bikini. Her legs parted, showing white lace and invitation. Both their auras blazed as he reached between her thighs.

"I had no idea it got this wet," Blue said, as innocent as a kid in science class, rubbing the sodden lace and bending closer to examine her. Slipping his fingers under the elastic, he began probing and petting her as if this were the job he was born to do. She writhed with intense pleasure, dangerously close to the edge of release.

When he yanked the fabric aside and lowered his mouth, she grabbed his hand, pulling it gently away. She had a different position in mind for their premiere sexual encounter. "I want to come together the first time."

He sat back, seemingly reluctant to take his hands away. "Tell me what you want me to do."

Amber couldn't help laughing, he was so sweet and serious, horny and awestruck all at the same time. "You're really enjoying this, aren't you?"

He scrambled into her arms again, pressing her near-naked body into his luminous robes. "For the first time in seventy-three years I understand the meaning of the word pleasure! It's suddenly clear that the most profound experience of it lies in pleasuring the beloved."

"Hey, you should start giving seminars."

"So tell me," he persisted. "What do you want?"

"Now let *me* strip *you*," she answered quickly. "I believe in equal opportunity loving."

"Okay." He sat up and reached behind him to release his robe, then allowed her to push him down on his back.

She knelt beside him and peeled purple from his white skin; he sank back into the satin. His shoulders and chest emerged, studded by the cobalt nipples, and Amber marveled again at his gorgeous shape. She sent her hands gliding across his clavicle, then pulled the sleeves down to free his arms. He stretched them over his head, and this gesture of surrender set her aflame.

Wrestling the robe towards his waist to afford her a better view of his tight abdominal ridges, there was no longer any way to ignore the purple tent that sprouted under the remaining cover. *No fear!* She stretched out her hand and wrapped it around the protruding shaft.

Blue twitched and shivered. Electricity raced from the captured organ up Amber's arm. It was already extremely hard, a blood-filled joystick that fit her grip as if custom-made. Their eyes locked as she brought up her other hand to help tear away the rest of the material.

None of the night's spacey revelations could have prepared her for the impact of the vision that now burned into her retinas. Blue lay exposed, his skin burnished tawny gold by the intimate lighting, but there was no mistaking the color of his displayed Martian manhood—it was undeniably, shockingly, bulbously blue.

Otherwise it was quite similar to the Earthling variety, except for the flared and fluted glans which made the tip look like a purplish Triceratops. The lack of hirsute cover enhanced the appearance of length; from the bottom of the blue balls it seemed to tower above his smooth stomach, a stomach that showed no sign of umbilical indent.

But it wasn't just the aesthetic appearance of the Martian penis that had penetrated her to the core of her being; it was the unshakable feeling of familiarity that resonated deep in her psyche, somewhere far below the logical mind. An ancient key turned in a hidden lock, and a dim recognition filled her. The image before her was not just a symbol of wanton lust, more a long-sought icon, and she bent over it like a pilgrim regarding the holy grail.

Her hair grazed his hips as she swung closer; he didn't seem to be capable of doing anything other than wriggle deeper into the bed. Her left hand wrapped around the warm, vascular pillar and they moaned in unison. She guided the dinosaur-head toward her descending mouth.

The blueberry knob shivered as she raked it with her raspberry tongue. Red and yellow energy flares were erupting from his groin and wallpapering the room. Blue abandoned telepathy and began using the international grunt-language of love. Amber gave up any pretense of tease, pushing his thighs apart with her knees as she climbed between his legs.

The smell roiling up from his crotch was voodoo perfume designed to drive human women wild. Amber buried her face in his lap and inhaled it greedily. She gave his dick a tender tongue-lashing, both hands busy caressing every part of his exquisite apparatus.

Blue was so lost in rapture, at first he didn't register the significance of Amber's actions as she sat up and ceased her ministrations. In a split second she stripped off her soaking thong and straddled Blue's body on all fours.

Then he understood. "I thought women liked to savor sex, make it last a long time," he protested feebly, though making no move to change his position.

"Baby, we're married," she reminded him hoarsely. "We've got plenty of time to savor it. Right now, if I can't get you inside me I'm gonna explode."

She slithered onto his chest, pink nipples sliding against blue ones. They kissed deeply while she gyrated against his erection, guiding it so it pistoned in her slippery groove. It only took one well-placed thrust to catch it on the edge and propel it into its sheath.

And just like a sheath made for its sword, they fit together. *Completion*, a voice said in her ear, or maybe it was just her own breath, rushing out in a tiny cry as he rested inside her, impaling her to the hilt.

But their hips couldn't stay still and they began to buck together, their auras flashing like funhouse lights on the fritz. Riding him from above, it felt like every stroke was going to send her off. She sat up, still pumping, longing for a glimpse of the blue stick invading her. Arching her back, she looked down and watched the otherworldly pole sliding in and out. The sight unhinged her; sent her spiralling toward the peak. *Just need one little push....* Blue reached between them and pinched the swollen knob in her pubic hair, pulling and rolling her clitoris between his fingers.

Amber shuddered as the wave of orgasm crested and broke. Her eyes snapped shut and she felt herself fall back into an abyss while a shower of stars erupted from the spot where they were connected. As each contraction wracked her, a sunburst of color streaked through her inner vision. At last she lay quiet, deep in blackness, the explosions of color mere dots far above her consciousness.

Lying on Blue's prostrate body like a sleeping leopard draped on a branch, Amber lost awareness of her physical surroundings. She might have drifted in an altered state for hours if a gentle slapping of her pelvis hadn't brought her back to 3-D reality. Remaining limp, she allowed him to rock her up and down to meet his thrusts and was soon aroused once more.

"I'm sorry," he said through gritted teeth. "I know you wanted to climax together, but I guess I don't understand the timing."

"Oh, baby, don't apologize! I must be dreaming because you are too good to be true." She kissed him on the cheek and said low in his ear, "Now shut up and fuck me."

Instinct took over and they began to pump in an ever-increasing tempo. The blue stone slipped from Amber's head and the room was suddenly muted; no more pulsing auras, just two citizens of the universe who were crazy about each other and showing it.

When he came, he grabbed her tight and convulsed into her, barely uttering a sound. Minutes passed as they rested, exhausted and content.

"I love you," he said finally, rolling her off his chest and tucking her under the satin covers. "Stay warm, I'll be right back." She watched him walk naked to the other side of the cave, then wrap himself in another gossamer robe.

"Hey, Blue," Amber called, propping herself up on one elbow.

He halted and spun around. "Yes?"

"I love you, too."

A smile lit up his face. "Yeah, I know. Isn't it cool?" He turned and exited the porthole.

"No, it's hot. Hotter than hell," she said softly to herself, burrowing back down into the silky sheets. It dawned on her that this was not just some wild adventure, it had escalated beyond that into the realm of life-changing developments. Whether anybody recognized Martian marriage or not, she was in love with Blue, no use denying it now. And that would have to be dealt with, integrating a Martian husband into a decidedly paranoid society. If they didn't like aliens from Mexico in Arizona, how were they going to react to one from another planet?

Amber lay back and gazed up through the windows. Moonlight still shone on the rocky peaks, though she could swear it was close to sun-up. The real world of traffic and buildings, work and paychecks, seemed an infinity away. The attitude of the man wasn't lending any reality to the proceedings, either; no guy on Earth said the things Blue did. It was as if he had a team of women writing his dialogue.

As she watched the landscape, another glowing disc began to emerge from behind a crag. There were two moons out there! She reclined, observing the slow ascension of the other moon, and wondering where in the universe they were now.

Blue returned, carrying a large basket. "Are you hungry?"

"Totally starving," Amber said, sitting up.

"I brought a few things from our artificial Martian farm, just to give you a little more flavor of where I come from." He held out a green fruit about the size and shape of a hand grenade. It had pointed spikes all over it that looked dangerous, but when she took it from him she could feel they were rubbery and harmless.

"What am I supposed to do with it?"

"Break it open, like this." He demonstrated with another one, digging his thumbs in and prying the skin apart. She followed suit, found the flesh inside a bright magenta color with tiny black seeds. He showed her how to eat it, chomping and licking out the middle until the husk was the only thing left. "Don't worry about the seeds, you don't even notice them going down."

She dutifully took a bite and chewed. It was amazingly light, dissolving in her mouth almost like ice cream. "Tastes like peach sherbet!" Soon they were several hulls piled on her plate.

"Now this is a traditional dish from the old country. It's a paste made from a white bean, spiced with indigenous herbs. You dip pieces of baked, grain-based items in it."

"You mean, like bread?"

"Right. Or these." He showed her a bowl with the dip and a platter with small pieces of toast.

"These taste just like bagel chips," she exclaimed, testing one out.

"That's because they are. I picked up a bag on the way over to your house."

Amber laughed, feeling thoroughly wonderful from head to toe. Picnicking in bed with an outrageous man who was intent on satisfying your every desire? It did not get any better than this! "Hey, what's with the two moons in the sky?" she asked, suddenly remembering. "Am I seeing double?"

"These windows are more than a thousand feet below the surface," he answered. "That is a holographic image, sort of like a television picture, of my home world before the disaster. Mars, of course, has two moons."

"Oh, of course. Every dimwit knows that," Amber said. "So what did happen to Mars? Did you get smacked with a meteorite, like the dinosaurs, or was it the people's fault, like a nuclear holocaust?"

"It was an asteroid, and not our fault at all. The populace was actually learning to do things in partnership with the planet instead of exploiting it. That's one of the reasons I don't understand Prime Creator's motivation in eliminating my world. Anyway, the asteroid didn't even impact the surface of Mars, it merely shot through the outer edge of our atmosphere."

"So, that sounds good. It missed you," she observed.

"Yes, but its size was so mammoth, it tore an extensive hole in the atmosphere, which reverberated with the disturbance. A wave started, then spread in both directions around the planet until it met itself on the other side. When it impacted, it created more waves in the other direction. The gravity is much less than that here on Earth; it couldn't calm the action of the ripples. In fact, they grew more intense."

"So they just kept bouncing off each other?"

"Yes. Until pieces of the atmosphere started being flung off into space. It took several years for it to manifest; the planet became more and more of a dust world. Enough time, at least, to perfect underground living and to plan an escape to a more hospitable environment."

"Well, Earth will be that for you as long as you stick with me."

He grinned and scrambled on top of her, starting the mating dance over again. It was longer this time, more bold and passion-fueled. Then mutually spent, they cuddled together and fell into deep sleep.

Some time later she became dimly aware that his cock was inside her again. But before she could swim up to waking consciousness, it was over and she drifted away. What must have been hours later she opened her eyes and found herself still wrapped in his arms. Blue was watching her, relaxed and happy.

"Damn, how many days went by while we've been in paradise? I bet they really wondered when we never showed up for work on Monday morning."

"I put us in a nexus," Blue said. "For lack of a better word you might call it a time bubble. Monday morning hasn't happened yet."

"Oh, I see! So are you saying we have time to do it once more before work?"

Blue told her that was exactly what he had in mind, and they set about enjoying their eye-opener. This time the spasms of her orgasm triggered his and they growled to heaven in sync.

"Ah, now we're vibrating on the same wavelength," he murmured as they fell back into dreamland.

Later, when Amber woke up, a sunbeam was streaking through the window, making her squint. She sat up, groggy, trying to locate herself on the grid of reality. Of all the freaky occurrences she had witnessed lately, this was perhaps the most unsettling: She was at home in her own bedroom, and the clock on the nightstand read 6:45, Monday morning.

9

Crazy Dream

For one panic-stricken moment, Amber thought it had all been a delirious dream. After all, here she was in her own bed, with no memory of the trip home. Not that it had never happened before, but copious amounts of alcohol had always been involved in those scenarios, and she felt fine with no hint of a hangover.

She sat up, noticing she was completely nude; usually she at least threw on an old T-shirt before bed. Then a subtle buzz from below captured her attention. She felt between her legs and there was no longer any doubt—her wedding night had left her oozing and deliciously sore.

"Thank you, *Jesus!*" she shouted, flopping back into her pillows. Then she saw her clothes from the night before, folded and piled on her rocking chair. On top lay the woven headpiece and the blue stone.

"Wow," she breathed, scrambling out of bed. She held it up gingerly, as if it might dissolve under scrutiny. In her ever-so-normal human bedroom, it seemed like a prop from the wrong movie.

The phone shrilled and Amber threw on her robe and raced for it. Who in the hell could be calling her so early? Her thoughtful and considerate husband, wondering if her molecules transferred home okay?

"Hello," she said breathlessly.

"What? This isn't a recording? Girl, have you been out all night?"

"Hi, Krystal!" Amber said cheerily. "Oh honey, I've been to Mars and back!"

"Well, at least we're thankful you are back! I've got my coffee right here, so you might as well start telling me."

"Oh, man! I don't know if I can do this over the phone; it's going to take hours to fill you in." Amber settled into the couch.

"Okay, how about the condensed version? Can't you see I'm drooling here?"

"All right, all right," Amber consented, giggling gleefully. "It's all true; the Martians live in a gigantic underground tunnel system, they talk through telepathy, they see energy fields, and their men are every Earth woman's fantasy!"

"Yeah, and the moon's made of green cheese, right?" said Krystalee.

"No, I'm serious! I was there, Krystal. I saw it with my own eyes. It's totally incredible but true."

Krystalee made a snorting sound. "So what happened? Did you marry him?"

"Yeah. In front of a Martian priest and everything. It turned out the priest was a woman, a really cool lady, too."

"This is nuts. You didn't happen to drink anything before this, like, where he could have slipped you a peyote button or something?"

"No! I swear! It was all real!" Amber protested.

"And then what? You fucked his brains out?"

"Well, yeah. It was our wedding night, y'know."

"This is too hilarious, this guy is just too much!" Krystalee exploded. "You should've just told him in the beginning he didn't need to go to so much trouble to get you into bed!"

"Okay, scoff all you want, but he really loves me," sniffed Amber. "And I love him, too. I know it sounds fast, but I've fallen like a rock."

"Hey, don't make me puke up my coffee, okay? You've gotta be kidding me! Your one-week anniversary isn't 'til Thursday, and already you're in love and married? I think you've finally lost your mind."

"Maybe so, but I don't miss it," Amber returned. "Listen, I have undeniable proof. When can we get together?"

"Lunch. I'll call Quinn. Call you back when we've got a plan. I'm worried about you, girlfriend." With that ominous remark, she hung up.

This was not the sort of enthusiastic response Amber had been anticipating from her friends! Were they going to hold his background against him? Then she realized it was quite a stretch for anybody to believe what she had just said. She barely believed it herself.

Now what was she going to do? Go to work? In one night, everything had changed. Her interest in illustrating a book which speculated on the existence of extraterrestrials had totally flown the coop. Why speculate when you could palpate the real thing?

Even though it was barely past seven o'clock, Amber put on music and began doing her chores, watering plants, feeding her goldfish, straightening up the house. Somehow she figured this would also organize her mind. She sang along, throwing in a few dance steps as she worked, basking in an afterglow of satisfaction and happiness. When the clock read a civilized 8:00 A.M., she picked up the phone and called home.

"Well, hi, sweetheart," Mom said with a note of surprise in her voice. "I never thought you'd be up this early after a big date. Don't tell me it fell through."

"Not hardly! I had an unbelievably wonderful time, and...I think I'm in love."

"In love! That was quick."

"I couldn't help it," Amber admitted. "He's so beautiful and sweet and caring and sexy! Mom, he's really different."

"That's a plus. Some of the ones you've picked in the past were real winners."

"I know, but obviously they were the dues I had to pay to deserve this."

"Well, honey, I think that's marvelous. When do we get to meet him?"

"Soon, I hope." Amber suddenly realized she had no idea when she would see him again. Surely he would call. Surely he missed her as desperately as she already missed him.

"So you're seeing him today?" her mother asked.

"Well, uh, I'm sure I am, but I don't think we really set up a meeting."

"What do you mean? You didn't discuss it when he brought you home?"

"See, he didn't bring me home...he sent me." How do you tell your mother your boyfriend is a Martian and rearranges your atomic structure instead of driving you?

"In a cab?"

"No, not really," Amber stalled. She had always prided herself on being totally open and honest with her mother, but this was way worse than telling her about getting a tattoo. "Mom, listen. When I said he was different, I mean really, really different. Like, out of this world."

"Uh-huh," said Mom amiably.

"I mean, like, not from here."

"Amber, for crying in a bucket, we had an exchange student living with us when you were in high school, remember? Your father and I don't have a prejudiced bone in our bodies! What's wrong, is he black?"

"No! No, nothing that mundane." If she told the truth, her parents were going to have her committed.

"Amber, stop worrying. Bring him around. I would love to see you find somebody nice," her mother said reassuringly.

Amber could picture it, the Martian and the Voss family. *You guys don't mind if we move to Alpha Centuri, do you?* Better to let them meet him and be won over by his charm. "Well, I think he's a keeper, Mom,'" Amber said.

"Wait a minute, Dad just finished his second cup of decaf and it looks like he's got some wit and wisdom for you." There was a short pause, then she said, "You're not going to like this, but he says, 'Fools rush in where angels fear to tread.'"

Amber laughed. She hadn't expected any different. "Well, tell him I'm no angel, in case he hadn't already figured that one out!"

"Don't listen to him, honey. What does he know? He's only had one partner in his whole life," Mom counseled.

"The lucky dog."

Her mother laughed. "Just let me know ahead of time when you're going to bring your new young man and I'll fix something special for dinner."

"You *are* an angel," Amber answered. She promised to be in touch soon and they hung up.

And now, at 8:23 A.M., the question really was—when would she see him again? If telepathy existed, why couldn't she send for him in her head? She sat with her eyes closed, and sent out the message: Blue, my love, please, please contact me today!

The phone rang and Amber jumped. *Dang, that was pretty immediate response!* "Hello?"

"Hey, it's me again," said Krystalee. "I talked to Quinn, got her out of bed, really, and she says lunch is cool. We're lucky, she only has one appointment this morning, and then she's off."

"Killer. Where do you want to meet?"

"The Greenhouse at 12:30. How does that sound?"

"Perfect."

"Oh, and I better warn you," Krystalee cautioned. "I told her you were married and she's pissed!"

"Ooh, I'm so scared," Amber returned. "Geez, I spent the whole night in an alien stronghold! I'm not gonna tremble before her."

"We'll see about that. Can't wait!" Krystalee said good-bye and Amber looked at the clock. Shortly after nine. How was she going to kill three and a half hours? It was true she had another drawing to do for the book, but her motivation was gone. All she wanted to do was talk to him, or talk about him, if she couldn't actually be in bed with him making love.

She took a shower, dressed, and did force herself to sit down with her drawing pad. "Extraterrestrial contact," she said slowly, enjoying the sound of the words. Her hand began to sketch two figures, across from each other on the paper. One was bald, but handsome, wearing unusual clothes: Blue. The other was female, red hair flying electrically, a look of stunned fascination on her face: Amber. Their hands were together, surrounded by a golden glow that beamed from between their palms. Another golden streak connected their foreheads. She hoped they liked it at Superstition Press; something told her it was the last drawing she would do as her former self.

"Where is he? Why doesn't he call!" she yelled to her fish. Absorbed in her drawing, the time had flown, and soon she could go meet her girlfriends. She resisted calling him at work, trying not to seem like a leech. *I always thought marriage eliminated insecurity. Guess not!* Quickly she changed clothes, stuffed the headpiece in her purse, and left the house.

It felt good to be outside, the hot sun grounding her. She drove to the restaurant with the windows down, savoring the atmosphere of good old Mother Earth. Still, the air conditioning was welcome when she breezed into the Greenhouse and spotted her friends at a table in the atrium in back. Krystalee grinned and waved when she saw her, but Quinn sat stone-faced, a statuesque African queen.

"It's Mrs. Martian!" Krystalee squealed as Amber sat down. "You don't really look mutated."

"Please do not humor her," Quinn implored. "She has totally wigged and encouraging her schizophrenia is not going to help."

"Well, hi, Quinn. Nice weather, isn't it?" Amber said sweetly. "Man, nothing like cutting to the chase!"

"Listen, I would love to be making idle chitchat, but you are the one who keeps dropping little bombs like, 'Oh, I'm marrying an ET.'

Now, honey, it wouldn't be such pressing business except that I happen to care about you, therefore I'm a bit concerned when I see your mind erode." Quinn really was an impressive sight, nostrils flaring, muscles bulging under her spandex top. Still, Amber laughed.

"You guys just don't get it, do you? The Martians live here on Earth with us, they have for a long time, and now they want to come out of the closet! This is the frigging event of the century!"

"K-lee, maybe the guy hypnotized her," Quinn mused. "You know, like in those fucked up cults where they get you to believe some complete asshole is the new incarnation of Christ."

Fortunately the waitress defused the tirade; when Quinn started using swear words, her anger was escalating into rage. As they ordered lunch, she couldn't resist asking for a "tall glass of Thorazine for my delusional friend here."

"Look, there's only one way to settle this: We have to meet the cat and decide for ourselves," Krystalee declared.

"The sooner the better," Quinn agreed. "I've got a whole suitcase of questions for him. For instance, how can he so shamelessly take advantage of my girlfriend's naiveté just to get into her pants? I don't trust a man who lies."

"Hold on a second, Quinn. Maybe he really is a Martian. Look what I cut out of the paper today." Krystalee retrieved a clipping from her purse and unfolded it. The headline read, "Scientists: Meteorite analysis suggests onetime life on Mars."

"Oh yeah, I heard about that this morning on CNN. And ancient organic trash is a far cry from a man who can bullshit you into bed," Quinn said with disgust. "That don't prove a thing."

"Let me see that." Amber took the clipping and scanned the first paragraph. "Wow, NASA says it's 'unequivocal evidence.'"

"Yeah, of there once being some moss on a rock up there. Doesn't mean your boyfriend came from another planet," reasoned Quinn.

"Husband," Krystalee reminded. "And I'm getting real sick of all this philosophizing when I want to hear what the hell happened last night!"

"Oh God, you didn't really marry him, did you?" Quinn whined with a grimace.

"In the eyes of Martian law, I guess I did," Amber said.

"I'm gonna smack her, Krystalee," Quinn warned.

"Would you please chill! Just hush 'til she finishes telling us and then we'll have the debate."

While Quinn and Krystalee ate, Amber picked at her fruit salad and tried to remember everything that had happened. Even to her own ears it sounded outrageous, but the story poured out, Amber in Wonderland with a decidedly X-rated finish. Quinn listened in silence, fixing an icy stare on Krystalee whenever she gasped, laughed, or interjected a comment.

When Amber paused after describing awakening in her own room and momentarily thinking she'd been dreaming, Krystalee jumped in. "Now don't tell me your sore puss is the undeniable proof you were gonna show us."

"No! I almost forgot!" Amber pulled out the headpiece and laid it on the table. Just seeing this artifact from last night made her tremble to be with him again.

"So?" Quinn was not impressed.

"So this is it, the stone they hung over my third eye so I could see auras and be telepathic."

"Your third eye, huh? Honey, you better stop getting more eyes and try to get that one pitiful brain to work! Let me see that thing." Quinn snatched it across the table and held it up.

"Try it on," Amber urged.

"In public! Are you out of your mind? I'd look like a fool."

"Here, I'll try it," offered Krystalee. "Been a fool in public many times and lived to tell about it." She arranged the stone on her forehead. "Like this?"

"Yeah, a little bit further toward the eyebrows," Amber coached. "What do you see?"

"Not a damn thing," she reported. "But I admit I've never seen this rock before; it's such an intense color of blue. I'd like to take it to the lab and get a closer look."

She passed it to Quinn who quickly held the stone up to her forehead without draping the net over her hair. "Real pretty. But it doesn't work."

"Let me see that! It sure worked last night." Amber took it back and put it in place on her head. Immediately Blue spoke telepathically, "Finally! Please phone me at work, darling, I can't wait to talk to you!"

Both her friends were watching Amber's wide-eyed look. Krystalee was bathed in bands of green and violet, and Quinn's aura was shooting streaks and spots of red from around her skull. It was one thing to experience paranormal abilities in a Martian temple, and quite another to be doing it in a restaurant in broad daylight.

Amber slipped off the headpiece. "Gotta make a phone call."

"Oh, what happened, did a transmission from the Starship Enterprise come through when you put on your macramé space cap?" Quinn called as Amber hurried to the phone.

"No, obviously it was Blue," said Krystalee.

"Don't you start believing in this crap..."

The sound of her friends' bickering faded as she closed the door of the old-fashioned booth and dialed Blue's number at Superstition Press. She asked for his extension and sighed as his voice slid down her ear. "This is Blue," he said. "Is that you?"

"Yeah. Hi, baby," she answered. "How are you doing?"

"Much better now. I am just so in love with you I don't know what I'm doing. I can't think about anything else."

Amber's heart soared. That was definitely the right answer!

"It's totally useless for me to be here," he confessed. "Every time I think about you I get hard, and that's about every ten seconds, so it's difficult to walk around the office. I can't go on like this."

His words sent shivers rippling down her belly. "What do you want to do?"

"Go on our honeymoon, of course! Immediately if not sooner."

"How are you going to get time off? It's your third week!"

"Tell them I got married and need to go on a honeymoon. Simple. By the way, ever been to Sedona?"

"No, but I've heard of it. You mean the place that's supposed to have magic powers?"

"Right. Energy vortexes. There are many of them at Sedona. I think it would be electrifying if you and I get near them."

"Honey, whatever you want to do, though I doubt if we need a vortex to get electric. I'm about ready to spontaneously combust right now."

He laughed. "I'm leaving work early. What are you doing and how soon can I come get you?"

"I'm finishing lunch with my girlfriends. They're dying to meet you, by the way. Then I'll go straight home and pack."

"I'll pick you up in two hours. And tell them I'll meet them when we get back, okay? I don't want to be rude, but this is our time and I want to be alone with you."

"I second that emotion," she assured him. "I can't wait to get my hands on you and show you what I mean."

"I'm all yours, Amber. Every part of me, body and soul," he declared.

Amber felt as if her bursting energy field was about to shatter the glass in the phone booth. "I love you, Blue. So much."

"Thank the angels!" he exulted. "I am the most fortunate organism in the galaxy!"

After several good-byes, Amber hung up and returned to her friends. The lunch dishes had been removed, but three cups of coffee steamed on the table.

"Sit down," Quinn directed. "We still have a lot of talking to do. Was that Mr. Spock?"

"Quinn, I thought we agreed that ridiculing her was not going to help," Krystalee said. "Let her talk, if that's what you want to do."

"Yes, that was Blue," Amber offered. "He wants to meet you guys, of course, but after we get back from the honeymoon."

"The *honeymoon*?" Quinn's eyes rolled dangerously. "Let me get this straight, you're going away with this maniac again tonight?"

"Yeah, he wants to go up to Sedona to check out the energy vortex."

"In other words, lean over a canyon and pretend you feel something, giving him another way to bamboozle you. And child, it's a pretty sad thing to see how easily he's doing it to you." Quinn shook her head slowly. "I can tell nothing I say is going to change your mind."

"Doubtful," Amber answered. "Especially after that phone call, I am officially, madly in love."

"Is that so?" Quinn snapped back on the offensive. "Let me interrupt your wet dream to ask you this—when you saw that his...thing...was a weird color and shape, you did remember to put a rubber over it, didn't you?"

"Quinn, he was a virgin! If anything he needed protection from me," Amber said.

"Honey, if he was a virgin, I'm Vanna White." Quinn stood up. "I told you, Krystalee, we need to call either the Betty Ford Clinic or the cuckoo's nest." She threw several bills down on the table. "You call me when and if you get back, and tell your old man I'm real anxious to meet him."

"Come on, don't get mad," Amber implored to Quinn's backside as she strode for the exit. "Shit! She's a little touchy today, don't you think?"

"Yeah, well, the bitch gets like that when her friends marry extraterrestrials," Krystalee stated, draining her coffee. "I, on the other hand, am a little more open-minded and I'm way more into joining you in your delusion than trying to talk you out of it. Come on, don't we have a honeymoon to pack for? We can hit Victoria's Secret on the way home and you can fill me in on some more of the juicy details."

10

Honeymoon Typhoon

The stone," Krystalee said. She and Amber were in the mall's parking lot, saying good-bye after their shopping trip.

"What about it?" Amber replied.

"Come on, just let me take it for a couple hours. Maybe I can tell if it really is Martian or not."

"I don't know; it's almost like my wedding ring...." Even though she would be seeing Blue in a little more than an hour, the Martian artifact connected her to him in a comforting way.

"I'll guard it with my life," Krystalee promised. "You're going to be right with him anyway, so you don't need to read his mind."

This was a good point, and even though auras were fascinating, it was still going to take some time to get used to seeing everybody in the center of a light show. "Well, okay, but only because scientific proof might convince Quinn."

Krystalee smiled as she took the headpiece and folded it carefully into her purse. "Hey, all we have to do is get them together and have him turn his hair on and off. That ought to do it." She gave Amber a hug. "Have a happy honeymoon. Get a piece for me."

"Oh, right. Like you have trouble in that department."

"Hey, it's a desert out there." Krystalee climbed in her Mustang. "Appreciate what you've got, even if he isn't human."

"Believe me, I do!" Amber called. "Mainly *because* he's not human!" She waved good-bye, jumped in the Toyota and raced home, wondering what else she was going to need to pack besides the black lingerie that was smoldering next to her on the front seat.

Appreciative? Her joyous state of shock had to be what the people feel when they answer the door and the Prize Patrol is standing there with a check for millions of dollars. The overwhelming reality of it puts everything else about life in perspective. Endlessly running instant replays of last night, she thrilled to the memory of Blue's body and his tender words. She examined the implications of what had happened from every angle, turning it like a gem and admiring each facet. Would she really go live with him in an underground cave? Sure, a cave would do fine. An igloo? A little chilly, but if that's what he wanted. A grass shack, a tree house, a mud hut, as long as they were in it together. Her love had taken her over like a fever and lifted her to another level of existence, where the events of what he called 3-D could not touch her happiness.

At home she packed and closed up the house. She didn't know how long she would be gone, but she could always call Mom and have her come tend the plants and fish. Until that became necessary, nobody else needed to know she was going. She checked her outfit in the mirror, blue jean shorts and flowered cotton top; despite the fact that it was officially autumn, the heat of summer ruled the desert.

When the truck finally pulled up in front, Amber's heart lurched and began to thump wildly. She felt her aura detonate into fireworks as she watched him walk up the driveway, a sensuous panther in black denim and purple T-shirt. He was sporting an even longer ponytail than before, a thick tassel that hung halfway down his back. A simultaneous mixture of affection, animal mating frenzy and extreme nervousness sizzled inside her.

She held the door open for him and he stepped politely inside. Then he grabbed her and pressed his face into her hair. "Don't ever stay away from me so long again!"

Amber wrapped her arms around him and tried not to tremble, but his presence had already seized control of her body. Blue slid his hand against her cheek and steered her into his mouth. The kiss was long, deep, passionate and utterly delicious. Amber burst into a fireball of giddy love and desire.

"This must be what drug addiction is like," Blue said, leaving her lips to plant little kisses along her jaw. "I'm so captured by this...by you, by us. The emotions created by it are changing me down to my DNA."

"Well, I'm high as a kite! Not looking to sober up, either." She raised her face and he kissed her again. The energy between them prickled and surged.

"Come on, let's get on the road before we get too drunk with this," he said, laughing and pulling away from her with obvious effort. "Two hours and we'll be there, in plenty of time to see the sunset."

They walked hand in hand to the truck, like two teenagers in the throes of first love. "I like your shirt," Amber commented. It showed a drawing of Earth above the words, "Love Your Mother."

"Yeah, isn't it great? I went crazy at the Kmart, wait til you see all the neat stuff I got. I'm really starting to get attached to this planet." Blue stowed Amber's satchel, then helped her inside. "There's a seat belt in the middle," he suggested. "I don't want to be reaching to touch you."

She scooted to the center of the seat. "Why don't you just beam us up there?"

"The same reason I put my hair back on. When on Earth, do as the Earthlings do. I'm not quite ready to openly proclaim my heritage." He climbed in beside her and cranked the ignition.

They rode out of Phoenix in rush hour traffic and headed north on Interstate 17, Amber sitting so close to Blue that resting her left hand on his right thigh was completely natural. Her mood was hyper-jubilant, like having her birthday, Christmas, and a lunar-landing all on the first day of vacation.

Soon they were cruising through wide, flat expanses populated by the giant Saguaro cacti, their thick arms raised as if in greeting. Rock formations in the distance projected layers of color against a deepening, clear blue sky.

"Television doesn't do your planet justice," Blue said. "Look at the size and expanse of the place!"

Amber smiled, trying to imagine what it would be like to emerge from a cave after seventy-three years and experience the wonders of the world. "Those cartoon cactus marching across the desert look way more like the green men from Mars than you do."

"You never know, maybe they are aliens. Many species can appear in whatever physical vehicle they want to."

"Uh...explain, please."

"Okay, to put it simply, there is more than one type of extraterrestrial. Some have their own physical shells, and some must borrow one if they want to manifest in 3-D," he said, sliding his hand onto her thigh. "There are Walk-ins, who enter an existing body after its birth, and Crawl-ins, who become the entity's consciousness as a fetus. There are also times when a spirit takes on nonhuman form. The lizard on your windowsill could be an ET."

"Hey, I'm having enough trouble adjusting to the man beside me being an ET!"

"I know that and I'm trying to take it slow. But there's so much for me to teach you, and so much for me to learn from you, I'm afraid I'm going to challenge your understanding sometimes. On the other hand, you already believe Martians exist, while the rest of the world is fascinated over polycyclic aromatic hydrocarbons in a meteorite."

"You mean the Mars rock? Yeah, what's up with that? Your planet is all over the news."

"It's another step in preparing humankind. I knew it was coming, but I didn't think it would be this soon. There are many minds that will need time to absorb this information and grow."

"Yeah, like my friend Quinn. She thinks you're a fake and that I'm insane."

"Well, that has been the official stance of the mass consciousness for decades. That's all changing now, as more and more people validate actual sightings or question the integrity of a government that continues to deny knowledge. The mass vibration rises, making the human race increasingly ready for contact."

"So is that why Quinn and Krystalee couldn't see auras with the stone?" asked Amber.

"Exactly. The stone only boosts the frequency of the wearer. Not everybody makes the leap to telepathy and clairvoyance. You're just on the cutting edge." Blue rubbed her bare leg above the knee. "Don't worry, your friends will catch up eventually, along with the rest of humanity."

"And then what?"

"And then the world as you know it will be over." He laughed, but Amber didn't think that sounded too funny.

As the road climbed steadily into the central highlands, they began to see the red rocks that are one of Sedona's landmarks. Blue asked why she had never been there before.

"I guess words like 'vortex' never meant anything to me before. Besides, I haven't spent that much time in Arizona since high school." She went on to describe her college years on the east coast and her subsequent nomadic lifestyle as she chased around after the pot of career gold, including a long stint as starving artist in New York.

"Finally I figured out what really mattered to me was being nearer to my family; I got tired of seeing them once or twice a year," she finished. "So with Mom and Dad here, and one of my sisters, Phoenix was the logical choice. What luck for me that it's also the home base of single Martian men!"

"Not luck, synchronicity," he said with a smile. "Not single anymore, either." He caressed her leg again and the butterflies beat against her belly.

"So what about your parents?" she asked. "Don't I get to meet them? They must be curious about your alien bride."

Blue paused and looked out to the horizon. "Amber, it has been many years since my people reproduced through sexual union. Even in those days it was something that was done at certain times and only for the purpose of procreation. I guess I should have told you this before, but my parents were a cylinder of green slime."

Amber considered this news for a few moments. "Well, so much for dinner with the in-laws," she said. "Is that why you don't have a belly button?"

"Yes. I'm sure they could have fashioned one for me, but at the time of my birth it wasn't known that my body would later be subjected to such intensive investigation."

He glanced over and smiled.

"Ha! I'm just getting warmed up!" Amber crowed. "But I still don't understand. Why did Martians stop reproducing naturally?"

"It happened when Mars got so hostile that the only life existed in underground caverns, much like the ones we built here. They knew they had to evacuate the planet, so they filled ships with people of all ages. But on the way to Earth, it was the children who couldn't adjust to the changes in atmosphere and gravity. Many died on the journey; none survived long after arrival. Other means had to be employed to ensure continuation of the species."

"Genetic engineering."

"Right. Ability to withstand the idiosyncrasies of Earth could be programmed right in to the physical circuitry. I am one of the first Martian sentients in millennia to be able to copulate. Certainly the first to successfully mate with a human."

"Successful? Oh, honey, that's putting it mildly!" Amber burst out, laughing. "Last night was magical!"

"Last night shattered everything I've ever professed and believed!" he agreed. "I have a whole new world view now, one where the mission is no longer my only reason to exist. There's something more important now, something entirely personal. For the first time in my life, I want something just for me."

"Well, baby, what's wrong with that?"

"Nothing, I suppose. I mean, it must be part of the emotional-hormonal programming. But I never realized...how powerful...how utterly absorbing it is! You are the only thought in my head, and when I'm with you, I'm blissfully happy."

"I know exactly what you're talking about." Amber snuggled closer to him. "This is cloud nine at its finest."

"No, it'll be even finer when you're lying in the tent in my arms," he said. "We must be getting close. I feel it."

"You feel what?"

"The vortexes. They're disturbing the normal energy pattern. Or I should say, elevating it."

"Okay, what are they, and why are they?" she asked.

Blue took a deep breath. "The entire globe is covered with an energetic grid called ley lines. They resemble your imaginary lines of latitude and longitude, except that these describe the actual flow of your world's biomagnetic field. Where these lines intersect they create a vortex, a huge energy whirlpool."

"So it's not just in Sedona, they're other places, too?"

"Yes, but Sedona is special because it has many vortexes in one ten-mile radius, and the red sandstone contains iron oxide and crystalline silica, which anchor the frequency and lend tremendous power to the rocks themselves. Each vortex has a charge, too, so they are either negative, female, and soothing, what's known as yin in some of your traditions, or positive, masculine, and stimulating, also called yang."

"Which kind are we looking for?"

"Maybe we should just let the spot pick us," he suggested.

"Aye-aye, Captain Kirk," she replied.

They exited onto Highway 179 and were soon deep in red rock country, entering Oak Creek Canyon. The sinking sun illuminated the towering sandstone formations while it threw long, dark shadows across the canyon floor.

"I don't know for sure because the energy is always jumping around when I'm with you," Amber said, "but I think I feel the vortex, too. I mean, I'm even higher and happier than before. I feel like a kid driving into Disney World."

"This is even better; it's the real thing. We'll probably start levitating soon," Blue remarked with a laugh. "Look at that one, it must be Bell Rock. I sense that will be our big pillow tonight."

"We're sleeping on a rock?"

"Not right on top, but on the slopes of it, yes. I've got a tent in the back, along with a cooler full of ice, your favorite wine, and an assortment of provisions. I hope you brought long pants; it could get chilly tonight at four thousand feet. Once we're in the tent, you won't have to worry about staying warm."

A delicious thrill of anticipation made Amber shiver. "How could I possibly worry when I've got a clairvoyant, telepathic, brilliant and outrageously sexy Martian next to me?"

"Oh, you flatterer," Blue said, grinning with delight. He turned off the paved road onto a dirt track, then left the road entirely, shifted the truck into 4-wheel drive and continued across the darkening terrain.

"Uh, are you sure we're allowed to camp in here?" Amber asked uncertainly.

"Martians get to camp wherever they want," Blue responded. When he spotted a mesquite tree with twisted, low-lying branches, he swung the truck behind it and parked. "We'll have to walk the rest of the way. I don't think it will be far."

Amber felt as if she could walk miles towing an elephant. Instead she only had to carry her own bag and her purse. Blue strapped on a huge backpack, picked up the cooler with one muscular arm, and led the way up the sloping edges of Bell Rock's outer skirt.

"Is this where the vortex is?" Amber called. "I feel electricity coming up through my shoes."

Blue stopped and waited for her to catch up. "This is one of the main and most famous vortexes. I not only feel it intensely, I can see it! Can you?"

"No!" she cried mournfully. "I let Krystalee have my blue stone so she could study it! Now I wish I hadn't."

"Never mind about that! Soon you won't need it anyway." He put his arm around her and turned her toward the formation's towering spire. "You don't need anything but your own mind, your own intention. Now stand here and say to yourself, 'I intend to see the vortex.' It should look like a huge typhoon of swirling color."

"A typhoon?" Amber squinted up but saw only the rock against the sky.

"I guess you call it a hurricane in this hemisphere. Anyway, look for a spinning funnel shape. Like the chakras of the body that you saw during our wedding, only on a much larger scale." Blue set down his load and took her hand. "Go ahead and try it. Affirm your intention and let your vision relax."

She sighed, then stared at the rock again. Feeling slightly foolish, she began mentally repeating, *I intend to see the vortex, I intend to see the vortex....* Nothing.

"Don't give up," he whispered, just when she was ready to give up and remind him that most humans don't see invisible energy storms.

But she was beginning to feel the usual exquisite tingle of Blue's frequency as it bubbled out of his hand and zoomed through her limbs. With her gaze glued to Bell Rock, she continued to chant silently. Then he squeezed her hand and a flash of light appeared, a silver curl of energy that spiralled around the massive stone and winked out high above it. "Wow," she breathed, "I do see something!"

Blue smiled, keeping his palm pressed tightly against hers. "Now inhale deeply, and when you exhale, release all your doubts with your breath."

Amber gulped a lungful of desert air and blew it out. *I release all my doubts....*Suddenly the stone megalith was wrapped in a cocoon of whirling, writhing energy bands, their iridescence tossing colored sparks into the navy blue sky. Transfixed, her mouth hanging open, Amber gripped him tighter.

"You're breaking my fingers," he whispered.

"But I'm seeing it!" she hissed back.

"Then you don't need me anymore." He straightened his hand, keeping their palms touching. She let go, still staring at the amazing vision. It persisted, in full color, as Blue held his hand inches away and watched.

"Look! I'm doing it all by myself!" Amber shouted. Unable to stand still any longer, she turned and threw herself at Blue. He swept her off the ground in a twirling hug.

"See? I told you! All it takes is practice!" Blue clapped her on the back like a football coach.

"Aw! I wrecked it!" Amber wailed, looking up and seeing the rock returned to its ordinary majesty.

"Don't worry, sweetheart. This is just the beginning of your extrasensory adventures. You're doing great!" He hoisted the pack to his back and resumed trekking up the hillside. Before long he stopped and threw down his load, calling to Amber, who scrambled behind him, "Look at this beautiful little flat spot. I had a feeling it would be here!"

It did almost look man-made, this level place surrounded by steep inclines. With her back to the sheer wall of Bell Rock, Amber looked out over Oak Creek Canyon in the golden sun of late afternoon. She was so grateful, elated and in love with life, she felt like crying.

"Well, we'd better get the important things done soon before the sun goes down," Blue called, rummaging in his pack.

"You mean set up the tent?"

"No, I mean set up our altars to the four directions," he answered. "Come on, help me look for large, flat stones."

"Altars? Good idea, I'm about ready to praise God."

"Believe me, the entity you call God is not waiting around for humans to fawn over it! I'm talking about utilizing the natural energies of the universe to our advantage." Blue wandered and scanned the rock-strewn ground as he talked. "By honoring the four directions we attract the special qualities and elementals that accompany each one. Then we sit in the center, where we invite the axis of nine dimensions and let its vibrational information flow through us."

"Oh, why didn't you say so in the first place?"

"Here, this one's perfect." He picked up a foot-wide slab and held it out to her. "We need this flat surface to arrange our offerings on."

Amber smiled and shook her head. *Never a dull moment with this guy.* "I'm afraid to ask, but what the heck are elementals?" she said, scouting around for similar stones.

"Fourth-dimensional beings that work closely with physical manifestations in 3-D. For instance, every plant has its own deva, sort of a spirit sponsor. That's where your myths about fairies and elves come from."

"You mean there really are fairies? I swear, hanging out with you is too much! Hey, how about this one?" Amber hefted a rounded rock shaped like a huge hamburger.

"That one will be for the South," he said, taking it from her, "soft, inviting, with no jagged edges."

They quickly located the remaining two altar stones, and Amber watched as Blue arranged them in a square, about ten feet apart. "Now we need to find things to put on them," he announced. "Let's go in different directions and see what calls out to us."

"But what kind of things?"

"A flower, an unusual rock, anything. You'll know it when you see it."

Amber studied his back as he walked away, head bent toward the earth, long hair waving like a mustang's tail. "Yeah, I see it all right," she muttered. Tearing her attention from him, she turned and wandered across the dusty terrain. How was a flower going to grow in all this rock? Well, she had to find something, otherwise they'd never get to the romance portion of this program.

She closed her eyes and took a deep breath. Maybe a little shot of that intention stuff would work again. *I intend to find the perfect items for our altars. Right now!*

When she opened her eyes she was reminded of Mars; the last view of the sun was turning the red rocks even redder. And there he was in the distance, the Martian altar that she really wanted to fall on her knees for. Heart racing with expectation, she turned back to the task at hand.

"Let's get this show on the road, fairies." She strode into the sunset, thoroughly enjoying the freedom of nature's expansive domain and the sweet solitude it afforded.

"This rock looks pretty cool." She picked up a lemon-sized stone with layered stripes. A few feet later she found a gray stone in a rough pyramid shape. She put both in her pockets and scanned the area. There wasn't much to choose from in this landscape of rock and scrubby bushes.

"Hey! There is one up here after all," Amber said as she ran to pluck the tiny flower she'd spotted growing out of a crack. She was holding it up and admiring it when a shape on the ground caught her attention.

"Whoa," she breathed, sweeping up a long feather. "This is a sacred object if I ever saw one!"

Hurrying back in Blue's direction, she passed a low-lying bush and couldn't help noticing a small rectangle peeking out from under its branches. At first she thought it was a scrap of litter, but when she bent to retrieve it she saw that it was a playing card. On the back was a picture of an owl. She turned it over and smiled; its face showed the two of hearts.

"Any luck?" Blue asked when they met back in the circle of rock altars.

"Are you kidding me? Luck is my middle name since I met you!" She showed him the stones and the feather. "I know this isn't exactly a product of nature, but this seemed appropriate," she said, holding out the card.

"Two hearts for our honeymoon; the elementals have such a sense of humor! Look, I got a feather just like yours. Guess things are coming in twos for us." They examined the almost identical feathers, both copper-colored with a tip of cream. He showed her the other objects he'd found, several stones, a hollow bone and a butterfly wing.

"Now we can begin," he announced, "although I feel very connected already." His arm snaked around her and pulled her close. Amber snuggled against him, her chest bursting with happiness. *Connected, signed, sealed and delivered!*

Blue let her go with a quick kiss on the forehead, then pulled out a drawstring pouch, opened it and placed a small mound of its contents in front of each altar stone. These piles seemed to be nuggets or crystals of some kind.

"We petition the spirits of this land's indigenous people, who value their planet and honor their relationship with it," he said grandly, sweeping the horizon with outstretched arms. In the waning light he really did look like an Indian brave surveying his territory. "I'm making up this ritual based on your teachings, so please send me lots of inspiration." He faced the altar to the north and motioned for Amber to join him. Then he knelt and cupped his hands around the mound of pellets, his palms several inches away.

Amber strained to see what he was doing in the dark. "I can't see a thing," she whispered. "Are you praying?"

"No, trying to help you see," he answered. "Just a second, I've almost got it..." The pile burst into flames and Amber jumped back.

"Wow! That was pretty impressive!" she squeaked.

"That's another parlor trick you'll be doing soon," he laughed. The fire toned down but continued to illuminate the scene.

"Now, we'll place these rocks on the altar to invoke the north's rugged strength." Blue picked out the stones that were sharp-edged or pointed. "And the bone to remind us that death of the physical body is only a phase in life, just as in winter the land seems dead but is really waiting to emerge in a new form."

Amber turned with him to the east altar and watched him ignite the mound of granules in the same fashion. "The east is the origin of new beginnings, the direction where the sun rises to start a new day. We'll place the feathers here, symbols of the joining of our wings in single flight." He positioned a yellow rock on the two feathers to hold them in the evening breeze.

"Come here, help me light the south fire. I know you've got it in you," Blue said.

"Yeah, I've got the fire down below," Amber drawled. She crouched beside the altar and framed the granules with her hands. At this point, she was ready to try anything.

"Think heat. Send it from your palms into the powder," he advised.

Amber concentrated for a solid minute, and though she could feel energy pouring from her hands, the material on the ground remained inert.

"Here," Blue said, "let me help." He knelt beside her and slid his hands around hers. Immediately she felt the vibration intensify. "See, you use your mind to funnel the power into a single tube, like a drill." The intense tingling in her hand drew itself into a pulsating dot in the middle of her palm. Five seconds later the pile blazed alive in a shower of sparks. Amber flinched with a yip and they both laughed.

"See? The south likes you, it's so warm and easygoing. We'll give it the smooth rocks and the butterfly wing, and ask it to bring the sensuous summer energy to our love."

"Amen to that," Amber said.

"For the last altar, the west, where the sun disappears every day and continues its adventures beyond our sight, we offer our card of two hearts. May we use the spirit of the west to extend our own adventure far beyond the limitations of Earth," Blue intoned. "Amber, light the firesand."

"Firesand? Is this stuff from Mars, by any chance?!"

"Of course. I had to add some element from my home planet to make our ceremony complete, and this seemed the best because it's so functional, too."

Amber squatted in front of the final altar and held her hands around the firesand. "It's incredible," she said, bending close to inspect it. "But I don't think I'm strong enough to do this alone."

"We'll see. Think of intense heat, channel it through your hands," Blue urged.

"Okay," she replied, "I'm thinking of you with no clothes on." She closed her eyes and moistened her lips.

"Good start," he said, laughing. "Think of me, with no clothes on...and, my head between your legs."

The firesand fizzed and puffed out a curling smoke trail. Abruptly it burst into flame. "Yow!" Amber yelped, jerking her hands away and flapping them in the air. "That one singed my skin!"

"Let me see," he said, taking her hands in his. "I didn't mean to hurt you." He bent and pressed his lips to her palms, kissing them repeatedly. Amber's heart rate soared off the scale.

Suddenly the ceremony was forgotten. The lovers looked in each other's eyes and were sucked into a maelstrom of urgent desire. Blue left Amber's hands and burrowed his tongue between her lips. She kissed him gratefully, stroking his temples and jaw.

"We need to prepare the tent," he croaked, as he nibbled on her earlobe.

"No problem; I used to go camping a lot with my sister Rose when she lived in Washington state. This should be a piece of cake."

They quickly erected the tent in the center of the four firelit altars, padded it with sleeping bags and covered them with a brightly-woven Indian blanket. Then Blue reached in his pack and brought out one of the shining glass-like spheres that had illuminated their wedding chamber the night before.

"Ooh, you brought a crystal ball; they are so awesome! Is that from Mars, too?" She took it and turned it around in her hands.

"Yes. The word for it in Martian would translate to something like 'bug light" in English. It's a hollow crystal globe filled with water and millions of incandescent microorganisms that used to exist on Mars." He plucked it out of her hands and tossed it inside the tent, where it settled into the covers and filled the interior with a cozy, peach-colored glow.

"So shall we test it out before dinner?" He asked, slipping his arm around her. "I don't think I can wait another nanosecond to have you."

"I like the way you think," Amber said, and they locked together in another hungry kiss.

They shed their shoes, crawled inside and headed for home, gliding naturally into an embrace. Blue slid his hands under Amber's shirt and caressed her back while they kissed and wriggled against each other.

"I'm completely humbled by your power," he confessed in her ear.

"Believe me, honey, it's a two-way street. I can't think about a thing but you anymore," Amber whispered.

"Why do humans ever get out of bed once they learn about sexual love?" he said, nuzzling her shoulder. "This ritual is so acutely compelling."

"Good question. I'd love to freeze this moment and stay with you in this tent forever." Her hands tugged on the edge of his shirt.

"It's too hot to freeze," he grunted, helping her pull off his T-shirt.

To see his bare chest again, with its powerful curves and blue nipples, drove Amber's passion toward madness. *I can't believe this is my man!* She ripped off her own shirt and they both moaned as they pressed together, skin to skin.

Blue slipped his hand between her legs, petting lightly along the center seam of her shorts. "Is it hurting from last night?"

She laughed softly. "It's a little tender, but it hurts good. Aren't you sore?"

"Not in the least," he answered, sitting up and popping the button on her fly.

"Good old Martian engineering," she sighed, as she arched her back and stretched like a cat.

Blue unleashed his hair and let it fall across her while he pulled off her pants. She was almost embarrassed for him see her skimpy underwear, all black lace and sheer fabric. Bordello-wear was not really her thing, but Krystalee had insisted.

But Blue acted as if he'd just unveiled a priceless art object, kneeling between her legs in an attitude of adoration. He bent closer, gently swinging his head to lash her thighs and belly with his hair. "You are the most flawless creation ever dreamed up by the Cosmic Mind," he pronounced.

Amber giggled, happily burning up.

He grabbed the light-globe and placed it closer to her parted legs, then crouched low and began grazing her flesh with his fingertips. When they reached the damp curls peeking out from the edges of lace, he skated them across the fabric's thin barrier.

"There's a clasp on either side," she urged, losing all interest in the tease.

Blue released the strings and reverently lowered the garment to expose her completely.

"Oh, Blue..." she groaned, seared by his stare.

"Oh, Amber!" he returned. "Now I see why the ancient wisdom always says to explore within!" A tiny whimper escaped her as he slid his fingers against her swollen lips. "I've never seen anything so wildly beautiful." He lowered his face and watched himself examine and stroke her. Quivering with pleasure, she silently begged for his tongue.

As usual he responded to her thoughts promptly. "Mmmm...cunnilingus tastes as good as it sounds," he declared between licks.

Amber surrendered to the intense sensations, eyes closed in ecstasy. A constant stream of love noises growled from her throat. Blue became more agitated as he ate her, spreading her legs wider and increasing the pace and pressure. She felt the rising, sharp pangs and managed to call his name once more before the orgasm wracked her body.

As each exquisite spasm quaked through her, she seemed to fall deeper into darkness. Neon flashes in geometric shapes rocketed by her as she tumbled in black inner space. She tried to open her eyes when she felt Blue climbing on top of her, but the whirling images continued. She could still feel her body lying under him, could vaguely hear him say, "This is going to be so enjoyable," as he penetrated her. Somewhere far away in her consciousness she acknowledged the sensations of his pistoning hips, the sweet violence of his release, and the weight of his body as he collapsed on top of her.

A loud crack, like thunder or a falling tree limb, snapped her awake. She struggled to unglue her eyes and was surprised when they gave way and flew open. But she was no longer in the tent, she was perched in a tree on the side of a mountain, in broad daylight. A loud thundering still assaulted her ears; she scanned the sky to locate the storm. Then she looked across the valley and saw the source of the noise— no piddling storm but an erupting volcano, spewing lava down its cone and ejecting smoke for miles into the atmosphere.

This would have been traumatic enough, but then she looked over at Blue and saw that he was an owl.

11

Bell Rock Tolls

Amber screeched when she tried to scream. "That's right," Blue's voice echoed in her head, "you didn't exactly crawl up in this tree, either."

The huge bird next to her returned her stare, his golden eyes unblinking under arched, bushy eyebrows. He had a white ruff around his neck that ended in a downy patch on his chest; otherwise, his feathers were coppery gold. Strong, curved talons held him to the branch.

Amber squawked again, then remembered to think what she wanted to say. "You're an owl!"

"So are you," Blue's voice said. "I guess that nine-dimensional axis worked a little better than expected."

"What are you saying?" Amber flapped her wings in frustration, swiveling her head to look at her own body. Golden feathers filled her view. "What *happened*?"

"Offhand I'd say the altars and the vortex—and the sex—arced us into the space-time continuum. We're in another dimension."

"Oh, that explains everything," Amber snapped, her panic growing. "And why are we *birds*?"

"Look around you down there. Perhaps this is the most efficient physical vehicle given the present conditions."

Amber did look, and it was not a pretty sight. Land that the lava had already scoured over was wiped clean of any sign of life, and the edge of the moving flow cracked and glowed as it cooked the surface of the earth.

"This is only a recent eruption," Blue commented. "Look at the trails left by earlier lava and mudslides. Let's get closer."

"Are you nuts? I don't like volcanoes and I'm afraid to fly!" Amber shivered and her feathers fluffed out like a pine cone.

"Come on, we're here in this dimension, might as well make the most of it," he reasoned. "Didn't you ever wonder what it would be like to fly?"

"Not particularly." She began to preen her pinfeathers.

"Well, then, I'll go and report back to you," he decided, unfolding his impressive wingspan.

Amber screeched out loud in protest. "No! There's no way I'm letting you out of my sight!"

"Come on then," he called, and swooped off the branch.

She watched his shape quickly diminish as he dived into the valley. *Goddamit, I'm fucking afraid to fly*, she muttered as she pranced back and forth on the tree limb. *Always have been....* Blue was a mere golden dot far below, and her view of him was already becoming shrouded by the smoke and ash billowing from the volcano's tantrum. *Always will be.* She stretched out her wings and looked down. Blue wasn't visible at all anymore. *Trust your birdness*, popped into her mind as if written. She launched herself into space.

Amazingly, her body knew exactly what to do; she tucked her wings, went into a head-down dive and rushed toward the valley floor. Air roared in her ears as she plummeted, fear-stricken at first, then excited when she realized her owl exterior could be depended on to run the controls. Punching through a cloud of smoke, she spotted Blue cruising below her, wings held motionless, gliding on a current. She came out of her dive and swooped toward him.

With a turn of her tertiaries, she avoided collision with him and rocketed past, deftly plucking out one of his tail feathers with her beak as she streaked even further downward.

Blue squawked in surprise. "Amber! Come back up!"

"Gotcha tail!" she sang, her head almost turned backward. "This is a gas!"

"Look where you're going!"

She jerked her head back around and saw the ground rushing up way too fast, ground covered by molten lava. *Bird-body, flap these things!* Instinctively she threw open her wings, two mammoth fans of gold and white, and began to rapidly scoop the air with them. They pulled her stout body effortlessly upward, and with no problem she maneuvered herself to Blue's side.

"Never thought I'd be a skydiver! What a trip!"

"Would you please be careful!" Blue said sternly. "I have no idea if you could get back to your human vehicle once you wreck this one."

"Hey, what's with you? You said take advantage of being in another dimension. Now you don't want to have any fun."

"Look where we are. I don't think we're meant to have fun here."

Amber looked down again and saw something man-made for the first time in this strange dimension-dream: A road. Cars were parked all along the edges, and some were stacked up on the asphalt. No moving traffic could be seen, and it was obvious why when she scanned the distance. Many sections of the highway were completely covered in mud and debris.

"Were they trying to get away?" she said, and then felt silly to be asking the obvious.

"They came from over there."

She followed his gaze to the far horizon, where a city skyline glowed like a beacon in the smoky sky. "Looks like a pretty big town. Think we should check it out?"

"We don't have a choice," Blue pointed out. "Here there's only desolation." He continued to fly in the direction of the city.

"Wait a minute! Can't we just go back?" Amber flapped nervously behind him. "You know, like call Mister Wizard and poof back into the real world? Isn't there a reset button?"

"I don't know, Amber. It's my first time in this dimension, too. We just have to trust, and the reason for this will be revealed."

"Spoken like a wise old owl," she said, calmed for the moment. But her uneasiness returned as they continued to fly over roads lined with abandoned cars, the countryside all around showing scars of nature's wrath.

Amber was torn between fascination with her shamanic transformation and horror at the context it was taking place in. This didn't feel like a dream at all; the chaos and destruction were real and crystal clear. When she saw a dark, jagged streak in the distance, and minutes later realized it was a huge crack in the earth, an icicle of fear pierced her heart.

"Is that a canyon?" she asked anxiously.

"Not likely. Look at the pavement." A ribbon of road ended abruptly at the crack's edge; hundreds of feet away, on the other side, it resumed again.

"Maybe the bridge just burned up." Just as Amber transmitted this desperate thought, the city's skyline caught her eye. They were close enough now to see that it was not electric lights illuminating the city, but hundreds of fires.

"Earthquake." Blue said simply. "Part of the seismic show."

"Please, honey, let's not go any closer! I have a really bad feeling about this." As soon as she said it, they were deafened by the roar of the exploding mountain. They circled, then looked toward the cone, but there was no cone left. The upper half of the peak had just been jettisoned into the sky. An enormous, boiling cloud rose like an evil genie from the shattered mountain's remains.

"That's a pyroclastic cloud," Blue informed her, "and it's headed this way. Let's get out of here before we become barbecue. Look, there's water beyond the city."

Pumped with adrenaline, Amber flew after him, though she dreaded seeing the disaster up close. Beyond the smoking buildings she could clearly see the shore now, and she longed to be over the cool, nonflammable water. She stared at the shapes of the man-made structures against the horizon and suddenly realized she knew this place. City on the seashore, mountains on the other side, and a distinctive structure rising up higher than the others around it, like a flying saucer on a stick.

"It's gaining on us! Fly faster!" Blue urged, darting in front of her to lead the way.

They were passing over the edge of the city now, beginning to smell the salt spray from the bay. Amber blinked her huge golden eyes, but it didn't change what she was seeing, spotlight beams of color that were rising from the cityscape like rain in reverse. Each one left a luminous trail as it ascended, creating a rainbow forest of undulating comet tails.

"What's that?" she asked. "It's beautiful!"

Blue hesitated, then said, "I sense that we are perceiving departing souls."

"No! There are so many of them!"

"Going to a better place," he reminded quickly. "Now fly!"

She looked behind her and saw that the cloud of hot gas, ash and rock was rapidly overtaking them. Squawking and flapping her wings crazily, she focused on the ocean and prayed she could outrun death.

There was no sound from the cloud behind them; its lethal pursuit, though visually spectacular, was completely silent. All Amber felt was a flash of heat as she instantly lost consciousness.

It seemed that she rested in a disconnected limbo for a long time before she finally awoke, tears pouring down her cheeks. A sob tore from her throat like a baby's first cry.

"You're alive!" Blue's voice said above her, and she slowly realized she was lying in his arms. She squinted up and saw his face, in all its hairless Martian splendor, also gushing tears from his red-rimmed blue eyes. "Oh, thank the Creator!" he wailed and clutched her tightly. "You've been cold so long, I thought you weren't going to make it back."

"What..." she muttered. "What the hell happened?"

Blue was crying too hard to answer, rocking her and covering her face with kisses. "I've got to warm you up!" he said suddenly, snapping out of his shock. He began vigorously rubbing and slapping her limbs, then dragged the blanket around her half-nude body. "I'll make some hot tea. Wait here."

He unzipped the tent flap and went outside. It was dawn, and Amber could clearly see him scurrying around, still naked, pulling things from his pack. They had been asleep, or away, or whatever you wanted to call it, for almost twelve hours.

She watched him pour water in a cup and heat it by holding it between his palms. Then he dropped in a combination of herbs and stirred. Amber snuggled into the blanket and thought how wonderful it would be to eternally watch him move, muscles wriggling like snakes under the flawless white skin, those hypnotic blue spots for punctuation. Her eyelids began to slide down.

"Amber! Don't sleep!" Blue barked as he entered the tent. He managed not to spill the tea as he grabbed her. "Please, please, stay here with me in 3-D."

"I don't know why, I just feel so tired..."

"No! Sit up and drink this," he commanded. Amber obeyed, and felt better after a few sips.

Blue left her side long enough to get dressed, wordlessly and with a serious expression. He glanced at her every few seconds, obviously worried.

"What happened, Blue?" she asked again. "Where were we?"

"I'm not completely certain, but it felt like the future." He looked at her and their eyes locked.

"The future? Blue, I recognize that town! The mountains, the sea, the Space Needle. That's where Rose lived—Seattle!"

"Well, it's a good thing she moved," he replied.

"What? Do you really think that's going to happen? To *Seattle*?"

"There's always the element of probability when time-traveling forward," he mused, "which means there may be a way to prevent the actual occurrence. However, if I remember my geography correctly, the city is situated right in line with the Ring of Fire, the huge arc of volcanic activity that extends up into Alaska and down to Japan on the Pacific's other side. And it seems to me there are several volcanic peaks near there, too."

"There's Mt. Rainier, and Mt. Baker, but I think they're extinct volcanoes."

"Remember Mt. St. Helens? It's in the same state!"

"Blue, you're scaring me! What is going on?"

He sighed, sat down and put his arm around her. "Drink your tea," he urged quietly, and waited until she took a slurp from the cup before he continued. "There are some things I haven't told you, only because I considered them to be non-immediate events."

She looked at him expectantly, forehead creased.

"Okay, what I'm trying to tell you is I knew what was going to happen, only I didn't know when, exactly, so I didn't think you needed to know right away," Blue stammered.

"That makes absolutely zero sense. Baby, just tell me!" she pleaded.

"I never thought it would be this hard..." he said, almost to himself. "When I told you before that the planet was in critical shape and needed everyone's love and attention, I fudged the truth a little. The planet will suffer, but it will be just fine. It's human civilization that is due to take a serious fall."

"And you think the destruction of Seattle is part of that?"

"No. I think the destruction of every city is part of that. For fifty years we've been working behind the scenes, hoping to inspire a responsible attitude in humans, hoping to avert global disaster. But even though some progress has been made, and some raises in mass consciousness are evident, it hasn't been enough. At this point in time we have resigned ourselves to the inevitable reaping of what humans on this Earth have sown: Planetary restructuring on an apocalyptic level."

"In other words, we're all going to die?" Amber squeaked.

"Not necessarily. There may be pockets of survivors; given the density of population, it's almost certain unless nuclear winter is the cause. The planet eventually gets another chance to support life, and the society of today...." Blue's lecture trailed off when he looked down and saw Amber's stricken face. "It may be far, far off in the future! It hasn't happened yet, so maybe it never will happen. And yet, the vision we had..."

"It was so clear," she finished. "So real. I was completely terrified. Look, I'm still shaking!"

Blue drew her close again. "I have to call in to headquarters. This must be reported. Then maybe we'll get more information."

"We can find a phone in town," she said.

"I don't need that! I just have to sit quietly, go into another brain-wave pattern, and I'll be able to check in." He crawled out of the tent, then stuck his head back in. "Don't snooze. Please. Right now I have an intense desire to keep your third-dimensional vehicle and its soul together. Okay?"

"Okay," she replied with a wan smile. He sat directly outside the tent's opening, flipping the flaps up so they could keep each other in sight. Then he closed his eyes with his hands held over his abdomen.

Amber continued to watch and sip her tea. As her strength returned, she turned her mind to what he had said about the fate of planet Earth. It wasn't fair! It wasn't right! How could our planet be jerked out from under us just when we were beginning to figure out how to take care of it? And why did one volcano signify the end of the world? Weren't there volcanoes going off all the time? It was just another item on the morning news, and only those who lived nearby got to call in late.

More importantly, how could the very ground be pulled from under her just when she had found someone worthy of marrying? How could Mr. Right finally arrive—on the Titanic!

It was difficult to believe in Blue's dire predictions as she watched the sunrise setting the canyon aglow, the peaceful silence studded with bird music. Maybe it really had been just a crazy hallucination, inspired by the vortex-sex. Maybe human beings would get their environmental shit together and the planet would continue the way it was, only sweeter, because she finally had what she'd been looking for since she was thirteen.

Blue sat motionless, and as she admired his shape she could feel his life force radiating out and capturing her. A little prayer formed in her mind, *Please, please, Lord, let this love last.*

The tea was long gone when he finally rose and returned to her side. His face was somber, not the way a man should look on his honeymoon.

"Well, what did they say?"

"They were quite disturbed. Apparently there has been much corroboration of our vision," he reported. "I'm sorry, but we have to go back immediately. The Martian Council convenes tomorrow."

"But even if Mt. Rainier were going to erupt, how can the Martian Council stop it?" Amber pointed out.

"There are all kinds of technologies that humans cannot yet fathom, let alone duplicate. But we have them. And some of the other extraterrestrials are even more advanced! Of course, humans would have to accept us and cooperate with us for it to work, but the oceans and the air really could be renewed. Unless...."

"Unless what?" Amber had been enjoying this Utopian scene.

"Well, if it truly is the fate, the karma of the people of Earth to pay dearly for their destructive lifestyle, then it's a violation of divine order to interfere from outside. Or at least that's what I've always thought, until I fell in love with you. Now I'm very motivated to give western civilization the benefit of the doubt."

"Yeah, isn't there some hope we could get it together and keep the planet from popping at the seams?" Amber asked.

"There's always hope. I had a lot of it in the sixties, when peace and love actually became a trend. We Martians thought the planet could only benefit from so many young humans opening their heart chakras. But we underestimated the power of the ones who feed off the vibrations of chaos and fear. They still rule."

"But isn't it possible to change that? Nothing is written in stone!" she insisted.

"Until I came to the surface, I never even wanted to believe that," he admitted. "The so-called civilization that I witnessed through television and written media did not impress me. I considered it just and due that Earth would wreak her changes and shake off the human parasites like fleas. You changed all that."

"I did?"

"Yes." He bent to kiss her gently. "Now I believe in a different outcome for Earth, and a happy ending for you and me. And that's what I'm going to advocate at the Council tomorrow—overt Martian intervention on a global scale."

12

Delight Delayed

Dang, girl! You have the shortest courtship in history, your wedding happens in a heartbeat, and now you're already back from your honeymoon?" Krystalee's piercing twang made Amber hold the phone away from her ear.

"Well, he had like an emergency. They wanted him to come back to headquarters," Amber explained.

"*Like* an emergency? And you say you spent the night in a tent? He probably has zero money and was too embarrassed to admit he couldn't get you a hotel room."

"I don't think so. When I was unpacking the coolers, which we never got to last night, there was a bottle of Dom in there! He said he'd bought my favorite wine."

"You mean Dom Perignon, as in the champagne? He must have seen your collection," said Krystalee. "Little did he know those bottles were all empty when you got them!"

"Hey, one of them really was mine. Celebration of my first book illustration job, given to me by...never mind, who wants to think about *him* right now? The point is, Blue is obviously not destitute." Amber wondered if she should try to describe their vision, but it was hard to know how to begin. *By the way, last night we time-traveled.*

"So let me get this straight," her friend pursued, "you hauled a bottle of Dom to your campsite and never drank it?"

"Well, we kind of got distracted."

"I bet! Damn, I'm envious, you lucky, horny bitch! Listen, bring him to my brother's birthday party tonight. There'll be all kinds of weird people there, so your Martian will fit right in."

Krystalee's younger brother, Farley, was a computer technician by day, a bluegrass musician by night, and he seemed to know half of Phoenix. Amber's heart fluttered when she fantasized showing Blue off in public. "Sounds like fun. What time?"

"It'll probably start mid-afternoon, but I'll be there around five or six. I'm sure Farley's gonna fire up the barbecue—and the band—early."

"And what about Quinn? She coming?"

"I'm sure she will if she hears you're gonna be there with your spaceman," Krystalee giggled. "We are absolutely dying of curiosity!"

"Well, I'll see what I can do. He already left to go back...home."

"Must've been pretty important for him to break off the honeymoon. They're not planning an invasion, are they?"

"Of course not!" Amber snapped, then realized that Blue's plan could be interpreted as exactly that.

"Whew! I'm relieved now—so make him come, okay? I mean, to the party."

"Very funny," Amber replied. "If I'm there, he'll be with me. And what about the stone? I'd really like it back."

"Oh, the stone! I almost forgot! I did take it in to the professors today and you know what? None of them had ever seen anything like it before. They were fascinated!"

"See, I told you it was from Mars! Wait til you hear about the other Martian stuff I've seen....So, where is it?"

"Uh...well, I left it with them for the afternoon and, without even asking my permission, they sent it off to a lab for further analysis."

"Oh, great! What lab?

"Uh, I think it was the Natural History Museum...in, uh...London?" Krystalee squeaked.

"Now my telepathy stone is in England?" Amber shrieked. "No way!"

"Way, I'm afraid. But they're going to send it back, relax! It's just that they were all so excited, they think it's a new mineral. They talked me into it!" Krystalee confessed.

"I thought you said they didn't ask your permission!"

"Well, they didn't, really, they just kind of informed me, and when I tried to argue...I mean, I didn't figure you wanted me to risk my job over it."

"It's just that I don't have anything else he's given me," Amber said.

"Honey, you still have the glow. And that's worth more than any old rock."

This incisive statement made Amber smile. "Well, you got that right; I'm glowing like a lighthouse."

"More power to ya! Can't wait to meet your battery charger tonight. And I will get the rock back, I promise."

"I know you will. See you soon." They hung up and Amber looked at the clock. It was 1:45. Not even an hour had passed since he'd left and she was ready to chew the woodwork.

They had only stopped in the town of Sedona to eat breakfast, then Blue wanted to drive straight back. He'd said something about how Martians can absorb life-force through air, sun and earth, and only ordered a glass of orange juice while Amber devoured a gigantic cheese omelette. In Phoenix he'd dropped her off, hastily kissed her and left, obviously preoccupied and disturbed.

Now that he was gone and she was safely in her own living room, erupting volcanoes seemed much less threatening. She just wished for this to be all over, for Blue to go back to being the carefree, laughing man who was in love with her, and for their honeymoon to resume.

The phone rang and she caught it on the first ring. "Hello?"

"Hi, sweetheart," said Mom. "How's everything?"

"Fine," Amber replied, almost meaning it.

"I didn't really expect you to be at home this afternoon."

"I'm kind of in between things right now, so I'm doing a little housework."

"Well, I just wanted to tell you that there's a program about outer space visitors on tonight. You might want to watch it for ideas."

"I'd like to see it, but I think I'm going to Farley Collins's birthday party with Blue tonight."

"Oh, now it's every night together?"

"Yeah. He's barely been away an hour now and I'm mooning around like a sick puppy," she admitted.

"Hmm, this does sound serious."

"Extremely. I've never felt so sure in my life, even though it makes no logical sense at all. I'm just crazy about him."

"Well, I guess it's time we...wait a minute, here comes Dad's two cents..." Amber could hear muffled voices, then her mother protesting, "Oh, come on, don't be like that!"

"What'd he say?" Amber insisted.

"He was saying what I was about to say, only not as politely...."

"Come on, tell me."

"Well, he said to ask you when we get to meet your new sex partner. Now, that's not my choice of words!"

"Always the cynic," Amber laughed. "But he'll see, this one's different. *Really* different."

"So when are you bringing him for dinner? How about tomorrow?"

"I guess that would work. Let me check with him and call you back later. Oh, and I think he's actually a vegetarian."

"That's all right. I'll make my famous spinach low-fat lasagna."

"And we'll bring the wine," Amber offered, envisioning popping the cork on the ultra-expensive champagne and unveiling their marriage.

After checking in with her parents, Amber felt even more back to normal. She busied herself with little chores around the house, playing music and trying not to strain too hard to hear the phone. The traumatic events of the night before were pushed into the back of her mind to await explanation, and she focused on the feelings in her heart. Her family and friends were just going to have to accept Blue's Martian origins, and then they would live happily ever after.

When Blue finally did call, her optimism evaporated at the first sound of his voice. "This is going to be more complex than I thought," he said, clearly distressed.

"What's happening?"

"It seems there are two factions developing—those who favor escalating the contact program and those who believe the time is not yet ripe. There is also talk of vibrational evidence that a disaster like the one we witnessed is possible, but I won't be able to sort the truth from the rumors until the Council convenes in the morning. Meanwhile, I ache to be holding you."

Amber wasn't ready for that, and it sent a tremor of delight down her spine. "Please say you're coming back tonight," she said. "We're invited to a party and my girlfriends really want to meet you."

"Of course I'll be back. I don't even want to think about spending a night without you. But I might have to meet you there."

Amber gave him directions and said she would ride over with Krystalee, imagining going home snuggled next to him in his truck.

"I'll be there as soon as I can," he promised. "I love you."

With a click he was gone. She dialed Krystalee's and left a message, then went into the bedroom for her most un-favorite game, standing in front of the closet wondering what to wear. This was a critical choice, too, since she would be parading with her new man and standing next to young, interesting Earth girls. It was her intention to keep Blue's attention firmly on his wife.

Finally she picked a silk halter top with a matching wraparound skirt. After eating no dinner last night, her stomach was, for once, pleasingly flat and the outfit molded to her curves. *Now you might even pass for being the same age!* The thought prickled a little, seeing as how he was actually over thirty years older!

Krystalee called, and when she found Amber was sitting alone being a nervous wreck, she came right over to pick her up. "Let's go to Farley's a little early, see if we can help him with anything. For a brain he sucks at organization," she said.

When they pulled up to his house, the street was already lined with cars. A rather unassuming structure from the road, Farley's house kept its main jewel in the back, the large, enclosed pool area. They came through the foyer and found the birthday boy in the kitchen, packing more beer into the already crammed refrigerator.

"Hey, big sis!" he shouted, jumping up to hug them both. "Can you believe I'm turning *thirty*!"

"No, I can't," Krystalee returned. "You still act your shoe size. Anything we can do to help?"

"Two gorgeous women help a party just by being there," Farley declared. "Mingle and look beautiful."

"Well, he's certainly learned to be charming in thirty years," Amber observed.

"Learned to kiss ass, you mean," Krystalee replied, laughing. "However, I brought my famous southern potato salad, and that is about all the work I want to do. Unless you need my help to blow out all those candles."

"Hey, if I look like I'm chokin', jump in there," Farley invited. "Okay, there's beer in the fridge, a bar set up by the pool, couple bowls of chips floating around somewhere, and my derelict roommate is presiding over a bag of purple haze back in the digital den, if you're interested in doing a radical attitude adjustment."

"No thanks," Amber laughed. "I couldn't possibly get higher than I already am. I will take a beer, though, just to be social."

"She's in love, little brother. Don't stand too close or you'll get crispy on the edges," Krystalee advised.

"Yeah? Anybody I know?" Farley asked as he reached into the fridge.

"No, I doubt if you've ever seen this one around before," Krystalee said with a wink to Amber. "He's supposed to show up tonight, so maybe we'll get to meet him."

The women exited through the back door and onto the deck that bordered the pool. It was a large oblong, intricately tiled, with a mosaic dolphin on the bottom of the shallow end. People were already swimming or socializing in the jungle of potted plants which surrounded the water. A hidden stereo system piped lively bluegrass music.

Amber and Krystalee sat near the backdoor, sipping their drinks and chatting briefly with whoever came in and out. The crowd slowly grew until it filled the pool enclosure and spilled out into the backyard where the grill was being stoked.

"Man, Farley sure has a big fan club," Amber remarked.

"This is nothing; it's barely five. Wait til people start pouring in after work," said Krystalee. "What time's your man coming?"

"When he gets done, I guess. Hope he doesn't get lost."

"Honey, if he can navigate the cosmos to get from Mars to Earth, I think he'll be able to find this place."

A slender black man walked up and interrupted them. "Excuse me, aren't you Farley's sister?"

"Oh, God, and I thought my disguise was working so well!" Krystalee joked. "Yeah, I have that unique distinction."

"I'm Dab Mitchell," he said, shaking her hand. "I was a year ahead of Farley in high school."

Krystalee had gone to the same school, but had graduated so far ahead of him, she didn't know many of her brother's friends. "The name sounds kind of familiar...."

"I write for the *Gazette* now. Once in a while they let me have a byline."

"Oh, yeah! I read your column all the time. And this is my girlfriend Amber, whose last name I don't know because she recently married a Martian."

"Krystal!"

"Well, it's not a secret, is it?" Krystalee reasoned. "You didn't hesitate to tell me and Quinn."

Dab shook Amber's hand. "This sounds intriguing. Is he from the underground colonies on Mars or their transplanted version here on Earth?"

Amber's mouth fell open. "How do you know about that?"

"Well, I've been what's known as a UFO nut since I was a kid. I read a lot."

"You read a lot?" Krystalee mocked. "Amber's been in the underground fortress! She's seen everything, in person."

"You can shut up any time," Amber warned.

"Come on, have you been there or not?" Krystalee demanded.

"I'd love to hear about it," Dab cut in. "You shouldn't be afraid to talk. I should know; when I was eleven I was abducted by the Grays."

"Guys in flannel suits?" Krystalee quipped.

"No, those short, bulb-headed guys with the big eyes," Amber said. "But this wasn't an abduction—"

"No, you let him put the blindfold on you willingly," Krystalee reminded.

"Well, naturally the aliens don't view it as abduction," the reporter said. "They're only gathering information, and their interior structure has no place in it for emotional response. They don't mean to be terrifying."

"That wouldn't make me feel any better about getting the anal probe," Krystalee said. "You two space cases discuss this while I go get more beers. Want anything, Dab?"

"No, I'm fine, thanks," he replied, holding up his bottle of mineral water. He sat down and leaned forward, smiling. "Did you really go underground? I've believed it existed for so long but never had proof! Are Martians really humanoid, almost indistinguishable from us? Is your husband here tonight?" He looked around quickly.

"Whoa, wait a minute! I don't think I should be discussing any of this with you until I talk to him first," Amber insisted. "I'm still amazed you even believe this."

"As I said, I've looked an extraterrestrial in the face." He shrugged. "Ever since then, believing was easy."

"You can't write about any of this, though. Please, we've only been married two days! I'm not ready to give up my privacy!"

"I respect that, of course. I won't write about it until you say it's okay. But you must know that the first Earthling-Martian marriage would make a pretty newsworthy item."

"In the *Enquirer*, you mean," Amber asserted. "The mainstream media wants to keep the space aliens in Hollywood, so they get relegated to the tabloid press."

"It's not really that way anymore," Dab said. "Or at least it's in the process of changing. I think people are going to be ready to accept that we're not alone in the universe real soon."

"Huh! That's what Blue says, too, that the consciousness of the masses is elevating, and we're getting ready for a big change."

"Don't you think seeing irrefutable proof that extraterrestrials exist would blow a few minds sky-high?" he asked, chuckling.

Krystalee returned with the beers and the conversation turned to other topics. Dab got up to greet some friends, then wandered off.

"Hope that guy doesn't put me in the paper," Amber commented. "And keep a lid on it, would ya? Let me see how Blue wants to handle this."

"Okay, but I know from experience it's not always best to let men handle things," Krystalee said. "That's why I'm gonna go take care of serving my potato salad."

Amber nipped at her beer can and focused on the dolphin at the bottom of the pool, which undulated hypnotically as people splashed the water. Her mind rushed to linger on its favorite subject. When Blue was out of her sight, he seemed too outrageously, impossibly wonderful, and she needed to see him again to make sure he was real. She silently prayed he'd be able to ditch the meeting before too long.

"Hey, Amber!" Farley yelled, popping his head through the back door. "There's a big bald guy in the foyer says he's your husband!"

13

Nothin' But a Party

Amber's face lit up as she shot out of her chair. "Course, I told him that was impossible, because you ain't married!" Farley chortled, gesturing with his drink.

"Little bro, that statement is not entirely accurate," Krystalee volunteered.

Amber was already past Farley and dashing through the kitchen. When she saw Blue standing there, wearing jeans, a shirt with cacti and coyotes all over it, and an adorably uncertain expression, she felt like crying for joy. She leaped into his arms and they clamped together like barnacles.

Krystalee and her brother stood in the doorway, waiting for them to finish kissing. "Excuse me," she said finally, "the honeymoon suite is to your right."

Amber giggled and gave Blue a final smack on the lips. "Honey, this is Krystalee, one of my best friends in the world."

Blue stepped forward, extending his large, pale hand. Krystalee took it, smiling but giving him a rapid once-over. "Hi, pleased to meet ya," she said. "Well, he sure is affectionate! I like that in an alien."

"Watch your mouth, big sis! That's no way to address people from other countries." Farley stuck out his hand. "Hi, Farley Collins. Welcome to the den."

"Blue Robinson."

"Robinson?" Farley echoed. "That's odd! From your appearance, I would've guessed some kind of mongolian moniker. Now don't tell me—let me guess."

"He loves geography games," Krystalee explained. "This oughta be a good one. Care to take a bet?"

"Save your money, I always figure it out in the end," Farley declared. "What I can't figure out is how our little Amber could run off and get married and not even invite me to the wedding! I didn't even know she had a boyfriend."

"We fell in love quickly," Blue said, gazing raptly at his bride, "and the traditions of my culture dictated that we marry at once."

"Aha! A tradition of purity—another clue to go with the shaved head!" Farley trumpeted. "Come on, let me get you a drink and we'll continue this." Blue looked questioningly over his shoulder as he was steered away.

"We'll be right out," Amber called.

"Wow, girlfriend," Krystalee said, "he is *way* fine! Even without hair!"

"Yeah, I like him better this way, too. The ponytail was fake and it kind of looked that way."

"Wish I could've seen that! He really does look...different, though, doesn't he?"

"That's because he's *really* from Mars. Don't you get it?"

"I can almost believe it," Krystalee sighed as she went to the fridge and got two more cold beers. "He's handsome, polite, and he treats you like gold. Can't be from *this* world."

Blue and Farley had been joined by several other people and were standing around by the pool when the women walked up. "Maybe one of the Hunzas from the mountains of Pakistan," Farley was saying. "An albino Hunza! Come on, am I hot or cold?"

"Not even on the proper planet," Blue laughed.

"Stumped, are we?" Krystalee goaded.

"No, no, for once I have a challenge," Farley corrected. "But this is a toughie. Amber, how did you find this guy?"

"Sheer luck," she answered happily.

"Sheer bullshit!" said a voice. They all turned to see Quinn striding up, her muscles threatening to burst her tight sheath dress.

"Uh, Blue, this is my good friend Quinnsetta," Amber attempted.

Blue stepped forward, smiling and offering his hand. Quinn jerked hers away, long nails flashing. "That's okay. Wouldn't want to contract any outer space microbes."

"I don't believe this!" Farley erupted. "How can you two be so rude to a foreign guest? Especially the one Amber chose for a husband!"

"Amber chose this? No, he hypnotized her, and now she's ad-dickted," Quinn accused. "Farley, for Lord's sake, he claims to be from Mars!"

"Mars?" Farley repeated. "And here I was over in Asia! Krys, is this one of those offbeat birthday pranks?"

"No, it isn't," Amber piped up. "The strangest part is that it's all true. I'm married, and my husband is Martian."

Everyone looked at Blue. "Martians are from the humanoid family," he said. "Millennia ago we had the same ancestor. Unlike humans, we only come in one color, and we don't have hair."

"Well, I for one want a little more proof than a headful of Neet and a bunch of New Age razzle-dazzle," Quinn sniffed, studying him carefully.

"Yeah, show us the blue tit!" Krystalee squealed.

"That's just how television manipulates your people!" Blue pointed out. "You think visual perception equals reality."

"Seeing is believing, isn't it?" Quinn said.

"No, it's not!" Blue countered. "Believing is seeing. You humans have it backwards. It comes from inside first, the way you use your thoughts to shape universal substance. When you believe in something, you open your mind to the capacity to perceive it."

"Come on, you guys," Farley said, laughing. "This isn't one of those surprise strippers, is it? Somehow I think I would've preferred a chick."

"What kind of dork do you think I am?" Krystalee snapped. "Amber's been talking about this guy for days."

"Yeah, I'm getting real worried about girlfriend's mental state," Quinn added. "She actually believes him."

"There's a friend of mine here tonight who says he was kidnapped by aliens twenty-some years ago. Been a raging maniac ever since, but he reads everything about UFOs and all that paranormal stuff. I'm sure he'd love to meet you; come on," Farley said, leading Blue off into the crowd.

"Sorry, but I do not call that convincing," Quinn said stubbornly, frowning and folding her arms.

"Aw, you just don't like anybody with bigger biceps than yours," Krystalee accused. "I think he's kinda cute."

"I think he's weird-looking, and the shit he says don't make much sense either."

"Come on, you guys, we're talking about the man I'm honeymooning with," Amber broke in. "Quinn, let me get you something to drink."

"Okay, white wine." Quinn stretched her elegant physique on a poolside chaise. "And don't make it that cheap box stuff."

As the three friends sat and talked, new arrivals poured constantly through the back door, some of them with musical instruments. The enclosure's far corner was being turned into a stage. Barbecue spice and chattering voices hung in the air.

"I'd better go look for Blue," Amber finally said, standing up. "He's been gone for a while, and when that happens I start getting withdrawal pangs."

"Pity the fool," Quinn snorted.

"Go, girl," Krystalee said, laughing. "Quinn, don't you have at least one romantic bone in your body?"

Amber worked her way around the pool, then went inside. The kitchen was full of people reloading the beer supply and preparing food, but she didn't see anyone she recognized. Distant voices lured her through the empty living room and to a closed door.

She knocked loudly and the door swung open, belching sweet, pungent smoke into the hallway. "Enter, if you dare," said a voice.

Fanning her hand in front of her face, Amber advanced into the cloudy, dimly-lit room. Every surface not covered with computer equipment had someone sitting on it or standing nearby. In the corner on an old couch, Farley and Dab sat on either side of Blue, who was staring down at a giant marijuana bud in his cupped hands.

"Aw, geez, Farley, do you have to corrupt him?" Amber put her hands on her hips and tried to look stern.

"You just want all the fun to yourself," Farley shot back. "Besides, he's only looking at it. Didn't want to take a hit."

Blue looked up at her and his face melted into a smile. "It's so good to see you again," he said dreamily.

"Eyes at half-mast, red around the blue," Amber observed. "He's wasted!"

"I swear, he did not inhale!" Farley said. "Right, guys?" Everyone swore.

"I don't have to smoke it, just let its vibrational essence interact with mine." Blue turned his attention back to the aromatic herb.

"Something I don't understand about your culture—this naturally-occurring plant is banned, because drugs are bad. But western medicine is based on pharmaceutical solutions, therefore drugs are good."

"It's just more Big Brother bullshit," somebody said.

"Right. All the land-of-the-free lip service keeps people from recognizing that we're under the thumb in America," Dab interjected. "Maybe not in the same blatant way as people in a dictatorship, but it's just as insidious."

"Like the government conspiracy theory," Farley said. "Yeah, that's a good question. What's the scoop on that, Blue, do they really have pickled extraterrestrials they're not telling us about? I cannot possibly believe the aliens were crash test dummies."

"I assume you mean the Gray telemetership that impacted the New Mexico desert," Blue answered. "It was similar to what we are trying to do now; they crashed deliberately as a kind of wake-up call. Unfortunately, in the 1940s humans had not matured enough to embrace contact. The ETs were seen as a threat, and their existence covered up."

"So do they really have a saucer in Area 51?" someone asked from a smoky corner.

"They had a craft and several bodies of the Grays, and were able to study them for a short time. Then, realizing that their mission to connect with Earthlings had been thwarted, the Grays came back to collect their trash. So now the government can truthfully claim it does not possess remains of an extraterrestrial ship. But their secret records show they once did."

"Whoa," somebody said, "he is really stoned!"

Amber reached down, took the bud from Blue's hands, sniffed it and handed it back to Farley. "Most of my friends' kids have already gone through their phase and stopped smoking this shit."

"Hey, call me retro," he replied happily. "Now let's go check the barbecue. I don't know about y'all, but I'm starving!"

The door opened again and everyone filed out in a fragrant cloud. When they came out of the living room, Blue pulled Amber into the darkened foyer and then close against him. He kissed her, slow and deep.

"So are you enjoying the party, honey?" Amber asked, still hugging him and smiling so hard she thought her cheeks would pop.

"Tremendously, because you're here," he whispered, nibbling her ear.

She persuaded him to eat food first, and they joined the throng around the pool. There was plenty of vegetarian fare besides potato salad, and Blue took small samplings of everything. For once, he seemed to be hungry. They joined Krystalee, Quinn, and two other friends at a round table.

Amber was relieved that the conversation stayed away from the cosmos and its possible inhabitants while they ate. Blue concentrated on his plate, obviously intrigued by every new taste. The barbecue was excellent, she was halfway through her fourth beer, and a sweet, sultry glow flowed through her like the molasses of love.

Suddenly Quinn's voice punctured her euphoria. "So, Mr. Spaceman. I haven't forgotten about you. I'm still waiting for some proof that you are what you say you are."

"Come on, Quinn," Amber began.

"No, if he's really Martian, it oughta be *easy* to prove it. Right?" She looked around at the others. Krystalee's eyes were glued to Blue. "And if you start taking off your clothes I'll slap you."

"All right," Blue said simply. He snatched a steak knife from Amber's plate and quickly jabbed it into the tip of his index finger. Everyone gasped as he grabbed a napkin to catch the first drop of blood. It fell to the white paper and spread, a dot of deep, midnight blue.

"Incredible!" Krystalee gasped as the other witnesses gaped in amazement.

"Haven't you guys ever seen a magic show? It's a trick!" Quinn declared.

Blue held out his finger and pulled the edges of the cut apart using his other hand; more liquid splashed to the napkin. Then he wrapped his fist around the torn digit. "Now I mentally assemble the skin molecules to accelerate healing."

"I bet next he saws Amber's heart in half," Quinn sniffed in a mock whisper.

He closed his eyes while everyone else stared at his hands. Even though Amber believed in him, she nervously hoped this impromptu faith healing was going to work. If it didn't, her friends might really think she'd lost her mind.

His eyes popped open. Smiling, he opened his fist and displayed the perfectly white, unscathed pad of his fingertip. Suddenly an amplified guitar chord silenced any comments. Farley was on stage with the other members of his band, clearly in his element. "Par-tay!" he yelled, jabbing the neck of his guitar into the air. The bass, mandolin and fiddle joined him in a blistering bluegrass riff.

Since talking was altogether impossible while the band played, harmony settled over the table. Amber scooted closer to Blue and scooped up his hand, full of satisfied contentment. After six or seven songs, Farley announced a short pit stop and voices could be heard again.

"I guess there's nothing quite like that on Mars," Quinn remarked, scowling in Blue's direction.

"No," he admitted. "It vibrates on an intense level."

"Puh-leeze! Would you just cut the bullshit and tell us who you really are." Quinn drilled him with a skeptical stare.

"Quinn, he really is from Mars!" Amber testified. "What in hell would it take to convince you?"

"I don't know, how about showing me the flying saucer he came in?"

Blue took Amber's wrist and looked at her watch. "We've got just enough time to intercept the evening patrol."

"You mean, you could take us to see a spaceship?" Krystalee asked in surprise.

"I can't promise anything, but if we leave now there's a good chance we could catch them," Blue said.

"Oh, no!" Quinn exclaimed. "I'm all relaxed here, listening to some good music, food and drink all around, and you want me to leave? No way."

"Come on, dammit!" Krystalee urged. "Do you want to see a UFO? I do! Let's go!"

"You've lost your mind! Leave on a wild-goose chase?" Quinn laughed and sipped her wine.

"Okay, then we'll go without you," Amber decided. "Come on, Blue."

Krystalee, Amber and Blue got up and headed for the house.

Quinn stood up. "How rude! What about your brother's birthday?"

"This won't take long," Blue said over his shoulder. "We'll be right back."

"Absolute waste of time," Quinn muttered as she picked up her purse and followed.

14

Sighting is Believing

A late arrival to Farley's party was hustling up the sidewalk with a birthday package under his arm just as Blue was loading Amber, Quinn and Krystalee into his truck.

"Hey, man!" he called. "What kind of cologne do you use?"

Amber and Krystalee laughed, but Quinn wasn't amused. "Please, Lord, do not let me be seen as a Martian's concubine," she muttered.

"That part will be played by *me* tonight, thank you!" Amber said as she slid to the middle of the seat. Krystalee climbed in beside her and Quinn sat next to the passenger door. "Besides, I didn't think you believed in Martians."

"I don't," Quinn answered quickly. "I'm only going on this fool's errand so I can bear witness to your shattered illusions."

Blue got in and started the engine.

"If it's all illusions, and I wasn't in the Martian's underground colony the other night, where was I?" Amber asked.

"The Lost Dutchman Mine? Under the influence of powerful narcotics?" Quinn spat. "I don't know, but anything would be a better explanation than a secret hideout built by men from Mars."

"Why is it so difficult for humans to believe there are other intelligent creatures in the universe?" Blue said. "Earthlings celebrate logic, but fail to see how logical it is that an infinite universe would contain other sentient life. It's so arrogant!"

"Oh yeah? Well, if Martians are so damn smart, how come nobody believes in them?" Quinn returned.

"Wait a minute; you're both wrong!" Krystalee broke in. "I saw a poll on TV where they were asking people their UFO views, and something like sixty-two percent said they believed aliens had contacted us."

"Maybe Earth *is* more ready than I thought," Blue mused.

"And another thirty-seven percent believed the government had made contact and was covering it up," Krystalee added.

"Oh, that's absurd!" Quinn said with disgust. "As intrusive as the media is, we know the color of every politician's underdrawers, but they manage to cover up alien contact? It doesn't leak out?"

"It's leaking everyplace, but only some have the eyes to see it," Blue said. "What's needed is an event that will cut through people's belief systems, and cause a massive change in consciousness. I guess, on a small scale, that's the experiment we're doing tonight."

"Better watch what kind of experiment you try to pull on me," Quinn warned.

"Don't worry, I know Kung Fu fighting," Krystalee said.

"Bullshit! You don't know any martial arts!" Quinn scowled at her.

"No, man, the song! Trust me, when I start singing that, people run."

By this time Blue had them hurtling along the highway, under the star-sprinkled night sky.

"We don't have to go to the other side of hell's half acre, do we?" Quinn finally queried.

"No," Blue responded, "just to a place where we can intercept their trajectory. Not too much farther."

"That's good because I *was* having a good time at the party."

"Quinn, listen to me," Amber pursued. "If he says there'll be something to see, you can bet it'll knock your eyeballs out. That underground colony is absolutely amazing, you can just feel that it wasn't made by humans...."

"Yeah, right, I know, and then the energy starts to swirl and change colors," Quinn mocked, drawing tornadoes in the air with her long nails. "Somebody bring me my magic crystal."

"You can't say energy doesn't exist!" Amber said.

"Sure, energy exists, as in electrical power, but I thought we were talking about the aura. Now, this I can believe in." Quinn thumped her thigh. "But an invisible halo around it? That's a little hard to swallow."

"Yes, many people think matter and energy are two entirely different things, but in reality they are the same," Blue said.

"How do you figure that?" Quinn challenged.

"All right, what's the smallest known component of matter?"

"You mean the atom?"

"Right," Blue said. "You learn in grade school that everything is made of them. Okay, and what is the atom made of?"

"Well, protons and electrons," Quinn answered uncertainly.

"And what are protons and electrons made of?"

"Let's see, they're little balls of...."

"Energy," Blue finished for her.

"It's all the same stuff," Krystalee said.

"What looks like solid matter," Blue concluded, "is really just different arrangements of energy. Which is why it is possible to manipulate matter with the mind, like I did when I healed my finger. Here's our road." He took the next exit off the highway, passed through a small group of buildings, then headed into the desert.

"I've never been out here before," Amber commented as he turned onto a dirt track that wound steeply downhill.

"We're going down by the riverbed; it will probably be dry at this time of year," Blue answered. "The moon's coming out from behind that cloud. Now we can turn off the lights." Suddenly they were surrounded by blackness.

"What the hell did you do that for?" Quinn erupted. "You're gonna get us all killed!"

"I can see fine," said Blue. "You'll need a few minutes to fully activate your night vision. Better to start now in case Amber's watch is slow."

He steered carefully down a slope and a hairpin turn, then the terrain leveled out in a wide, flattened area, where he pulled the truck in to park. In the dim moonglow they could see the curving trench of the stream, filled with smooth, rounded rocks.

"Hurry," Blue said as he killed the engine. "I think we're just in time."

Quinn mumbled something as she jerked open the door, and they got out and followed Blue toward the streambed. It was pleasantly warm, the sky was clear and star-strewn, and the peace of nature reigned.

"Sure is beautiful out here," Amber whispered. "Look at these stones; it's like they were all polished."

"Some time in their lives they must have been rolled around by a lot of water," Krystalee replied in a hushed tone.

"What are we whispering for?" Quinn shouted. "It's the friggin' middle of *nowhere!*"

"I don't know, I feel like I'm in a church," Amber said. "Like something profound is about to happen. I'm getting this tingling down the back of my neck..."

"Yes, it is coming! I feel the vibrational disturbance, too." Blue grabbed her by the hand and pulled her down the embankment, picking out the biggest stones to step on. Krystalee bounded after them and Quinn reluctantly followed, grumbling to herself. Finally they all stood on the level expanse of river bottom.

"Where should we be looking?" Amber asked.

"Out that way, to the north," Blue directed. "We should get a good view of them crossing the horizon. But it will be fast, so don't blink."

"Just hope I don't yawn," Quinn said. "This could be like waiting up for Santa."

"No, I feel it coming closer!" Amber insisted. "Now I'm tingling all the way down to my toes!"

"There!" Blue pointed to the sky.

"Where? I don't see a thing," Amber heard Quinn say, but her attention was on the dot of bright light at the end of Blue's finger, and it was drawing her like a magnet. Blue was still holding her hand, and she felt his energy sizzling up her arm. The dot began to move in slow motion, pulsing slightly.

"Do you see what he's talking about, Amber?" asked Krystalee. "I don't see a fucking thing either!"

"Yeah, I see it, and it's moving this way. I think there's two of them." A second blip now trailed the first.

"Right. We always patrol with two vehicles," Blue affirmed. "The timing is perfect."

"Yeah, I'm just so excited to be out here watching some airplane lights," Quinn scoffed. "Which I can't even see! All I see is stars."

"Hold Amber's hand; our combined fields will help alter your focus. Krystalee, come to my other side," Blue instructed.

"They're speeding up," Amber reported.

"No, they're just getting close enough for you to perceive how fast they're going." They stood in a line, hands linked.

"I do see something!" Krystalee screeched. "And it can't be plane lights because they're getting so big."

For once Quinn was speechless, watching the bizarre show unfold. The dots were growing bigger as they approached, until it became plain that each light-ball was really a glowing row of lights. The three women stared at the oncoming ships.

"Oh...My...God!" Krystalee choked.

The two craft swiftly approached, their disc-shaped, silver hulls glinting in the moonlight. Except for the row of lights marking the circumference, their smooth contours were completely featureless. They made no sound at all, simply sailed along like a computer-generated special effect superimposed on reality. The strong smell of ozone flooded the atmosphere. Amber could feel every hair on her arms standing straight up.

"What is it?" Quinn hissed, squeezing Amber's hand.

"I tried to tell you guys he's for real," Amber whispered.

"The odor is caused by chemical changes in the air due to the propulsion system," Blue volunteered. "It's harmless."

The ships passed quickly and surged away, within seconds becoming dots in the distance again. Everyone still stood, mutely looking after them.

"Well, that's about it," Blue announced. "See? It didn't take long."

Krystalee let go of his hand and spun Amber into a bear hug. "Whoa, we just saw a UFO!!" She was laughing and shaking with excitement.

"Technically, no, since UFO means Unidentified Flying Object, and these were definitely Martian patrol transports," Blue corrected. "Nine-person craft, I'd say on a par with your sports cars."

"They were awesome!" Krystalee exclaimed. "Beautiful!" She sat down in the riverbed. "God, my knees are like jelly!"

Quinn sat down in the stones, too, shaking her head. "This just isn't registering in my brain."

"It's registering in your heart, though, and that's the important thing," Blue said cheerily. "Well, shouldn't we be getting back to the party?"

All three looked at him in amazement.

"How are we going to go back there after...*this*?" Quinn asked. "One look at us and they're going to think we've been off doing fairy dust."

"You mean 'angel dust,'" corrected Krystalee.

"Some kind of dust. All I know is my whole world view is a duster..." Quinn said softly.

Krystalee started laughing hysterically. "This is just so unbe-fucking-lievable!" She rolled onto her back in the rocks, staring up at the star-sprinkled sky as if the ships might come back to take a bow. "He's a Martian, Quinn. Our fucking brother-in-law is really a fucking Martian!"

"Earth girls sure do swear a lot," Blue observed.

This comment sent Krystalee into another fit of giggles. "Hey, while you were in a cave all those swear words went mainstream. Cussing is as American as apple pie."

"Blue, don't listen to her, and please don't go around using those words." Quinn stood up and walked to where Blue stood with his arm around Amber. "And please accept my apology," she said, holding out her hand. "I'm sorry I was so mean, but I get pretty maternal about my girlfriends."

Blue grabbed her hand and pulled her close. "I'm honored to play a part in the expansion of your consciousness. This experiment has been a resounding success!"

"Group hug!" Krystalee squealed, jumping up to add to the cluster, and they all clung together for a moment.

Amber had no trouble feeling the intensity of their combined fields; her energy was spitting and popping like a shrimp on the cosmic barbie.

Finally Blue said, "Re-entry into 3-D life may be difficult after this experience, but we can't stand out here in the dark forever." They slowly released each other. "Besides, I need to put my wife to bed soon."

Lovebirds swooped through Amber's stomach. "I *am* feeling a little bit sleepy," she giggled.

"Yeah, let's go," suggested Krystalee. "I could really use a fucking drink."

The mood in the truck's cab was loudly exuberant on the way back. Blue didn't say much, simply smiled and listened to the women marvel over what they'd seen. Every five minutes one of them came up with a new angle on how the knowledge would affect their lives, and the lives of all Earthlings when the truth was universally known.

When Blue parked in front of Farley's house, Quinn and Krystalee piled out onto the sidewalk.

"Doesn't it seem like we've been gone for days?" Krystalee asked, looking at the house. Party noise blared from inside.

"That's a typical reaction," Blue called out the window. "Welcome to the dawn."

"Aren't you guys coming back in?" Quinn said, noticing they hadn't budged. "It's not late at all."

"I really do have an early meeting to attend. And we are still celebrating our marriage," Blue said with a glance at Amber. "Please thank Farley for us."

"Hey, thank you," Krystalee returned. "Come on, Quinn, let's go get that drink. Have fun, Amber!"

Amber waved and watched her two friends go into the house. "What a difference a sighting makes, huh?" she said.

"Yeah, that worked out quite well. I would have looked pretty stupid if we'd gotten there five minutes later."

They drove to Amber's house and walked up to the door, hand in hand. She was thrilled to have him in her humble abode, no fantastic cavern or tent on the edge of the vortex, just her double bed with the homemade quilt, and pictures of family and friends on the wall.

She lit one vanilla-scented candle before they threw their clothes on the floor and slipped between the sheets together. Then the moth plastered herself to the flame, knowing she was home, whether it burnt her to a crisp or not. They tried to linger over their love-making, but there was now no shyness to slow them down. Greedily, openly, they devoured each other and climaxed quickly.

Afterward, Amber held herself tightly against him, wanting to go to sleep with his penis still inside. "Oh, Blue, I love you so much," she told him. "I've just never felt this kind of connection; I've never been so much in love."

He stroked her hair, saying, "I know. It seems we are soulmates."

"Whatever that is, I'm into it."

"I have a secret to tell you, then," he whispered.

"What is it?" she whispered back.

"You know how when I start talking about things that you'd ordinarily consider crazy, you understand exactly what I'm saying? And the way you feel about me; when you saw me with no hair—and especially with no clothes—didn't you sense a deep recognition, an attraction that was not based on the conditioning you received in this society?"

"Get to the point," Amber said sleepily.

"You're not from here either."

She was too happy and satisfied to take this message seriously. "Yeah, right," she murmured. "I'm really from the planet Nympho." Her pelvis bumped softly against him.

He chuckled and kissed her forehead. "In that case I'd better stay close by."

"You got that right, baby." She made one more sound, a tiny moan of contentment, before drifting to sleep in his arms.

15

There He Was, Gone

"Dammit," Amber muttered, waking to find she was alone in her bed. Lovemaking in the morning was her favorite way to start the day, and she had been planning to send Blue to his meeting with a satisfied smile. She hugged the pillow he'd slept on, sighing wistfully into the last traces of his presence. *This better be a quick-ass Martian Council meeting or I'm gonna lose it!*

Then she saw a note on the bedside table. Scrambling upright, she snatched it and grinned broadly as she began to read: "Good morning, darling wife and daring lover. You add a whole new dimension to 3-D! The meeting begins early and I did not want to disturb your sleep, you look so beautiful and peaceful. Expect me to contact you at the first opportunity. All my love, always." He'd ended it by drawing a smiley face with oversized, alien eyes.

Amber squealed with delight and bounded out of bed. She threw on her robe and glanced at the clock. It was eight already, but so what? The illustrations for Superstition Press were ready to be viewed and approved, and nothing more urgent than dinner with Blue at the folks' was on her calendar. Humming while she made coffee, she marveled at the fairy tale turn her life had taken in one short week. Maybe she should be thinking about where her next job was coming from, but that issue would be going on the back burner today. First priority: Enjoy the magic of being madly in love.

"Besides, I'm still honeymooning, even if he's not here," she said to herself as she opened the door to collect the newspaper. She sat down at the kitchen table, unrolled the paper, and took a sip of coffee. She almost spit it out again when she saw the blurb across the bottom of the front page: "Alleged UFO Sighted by Phoenix Residents, p. 7."

"Damn, the girls must've been flapping their lips already," she muttered as she turned to the article. In it were quotes from two people who claimed they had witnessed the passage of two spacecraft. When asked if there was any chance the sightings could have been airplanes, one source commented, "No way. We happen to know they were Martian ships." That had to be Krystalee, putting mouth in motion before engaging brain.

"Damn," she said again, shaking her head. Media publicity was not exactly what she'd had in mind last night, and she began to realize how it could complicate things. But what did Blue expect? That his campaign to strike up a friendship between Martians and Earthlings wouldn't cause a stir in the press? Well, the genie was out of the bottle now.

The phone rang and Amber grabbed the kitchen extension. Krystalee was on the line, excited and breathless.

"Have you seen the paper? Oh my God, we're famous!"

"I'm reading it this second. Now how are you gonna be famous when you spoke on condition of anonymity?" Amber asked sharply.

"Well, you know, I don't want to be branded a nutcase. Besides, I didn't want to cause any hassle for you and Blue."

"Huh! Nice of you to think of that, now that it's all over town."

"Hey, listen, can I help it if one of my brother's friends is a reporter and a UFO nut? You want me to keep quiet after you take me to see *that*?"

"I don't know!" Amber wailed. "I'm just worried; I liked it when Blue was just my private secret. I don't know if I'm ready to share him with the rest of the world."

"Nobody's trying to get him on the cover of the Rolling Stone! Dab said he wouldn't mention that we actually saw a Martian to go with the spaceships. How much Blue is involved with the media is up to him."

"Yeah, I guess so," Amber sighed. "I just wish he were here right now to tell me it's all right."

"It's all right! It's all right!" Krystalee insisted. "Forget famous, we are gonna be rich!"

"Now what are you talking about?"

"Thought you said you read the paper! Flip to page eleven."

Amber did and saw a large photo of a bespectacled man holding up egg-sized stones for the camera. The caption read: "Martian Rocks Go On Block."

"That's right," Krystalee continued, "there are only twelve of these babies in the world, that they know of, and they're expecting to auction them off for between one and two million. *Million!* And guess what? We have the thirteenth!

"You mean my wedding stone? Oh, no we don't, because you had to send it to Europe!"

"So what? They're gonna send it back! And it's way more beautiful than these gnarly meteorite chunks in the picture. Probably worth five million, at least."

"If it's worth that much, do you really think they'll just give it back to you?" Amber couldn't believe her friend was turning her marriage into a marketing opportunity.

"What can they do? Steal it?" Krystalee reasoned. "They'll send it back, but forget selling your stone; I realize it has sentimental value. You said Blue had a lot of rocks and crystals in his underground bedroom, maybe some of them are from home. One about the size of a golf ball would mean none of us ever has to work again."

Amber chuckled softly. Her friend's attitude suddenly made things clearer in her mind. "You can't just look at the flashing lights on the spaceship, you have to listen to what Blue is saying, too. Everyone basing their worth on the size of their bank accounts is one of the fucked-up things about this country! It's about raising your consciousness, not your checkbook balance!"

"Well, I don't know about you, sweetie, but I find it much easier to meditate when the bills are paid. Speaking of which, gotta get to work," Krystalee announced. "Then I'm meeting Quinn at the library this afternoon; she wants to do UFO research. I swear, it's like she had a religious experience last night! Never seen her so fired up about anything, and she doesn't know yet that the rocks from up there are worth a fuckin' fortune!"

"Oh, Lord, I've opened Pandora's Box!" Amber said.

"You better believe it! This is the hottest thing that's happened to Quinn since chromium picolinate. She may even skip her workout today! And what are the newlyweds doing?"

"I don't really know," Amber sighed. "Blue's off to save the world. Then we're supposed to have dinner at my parents'."

"So he's gonna meet the family. They'll flip when they see that bald head!" Krystalee hooted. "You gonna tell them the truth?"

"Well, I'm working on telling them we're married, but I'm not sure they're ready for the ET rap."

"Hell, they're never gonna be ready for that! Hit 'em with both barrels right off the bat. Blue will charm them; if he can convince Quinn, he can convince anybody. And see if he'll give up a geode or two, okay?"

"You're unbelievable. Don't you know money can't buy love?"

"Then be thankful *you* already got that! Me, I'll take money and a good lay. Talk to you later."

Amber hung up and sighed. It was only 8:30, and an eternity of time stretched before her. She wanted to kick herself for not making a plan with Blue before, but last night she'd been thinking of other things than synchronizing watches with him. Of course, who knew he would vanish from his side of the bed without a sound? She wished they could spend a normal night and wake up together without somebody's molecules zipping through hyperspace.

So now what? She looked around at her house, which wasn't a total mess but on close inspection would never pass the white glove test. Maybe if she cleaned and organized her surroundings, it would have a similar effect on her thoughts.

Too nervous to be hungry, Amber got dressed and attacked her chores right away. At least they would serve as excellent time-wasters. She loaded the washing machine, scrubbed the sink and stove in the kitchen, and was deeply involved in the living room carpet when the phone managed to shrill through the vacuum's roar.

She shut off the noise and raced hopefully for the phone. "Hello?"

"Is this Amber Robinson?"

Amber felt a tremor jolt through her as the caller spoke her new name for the first time. "Uh...," she stammered, "who is *this*?"

"Dab Mitchell, from the *Gazette*. We met at Farley's party last night?"

"Oh, right, I just read your article. Thought you said you wouldn't write anything without permission."

"I said I wouldn't write about your husband without permission. And as you can see, there's nothing about him at all."

"Okay, great, you managed to write about him without writing about him. Now what do you want?"

"The exclusive interview, of course," he replied. "Speaking as a journalist and an old flying saucer buff, this has to be the news story of the decade. No, the century!"

"Interviews? No, I don't think so."

"Why not? Krystalee and your other friend said he mentioned that Earth and Mars should formally acknowledge each other. You know, like establish diplomatic relations. I can help."

"Well, I'll pass the offer along."

"Is he there? May I speak with him?" Dab persisted.

"No, he isn't," Amber said icily. "And we're actually on our honeymoon right now. Do you think you could refrain from bugging us til we're done?"

"Oh, sure! I'm really sorry if I'm intruding," Dab tried to soothe her. "Just one more thing about the interview—there could be money in it. A lot of money."

"Good-bye, Mr. Mitchell," Amber said sweetly, then hung up on him.

This was the second time this morning someone had proposed making money from Blue. What sort of cat had they let out of the bag last night? She slumped into her chair, feeling as if things were spiralling out of her control. She began to see that the first extraterrestrial to openly visit Earth would certainly be inundated in a media flood, his name a household word all over the planet. That was simply the nature of twentieth century communications!

And how could she really blame Quinn and Krystalee? Blue had flaunted his true color in front of a bunch of people last night! Surely, he had already thought this through. *On the other hand, it's hard to get street smarts in a cave.*

Three hours later, the house was spotless but Amber was still distressed. No phone calls, no telepathic messages, no discernible signs from heaven had arrived. As she collapsed on a kitchen chair and splashed down a glass of cold water, the only sound she heard was the rumble of the air conditioner. It was another scorcher outside. And inside, she burned up with the desire to hear from Blue.

The phone suddenly split the silence, making Amber jump. But it was only Mom, wondering what time to expect them.

"I'll call you when he gets back from his meeting," Amber told her. "He didn't really know what time it would end."

"Well, it doesn't matter. Lasagna gets better with age," her mother replied. "Just come as soon as you can. Violet's coming; she sent Bill to the latest Disney with the kids. She's looking forward to meeting your new friend."

Amber could just imagine her persnickety sister's reaction to her new husband! This would be one for the record books. "She'll meet him. We're going to be together for a long time."

"Are you really that sure, after knowing him one week?"

Amber answered unhesitatingly, "Without a doubt. He's really different, Mom, like I said. You'll see."

"As I said," she corrected. "And I'm certainly rooting that you're right. So call me when he gets...home. Wait a minute, there may be input from the peanut gallery." Amber smiled as her parents went through their familiar routine; then her mother came back on the line. "This one's sort of a cliché. 'All that glitters is not gold.'"

"So he doesn't think I have the genuine article," Amber snorted.

"Honey, he's a skeptic from way back. He can't help it!" Mom said, laughing. "But he's also capable of admitting when he's wrong, and I'm sure your young man will prove that to him."

Young? Mom, the dude is seventy-three! "I sure hope so," Amber said instead. "I'm a nervous wreck."

"Oh, sweetie, don't be. Everything will be fine and your father will behave. I promise," she added with emphasis, and Amber could envision the exaggerated look of warning she was faking for him.

"Good. I'm jittery enough. And you'll like him, I really think you will!"

"Don't worry, I have an open mind."

They hung up and Amber looked for the zillionth time at the clock. Was he ever, *ever*, going to call?

When the afternoon finally dragged toward evening, she was still thinking the same thing. The phone seemed to have died in the meantime, lying there lifeless, hour after hour. A gnawing uneasiness was beginning to brew deep in her gut. Sure, Blue had an important mission, but couldn't he take a minute out to contact and reassure her? What was happening back at the underground ranch?

There was nothing to do but go over to Mom and Dad's by herself. As usual, being there was like returning to the nest, but there was a note out of tune tonight. The family was buzzing about Amber's new love, and here she was, without him.

Her sister Violet got right down to business. "So what's with the man of your dreams? I sent the rest of the tribe off so I could interrogate him personally."

Amber sighed, realizing it was useless to hide her feelings from the people who knew her best. "I just don't get it," she admitted. "He's been stuck to me like glue for three days, and now, not a word."

"Let's see, it's time to meet the folks and suddenly he has an important meeting to go to that he never comes back from. I smell something slightly rotten in the Garden of Eden," Violet said, arching her eyebrows.

"Come on, give her a break, Violet," said their mother, the eternal peacemaker.

"It *was* an important meeting!" Amber insisted. "If you only knew what it was about...."

"Okay, so tell me, what was it about?" Violet pressed.

Amber paused. What could she say now? That it was about the survival of civilization as we know it?

"Yeah, it was probably a meeting of the 4-F Club," her sister continued.

"What's the 4-F Club?" Dad asked innocently.

"You remember that one, don't you, Amber?" Violet asked. "French 'em, Feel 'em, Fuck 'em, Forget 'em."

"Violet!" Mom warned, feigning shock.

"Very funny, but it's not like that at all!" Amber wailed. "You don't understand, he really loves me!"

"Then where is he tonight?" Violet gestured at the clock.

"That's enough now," Mom declared with finality. "Help me set the table."

But Amber didn't hear her; she was staring at the television set while adrenaline flooded her veins. The sound had been muted, but the picture told an unmistakable story, that of a cone-shaped mountain emitting a plume of smoke.

"Dad, give us some V," Amber said loudly. Violet, seeing her stricken expression, snatched the remote and punched up the volume.

> "...unexpected that any activity would originate at this time in the long-dormant volcanic peak. Scientists are closely monitoring developments but do not think it is yet necessary to investigate the possibility of an evacuation plan."

"Where the hell is this?" Violet demanded.

"Seattle," Amber recited like a zombie. "And the evacuation needs to start right away."

16

Blue Mood

All Amber could see was Blue looming above her, naked, immense erection in his hand; everything else was darkness. She watched as he plucked his prick like a guitar string, letting it smack his belly and quiver invitingly. Lowering her hand to the blue shaft, she covered the knob and savored the warm, soft skin against her palm. Then she woke up.

The dream slowly dissipated, her fuzziness grew clear, and reality rushed back in like thieves into the temple. A disappointed whine escaped her throat. On top of the emotional trauma of twenty-four hours of forced separation from her mate, Amber now realized she was also terminally horny.

She wriggled into the pillows, letting delicious memories flash through her head. It felt as though every cell of her epidermis were longing, crying, begging to be touched by Blue. She thought of the dream again and an eddy of lust swirled through her stomach and cascaded between her legs. But the sensation wasn't really pleasurable; it was a clutching ache, empty and erotic at the same time.

Her hand slid under the covers, toward the tender center of her pain. A bittersweet thrill raced through her as her fingers expertly kneaded the need. *I sure thought the days of resorting to this were over!*

The phone screamed demandingly from the kitchen, jerking Amber away from the task at hand. She shot out of bed, completely convinced that concentrating on him had summoned Blue's ring. When the voice on the line turned out to be Quinn, her heart nosedived.

"Honey, what you doing up so early? I was just gonna leave a message."

"What the hell time is it?" Amber groaned.

"Almost seven. I have an early session, but I sure didn't mean to disturb your sugar session with your man."

"Yeah, well, there've been some technical difficulties with that."

"Don't tell me he had another early meeting today!"

"Quinn, he never came back from the last one!" Amber wailed. "I'm losing my mind over here."

"Lord have mercy, that doesn't sound right. Didn't call or anything?"

"Not a word. I had to go to dinner at my parents' by myself. Needless to say, they were not impressed."

"Well, maybe he just got tied up; sounded like the thing was pretty important. You know how men are when they get involved in something—all else flies out the window."

Amber wanted to cry, *including me?* Instead she said, "I just hope he's okay."

Quinn laughed lightly. "Don't worry about that; I think boyfriend can take care of himself. And he'll contact you soon, I'm sure."

"Damn, you sure changed your tune in a hurry."

"Honey, don't get jealous, but that man of yours has turned my world upside down! I just can't get over those spaceships! It's like being an atheist all your life, and then, boom! You see God!"

"I know what you mean...."

"Listen, I gotta go or I'm gonna be late to my appointment with the sunrise crew."

"Well, what was the message going to be?" asked Amber.

"Oh, right, almost forgot. Krystal and I are meeting with that reporter this afternoon, if you want to join us."

"*What*? Please don't tell him anything else!"

"Cool your jets, child, it's gonna be the other way around," Quinn assured her. "*He's* going to school *us* on this flying saucer stuff. Guess he's been queer on the subject for years."

"Come off it, his motivation is the big scoop! Why would he waste his time telling you guys anything?"

"Because, my dear, we all have one thing in common—the planet we're standing on and an interest in keeping it there."

Amber was so surprised to hear this coming from Quinn, she couldn't even think of a smartass comeback.

"Anyway," Quinn continued, "We'll be at my place at around four if you're not doing anything."

"I had sort of planned to get back to my honeymoon," Amber pouted. "Meanwhile, the waiting is killing me."

"Well, what doesn't kill us makes us strong," Quinn quipped. "Later, sweetheart."

Amber hung up, eyeing the phone sourly. Blue would probably not resort to such primitive technology to contact her. Besides, hanging out in the house waiting for him to call would really tip her sanity over the edge.

"I've gotta get outta here!" she resolved, running into the bedroom to throw on shorts and a T-shirt. Ten minutes later she was stuck in traffic and wondering what demon had possessed her to make her go joyriding during rush hour.

All around she felt a harried, hurried vibration. Horns honked and drivers revved engines in frustration. It was no different than any other morning drive, but today it seemed so pointless, an enormous amount of wasted energy. Where were all these people rushing to, mindlessly poisoning the Earth with their carbon monoxide fumes?

Not that I'm any different, she reminded herself, and then what Blue had said flooded her brain. "Not from here...." What had he meant by that? She had hair, so that ruled out Martian citizenship, and she sure didn't look like a Gray!

Amber turned into the parking area at the Desert Botanical Garden, thinking of a soothing walk alone among the pathways. When she saw a school bus already parked there discharging raucous children, she eased the Toyota back onto the highway. The real desert would make a better destination anyway.

Driving out of town, a new idea occurred to Amber. It seemed stupid at first, almost impossible, but then it began to look brilliant in its simplicity. If he wouldn't come to her, she would go looking for him. She'd retrace their steps as best she could and scout around for the entrance to the Martian tunnels. Even if they were totally hidden, surely they had monitors of some sort that would spot her. No way was she going to be left pining away at home, tossed aside like space junk into orbit!

Okay, he said it was in the Superstitions, so it's got to be out this way.... But how long had they driven? She tried to remember the conversation, tried to recall any detail other than her heartbeat pounding against her blindfolded temples.

"Aha!" she shouted as the shoulder of the road became orange groves. Blue had turned shortly after she had smelled the blossoms that night; she wasn't surprised to see a sign for a recreation area a few miles later. Either this was a pretty accurate reconstruction of their route or a wild coincidence, and Amber was beginning to believe those did not exist.

No other cars were in the parking area this early. She locked up and headed off on one of the marked trails, anxious to be surrounded by nature. Zigzagging along the rocky paths, she felt better immediately. The open, peaceful desert was a welcome contrast to humanity's frantic pace.

She climbed to the top of a rise and looked out at the panoramic vista with a satisfied sigh. No people, no roads, just rocks and plants in an artful jumble as far as the eye could see. And, she noticed, there were at least a million possible hiding places for the doors leading to Blue.

She kept walking, and it felt good to be working her muscles in the morning sun. But after a half hour, all she'd really gained was a layer of sweat. She stopped and surveyed the magnitude of the landscape. Maybe this *was* a stupid idea; she could easily be miles from the right spot.

Suddenly a wave of fear and longing streaked through her, and she sat down on the nearest large rock. Burying her face in her hands, she caved in and cried.

"Oh, God, or Prime Creator, or Great Spirit or Guardian Angels—whatever you are—please, please don't take him away from me!" she prayed between sobs. It almost felt good to pour her anxiety out her eyes, and when the tears subsided at last, she felt drained but somehow cleansed.

She pulled up her shirt and wiped her face, then took a few deep breaths. Crying seemed to have activated her aura, and she stilled herself so she could focus on the tingling energy. Suddenly the sensations jumped in intensity, flooding her body with an almost paralyzing current.

A peripheral movement jerked her attention to a jagged rock on her far right side. She gasped softly when she realized she was staring at a large iguana. Or, at least it was some kind of reptile, long and thick with skin of mottled green and a pattern of blue dots on its back.

Her energy surged as she looked at it staring back at her with its round, gold eyes. Her muscles contracted tighter and it dawned on her, *My God, this freeze ray is coming from him!*

They held each other's unwavering gaze, neither creature moving. Something Blue had said popped into her head: "The lizard on your windowsill could be an ET." At this insight a wave of dizziness overcame her, threatening to topple her into the dust. She steadied herself on her rock perch, never looking away from the iguana. It remained motionless, regarding her fixedly with a stare that she swore contained intelligence. At last she was able to move her mouth. "Talk to me, little dragon," she invited.

At this the lizard turned and posed facing away from her, switching its tail. Amber stood shakily and stepped toward him. As she got closer, the blue dots almost glowed, pulling her attention. They were arranged in unbelievable precision, two perfect circles on top of each other, each with its own distinguishing marks. The image seemed to burn into her cerebrum as she stooped over the large reptile, perilously close to his mouth if he'd been the unfriendly type.

Another power surge rocked her equilibrium and sent her to her knees. She reached for the lizard; it twisted its head around, darted its tongue out, then scampered away. Lurching upright, she tried to follow it, but it quickly disappeared, as if down a hidden hole.

Amber sat down on the ground until the electric sensations in her body ebbed and the dizzy nausea had passed. Then she got up gingerly and made her way back to the car. She felt confused and dazed, yet strangely calm. She looked down at her hands; they still buzzed as if she were wearing mittens made of bees. The desert floor appeared printed on cellophane, shiny and warped, and even the sun looked fake, like a bare bulb in the hazy sky. When she got in the car she found a scrap of paper in the glove compartment and quickly drew the design from the lizard's back. There was no doubt in her mind that this was a message from Blue.

Going back into human territory was challenging. Once again she felt the distance, watching people madly, angrily rush around the roadways. Her world had become a fantasyland of visions, messenger lizards, UFOs and impossibly fine love. These people could never relate!

She arrived home in a numb, trancelike condition. She kicked off her shoes, then noted with amazement that it was already two o'clock. Her desert trek had lasted longer than she thought. But that was good; every hour passed was an hour closer to Blue.

Unfurling the paper across the kitchen table, Amber smiled as she read the date. A week ago today she had met Blue because of a flat tire, and embarked on the seven most incredible days of her life. *May there be many more. Amen!*

She flipped the pages, skimming the headlines for something worth reading. More corruption in government, zillions of wars around the world, nuclear material falling in the ocean from a failed Russian Mars probe. When all along, the Martians had been right here!

Then came the headline that turned her blood to ice water: "Scientists Say Evacuation Not Likely." She'd almost skipped over it until the Seattle dateline caught her eye. It began, "Labeling the recent seismic activity on Mt. Rainier a 'fluke,' scientists say evacuation plans are being shelved for the time being. Yesterday's tremors and smoke-belching display subsided quickly, and volcano experts widely declared the event to be an isolated incident."

Amber was filled with a prickly rush of guilt. Here she'd been pissing and moaning about the lack of her lover all day, completely forgetting the double whammy of her vision and last night's news broadcast. Meanwhile, a lot of people could be in deep shit.

She dialed Rose's number, aware that her sister would be at work. When the machine picked up she said, "Hey, sis. Just calling because I want to talk to you about Seattle. I was there recently with my, uh, significant other. Anyway, call me as soon as you get home and I'll explain."

Amber slumped into the couch. The next thing she knew she was waking up two hours later. Whatever energetic freak-out the meeting with the iguana had involved, her physical vehicle had taken it on the chin. She ran her fingers through her frizzy mane, trying to get reoriented. Then she looked at the clock and remembered the volcano's spewing cone. She had to get over to Quinn's, talk to the newspaper guy, and have him write an article urging everyone within a hundred-mile radius of Rainier to take a quick vacation.

It was almost six o'clock by the time she pulled up in front of Quinn's cedar and glass A-frame. Krystalee's Mustang was there, in front of a beat-up, pea-green Impala. As she parked behind it she noticed its bumper sticker: "Shift Happens." Amber smiled to herself; maybe the reporter really was an ally.

"Hi!" Amber called, stepping in through the unlocked front door. Though sunlight poured through tall glass panels, inside the living room was air conditioned cool.

"We're in back!" Quinn shouted, and Amber walked soundlessly through the white carpet and into the rear atrium where her friends were gathered. They sat around a table in the glassed-in patio instead of moving further out into the screened porch; even though it was the end of September, the late afternoon sun burned brutally hot.

"Jesus, your face is fried!" Krystalee exclaimed.

"Is it? I took a walk in the desert today."

Quinn got up and pulled up a chair for her. "Ah yes, nothing like a walk in the desert to beat the ninety-five-degree heat."

"Well, she probably had excess steam to blow off, if you know what I mean," Krystalee giggled. "Still no word from Blue?"

Amber shook her head as she sat down. "Hi, Dab."

"Hello, Mrs. Robinson," he said cheerfully. "Glad you could make it."

She nodded, looking down at the books strewn over the table. They had titles with words like "cosmic" and "transformation" and "dimension," and some even had drawings of aliens or their ships on the cover.

"Amber, you just can't *believe* some of the things he's been telling us about!" Quinn enthused as she glided up with a glass of wine for her. "The government has been pulling the wool way over our eyes; they've known for fifty years!"

"More than that, really," Dab said. "It supposedly started in the early forties, when Einstein and Tesla were working on the atom bomb. But the military had another task for them, a secret one. They were trying to create a cloaking device for their ships and aircraft, basically an invisibility machine. The technology was based on generating an enormous electromagnetic field. And guess what? It worked!"

"You mean they made something invisible?" asked Krystalee.

"Yeah, that and a lot more. They made a whole ship full of men disappear, but they also ripped a hole in space-time, and instead of making them invisible, they shot 'em into the future."

"Time-traveling?" Amber said, with a little shiver.

"Uh-huh, and it worked real great, except when they came back from the future," Dab went on.

"What do you mean?" Quinn asked.

"Well, the people that survived were certifiably insane, and a lot of people did not come back the way they left," Dab explained. "The dead ones they could pretend were war casualties, but I don't know how they accounted for the ones that were sunk halfway into the bulkhead, like their flesh had combined with the metal."

"You really believe that?" queried Quinn.

"Of course it's all speculation; the government denies it ever took place. But that's the story of the Philadelphia Experiment, 1943." Dab leaned forward. "And some say that when they punched into another dimension, that's when the government first came in contact with alien life."

"Oh, please!" Quinn interrupted. "I do believe in alien life now, but this conspiracy theory I just can't buy! They can't conceal a sneeze, let alone this kind of information for over fifty years."

"They've done it by creating a campaign to discredit eye witnesses, making anyone who claims they've had a sighting an automatic lunatic," Dab insisted. "At Roswell, people say they were visited by government representatives who threatened to kill them, and their families, if they talked about it."

"Yeah, that makes you really proud to be an American," Krystalee commented.

"I still don't get it," Quinn continued, "why would they go to those extremes to keep it quiet? It's like we're a bunch of babies they don't trust with the information."

Dab trilled a laugh. "Now why would they want to admit there are alien forces penetrating our air space at will, abducting whomever and doing whatever they want with them, and our omnipotent guys in Washington can't do jack shit about it?"

"I see what you mean," said Krystalee. "If people knew that, it might be worse than a run on Beanie Babies."

"Exactamundo!" Dab agreed. "We wouldn't want citizens spinning out of control, now would we?"

"Uh, speaking of time-traveling—" Amber began.

"Yes, what's your question?" said the reporter.

"Not a question, an experience," she said. "See, I think I time-traveled with Blue the other night." They all looked at her, wide-eyed. "I mean, it wasn't like time-traveling in the movies because we happened to be owls, but it was definitely out of this world! Later, he even said it'd felt like the future."

"Okay, so what did you see?" Dab was obviously intrigued.

"Did you hear about the strange tremblings on Mt. Rainier in the Cascades?" Amber asked.

"That sounds vaguely familiar. What does that have to do with time travel?"

"Well, we saw that mountain erupting and annihilating Seattle! And then I read where they're not going to evacuate, they think it's a fluke and nothing more is going to happen. Dab, you've got to do something!" Amber implored.

"Like what? Say someone I know had a vision and everyone in the city needs to leave? Do you have any idea how complicated the logistics of that would be?"

"Do you have any idea how many people might die if I'm right?"

He considered that for a moment. "I'll check into it as soon as I get back to the office, see if I can light a fire. Okay?"

She smiled. "Yeah, thanks."

All at once the air conditioning wheezed off and fell silent.

"This cannot be!" Quinn declared, jumping to her feet. "That unit was new last year!"

"Look in the kitchen; the lights are out, too," Dab pointed out.

"The damn electricity's off! We'll boil!" Quinn tried several appliances to make sure it wasn't just a blown fuse. Then she opened the door and looked down the street, as evening began to settle in.

"Yep, whole damn street's off," she reported when she returned with a pile of candles. She pulled open the glass sliders, and they moved out onto the porch. "Come on, y'all, we gotta drink this wine before it gets warm."

She refilled everyone's glass and they continued their conversation. Mostly Dab talked, about parallel universes, quantum physics, and the different races of extraterrestrial intelligence. Amber listened attentively with the others, but an undercurrent of anxious fretting disturbed her concentration. The fact that Blue was missing in action did not help. She picked a pen up from the table and began to doodle on a napkin.

"That's cute," Krystalee said presently, leaning over to look at her drawing. It was a copy of the lizard's spot patterns, two stacked circles, the top one with a protruding arrow, the bottom one with a cross inside. "The geologic symbols for Mars and Earth, stuck together. Only I thought you liked being on top."

"Is that what this is?" Amber asked in surprise.

"As far as I know," Krystalee answered. "Where'd you see that?"

"In another one of my visions, I guess."

The wine bottle was empty now, and it was getting quite dark. "I was hoping to wait until the power came back on," Dab announced, "but I really have to go. The streets are going to be a nightmare."

"Wait!" Krystalee piped up. "The phones are probably still working. Can't you call in to the newsroom and see if they know what's going on?"

"That's a good idea," Dab responded. "It's probably just some computer glitch." He got up and Quinn took him inside.

"What do you think? Ain't he a fox?" Krystalee said to Amber.

"Oh, God! Is that why you wanted him to call, just to keep him here a few more minutes?"

"No, actually I'm kinda curious what the hell is going on. But he's still a fox. I got an exclusive scoop for him, too."

"Would you stop it?" Amber said, unable to keep from laughing.

"Oh, yeah, you're one to talk," Krystalee shot back. "You can't keep your mind off Blue for two seconds, can you? I smell rubber burning from here."

Before Amber could say anything, Dab dashed back out onto the porch and began to collect his things. "The whole damn western U.S. is blacked out!" he hissed as he shoved books in his briefcase.

"No shit! What happened?" Krystalee exploded.

"Just like your friend here said," he replied, straightening and looking at their faces frozen with fear. "There was a fluke all right, an unexpected and incredibly powerful eruption of Mt. Rainier. Seattle is history."

17

Dark Age

Amber slumped over the table, head in her hands. Since Dab had rushed off to the newsroom, she had been inundated by a tidal wave of guilt. "I knew this was coming! I could've done something!"

"Like what, supergirl?" Krystalee said. "Plug up the volcano with a giant tampon? Lighten up on yourself!"

"Maybe I could've called the governor, or the Civil Defense, or even the cops. Somebody!"

"Yeah, I'm sure they would've listened to some ditzy chick from Arizona seeing visions with her Martian husband!"

"Listen to me, Amber. Don't jump to conclusions until we know for sure what happened," Quinn advised. "Maybe it was only the power plant that was damaged."

"Then why do I feel so sick?" Amber asked.

"Because you haven't been laid in twenty-four hours?" Krystalee guessed.

"More like twenty-eight and a half," Amber sighed, "but who's counting?"

"I swear! How can you two think about sex at a time like this?" Quinn scolded. "Everything that's going on is just so incredible."

"Yeah, like the cute little butt on that reporter," said Krystalee.

"Now what is this?" Quinn demanded. "The lily-white southern belle is going to chase a black man?"

"Hey, I've always had a nondiscriminatory fun policy. Cute comes in all colors."

"Shit, I just wish it would come in the color Blue!" Amber whined. "This is killing me, you guys. He's got to know I'm freaking out right now! So where in the hell is he?"

"Maybe this whole thing is part of the Martians' plan," Quinn theorized. "Maybe that's why you had the vision when you were with Blue, and why you haven't heard from him since."

"I don't believe this," Amber said, staring at Quinn. "Are you saying Blue is responsible for blowing up that mountain?"

"Not him, but what about the other Martians? How do we really know what their agenda is?"

"Yeah, I saw an episode just like this on the *X-Files*," Krystalee chimed in. "The aliens were taking over by creating natural disasters."

"You watch way too much TV," Amber said. "Blue is trying to save the planet, and so are the rest of the extraterrestrials. Unlike humans, they operate on the principles of love and concern."

"Oh, right! What about the ones that suck people up in their ships and stick weird instruments in their orifices," Krystalee said. The phone rang, cutting her off, and she sprinted inside to get it.

"It's my house, y'know," Quinn called after her.

They heard her say hello, then, "Hi, Dab."

Quinn pursed her lips. "Trust her to turn disaster into a dating game."

"Oh, my God!" Krystalee exclaimed loudly. "Uh-huh...oh, shit...unreal!" Amber and Quinn waited anxiously, saying nothing while their friend listened. "So what are you gonna do?" she said finally. "Uh-huh...big time...total bummer...okay. Listen, do you have my home number?"

"See? She's unbelievable," Quinn whispered.

Krystalee reappeared shortly. "It's fucked up all right," she reported. "He says they're just starting to get helicopter footage of it. Get this, there's more than one volcano! He doesn't know details yet, but there're several volcanic peaks around there that could've blown."

"But what about the people?" Amber asked.

"I don't know; guess they're wishing they'd migrated south right about now. But the eruptions are still going bonkers, so nobody's been able to get close. He said there'd be more in the paper tomorrow, although it'll be out late if the power doesn't come back on. Oh, and he said if it isn't on by morning, the water will probably go out, too. Something about the pumps."

"Lovely," Quinn spat. "This is getting more fun by the minute. Now what am I gonna do all night with no electricity, no air, not even a fan!"

"Well, I know what I would do if I were you," Krystalee offered. "I'd get Darryl over here and at least make the sweating worthwhile."

"You are the queen of the one-track mind! I wouldn't ask him to come over here tonight, in the dark with all the traffic lights out. And you guys shouldn't drive, either. There's plenty of room here."

"Forget that," Krystalee twanged. "You're out of wine."

"I gotta get home, too. You know, in case..." Amber's voice trailed off.

"Well, he better get in touch immediately if not sooner," Quinn asserted. "I don't care if you're white, black, or blue, you should respect your wife's feelings and not leave her sitting around growing cobwebs."

"Yeah, homey don't play that!" Krystalee added.

"You guys are really cheering me up here." Amber got up to go.

"Well, if you have to leave, at least keep the windows up and doors locked, okay?"

They agreed and she led them out to the curb with a flashlight. The street looked strange, so black and silent, the soft glow of lanterns or battery lights scattered around the neighborhood like fireflies. When they got in their cars and turned on the headlights it wasn't bad at all, similar to driving on a country road were there were no street lamps.

But when Amber left the quiet residential streets and got onto the big six-lanes, traffic was in a snarl. Arriving at the end of rush hour, the power failure had delayed the after-work exodus and caused a tremendous pileup. As she reached the first intersection, she was relieved to see that the police were on the case, directing traffic and illuminating the area with flares.

Even though it was still warm, she kept the windows up as Quinn suggested, with the air conditioner on low and the doors locked. As she waited in line at the last traffic light before home, she was glad she'd been cautious. Someone rapped on the passenger side window and she jumped and looked over. A young man was smiling and pointing to the empty seat, shouting, "Hey, give me a ride?"

She shook her head quickly and looked forward again. The line of traffic wasn't moving. Suddenly another guy popped up to her window and knocked on it loudly. "You got room in there! Open up!" They were both laughing like hyenas, drumming on the sides of her car. Trapped and vulnerable, she thought of Oro in his fishbowl and prayed to be safely at home. Suddenly the traffic moved and she shot the Toyota forward. Before they could catch up, the traffic in her lane allowed her to accelerate, make her turn, and drive away into the dark. Just in case, she wound around and doubled back. Those derelicts were the last thing she wanted to bring home with her.

Parked in the driveway of her house, there were still more fears to face. Her heart hadn't even had a chance to slow down, and now she realized she hadn't thought about going in a dark house alone. She looked in the glove box. No flashlight, that was convenient. Not even matches in her purse. *Or a damn can of pepper spray, which Krystalee has been trying to get me to carry since the dawn of time!*

On top of everything, the moon was shrouded by clouds tonight, but Amber managed to get to the door and match the key to the lock. She made sure to lock it behind her right away. Now she felt her way to the hall closet and found a flashlight, then went to check on her fish. Oro seemed fine without his bubble machine.

Next she hunted for candles, assembling them in the living room and lighting enough of them to give the room a cheery glow. She went in the bedroom, checked her clock-radio for batteries, and found the compartment empty. Shining the light on the closed bedroom windows, she wondered how long it would be before she started cooking and had to open them. She shuddered, remembering the punks outside her car. If the windows stayed shut, it would be too hot to sleep, and if she opened them, she might as well forget slumber, too. Apparently perverts and thieves love a blackout.

Where, oh where, was Blue? If this went on much longer, she'd be a complete nutcase! She sat down and dialed her parents' number, anxious to find out how they were coping.

"Oh, we're actually enjoying it," Mom reported. "We've got the lanterns burning and batteries in the radio so Dad can still listen to the game. He says it reminds him of when we used to go to the lake when we were young."

Good. Presumably they hadn't yet heard that the blackout meant a city full of people would be camping out at that big lake in the sky tonight. "Well, I just wanted to check. Some creeps tried to get in my car on the way home from Quinn's, and it worries me to think about the nuts that want to take advantage of darkness. Lock up, okay?"

"Who were these guys? Did you call the police?"

Amber realized she had just waved a red flag. "No, they messed with me when I was stuck in traffic, then I took off. Think I got a couple dents, though."

"That's just awful!" her mother cried. "And where is your loyal new boyfriend when all this is going on?"

"That's a good question—even though I wish you hadn't asked me."

"You mean you still haven't heard from him? I hate to say it, honey, but he sounds like another swine to throw pearls before."

"Did Dad tell you to say that?"

"He doesn't have to, I know how he thinks. Just be careful, babydoll."

"I've got the damn windows shut and locked," Amber said. "How much more careful can I be? I'm roasting!"

"Go take a nice lukewarm soak," Mom advised. "And by the time you're done, the power will probably be back on. This can't last much longer."

Amber didn't even want to start tackling that topic. "Good idea. I'll talk to you tomorrow."

After hanging up, she carried a candle into the bathroom and looked at the tub. Then she shook her head and did an about-turn. Tonight, alone during a power outage, was no time for freaky out-of-body experiences.

She went into the living room and placed a votive candle in a red glass next to the fish tank, then curled up on the couch and tried to relax. Oro was glowing even brighter than normal in the rosy light, and she watched him flit and turn, his tranquil movements soothing her frazzled nerves.

All remained dark and quiet; no weirdos or looters rang the bell. Her pulse had returned to a normal, at-rest rhythm, when the phone shrilled in her ear.

"Hello?" she huffed, heartbeat already racing.

At first she couldn't recognize the voice; it sounded like a mewling kitten inside a burlap bag. "Oh my God! Rose!" she cried. She'd forgotten all about the flippant little message she'd left, seemingly an eon ago. "Please, honey, stop crying and tell me what's going on! The power's been out here for hours."

"You tell me what's going on, Amber. How did you know?" she sniffled.

"Jesus, Rose, I didn't *know* anything! I had a dream, or a vision—"

"Well, excuse me for thinking it's strange that you call me up and ask me about Seattle, six years after I left there, and about twenty-two minutes before the city was destroyed! Maybe you ought to tell me what the fuck is happening."

"Oh God, the city was *destroyed*?"

"They don't even know the extent of it yet. The ash in the air is too thick to fly in, and the stupid things keep erupting." Her voice trailed off and she started crying again.

Amber knew Rose was thinking of all the people she'd gotten to know there, the good friends she still kept in touch with, and the man she'd lived with for four years. *I never realized how much being a psychic could suck.*

"What about the power?" Amber asked gently. "Did they say anything about when the electricity would come back on?"

"Believe me, nobody gives a shit whether people in Phoenix can run their appliances."

Amber tried to comfort her sister as best she could, then said goodnight, and was once again alone. She didn't know what time it was; the only clock that worked right now was in the car, and she wasn't going back out there until morning. What did it matter anyway? The night was just a large, black, Blueless expanse that she had to get through—somehow.

She sat back on the couch, crossing her legs and settling into a comfortable position. "I'll get through to him by sheer force of will," she announced to the goldfish. "I'll manifest his ass by iron-willed intention!" Forcing her knotted muscles to unwind, Amber began breathing deeply, mentally calling her lover with every exhale. For a while she watched the flickering candle flames, then she closed her eyes and soon fell deeper into a trancelike state.

As she concentrated on him, the longing intensified, consuming her totally in body and soul. How could she have been so wrong about him? She just couldn't believe that he would leave her like this, to wonder and worry. Tears sneaked down her face, one on the left, then another on the right, plopping to her thigh with a soundless splash.

"Please don't cry."

It was Blue's voice, so clear and loud she thought she'd punched through to the next dimension. Her eyes flew open, but the room was the same, full of candles but not another soul.

"Blue?" she sniffled.

"I didn't want to alarm you by walking right in," said his voice again, "but I'm standing inside your front door."

18

Flying Sparks

Amber's startled howl could have passed for an alligator with its tail in the wringer. She leaped up, immediately banging her shin into the coffee table as she tore past it and into the hallway.

Incredibly, Blue was actually standing there in the dimness, dressed in human clothes, a sly smile on his face. She hurled herself against him and they clutched each other tight. Amber could feel herself shaking with emotion and relief as they pressed together, neither one saying a word. At last he released her enough to lower his face toward her mouth; her happy tears salted their kiss.

"Baby, where have you been?" she squeaked in his ear. "I thought I'd never see you again!"

He kissed the tears from her face, stroking her hair with both hands. "I'm so sorry, I didn't mean to do this to you! I should've known the time would seem eternal to you in this dimension."

"Every minute was eternal!" Now that it was over, though, this reunion was making it almost seem worth it.

"Please forgive me, darling, it's just that when I'm in a place with no linear time, it's hard to gauge the elapsed time in 3-D," Blue explained, still planting fields of kisses on her face. "And the things we were discussing were of the most serious and urgent nature!"

"Speaking of serious and urgent..." she said, steering his mouth back into hers. Kissing him was sublime pleasure after the last two days of doubt and fear, and he seemed to be enjoying it, too, sliding his hands around to everything they could reach on her back side. All she could think of was rolling him into bed. Then somehow he noticed the red mark on her leg.

"What happened?" he asked, stepping back and looking down.

"Just a flesh wound," she assured him, although the skin was gouged back and dots of blood were appearing.

Sweeping her up and carrying her into the candle-lit living room, he landed on the couch with her sprawled in his lap. He rubbed the palms of his hands together, then cupped them over her cut.

"Forget my damn leg and get back over here!" Amber wrapped her arms around his neck and kissed him while he held her shin. Her grateful fingertips slipped over his anatomy while she fantasized about a splendid night adhered to his skin. She knew she should be more inquisitive about a meeting that supposedly concerned the survival of the planet she lived on, but at the moment it was time for instant gratification.

"I gotta have you right now," she informed him. From her perch on his lap, it was easy for her to tell that he was interested, too.

"I'm sorry, there's no time for that," he said, then lifted his hands from her leg. The skin beneath was free of any mark save for the three-day stubble.

"Whoa, Jesus!" Amber exclaimed. She looked at him in amazement. "Yeah, just like Jesus...."

"He was simply pointing out a natural ability which so-called civilized man has forgotten. Don't give me a deity complex; you'll be doing it soon," Blue said. "Now, we really need to get going."

"Where to this time? Someplace with electricity, I hope."

"I wouldn't advise getting too attached to that technology," he chuckled.

Amber wrapped herself tighter around him. "Why do we have to go somewhere? The bed is right in the next room!"

"You are such a temptress, I could forget my duty!" He hugged her close. "But I promise, we will have our satisfaction tonight."

"More waiting," Amber sighed.

"Not much more, I'm afraid, at least not for Earth. An emergency session of the Galactic Federation has been called, and as a Martian envoy, I am obligated to attend."

"So where is this meeting supposed to be?" Maybe being a galactic diplomat's wife would have its advantages.

"Actually it takes place in another dimension, but to access it I will need to travel to the Martian Earth-Headquarters and embark from the Crystal Hall."

"Sounds like a concert venue from the seventies."

"It's a subterranean network beneath Puerto Rico, an island one hundred miles long. Only a small portion of the caves has been discovered by humans, so it was a perfect, ready-made base for the first colonists."

"We're going to the Caribbean?" Amber was excited now. Hell, if the world was going to end, why not go out on vacation? "Are we going by plane or spaceship?"

"Commercial airlines are far too dangerous!" he objected. "Many of the protective spirits who guard Earth are now leaving what they consider a lost project, and accidents will be increasing."

"Oh, that's comforting! In case the volcanoes don't get you! So what does that leave us with, transport by UFO?"

"No, I have another idea." Blue slid her off his lap and stood up. His mind may have been on duty, but she was happy to see his dick was still focused on her. He saw her looking at the bulge and said, "I just can't control it around you. Come here." He held out his hand and she hurried to mold herself to his body.

"I'm going to try something I've never done before," he said softly.

Amber's mind spun, trying to fathom what that comment might mean. If he'd only been on the planet for two weeks, he could be talking about almost anything. On the same hand, if he'd never had sex before a few days ago, he could be talking about any number of things involving his oversized, dinosaur-headed phallus. "Honey, whatever you want to do, I'm sure I'll try it," she decided.

"Good," he said. "I want to attempt to take you with me in my external merkaba."

"Excuse me? Did you sneeze?"

"It's a construct of sacred geometry, a personal space-time vehicle."

"Oh! That clears everything up," she laughed. "So where is it?"

"I'm going to breathe it," he explained. "Are you ready?"

"Right this minute? I'm not even packed!"

"Everything we need will be provided. Let's put out the candles and go outside. The merkaba likes to be built in unencumbered space."

Reluctantly she released him and helped him extinguish the candles. Then they went out into the darkness of blacked-out suburbia and stood on Amber's front lawn. Above, normally obscured by the city's electric glow, the stars sparkled in quiet sovereignty.

"Power failure has its pretty side," she remarked.

"I've been trying to tell you human technology is overrated." He pulled her close. "Let's balance our energy fields first. I sense that will aid in making it possible to transport two in the merkaba. And try to focus more on the heart chakra than the one in the low abdomen, if at all possible."

"Yeah, right," Amber said, but as she closed her eyes and felt the stirrings of their combined vibrations, it was easy to think with her heart. Love was pouring out in such purity and abundance, it made every other relationship she'd ever had seem pitifully weak by comparison. She almost didn't recognize the person who had existed as herself up until a week ago! This man, this sweet, loving, intelligent, insanely sexy hunk of Martian had already done some transforming work on her, and she liked the result—from cold and lonely to happy and hot. Right now she felt like loving him hard til the end of forever.

"Amber," he said, lips in her hair, "it's incomprehensible, but I'm grateful you love me that way."

She squeezed him happily. "This mind-reading stuff is unnerving, but I guess I'll get used to it. When are you going to start building the whatchamacallit?"

"Already done; it worked!" he announced, releasing her.

Stunned, she opened her eyes and found herself in another silvery tunnel, this one much larger than those she'd seen on her wedding day. Blue stood with outstretched arms, grinning proudly. "Don't you just *love* subverting the space-time continuum? Amber, you are advanced beyond your humanity!" He swept her up in a giddy hug.

Flushed with the double thrills of love and adventure, Amber figured she'd finally hit the big time. Now things would start going her way; she could taste it!

Suddenly an eruption of skittering footsteps echoed down the tunnel. Amber's triumphant mood vanished. It sounded as if a herd of giant cockroaches was rolling out the welcome wagon.

"What—" she started to ask, then was robbed of speech as the noisemakers bounded into view. Two large, furry animals lunged toward them, snarling and flinging spittle from their flapping tongues.

Amber screamed, her throat finally unhinged by the sight of Blue throwing himself on his knees in front of her. Paralyzed with terror, she fully expected to see the spilling of his blue blood.

Instead the beasts knocked him over, flogging him with their long tongues while they squeaked like a pair of bats. Blue rolled on the floor, laughing and grabbing their enormous ears.

Amber peeled herself from the tunnel wall and slowly stepped closer. "Uh, I take it you all know each other?"

"These are Rana's pets, Phobos and Deimos, named after the English words for the moons of Mars. Hey!" he shouted, fending them off with a laugh. "I guess you'd say they're the equivalent to domestic dogs."

"I sure wouldn't want to get on their bad side," Amber said. They were as big as Afghan hounds, with a thick, wiry coat, a monkey-like tail, and thin, pink tongues that lolled at least a foot out of their pointed snouts.

"No, look, they're perfectly harmless," Blue insisted, grasping the nearest one's mouth and pulling back the gums. "No teeth!"

"So how do they eat?"

"They exist on blood. No, not mine!" he shrieked, laughing as he fell over again under their slobbery kisses.

A voice spoke sharply from the tunnel and the animals immediately ceased their play. Rana strode into view wearing a shimmering robe of dark green, her head swathed in a turban of the same sparkling fabric. Phobos and Deimos ran to her, turned and sat politely on either side, never taking their adoring eyes from her face. Amber's heart leaped as if she were seeing an old, dear friend.

Blue uttered something in Martian , then said in English, "I am so pleased to see you are already here!"

"And I, too, am very pleased to see you both!" She glided forward, the dogs flanking her in flawless obedience. Blue got to his feet and hurried to embrace her.

Then Rana turned to Amber, her plump visage all dimples and smiles. "My daughter! This is indeed a joyous meeting." They hugged, and Amber felt the priest's energy tingling through her.

"But Rana, a few days ago you could barely speak English!" Amber marveled. "And I'm not wearing my stone!"

"Given the situation, do you not think it was time to put away my stubbornness and begin to study?" Rana tittered merrily. "I see you've met my babies. Aren't they dear?"

"Cute as a button," Amber said with a skeptical look at the big beasts.

"Hmmm...strange expression," Rana mused. "Is a button not a garment fastener?"

"Rana, can't we discuss English idioms later?" Blue moved to Amber's side and drew her against him.

"Ah! Of course! I am forgetting the most important agenda—human passion!" She winked at Amber. "Do not worry, my son; all is arranged. Come." Rana swept quickly down the passageway, moving more easily and elegantly than her bulk would seem to allow, her pets matching her stride.

The tunnel grew even larger until it widened to the size of a city street, and they began to pass other Martians. All greeted them silently, with a bow of the head and a polite smile, but it was obvious they were containing their excitement with much effort. The softly glowing walls reddened Amber's curls and heightened the flush in her cheeks, emphasizing her unique appearance among the pale, hairless beings. Blue couldn't tear his eyes from her face.

"No human has ever walked in the Catacomb before," Rana told her in a low voice. "Everyone senses that a bridge has been crossed, and a new era dawns."

Blue said something in Martian and Rana answered in the same tongue. Then leaning toward Amber she said in a mock whisper, "Your beauty is all he speaks of! He has become enamored of third-level density, ego-centered pride, and the sensual pleasures of the flesh."

Blue laughed and squeezed Amber's hand. "It's all her fault."

"Yes, and thank the Creator for that," Rana asserted. "We may make a whole being of you yet."

They rounded a sharp turn in the corridor, and the floor began angling upward. "This is as far as my sweet guardians may accompany us," Rana announced. "Their presence would merely alarm our Earthling contact." She raised her hand and an undetectable portal slid open. Ordering her pets into the room, she sealed the door behind them with another hand movement.

"We must be extremely careful," Blue explained, "ever since Deimos sneaked out to the surface and couldn't find his way back. He created quite a stir, going around the countryside snacking on farm animals and leaving their blood-drained bodies behind like empty McDonald's containers. Now he's a Puerto Rican legend, the Chupacabra, or "Goatsucker.""

"I was frantic, to be sure, knowing he was lost and frightened on the surface," Rana added. "And when we finally got him back, his fur was matted, filled with burrs and insects, and the smell!"

They were walking up the ramp-like passageway now, steadily ascending until the tunnel ended in a hollow, rounded chamber.

"This is where I must leave you," Rana announced. "I have never been on the surface and do not intend to start now. However, I wish you two much enjoyment." Her eyes crinkled and twinkled. "Lumi, your contact, awaits you on the outside."

"But what about the people in the United States, Rana?" Amber blurted out. "The volcano? The earthquakes?"

Rana placed a hand on Amber's shoulder. "It is well this should concern you, and indeed it is of the highest priority. But there are many preparations to be made before an entire galaxy comes together to exchange views. Meanwhile, there is time for you two to swim in this ocean of love. Until *mañana*." She kissed Amber's cheek, then Blue's. "I will help you exit," were the last words Amber heard. Immediately Blue hugged her and she felt the same whirling sensations that had ushered her into the cave at the Superstitions. Then they were outside in the Puerto Rican night, dark as ink and spitting rain.

"Hey, I thought this was the tropics!" Amber complained as the wind whipped her hair.

"*Bienvenidos*! Welcome!" A man materialized from the gloom, holding a lantern above his head. "I am Lumi. Please, keep yourself warm." He held out thick ponchos like the one he was wearing, and Amber slipped hers on. "This is nothing but a cold front, passing over the island. Very unusual weather for this time." He turned to Blue and bowed low. "Sir, I am honored. At last! I mean, I have seen the ships before, but you, sir, are magnificent!"

Blue barked out a startled laugh. "I think you mean to address that comment to my wife."

"*Seguro que sí!*" Lumi hurriedly agreed. "And I fill with pride at being chosen to escort you. Please follow." He whirled and hustled away, leading them into the underbrush with his lamp.

Movement on her left side caught Amber's eye. Through the blackness she saw two angular, white shapes hovering near the trunk of a tree. "What's that?" she whispered.

Lumi didn't answer, just held the light high and moved closer to the ghostly apparitions. When she saw that the odd patches were different ends of the same pinto horse, she sighed with relief. Two other horses were tethered with him, one brown, one black with a white blaze, and all three wore bridles and English saddles.

The rain began to pelt them harder now, bouncing off their ponchos and making further conversation impossible. Many aspects of the past week had challenged Amber to her limits, but she had taken riding lessons for years as a kid and this part of the adventure looked fun. Without hesitation she walked up to the spotted horse and Lumi boosted her into the saddle. Then the Puerto Rican man vaulted effortlessly on top of the bay.

They both turned to look at Blue, who still stood on the ground with the reins of the black horse in his hand. "Are you sure this is safe?"

Amber erupted in laughter. "What, the guy who flits around in space-time vehicles is scared to get on a horse?" Blue looked so much like a cute little boy with his white face glowing under the poncho hood, she thought she might have to get down and hug him again.

"Not too many horses live in caves," he said, wiping the rain from his face.

"Sir, don't worry yourself, these animals are extremely well-trained," Lumi called, though his own horse pranced with excitement.

Blue lifted his foot to the stirrup and swung up quickly, his poncho skirt swirling behind him like Zorro's cape. The black stallion whinnied as the weight settled onto his back. Lumi seemed to take this as a signal; he blew out the lantern flame and spurred his horse to a smart trot. Amber and Blue only had to hold on as their horses fell obediently in line.

Lumi led them down a narrow dirt trail. The clipped gait of the horses made for a smooth ride, and Amber found she could sit comfortably if she relaxed her spine and let her body be taken by the motion. Before long the rain diminished, and her eyes became more used to the dark. She could see the treetops on either side and the gray stripe of sky that marked their downward path into the jungle.

They emerged abruptly onto a paved road, but Lumi didn't stop or slacken the pace, just guided his horse to the right side and continued to descend. Fortunately it was late at night and they had the asphalt to themselves, curving down through the hairpin turns, hoofbeats drumming a Latin rhythm. They passed under a streetlight, then another, and then houses began to appear, most of them concrete, brightly-painted, and constructed right on the edge of the road. In the dim light Amber could see the reason they built that way—the ridges were razor-thin, flattened on top to make roads, and the land sloped away so steeply that most of the houses needed the support of concrete stilts. When the trees allowed her to look into the distance, she could see rows of these ridges lined in lights.

Soon they began to hear the thunder of the waves, crashing in slow cadence and reverberating up the valleys. The horses trotted to the beat, arching their necks and lifting their tails like flags. At last the road leveled out and intersected what appeared to be a main thoroughfare, though it was barely wide enough for two cars to pass. They crossed it and headed down a dirt path in the direction of the ocean's roar. In minutes they burst onto the beach, the horses picking their feet up even higher as they plowed into the deep sand.

"Not far now!" Lumi screamed over the pounding surf. He led the way down the beach, sand flying as his horse churned through the shorebreak.

The clouds had thickened but Amber could still make out the seashore and the dense foliage that crowded to the edge of the sand. Holding on tight to the pommel of the saddle, she looked back at Blue astride the black stallion and felt her spirit soar. There was nothing else she'd rather be doing, no place in the galaxy she'd rather be! She turned her face back into the ocean spray and filled her lungs with its clean, salty tang.

Light drizzle began to fall again; Amber was just wondering how long they'd have to ride in a cold shower when Lumi veered his horse and entered a thick coconut grove. As if programmed, Amber and Blue's horses followed close behind. Suddenly they were running under trees that soared a hundred feet up, arranged in rows no more than ten feet apart. Only occasional drips of rain made it through the canopy of leaves to the ground below.

Lumi slowed his steed and threaded them through the columns of tree trunks. The sound of the waves faded; the trilling and chirping of night insects grew louder. Before Amber could see it, she was fending off a low-growing palm frond that Lumi had disappeared behind. Then she saw they were in a small clearing where a tiny wooden house was wedged among the palms. Soft lavender light glowed from the open shutters and spilled out into the surrounding yard.

Lumi slid off his horse and looped the reins around a nearby sapling, then knelt with the lantern. In spite of the wind, it ignited at once. "Zippo!" he said proudly, brandishing the lighter. Then he hurried to Amber and held her horse while she dismounted.

"This is like a fairy tale!" she gushed. "The house is perfect! And what is that whistling? It sounds like hundreds of birds singing the same two notes."

"Hundreds of frogs, *Señora*," Lumi laughed. "That is the coquí frog, the mascot of Puerto Rico. This island is the only place on Earth where it lives."

Blue had slid from his horse and secured its reins, and now he hurried to share his excitement with Amber. "That was certainly exhilarating!" he declared, mashing their wet parkas together. "The surface is so full of unexpected pleasures."

Like a doting uncle, Lumi watched them kiss—until a rumble of thunder diverted his attention. "The rain will come again, we must close the windows," he interrupted them. "Inside is better for this by any means."

Arms around each other, they followed him to the front of the house. It rested on short stilts, and they climbed several steps between lush flowering bushes that perfumed the night. Lumi opened the front door, revealing the interior of the one-room cottage. It was just as enchanting inside as it was out, the scant furnishings made of bamboo and wood.

"Like this, sir." Lumi demonstrated how to pull the shutters in and secure them, and Blue and Amber went to work on the other side. It was impossible to ignore the bed, a four-poster draped in white netting, fashioned from enormous lengths of bamboo. On either bedside table an oil lamp with a purple glass chimney provided the pastel glow. Amber wanted to dance with the joy of anticipation.

As soon as they finished the drops began to plunk on the tin roof. "Brilliant timing!" Lumi smiled broadly. "I believe you will have everything you need tonight, but if I can help in any way, you have only to think of me and I will be summoned."

"Thank you so much!" Blue said sincerely, grasping the man's hand in both of his.

"For nothing! At your orders, sir! I will return at sunrise; until then, I wish you both *buenas noches*." With a slight bow he turned and hurried to the door.

"Lumi, wait!" Blue called, causing him to whirl and snap to attention. "Please call me Blue, not 'sir.'"

The man grinned again, his childlike face beaming. "Yes, of course! Incredible!" He turned back to the door, grabbed the knob, and with a final, "Goodnight, Blue!" disappeared into the rain.

"Alone at last!" Amber exulted, dragging the poncho over her head and tossing it on a chair. Blue followed suit and they quickly assumed the barnacle position. Within the span of several passionate kisses, she was wet, eager and impatient. "Hurry, honey," she panted in his ear, "I've gotta get you under that mosquito net."

"Oh no, not tonight," he said, running his hands over her back.

"Say what?"

"Eliminate the word 'hurry' from your vocabulary. I want to serve you and savor you the way you've always deserved."

"You're not from another planet by any chance, are you?" she laughed, leading him by the hand toward the big bamboo bed.

19

Rain Dance

The thunder crackled closer and the wind began to pick up, rustling the palm fronds and rattling the shutters. Too chilled and wet to play undressing games, Amber and Blue had quickly stripped and were now snuggling naked under the thick quilt. Tucked away from the world in their bamboo cocoon, surrounded by the storm, she felt safe and insanely happy to be in his arms again.

"Two days and an entire night away from you," Amber sighed. "It was torture! I think you've somehow altered my biology, and now the organism needs you just like it needs food, water and air."

"The same force is transforming my vehicle also. And what I considered an instrument for urination has taken on a completely different meaning!"

Amber giggled seductively and pressed her belly tighter against his erection. "Yeah, I like the new tricks it's learning." She slid her hand down his back and across his hip.

"Don't touch it yet," he whispered, capturing her wrist before she could reach between them. "I want our energies to gather and grow while we stimulate each other."

"That might be dangerous; we could burn this cute little house down."

"Or we could build an internal merkaba, which is much more powerful than the external variety."

"How do we do that?" Amber asked, though she was more interested in getting his external and her internal together.

"The external merkaba is pure technology, but the internal merkaba is constructed through emotion. Exactly how we attain that, I don't know, but I do believe that if we practice, we'll be shown the way."

"Well, let's get practicing," Amber suggested, licking his lips.

A gust shook the shutters and a few loud drops splattered on the roof while they kissed in blissful oblivion. Soft, low-speed smooches weren't slowing down her excitement in the least. Her heart pumped furiously, her skin was igniting under Blue's cruising fingertips, and the faithful geyser between her legs steamed and screamed for release.

"Damn! I feel like we already built the merkaba and took it up for a few barrel rolls," she wheezed in his ear.

"Yes, the frequency intensifies. Now just hold me, and concentrate on moving the energy up your spine."

"If you say so, baby." She stopped caressing him by brute will-power, closed her eyes and imagined a burning ball of red churning at the base of her backbone. Then she envisioned it rising, like water through a straw, up to the top of her head. The intermittent rain began to beat steadily on the tin roof, providing the sound effects for her spiralling energy.

"Don't stop it at the crown," Blue advised, speaking loudly to be heard over the rushing rain. "There are chakras outside the body; send the light up and out and into the cosmos."

Amber concentrated, and imaged the streak of red bursting through the top of her head and out into space. The noise on the roof was no longer individual drops but a dense blanket of sound, as if their little cottage had slipped under a waterfall. She clung to him and breathed deeply. The intense sensations of her body began to drift away, and she felt herself rising, being siphoned up the straw with the pulsing red energy.

Suddenly her awareness snapped back into 3-D. Blue's hand was gliding down her low back. Gently he caressed her cheek, letting his fingers patter down into the cleft. She groaned appreciatively but neither could hear it over the clatter of the storm. Bending her leg on top of his thigh, she offered mute invitation to his touch, and he graciously accepted.

First he brushed along her inner thighs, going into the edges of her hair patch but carefully avoiding anything else. By now her mouth was open and sounds were continually rumbling from her throat, but they were lost in the thrashing of water against tin. She strained to open her legs wider, and the merkaba be damned. Satisfaction, carnal union with her beloved, was her only thought.

But Blue continued the tease, withdrawing and leaving her throbbing vulva bereft. He said something, but whether it was English or

Martian, she couldn't tell. Then he kissed her again, harder this time, his tongue searching, and she knew he was losing control, too. *Excellent!*

She pulled away and arched her back, thrusting her breasts in his face. He smiled and brought up his hand, then reached out in slow motion to stroke them. As if in a silent movie, she shivered, moaned, and puckered to the pounding music of the rain. Watching him lean down and suck on one of her nipples, she thought, *This is what boobs were made for, not the pawing demands of an unappreciative infant!*

Blue released her nipple long enough to say something; it almost sounded like "We'll see about that," but it was impossible to know for sure with the racket from above. Then he went right back to lavishing her chest with every sort of worship he could think of. She ran her hands over his smooth head, his neck, his ears, and abruptly knew there was just one more piece of him she had to get her hands on.

She pushed him down, onto his back. If they had been able to hear, her nipple would have popped from his mouth with an audible smack.

Amber threw off the quilt and knelt above him, her body shiny with sweat in the lilac lampglow. Blue lay where she'd placed him, except to stretch his arms up over his head. She watched his muscles move and it was like drinking champagne, only headier. A thousand drumrolls beat on the roof.

His beautiful body squirmed as she finally reached out and wrapped the midnight-colored shaft in her fist. She could feel it swell against her grip as if it wanted to split at the seam. Her stomach fluttered with lust, imagining the sweet fulfillment of guiding it home.

Blue didn't let her play with his body long; seeming to forget about delay, he sat up and pulled her onto his lap. Their torsos welded, arms and legs wrapped around each other, there was only one more thing left to make it complete, the insertion of Tab A into Slot B. A well-aimed wriggle and Amber had him just where she wanted him.

He held her waist, urging her closer until they were completely locked. She crossed her ankles behind his back and savored being full of him. Every fiber of her being shouted with joyous passion, making it difficult to keep still. She swiveled her hips, trying to prime the pump.

"No," he said loudly, pressing her against him. The rain was finally slackening, making it easier to hear. "Let's see how long we can stay like this."

Amber wasn't so sure that sounded like a good idea. How long did it take to make a merkaba? Meanwhile, every instinct was instructing her to ride that thing!

"Picture the force of your desire rising up, through your head and into the heavens." Blue was clutching her so hard, there was no alternative; she focused on the feelings in her body and imagined them exploding upward. The tingling of buzzing energy permeated her limbs, and suddenly she felt as if she and Blue were moving, twirling together and streaking across the sky.

She opened her eyes and was shocked to see that she was in the sky, or at least floating in a uniformly blue field. It was as if she'd been sucked into a television screen, one that had no gravity. She looked at herself and discovered she'd transformed back to a lightball. Panicked, she searched frantically for a sign of Blue.

Then she saw him far, far below, through the roof of the cabin, calling to her. "Blue, I don't want to go! Grab me!" she yelled, even as she drifted further into space. The cabin was less than a speck now, and the Earth displayed its curvature. Amber was being drawn inexorably into the cosmos.

With a gigantic crash she popped back into her body and was flooded with relief to be again in Blue's arms, safely impaled on his cock. He began covering her face with kisses.

"What happened?" she asked groggily.

"You left for dimensions unknown without me," he told her. "Then, thank the Creator, a coconut fell on the roof and you returned."

"Can't we have sex like normal people?" Amber sighed. "Maybe I should just leave my kundalini where it is."

Blue laughed softly. "How could we ever be normal? We're the greatest lovers in the universe." Then he endeavored to prove it, rocking her to the rhythm of the rain until both erupted in orgasm. It might have been the lingering foreplay or the two-day separation, but Amber came like a rabid wolverine in a seizure of joy.

Spent and satisfied, they burrowed back under the quilt. Thunder still rumbled in the distance, but the storm had passed, the downpour reduced to a dripping drizzle. The last thing Amber heard before she fell asleep was the frog chorus outside, renewing their cries of "Ko-kee! Ko-kee!" in the rain's aftermath.

* * *

The room was shrouded in shadow when Amber slowly emerged from slumber, realized where she was, and immediately sensed that Blue was not beside her.

Heart hammering, she snapped awake. Then she saw him at the window, glowing like a naked ghost as he stood and looked out the open shutters. She relaxed, exhaling deeply as she propped herself up on her elbow to wallow in watching him. Seemingly unaware, he didn't move or acknowledge her. *This is it*, she thought, *that rare moment of perfect happiness! I could gaze at those beautiful buns forever!*

Blue coughed or sputtered a laugh, but didn't turn around.

"What are you looking at, honey?" Amber asked sleepily.

"The new world," he replied, turning his head to smile at her. "Or what I always imagined it would look like."

"Yeah, I like the way it looks, too," she said, her eyes having him for breakfast. "Now come back to bed."

"Dawn approaches, and Lumi will be here soon." He looked out the window again. "Hear the birds?"

"No, I just hear those frogs. It's still the middle of the night! Please come back to bed," she wheedled, unable to tolerate the thought of another day without him.

"It is morning," he insisted, turning around. "Would you distract me from my duty?"

She gasped as he came toward her, dick first. "Oh, hell! Planetary survival can wait!" Amber snagged him as soon as he came near and plastered her face to his abdomen.

A voice burst into Spanish song outside the house. Amber paused in mid-snuggle and clearly heard horse hooves crackling through underbrush and fallen leaves.

"I must go," Blue said, and her arms were empty.

He dressed quickly, went to the door and conferred quietly with Lumi. Then he came back, sat on the bed and gave her a deep kiss. "Lumi will return with food, and I will be back at the earliest possibility." She nodded. "I love you," he said, then rose and hurried out the door.

She listened to their hoofbeats disappearing into the distance. There was nothing to do but sink back under the covers, beat off, and go back to sleep.

Some time later she awoke to horse sounds again. Dark, rainy night had been transformed to sunny day.

"Miss Amber!" Lumi called. "*Señora!*"

Blinking rapidly, Amber wrapped herself in the quilt and rushed to the open window. Lumi was outside in the yard, astride his nervously-dancing stallion. The brown-and-white pinto stood beside him, saddled and ready.

"Dress yourself and mount your horse!" Lumi commanded. "Now!"

"What happened?" she shrieked, rushing to do what he said. "Is Blue all right?"

He shouted something in Spanish several times, but Amber didn't recognize the word. It sounded like "Ark Weeris!"

"What? What?" she chanted, feeling her blood pressure soar.

"Explain later!" Lumi shouted. "Hurry! Or we may be too late!"

20

Under the Arco Iris

Swept up in another adrenaline rush, Amber shoved her limbs in shorts and a shirt and ran barefoot out of the house. Scrambling into her saddle, she thanked God these horses were small.

"*Vamanos!*" Lumi shouted, flashing past her and ducking as he and his mount burst through the young coconut palms' wall of foliage. Amber's stallion whirled to follow with no urging on her part; she simply snatched two handfuls of mane, tucked her head and hung on. The heavy fronds scraped her on both sides, and then they were among the tall palms, racing down a long, grassy track between the rows.

Both horses were now in an open gallop, the tree trunks flashing by in a tempo that had Amber completely unnerved. One swerve, one stumble or hidden hole, and she would hit those palms like a fly hitting the swatter. But the horse muscles pumping beneath her continued to carry her in a flawless, straight path, locked in on the leader. They cleared the last pair of trees and thundered onto the beach, spraying roostertails of sand.

Lumi suddenly reined in his horse, causing it to half-rear and spin around. Amber's stallion locked his knees and skidded to a halt, almost sending her sailing. Sprawled up on the horse's neck, she looked up at Lumi and was shocked to discover him smiling broadly.

"We made it!" he yelled jubilantly. "See how beautiful!" Throwing an arm out toward the sea, he displayed the cause of their early-morning scramble—a perfect double rainbow, glowing against the solid gray of the retreating storm clouds. Its twin arches soared from the thicket of coconut palms and ended in the ocean, where it seemed to drill down into the water, making it boil with shimmering colors.

"You brought me to see a rainbow?" Amber cried, unwrapping herself from her horse's neck.

"Yes! In Spanish, *arco iris*. This one is especially fantastic."

"Lumi, I thought it was the end of the world!" Still, she laughed with relief.

"Oh, no!" he answered with a dismissive wave of his hand, "that won't be until at least the year 2012! Please calm yourself."

Amber watched the rainbow, willing her heart to slow down. A feeling of *déja vu* swirled through her, pulling her consciousness into the colors. Then she realized where she'd seen this before. "I dreamed this rainbow, Lumi."

"Then it must have been a dream of the future, because here you are, and there it is!" He chuckled happily as he slid off his horse and hit the sand with bare feet. "Come down and rest a moment."

Amber dismounted and Lumi tied the horses to an almond branch. The trees bordering the beach cast long, cool shadows, making each step a pleasant foot massage as Amber walked toward the edge of the water. She stuck her toes in the foam and shouted, "It's cold!"

"It only feels that way now." Lumi joined her at the waves' edges. "Soon the sun will be chasing you into the sea! But this is not a good place for a swim; the rocks here are home to the sea urchin. If you step on one of them, you will not have a good memory of the Enchanted Isle!"

"Don't worry, I'm staying right here on shore."

"Look! The angels have sent you another gift!" Lumi scurried a few feet across the sand, then bent and scooped something up. He ran over to her, holding out a fist-sized seashell. It was oval and smooth, with a jaw-like seam on the underside and a surface of light spots on shiny bands of brown.

"Wow! That was just sitting on the sand?" Amber took it and examined it, marveling at its gleaming polish.

"It's called a measled cowrie. A large one! Usually the big waves in winter bring up the shells, but lately the weather has not been so usual."

Amber was already looking around for more and discovering that the sand was littered with shells, most of them much smaller than the one Lumi had found. She picked up a pearl-white one shaped like a snail shell, a tiny orange scallop, and a miniature cone with a pink tip and bright, intricate patterns. "Wow, this one looks like it was hand-painted by elves."

"You come to the beach on a very fortunate day," Lumi agreed. "The storm stirred up the ocean's treasures." He walked over and held out his hand; lying in his palm was a precise equilateral triangle of cobalt blue.

Amber stared at it in wonderment. Was this another of Blue's unconventional geometric messages? "What is that?"

"Seaglass, also known as trash," Lumi explained. "The sea turns broken bottles into gems, and throws them up here for the collectors and jewelry makers."

"But how did it break in such a perfect shape?" Amber took it from him and held it up to the rising sun. The edges were rounded, the color a bright royal with the light shining through.

"Millions of bottles, millions of pieces." Lumi shrugged. "You will find seaglass in any shape you can think of. The white, green and brown glass is very common, the blue is harder to find, and red is very unusual. They say the red is antique, made by adding gold to the glass. But then, the people say a lot of things around here; many have no telephones, so we use rumor to pass information!" He accented this with a hearty laugh. "If you wish to stay and collect more, I will go back to the house and prepare the breakfast."

Amber straightened and looked out over the ocean, where the rainbow was still decorating the sky, and took a deep breath of clean, salt air. From here the damage done to the planet by human beings seemed erased and healed. It truly did look like the dawn of a new world. "I'd like to stay for a while, but are you sure I can find my way back?"

"It's not far, and Yinyang knows the way," Lumi said.

"That's the horse's name?"

"Yes, because he is both light and dark at the same time, just like the duality of life." He pulled a fat banana from his pocket. "Give him this and he will be your friend forever."

"I thought horses liked apples and carrots," said Amber, taking the sweet-smelling fruit.

"Paso finos eat bananas. They are a breed particular to Puerto Rico, and they have tropical tastes. They wouldn't think of eating an apple!"

Together they marched through the sand toward the tethered horses, and Lumi mounted up while Amber held out the banana. "He'll eat the peel," Lumi assured her, as Yinyang greedily snatched it from her hand.

"He sure snarfed that up in a hurry," Amber said, petting his broad, two-tone forehead. She felt so acutely alive, even the horse smelled wonderful.

Lumi called, "Enjoy yourself and know you are safe! *Hasta pronto*," then clucked to his horse and disappeared into the coconut grove.

Amber made sure the reins were tightly tied, then went back to beachcombing and admiring the rainbow. The temperature was perfect, warm and comfortable; the early breeze tousled her hair and caressed her skin. She half-expected to wake up at home in Tempe, since being here on this deserted beach was nothing less than miraculous.

By the time her pockets were full of shells and seaglass, the clouds had burned off and the rainbow had faded and evaporated. The day was growing warmer, but she wanted to look just a bit more for a piece of the rare red glass. Spotting a dark patch of debris a little way up the shoreline, she promised herself she'd check that area and then go.

"Stay here, Yinyang," she called to the horse, who was busy chewing the tall grass. "Okay, I need some red glass now," she said as she walked along, looking around her feet. "Hear that, universe? A nice souvenir to mark my first day in paradise." She reached the spot she'd seen and discovered it was mostly rocks, shell fragments and more glass. None of it looked red.

"Oh, well," she sighed, and turned to walk back. Stepping in the wet sand at the water's edge, she could paddle her feet in the lapping waves. Then something a few feet ahead sparkled and drew her attention. It lay all alone on the golden sand like a dark ruby, and as she bent and lifted it up she was astounded to see that her piece of red seaglass had been smoothed and polished into a perfect, tiny heart. Amber tingled all over as she stared at it in her cupped hand.

She was standing there, puzzling over the meaning of such a coincidence, when a loud voice said, "The universe loves you."

Amber jumped, almost dropping the glass heart. She wheeled around to see where the voice came from, but she was still alone on the long stretch of beach. Her heartbeat launched into a frenzied drum solo.

Okay, Lumi and Rana are always saying have no fear, and they should know, right? She breathed deeply and tried to calm herself, but the mellow mood of solitude had vanished. Minutes passed and all was silent; she began to think she had just imagined it, or said it to herself. After all, her mind had been producing an amazing array of new special effects recently.

"Yes, mind communication," said the voice again.

Amber yelped and spun around, even though she now realized that the sound was coming from inside her own head. But the voice wasn't Blue's, her telepathy stone was missing in action, and nobody else was in sight. She started to speak, then changed her mind and simply thought, "Who are you?"

"An old friend," the voice answered. "It has been a long time since I found a human I could communicate with."

Amber's heart started to pound again; she wasn't sure she was ready for a close encounter this early in the morning.

"Do not be fearful. I am of this Earth, just like you."

"Well, where are you then?" she thought. "On Earth a voice is usually attached to a body."

A splash in the water caught her eye. She turned to look at the place where the water still rippled, not far from shore. Then the flank of a large fish broke the surface, flashed silver and disappeared. Amber took several steps back up into the sand; the theme music from *Jaws* popped spontaneously into her head.

Suddenly the sea erupted, spewing spray and a large, gray animal from its depths. Paralyzed by the spectacle, Amber watched it leap and was hugely relieved to see it was a sleek, bottle-nosed dolphin. It crashed back into the waves, then reemerged with its snout waving skyward and chattered loudly. As Amber stared dumbfounded, she heard the voice say, "If you could understand my language, I just said I am not a shark."

Right, it's the fish talking, and I'm Dr. Doolittle! Although she'd seen and done many impossible things lately, telepathy with animals was still a shock.

"I'm not a fish, either," the voice insisted. "I'm a cetacean, an ocean-dwelling mammal." The dolphin's dorsal fin knifed through the water and he slapped the surface with his tail.

Amber sat down on a flat stone and stared as the big creature frolicked. It would have been awesome enough just to witness this show, but to interview the performer? "Sorry, I didn't mean to offend you," she thought.

"No offense taken. As I mentioned before, I am grateful to see a human who is vibrating at a high enough level to hear me." He twirled gently and came to rest, head up and out of the water, watching her with an unmistakable expression of mirth.

"I guess I really must be mutating now. This is too cool! Will I be able to do this with my goldfish?" Amber giggled, imagining how much fun it would be to talk everything over with Oro.

"Not unless the goldfish does some mutating of its own," the dolphin answered. "Cetaceans—dolphins and whales—are the only other beings besides humans that possess an individual soul. Therefore we share some abilities, though my tribe must be considered superior stewards of this planet."

"No doubt. My tribe has just about destroyed it."

"Sadly, that is so. Earth was meant to be a library, a living storehouse of biological forms, for all in this galaxy to access. Humanity was to function as librarians, forming the bridge between third-dimensional knowledge and the multidimensional entities seeking to use it. But instead of protecting and increasing the rich variety of life, humans are now reducing the number of species every day."

"I know, it's horrible. Why are humans so screwed up?" Amber wondered.

"There's nothing wrong with the basic design. My ancestors used to communicate like this with the native humans of the landmass you call Australia, until the white people arrived and drove them inland from the coasts. Their descendants are very connected with the Earth's spirit, as are survivors of the ancient tribes who still live according to universal laws. But these tribes are few, and the abusers are many."

"I've been thinking about this a lot recently. Is everything on Earth doomed?"

"Ultimately, no. There is an alternate library location being prepared and stocked; as Earth's species disappear, they are gathered and included in this new environment. Your race, and mine, are not destined for extinction."

"Really? What a concept!" Amber was startled tremendously by such an idea. "Who is engineering all this?"

"The entities assigned this task are not human in origin." The dolphin swam in a nonchalant circle, oblivious to the mind-blowing effect he was having.

"Not human? Let me guess—are they Martians?"

The dolphin made another real sound, almost like hilarious laughter. "Martian civilization has peaked and declined," the voice added. "Only isolated pockets of their relatives still exist."

She was astounded that a creature who had spent its life in the ocean would know something that very few humans suspected. "Then where is the new library going to be?"

"In another system entirely, one that revolves around two suns."

Amber shook her head. "Well, I might like to visit it, but I wouldn't want to live there."

"We may have no choice," the dolphin said, "but then I am not equipped to see into the future. If humans want to stay here, they must develop respect and love for their home, and quickly. Earth's patience has almost run out." He scooped up a plastic cup with his pointed nose and batted it toward the shore. "So has mine."

Amber leaped up and waded into the water to snag the cup. The dolphin's dorsal fin curved around and headed out to sea. "Hey, wait a minute!" Amber yelled out loud, forgetting her telepathic manners. "I didn't throw this!"

The dolphin showed off a few more times, leaping and twisting, and then he was gone. Amber now realized she'd been in another kind of altered state; she felt flushed and slightly dizzy, and a dull pain buzzed in the center of her forehead.

She sat down again and opened her right hand. The seaglass heart was still pressed into her palm, so tightly it had made a heart-shaped imprint in the flesh. She emptied her other glass and shells into the cup and stashed the heart in her pocket. After several deep breaths she felt recovered from her experience, except for an intense excitement. Sand flew as she hurried back down the beach.

The horse was still waiting, happily munching. Amber untied the reins and vaulted on top, careful not to spill her cupful of treasures. She prodded Yinyang with her heels and he set off at a leisurely pace, straight for the trail into the woods. Once they were among the coconut palms, Amber was amazed at how completely their cabin was hidden. Unless you were right on top of it, looking through the low-growing cover of the younger trees, it was camouflaged perfectly. Drips from last night's rain sprinkled down as they brushed through the fronds and into the clearing.

Again Amber felt as if she were starring in a fairy tale or a Disney feature. The little house, painted lime with lemon trim, was surrounded by tropical flowers of all sizes and colors. Butterflies and bees flitted about in the dappled sunlight, and birds added their chirps and tweets to the idyllic scene. Far, far overhead, the green, coconut-studded canopy rippled in the breeze.

She dismounted and looked for a place to secure the reins. Lumi's horse wasn't here; he must have grown tired of waiting for her. Just as she was wondering where he might have gone, Yinyang jerked his head and the reins yanked from her hand. Before she could grab them, the horse had turned and trotted off into the palms.

Hoping the horse would run home to be with his buddies, she went in the house and found a note from Lumi on the wicker table. It read: "Do not tie the horse. Set him free and he will return to the barn." Amber laughed, relieved. "I will return upon request," the note continued. "*Buen provecho*!" An echo from long-ago high school Spanish told her that meant "enjoy your meal."

Immediately she realized she was ravenous, and turned her attention to the long loaf of bread that lay on the table in an even longer paper bag. Next to it was a foil-covered plate filled with thick slices of pineapple, mango, papaya and avocado. A mug with a saucer on top held black coffee, still slightly warm, and a covered dish hid a softening stick of butter. Silverware and napkins had also been provided, and Amber wasted no time putting them to use.

When she was finished, content and zooming from the caffeine and the morning's adventures, she wiped the bread crumbs from the table and unfolded the newspaper Lumi had left along with the food. It was a copy of the *San Juan Star*, in English, and its headline immediately assaulted her senses. "Volcano Kills Thousands," it screamed above a photo of what appeared to be a mushroom cloud.

As Amber read the terrible account, tears began to pepper the newsprint. "...scientists have not yet determined whether an earthquake provoked the eruption, or the volcanic activity triggered the earthquake. Aftershocks and continuing ash clouds have severely hampered rescue crews...."

The worst-hit community was Orting, on the outskirts of Seattle and fifty miles from Mt. Rainier. When the mountain blew it sent a lahar, an avalanche of mud and rocks over a hundred feet thick, barreling through the White River valley. Traveling at 180 miles per hour, the lahar needed only minutes to turn this thriving town into something resembling the surface of the moon.

The article concluded by saying that power was being restored to western states, but that efforts were being hindered by the repeated occurrence of quakes, which were being felt as far south as San Francisco. As far as Amber could tell, scientists were scrambling to explain what was going on and why they had been so unprepared.

The rest of the paper was filled with related news. The challenge facing rescue workers was explored, the impact on the insurance industry was discussed, and prophets of every persuasion aired their views. Nobody in America was ready to comprehend a tragedy of such huge proportions.

Of course, thousands died all the time in foreign lands, victims of famine or monsoons, quakes or tidal waves. But here, in the United States, it was unthinkable that so many could disappear from the roster in one afternoon. The entire country was reeling.

Amber felt unsteady herself. She tossed the paper aside and tried to get distracted in domestic chores, but it didn't take long to wash one plate, make the bed, and open the rest of the windows. Meanwhile she agonized over the Seattle disaster and her connection to it. If only Blue were here; she really needed somebody to talk to. Lumi, the dolphin, anybody!

She looked around the house. Of course, there was no phone. Then what had Lumi meant when he said he would come back "on request?"

When she went in the bathroom to shower she found a new dress hanging up for her, a jungle print of thin cotton with spaghetti straps. It felt good to wash off the sand and sweat and put on clean clothes. She was brushing out her hair when she heard the rhythmic crunching of hoofbeats outside.

She got to the window in time to see Lumi burst into the clearing. "Sorry I'm late!" he called cheerfully when he saw her.

"Late for what?" Amber couldn't remember any appointment, but then she'd also been chatting with dolphins lately.

"You needed someone to talk to," he replied, jumping to the ground.

"So you've been in my head, too? It must be getting pretty crowded in there."

"*No, Señora,* I would never invade your thoughts. I simply felt you summon me, that's all." He smiled and went to tether the horses.

Amber came out to the front stairs and sat on a step. Lumi sat beside her and slapped his hands on his knees. "Now, what is your worry?" he asked.

"You don't already know?" She lifted one eyebrow dramatically. "I thought you were psychic."

"Oh, *sí* , but not from an accident of birth. When I was four years old I had my first sighting; all I really remember is a glowing ball of light. It seemed to burn into my eyes, but I couldn't look away. After that I was different, changed. That's when everyone began calling me 'Iluminado,' the illuminated one."

"Uh, did you say your *first* sighting?"

"Yes, there were many more. And other things, things I can't even describe. The light in the sky did something to my brain. Something that was meant to open and close was stuck open, and now I see into other worlds."

"Was it...Martians?" Amber asked.

"No, another species," he replied, "not nearly as humanoid as the Martian race. But I did not come to talk about me! You are disturbed by the beginning of the end times?"

"Shouldn't I be, if that's what it is? You talk like it's an upcoming Super Bowl game!" Amber shivered. "There's been a horrible natural disaster, the worst our country has ever seen."

"It all depends on how you look at it," Lumi insisted. "From a fourth-dimensional perspective, what humans call disaster is simply a necessary step in Earth's evolution. The planet and its inhabitants are about to make a giant leap forward; the Golden Age that has been predicted is at hand! Unfortunately, the transition may be experienced as death and destruction by those not attuned to the frequency."

"But it *is* death and destruction!" Amber protested. "When lava rolls over you it doesn't evolve you, it kills you!"

"Yes, but those it killed are currently in bliss. It is only the people left behind who are calling it tragedy. The ones on the other side will continue in a different form, doing their part to help the universe develop in the direction of light. They really don't need your pity."

"Well, that's a nice way to look at it, but I doubt if it would comfort anybody who lost a friend in that blast."

"Comfort is not the ultimate goal of living, despite what the advertisers tell you."

Amber had to stop and think about that one. This seemed to signal Lumi that the discussion had concluded; he stood up and clomped down the wooden steps.

"Are you leaving so soon?" she asked plaintively, unwilling to be alone with her thoughts.

"I must go, if I am to return with the one person who can make you feel calm and safe." He held his arms up as if he'd just presented a magic trick.

"You mean Blue's meeting is over? Boy, it sure didn't take them long to figure out how to save the world!"

"The message I received simply asked for my presence. Maybe they will assign me my part in the mission," he speculated with more than a little pride.

"Well, go then," Amber urged, standing up and waving her hands as if she were shooing away chickens. "Hurry!" *Mission, shmission; I just want to get him back within eyeball range!*

Lumi chuckled as he hurried to his horse. "Tonight my spouse and I would be honored if you would go with us to the *Fiestas Patronales*," he called from the saddle. "That is the festival of the patron saint that each town celebrates once a year. Lots of local color!"

"Sure, that sounds great. I'd go with Blue to a dogfight," Amber answered.

"Dogfighting is illegal on the island, but I could arrange a cockfight for you," he said helpfully.

"I'm kidding!" she wailed. "Now will you please just go get my man?"

Lumi let out a deep laugh and an *adios!* Then he flicked his heels against his horse's flanks, and they bounded off into the coconut palms.

21

Lost in Bliss

While she waited for Blue to come back, Amber rinsed the sand from her beach treasure and spread the pieces across a section of newspaper on the kitchen table. She separated the glass from the shells, then arranged them by color and placed the red heart by itself off to the side. Grouping the shells by type, she examined each one and was amazed by their different shapes and patterns. It was just so incredible to think that tiny blobs of protoplasm could produce an object of such intricate perfection.

"Prime Creator does nice work, don't you think?"

Amber jumped in surprise even as she realized whose booming voice it was. Blue was standing in the doorway, filling the frame with his gorgeous presence.

"Goddammit, baby, I'm never gonna get used to your entrances!" She knocked her chair over backwards as she leaped up and rushed into his arms.

"I couldn't wait for a slow-moving quadriped to bring me back to you," he explained, "so I just transported."

They reveled in their greeting ritual, kissing and stroking to the tune of Amber's tiny moans. "Being apart is so much fun when it's over," she said in between smooches. Just as she was thinking about getting him horizontal, he gave her a final smack on the lips, released her and began to describe the Galactic Council.

"Everything went so smoothly, as if meant to be," he reported excitedly. "The Seattle incident was just what I needed to convince them! Of course, there were several objections, mainly from the human delegation, but in the end the vote was overwhelmingly in favor of intervention."

"Wait a minute, did you say the human delegation? I thought this meeting was happening in another dimension!" She walked toward the window, then turned to glare at him, arms folded. "And I don't like the way you and Lumi are trying to put a positive spin on the worst tragedy of the century!"

Blue chuckled softly and pulled up a chair, motioning for her to sit on his lap. "Come here, honey, I have a lot to tell you."

Amber went over and slid onto his thighs, hooking her arm around his broad back. "Nice threads," she said, scrutinizing his outfit. He looked like a typical male tourist now, wearing shorts, flip-flops and a T-shirt emblazoned with the red, white, and blue Puerto Rican flag. The only difference was that the blindingly white legs seemed to be carefully shaved.

"You mean the clothes? Lumi picked them out," he said. "Something wrong?"

"No, they're great. You look almost human," she giggled. "Speaking of which, if humans were allowed at your meeting, why couldn't I go?"

"Because you were right, we did meet in another dimension, and you don't yet know how to access these realms, at least not deliberately. But there are humans who can. Unfortunately, most of them are employed by the intelligence branch of the U.S. military."

"I don't get it. The military is multidimensional?"

"I'm not exactly sure how they stumbled onto it, but they learned it was possible to enter the space-time continuum by altering brain waves," he explained. "They called it scientific remote viewing, and began training a secret staff of people to use it for information-gathering purposes. Some staff members also use tarot cards or channel spirit guides."

"Oh, come on!" Amber snorted. "Believing in extraterrestrials is easy compared to believing our government uses tarot cards to get information!"

"That's why their activities are still secret. Even when news about this does leak out, nobody can believe it. Most military personnel would never believe it either, except the members of one small group. Meanwhile, that group possesses knowledge and power more dangerous than any threat from outside."

"And you invited these guys to your meeting?"

"We don't invite them, they just show up. In a sort of a phantom form, of course, but we feel their presence. They are very alarmed that we would even think of revealing ourselves and spoiling their game."

"Reveal yourselves? How exactly are you going to do that," she wondered, letting her hand pet his luscious lats. "Call the tabloids?"

"No, but we discussed radio signals, which is the method humans have been using to attempt contact with ET intelligence. The largest radio-telescope in the world is located in a gigantic sinkhole in the jungle outside Arecibo, just up the coast from here. In fact, Martians were responsible for the choice of that site. We wanted it right in our neighborhood."

"Please, just let me be there to see the scientists' faces when they get your message!" Amber flashed back to the utter astonishment she'd felt when she first set foot in the Martian domain and realized the impossible was true.

"In the end that idea was rejected," Blue told her. "We decided a distant radio signal is not going to change many lives. So what if the scientists record some blips from outer space? This society is used to snarling aliens and advanced spacecraft on their movie screens! I argued that overt contact must be attention-grabbing drama—compelling, ultimately inspiring, and of course, televised."

"So what's your plan?"

"Simply land a ship. Someplace obvious and full of cameras. If it's on film, people will believe it."

"Don't tell me you're planning to participate in this." Amber could already envision her beloved surrounded by automatic weapons.

"Who else? I know Earthlings more intimately than any other Martian, being married to one." He gave her a quick kiss on the cheek. "The Zeta Reticuli, the Grays, are too strange-looking to bridge the gap to human understanding. Their appearance might provoke a violent reaction, but I look almost exactly like humans, and I speak the language. So it would be perfect for a Blue to introduce the Grays."

"And you think that will stop the whites from cutting you down with their guns? Believe me, honey, in all those movies you're talking about, the humans kill the ETs!"

"Well, it's time for humans to rethink that reaction." He picked up the tiny triangle of seaglass from the table. "This is the basic building block of the universe, the triad. Humans have got to realize that they are composed of body, mind, and spirit. That spiritual component is what links them to Martians, and every other creation in the universe and beyond. Soon attacking others will be seen as useless because it is the same as attacking oneself."

"Not soon enough for me."

"The triad is also formed when woman and man come together," he continued. "Then a third energy is created, one that would never manifest if they stayed apart."

"That reminds me, I've been meaning to talk to you about birth control," Amber interjected.

"Oh, we don't need that!" he declared. "We'd make beautiful children." He tossed the triangle back onto the table, then reached up to caress her face. "And think of it, they would be an entirely new species, the first of their race."

"Yeah, that would be great. They'd probably be transferring their molecules all over the place, reading my mind, and insisting on keeping Goatsuckers for pets." She stretched to pick up the red heart. "This is what I'm in it for. Just for love, baby, that's the only thing I want. Let somebody else start a new race."

"I've got all the love you'll ever need right here," he said, and pulled her into another kiss. The energy between them was so warm and intense, Amber could almost hear it sizzling. She felt the terrain stirring beneath her and was delighted to know he was getting as turned on as she was.

"Amber, I promise you, our sexual communion will never create a third life unless you and I both fully desire and intend it," he swore. "So let's take a blanket and go outside. I want to see you naked among the flowers."

"And you're going to provide contraception with your mind? At least you come up with some original lines." She kissed him again, relishing the renewed rush of passion. "You know," she whispered, "we wouldn't have time to be parents, we're too busy fu—, making love." She was reaching for his obvious erection when a sudden thought stopped her in her tracks. "Shit!"

"What happened?" Blue asked with a worried frown.

"My *parents*! I have to call them; they'll be frantic!"

"But you've only been gone one night."

"Yeah, but the electric may still be off, and they'll be freaked over the volcano. I had just told them that I thought it was going to erupt! Believe me, they've been trying to call."

"Well, let's go find a telephone, then," he offered. "We'll still have the rest of the afternoon to luxuriate in ecstasy."

"Okay, but you don't exactly look ready to appear in public."

Blue looked down at the erotic configuration of his clothing. "We'll have to walk through the trees to the road; maybe it will calm down by then, if I don't hold your hand."

They left the cottage and headed inland through the coconut grove, crunching through the fallen palm fronds. Soon the sounds of traffic filtered through the trees, and before long they could glimpse the cars zooming by between the tall trunks. They reached a barbed-wire fence, which he held open for her to climb through, and then they were standing in tall grass by the side of the road.

To the left the narrow strip of asphalt was bordered by lush almond trees as far as the eye could see. At least to the right several buildings were visible in the distance, and they made their way in that direction. Cars and trucks occasionally whizzed past as they walked single file on the overgrown shoulder.

The first structure they reached was a shabby-looking tavern with a neon Budweiser sign glowing in the window. Blue stuck his head in the door and asked, *"Hay teléfono?"*

The man behind the bar laughed and shook his head. *"Pero hay uno en la gasolinera."* He swept his hand several times to indicate the location.

"He says there's one at the gas station," Blue reported. He told the man *gracias* and they continued walking.

"How many languages do you know, anyway?" Amber asked.

"A few. I've had a lot of time to study. Never really thought I'd actually get to use them."

"There it is, over there," Amber said, pointing across the street. "That sign with the big shell."

This was not the kind of service station with a convenience store and a bulletproof cashier booth. It was a concrete block square with a tin-covered area on the side that served as a mechanics' bay. A driver sat in his car by the pumps while the young man filling his tank sang along to the salsa music from a tinny radio.

Amber spotted a pay phone on a post and hustled toward it, then suddenly stopped and whirled around. "Blue, it's a *pay* phone! I don't have any money, didn't even bring my purse with me. It's sitting in my living room on the couch!"

Blue fumbled in his pockets, but Lumi hadn't thought to leave any coins in them.

"Damn! Now what are we going to do?" Amber wailed.

"*Espera!*" yelled the man at the gas pumps, waving at them.

"He says to wait," Blue translated.

The man quickly finished his transaction, the car drove off, and he approached them with a smile. "Thanks a lot," Amber said as he dropped coins in her outstretched hand. "It'll be collect, so you can have this right back." Then her face fell when she looked down at two nickels.

"I hate to be ungrateful," she called as he strode away, "but this isn't enough."

"Phone calls are still ten cents in Puerto Rico," he shouted in perfect English, then hurried to tend to an arriving customer.

Amber frowned skeptically, but when she turned back to the phone there it was in print: 10¢. "This place really is like going back in time," she muttered as she pushed in the coins and punched the buttons. When the operator answered she said, "Yes, I'd like to make this collect from Amber."

There was a long pause, and then her mother's anxious voice. "Amber? Is that you? Are you okay?"

"I'm fine, Mom."

"We've been worried sick!" her mother exploded. "First a blackout, then the news about Seattle—Rose is just a basket case—and then nobody could get in touch with *you!*"

"I'm sorry, really, I just...." Suddenly Amber noticed she had neglected to work on a cover story before dialing.

"Where are you, anyway?" Her mother's voice was steely and definitely not amused.

"Oh shit, you're not gonna like this," she said by way of preface. There just wasn't any way to lie to Mom. "I'm in Puerto Rico."

"Puerto Rico? What in the world are you doing down there? I can't believe this! In the middle of a power failure you sneak off and fly to the Caribbean? You're down there with your new boyfriend, aren't you?"

"Yeah, he had to...come here on business. It was kind of a spur of the moment thing."

"I'll say. I talked to you early yesterday afternoon and you didn't mention it at all."

Amber wasn't about to get into the convenient spontaneity of traveling in external merkabas. Instead she said, "So, is the power still off?"

"No. Came back on a couple hours ago, but there's still lots of outages up in the Northwest. Don't try to change the subject! When are you coming back?"

"I guess that depends on how the business goes," she said lamely. "Right, Blue? We'll be going back soon?" He nodded. "Yeah, we'll be back in the next few days."

"What kind of business is he in?"

"Uh..."

"Amber, this all sounds like funny business to me."

"I know, I know. But it's a long story and you'll just have to wait til I get back. Then we'll come over and Blue and I will explain everything to you."

"I hope so. Hold on, your father wants to talk to you."

Amber rolled her eyes and got ready for a lecture, but her father was terse and to the point.

"Love is blind," he pronounced, "but does it also have to be dumb? But of course you know this guy well enough to run off with him."

"Dad—" Amber tried to protest.

"No, no, I don't want to hear the gory details," he interrupted. "You go off on your wild love affair. I just have to say this now, so I can say I told you so later. And at least pick up the phone so your mother doesn't drive me crazy with her constant worrying. Okay?"

Amber sighed. "Yeah, okay. Look, I'm really sorry."

"Right-o," he said briskly. "Here's Mom."

"Okay, sweetie, I'm just happy you're all right." This was typical Mom, unable to sustain anger at any of her chicks.

Amber promised to phone as soon as she knew their plans, said good-bye, then hung up with a huge sigh. "Whew! Those guys can't help worrying themselves into a frenzy, no matter how old I get," she sighed, shaking her head. "And you want to have kids."

"Our kids would be different." He grinned and took her hand.

"Yeah, mutant rug rats. I can't wait."

On the way back Blue kept his fingers entwined with hers while she told him about her magical morning. The rainbow, the glass heart, the dolphin encounter, and then the most awesome phenomenon, the arrival of an extraterrestrial god to claim her love.

Blue laughed and brought her hand up to press it to his lips. "I think calling me a god is taking it a bit too far. I still can't fathom that you harbor such thoughts about me!"

"Why not?"

"Because Martians get insecure, too," he admitted. "There's always the question of whether you'll ever want to go back to being with one of your own."

"Have you lost your mind? I've been trying out human males for a while and there's just no percentage in it! You're like an angel, or a wizard."

"Look at *you*! Your rapid development of paranormal powers borders on miraculous!"

Trading compliments in mushy mutual admiration, they made their way back down the road, through the fence and into the coconut grove. Something about the remoteness and simplicity of this place, set in such lush, natural beauty, was reviving wild fantasies from hippie days in Amber's mind. What if they just forgot about saving the world and dropped out of sight on a romantic tropical island? She could picture herself in a flowing skirt, barefoot and tan, picking hibiscus and fresh fruit from their garden. Blue would be running around in very little clothing, adding major scenic benefits, and surely the sultry, salty, steamy atmosphere would keep them happily in heat. She was walking with him in a blissful aura-meld, their arms wrapped around each other, when they entered the clearing of their secluded home.

"Now, where were we?" Amber said, more than eager to strip and roll around with him in the grass. Then she noticed something hanging from a tree on the far side of the yard.

"Look, honey, a hammock!" she squealed, and ran over to test it out. Made from a generous expanse of blue denim, it was suspended between two palms. Amber sat in it sideways and started to swing. Blue strode toward her, smiling. Every cell in her body revved its engine and began to purr.

"This looks like it could be more fun than a blanket," he observed, sinking in beside her. Their lip-magnets drew them instantly together and they abandoned their souls to serious kissing.

It didn't take many licks for their desire to burst into flames. She could detect the extreme vibration of their combined energies and the acute, thumping demands from the depths of her physical self. Blue reclined and pulled her down on top of him so that her back rested against his chest.

From this position he could touch her anyplace; he sent his hands out to take a careful inventory of her anatomy while he nuzzled her neck. The little dress she was wearing was already worked up her thighs and his fingers had no trouble finding their way beneath it. When he poked under her panties and into her moistened pubic hair, she shuddered, moaned and let her knees fall further apart.

They swung and swayed while they praised and petted each other, lost in sweet indulgence. At last he reached under her tailbone and fumbled to free himself from his shorts, then shifted her hips until his shaft sprouted from between her legs like a Martian mushroom. She reached down with both hands to grip it, and they moaned in sync.

Amber used every trick she knew to keep him inflamed, all ten fingers prodding and petting his rigid rocket. With a minor shift of her hips, she'd have the nose cone lined up and ready for lift-off.

At last she squirmed up, pulled her underwear aside, and pushed his awesome appendage into her groove. She reached her arms over her head, snatched handfuls of denim and lay back with her eyes closed while he did the rest. It didn't take long, between the thrusts and his fingering, for her to explode in another grinding climax.

"I love it when I make you do that," he said when she'd stopped shaking and shrieking. Slowly he hooked a hand under each of her knees, hiked her legs open and got the hammock rocking again. Several staccato strokes later, he joined her in the afterglow.

Then the hammock grew around them like a pea pod, and they seemed unable to get out. Changing postures so they could try out all snuggling combinations, they stayed swaying the rest of the afternoon, talking, laughing, even making love again, until they were finally interrupted by Lumi's arrival.

"Ah, I see you are having another shitty day in paradise," Lumi joked as he approached. Amber tugged down her skirt in an attempt to look decent, though it was obvious what they'd been doing by the love-drunk looks on their faces.

"Lumi, the surface is just so, so...I just don't know how to express it!" Blue gushed. "It's fascinating, astonishing, amusing! And intensely enjoyable." He looked at Amber in unabashed adoration.

"*Señor*, Blue, I mean, you are a very wise man. You came into our world and immediately discovered the most important element in human life, something that remains a secret to many here on Earth: *Amor*, love!"

"And it is stronger, more exuberant and spirit-filled than any force I've ever known," Blue testified. "It profoundly moves all three aspects of third-dimensional form—it inspires the mind, it uplifts the spirit, and the things it does to the body!"

"You are a poet, *señor*," Lumi laughed. "With this force anything can be created. It is the lifeblood of God Himself."

"Yes, Prime Creator has really outdone Itself on this planet. Especially here, in the peace of nature," Blue said.

"Then I hope you will accompany me and my wife to the fiesta tonight. It will not be so peaceful, because there will be wonderful music, but the love of the people for their town, each other and their patron saint, that will be worth the noise."

"That sounds great," said Amber.

"Also, my wife's cousin has two sons in El Gran Combo de Puerto Rico, who are performing tonight. It will be like a family reunion."

Something about his words snagged a loose thread in Amber's memory. Her woozy smile was replaced by a slight wrinkle across her brow. "Two sons," she repeated. "Two suns! Blue, I've been meaning to ask you, the dolphin said that some non-Martian ETs were making a new location for the plants and animals of Earth as they become extinct here. A planet not in this galaxy, he said. In a system with two suns. It sounded pretty crazy."

Utter silence followed this remark. Blue looked at Lumi, and Lumi looked at Blue. Then they both looked at Amber.

"What? Did I say something wrong?"

"No, it's just that I didn't really want you to find out about that yet," Blue ventured.

"Blue, if I'm your partner, you have to trust me with the truth."

"Okay, I'm sorry," he said. "You're right; you deserve nothing less than the truth. There *is* a colony being prepared by the Zetas on a class five planet in the Pleiades, to preserve disappearing life forms and to act as a safe haven if human civilization should fail. But that is being set up as a last resort, and we must meanwhile work as if our goal is achievable."

"Yeah, I prefer the salvage scenario where Earth is somehow reborn," Amber said. "I think I'm too old to relocate to another planet."

"Leaving the planet is out of the question for me," Lumi agreed. "I would rather stay and go to meet *El Señor* than travel outside the solar system."

"But that's insane," Blue insisted. "How could you pass up the chance to experience an entirely new world? Especially if staying here on Earth meant certain death."

"I am a Puerto Rican, unique to this island, just like the coquí," Lumi explained. "The little frogs know their home, and they will not thrive anywhere else. That is how it is with me, too."

"How can you tell whether frogs are happy or not?" Amber asked. "Do they change their tune and start singing the blues?"

"No, if they are removed from their island, they refuse to sing at all." Lumi explained. "And if not returned to their homeland, they will eventually decline, and die of a broken heart."

22

Hot Salsa

The clothes Lumi brought for them to wear to the fiesta fit Amber's fantasy almost perfectly. There was a long skirt with a floral pattern and a peasant blouse for her, and for Blue white linen slacks and a traditional men's dress shirt, the *guayabera*, this one in sky blue with matching, intricate embroidery on the front.

They dressed hurriedly, since Lumi's wife was waiting nearby in the car. There was a dirt road that bordered the grove on the south side, ending at the seashore, and they would reach it by walking out to the ocean and down the beach. By the time they made it to the sand, the sun was dipping low and painting the clouds in luminous pastels.

Amber slipped off her sandals to enjoy the sand's cooler temperature, and a sweet breeze fluttered her skirt and her loose-flowing hair. *Oh yes, I've died and gone to heaven*, she thought as she strolled along swinging arms with Blue. The sea, the sunset and the sensuous grace of the male creature beside her made a perfect romantic dream.

The road wasn't far and they soon arrived at Lumi's parked VW bug. A plump, pretty woman with long raven hair sat on the front bumper; she waved and smiled, then stood up as they came near.

"I am called Milagro," she said, and shook their hands. "*Mucho gusto.*"

"Her name means 'miracle,'" Lumi said. "And you can see it is a miracle that such a beauty would marry a dog like me."

Milagro laughed loudly and punched Lumi's arm. "My spouse is a big joker!"

"Now you'll have to drive, my arm is broken!" Lumi squawked.

They piled into the car, an ancient model festooned with dents, its once-yellow paint splotchy with rust. Blue could barely fold himself into the back seat.

"This Volky is a classic!" Lumi shouted over the sputtering engine. It roared even louder as he gave it gas, made a three-point turn and sent it bumping down the dirt track. Soon they turned onto pavement and drove along the road where Amber and Blue had walked earlier in the day.

"Milagro, let's turn on the air conditioning," Lumi said. They both reached up and swiveled their window vents outward, and air rushed into the back.

"Thank you," Blue called, scooting closer to Amber so he could encircle her with his arm.

"I guess the rear windows don't open because it's cold in Germany," Lumi said. Then he began to tell them about the town and the festival they were about to attend. "Our pueblo is called Esquina, which means corner. That makes sense because it's out here on the far west tip of this island. Every year we celebrate Santa Rosa, our patron saint, for two weeks starting at the end of September. It is the social event of the year!"

Milagro turned in her seat to look back at them. "It is mainly an event to benefit the liquor distributors, not the saints," she said with an impish smile.

"And what's wrong with that? What's good for Bacardí is good for Puerto Rico!" Lumi declared. "Besides, the concerts are free."

They drove by cow pastures and scattered houses, past fragrant jasmine hedges and towering mango trees, until buildings and parked cars were crowding both sides of the road. Lumi searched until he found a tiny gap to squeeze the bug into. Then they were walking down the sidewalk under thousands of tiny white lights suspended above the street, joining many more people on their way to the center of town.

Esquina's tiny plaza, no more than half a block long, was jammed with booths and rides and festive energy. Nobody seemed to notice the arrival of the town's first Martian visitor. The bands hadn't started yet, but recorded music blared and clashed from many of the vendor's stands.

"What do you want to drink?" Lumi said loudly.

"What do you recommend?" Amber asked.

Milagro spoke up. "Get them a *sangría*," she told him. "Sangría goes with *fiesta*." She nodded reassuringly at Amber.

They went to the nearest drink stand and ordered four glasses of the spicy wine. It came in a plastic cup with a straw and slices of citrus fruits, and all agreed it was delicious. A Ferris wheel, set up in the middle of the square, jutted above the buildings surrounding it, none of which were higher than two floors. The four of them stood next to it and watched as the people flashed by screaming.

Milagro said something to Lumi in Spanish, and he responded in English, "No, my love, I'm staying right here on the ground! She's crazy about these stupid machines, or maybe just crazy."

"Then go with me, Amber," Milagro pleaded. "The men are cowards!"

Amber looked up at the contraption. It seemed fairly sturdy, but who could tell? If she said no, it would be akin to saying that women were cowards, too. She slurped up the last of her sangría and handed the cup to Blue. "Okay, let's go."

Milagro clapped her hands, jumping up and down as she hurried over to the ticket booth. Amber could already see the headline, "Arizona Tourist Dies in Ferris Wheel Mishap," as she climbed in.

They waited for the wheel to fill, each time rising a notch higher as passengers loaded below. Milagro giggled and rocked the car as she pointed out friends of hers on the ground. Then they were above the rooftops, able to view beyond the fiesta's glittering lights. Blue's head was a whitish dot far, far below.

"I've walked these streets most of my life," Milagro said, "but it all looks so different from up here! Isn't it beautiful?"

Amber scanned the distance. "Where are the stars? It's so cloudy tonight."

"Not clouds," Milagro replied. "It's ash from the Soufriere Hills volcano in Montserrat. It's been smoking since 1995, but just now it's really heating up. Ooh!" she yelped as the wheel jerked and boosted them to its zenith.

"Not another volcano!" Amber wailed. "Where is it?"

"Montserrat is an island not far south of here; it's a British colony. The volcano can't hurt us, unless it erupts and causes a tsunami to hit Puerto Rico. They say that's not very likely."

Before Amber could explain how unlikely it was, just a few days ago, that Mt. Rainier would blow, the Ferris wheel creaked alive and started to spin. "Whoo!" she yelled as her stomach flipped into her throat.

Milagro screeched along with her as they hurtled toward the ground, then zoomed skyward again. Blue and Lumi were a blur in the crowd as they went by. In spite of her experiences with merkabas, molecular transfer and forays into the space-time continuum, Amber wished this particular trip would be over soon; this contraption felt a lot higher and a lot more rickety than it looked. Milagro wasn't concerned in the least, giggling and shrieking like a little girl.

When the ride ended at last, the women pushed through the throng to get back to their men. Blue seemed equally relieved to have Amber on the ground, gathering her into a hug and exclaiming, "Such anxiety! I do not trust that technology in the least!"

They refueled on sangría and sauntered on, pausing at an *empanadilla* stand to sample the filled, deep-fried pastries. Nearby was a rowdy booth where people were playing some type of betting game involving racing mechanical horses, but Lumi herded them past it, commenting that it was "not honest."

Several large stands displayed crafts and artwork from Haiti and the Dominican Republic, the two countries composing Hispaniola, the next island to the west. Amber was immediately attracted to the carved wooden statues and the woven baskets in all shapes and sizes. Her domestic fantasy bloomed again as she pictured decorating their island hideaway with shells, windchimes, and intricate Haitian paintings of tropical scenes.

Toward nine o'clock Lumi led them back to the center of the plaza, where the cement bandshell was being readied for the evening's featured entertainment. They sipped more wine while the crowd thickened around them. At last a spotlight hit the stage and an announcer stepped up to the microphone. He rattled off several sentences in Spanish, eliciting cheers and applause from the audience.

"Damas y caballeros, El Gran Combo de Puerto Rico!" he shouted. The lights blazed up and the band filled the night with a huge, overwhelming sound. There were at least fifteen people up there, including a brass section and every percussion instrument imaginable. The lead singer and his two backup vocalists were executing synchronized dance steps to go with the lyrics.

The crowd cheered and whistled, and bodies began to sway with the rhythm. Pockets of dancing began to break out, the people forming rings around the wiggling couples while they clapped and shouted encouragement. Soon Lumi grabbed Milagro by the hand, whipped her around in a double twirl, then pulled her tight against him and they launched into rapid, hip-swinging steps. They danced beautifully, with the relaxed confidence of partners who had been practicing for a long time. Amber watched them smiling at each other, their movements perfectly matched, and was aware of her heart chakra tingling with the joy of love.

"*Ay, Dios mio*, this is so much fun!" Milagro squealed when the song was over. She rushed to Amber and put a hand on her shoulder. "It's very easy to learn; come on, I'll show you." She backed away and began to demonstrate the steps.

When music thundered through the open-air hall again, the Puerto Rican couple urged Blue and Amber to the dance floor. Blue jumped right in without a trace of self-consciousness, glancing over to copy the way Lumi held his partner's arm up with one hand while planting the other one just above her rear.

Amber hadn't danced in forever and was enjoying herself tremendously. The utter freedom of moving to the seductive rhythm, the enchantment of this exotic little town on the seashore, and the close proximity of her dream man had her glowing with happiness. Everything else, all the pending drama and trauma, were forgotten as she totally immersed herself in the beauty of the moment and focused on the blessings at hand.

For the next few hours they stayed right in front of the bandstand, only occasionally sending one of the group to fetch a round of sangría. During breaks Lumi and Milagro gave them more lessons, showing them how to do spins and different steps. They danced almost every song until the band had collected their last round of applause, then made their way, perspiring but laughing, through the still-crowded plaza to Lumi's car.

"What an unbelievable chance to participate in human culture!" Blue enthused as they drove home. "Thank you so much, Lumi and Milagro."

"Everybody was so friendly and nice, it really renews your faith in the positive side of humanity," Amber added.

"Yes, the town was in a party mood tonight," said Milagro. "Lucky the volcano didn't explode and send over a tidal wave. The plaza is at sea level."

"Did you know about that, Blue?" Amber asked. "I'm getting a little paranoid about this volcano action. It's like they're following us around!"

"No need for paranoia, but don't be surprised, either," Lumi advised. "The increase in intensity and frequency of weather disturbances and other natural violence has been predicted and is a presently-occurring fact. Our challenge is to survive it. In fact, there is a storm headed our way from Africa."

"Oh, that's just what I need to hear!" Amber groaned.

"I thought that was just a tropical depression," Blue commented.

"Well, it unexpectedly organized and was upgraded to tropical storm Harold this afternoon," Lumi said. "Forget the volcano; let's just hope this guy doesn't become a hurricane."

"*Ay, por favor*! I haven't stopped shaking from the last one," Milagro said.

"Amber and I must return tomorrow anyway. The mission begins in two days and there is much to be done," Blue announced.

"So soon?" Milagro complained. "I was hoping we could hike to the waterfall tomorrow."

"I'm just convinced that every moment waiting is a moment wasted," Blue said. "The extraterrestrial community needs to stop treating humans like spoiled, violent children and start involving them in their own salvation. The sooner the better, because every day more trees fall, more land is poisoned, more whales are killed."

"This is true, sir, Blue," Lumi agreed, "but I'm also sad to see you go. Perhaps there will be a time someday for a carefree visit." He turned onto the dirt road to the beach and soon they were climbing out of the Volkswagen's back seat.

"I think you will have no trouble finding your house," Lumi said. "Watch for the leaning palm tree; the path is just beyond it. I will be awaiting your call in the morning."

Amber and Blue called goodnight as the car rattled away, then took off their shoes and walked up the beach hand in hand. The moon was a smoky crescent in the ash-laced sky, but it still cast a silver glow over the normally golden sand, allowing them to navigate around rocks and chunks of coral. There were no other people but hardly a feeling of being alone with the coquís and the insects singing, the waves lapping the shore, the leaves softly clicking in the breeze. Amber sensed that every object around them, every plant, stone, animal and grain of sand was conscious and vibrantly alive.

"It is indeed a planet of extraordinary diversity and beauty," said Blue. "And seeing it with you beside me is a truly rare privilege."

"Oh, honey, sometimes I just wish we could be together and have a regular life! This is such a cool place. The people are friendly, the beaches are beautiful—and the phone calls are only a dime! Wouldn't it be nice to just drop out of sight down here? I mean, we could build a hurricane shelter and live like Adam and Eve in the garden."

Blue laughed and squeezed her hand. "It's very tempting, but believe me, the transformation of Earth from the third dimension to the fifth is a show you don't want to miss. And we have been given a role to carry out."

"I hope you're not going to start talking about baby-making again."

"No. When I said before that a third energy is created when the first two merge, I didn't mean children. I meant this, what we feel now, the emotion that fills us when we're aroused and looking into each other's eyes."

"Come here and say that," she commanded, stopping and helping herself to a long, deep kiss. "Baby, this is so awesome, I feel like I've known you for a million years but we're really still so new! There are so many things to experience, so many things we haven't done yet."

He took her by the hand again and continued up the beach. "Oh yeah? Like what? What do you want to teach me to do?"

"How good are you in math?" she asked. "Do you know about sixty-nine?"

"Uh...does it have anything to do with bottles of beer on the wall?"

"No, that's ninety-nine!" she laughed. "Here, let me show you." She stopped and stooped to pick up a stick, then drew the number in the sand. "I never thought I'd be explaining this to a senior citizen."

"Hey, I've led a sheltered life! Educate me."

"*No problema,*" she answered with an attempted hispanic accent. "See, the six has her head down here, and the nine has his head up here on the other end."

"Oh, now I get it," he said, and he reached out to rub her bent-over backside.

"Let's get home and you really will get it."

They grabbed hands again and ran to the leaning tree. The path was easy to find from there, but once under the trees they were enveloped in inky blackness.

Amber thought she saw a light off to her left, but when she looked it was gone. Then another one flashed to the right. They must be fireflies, she reasoned. Then she saw one almost directly ahead of her and could readily see that it wasn't a bug. The light was tiny enough, but it glowed green without so much as a flicker.

Suddenly Blue stopped ahead of her. "Do you see it?" he whispered.

"Yeah!" she hissed. "What is it?"

The green dot popped up and zipped away to the right. They could see its glow from the underside of a leaf.

"I think it's a nature spirit," Blue said. "They are known to be very curious."

"Oh wow, now I'm seeing fairies?"

"They've always existed, humans have just lost their ability to perceive them. Except for a few advanced models who are beginning to view beings from other dimensions."

"This is wild!" Amber exclaimed softly. Now the woods around them were dotted with the glowing balls.

"They're just being friendly, giving us an escort," Blue said. "Let's go."

Amber's body tingled intensely, which was becoming a familiar feeling whenever other dimensions intersected with hers. It was like floating, her feet touching a foot or two above the ground. The glowing spirits followed along, surrounding them on all sides but never getting close enough to reveal their structure. When they reached the house, the spirits swirled quickly into the night.

Once inside they lost no time in slipping out of their clothes, diving into bed and between each other's legs. Blue exhibited mathematical genius, comprehending the numerology precisely. They lavished and ravished each other with oral delights, all inhibitions gone, until love's salty cream flowed down both their throats. She swore she could feel the life force of his seed as it entered her mouth and slid deep inside, its taste piquant yet sweet, like the sweat of a saint.

They snuggled sleepily together, windows open to the warm night air and the chirping nightlife. Wrapped up in his arms, buzzing with sangría and contentment, Amber fell asleep feeling happy and safe and loved, without the slightest inkling that this would be her last moment of peace on Earth.

23

Eyeing the Storm

They were awakened the next morning by the sound of horse hoofs in the garden. Blue untangled his limbs from Amber's, pulled on his shorts, and went to the door. She could hear the men talking outside in low voices, but couldn't make out the words. Maybe Lumi was just dropping off breakfast and telling Blue how to get to the swimming hole.

The grave look on his face when he came back in dissolved her day at the beach in an instant. "What's wrong?" she said, sitting up in bed. "Is it the volcano?"

"No, Lumi says the storm strengthened into a hurricane during the night. It's still a category one, but they're predicting an increase in speed and it's heading this direction. I think we should leave right away."

"That would be my guess. I was in a hurricane in Florida when I was a little kid, and I never want to see that again." She got up and scrambled into her clothes.

"I see that living on the surface has its drawbacks," Blue commented, gathering up their few possessions. "In the caves we never had to worry about weather."

They met Lumi outside where he stood holding the three horses.

"I'm sorry I didn't get a chance to clean up the house," Amber told him.

"No problem," he insisted. "Milagro and I will come back later to board up the house. We'll clean after the storm goes by."

"Are they certain it's going to hit the island?" she asked.

"With a hurricane there is no certainty, and many do curve north before reaching Puerto Rico. But not all, so we must prepare."

As they rode back up into the hills it was easy to see that everyone was already taking the threat seriously. Every house had people working on it, hauling panels of plywood to secure over the windows or cleaning the yard of anything that might fly in a wind. The sounds of drilling and hammering replaced the usual birdsong.

Except for the scurrying humans, there was no sign that bad weather was on the way. The sky was clear with only a few puffy clouds, and there was barely a breeze to cool them in the morning sun.

It was also difficult for Amber to feel much of a sense of urgency or impending doom; she was just too madly, deeply in love. Her trust in Blue was so complete, there was simply no room for doubt. If anything she was more worried about the grilling she'd get from friends and family about her recent sudden disappearance.

Settling into the pleasure of the ride, she focused on Blue in front of her, mentally projecting waves of pure love in his direction. When they left the paved road and set off uphill on a narrow trail, she recognized their proximity to the cave's hidden entrance. Amber realized she'd grown rather enamored of her island fantasy, and it was a little sad to think about going back to the real world.

When Lumi stopped and dropped to the ground, Amber was puzzled. There were no rocks around, and she had somehow pictured them entering at a stone wall. "Is this the door?" she asked.

"Yes, right there." Blue pointed to the ground as he dismounted. "Disguised well, don't you think?"

"Nobody will be stumbling onto it by accident," she allowed, climbing down, too.

Lumi walked over, gave her a hug and took her horse's reins. "May your path be blessed and protected," he said.

"Thanks for everything, Lumi. I hope we'll see each other again," she replied.

"We are on the same team, working toward the same goal. No doubt we will meet again." Then he turned to Blue and hugged him, too, saying, "Words are unnecessary. You know my heart." They looked at each other for several moments, telepathically saying farewell.

"Now I go to get ready in case Harold drops by. *Adios*!" He waved, smiling, as Blue embraced Amber and sent them into a blurring spin, the now-familiar method of morphing through stone. As soon as her vision cleared, they were standing inside the silvery tunnel of the Martian colony.

Blue kissed her before letting her go. She was about to tell him what a wonderful piece of their honeymoon this had been, when she heard the unmistakable snarl and skitter of the Goatsuckers. Whirling around, she saw them burst into view and head for Blue, intent on a repetition of their earlier wild greeting.

A sharp command from Rana, who followed close behind, halted them in mid-spring. They again hurried to flank her as she sailed up to embrace Amber and Blue.

"Welcome, children!" she boomed. "The dangers of the surface have an unexpected benefit as they drive you back to me!"

"It's terrible, Rana," Amber reported. "There's a volcano ready to explode south of the island, and a hurricane coming from the east."

"Yes, the pressure is increasing, and with it the violence of the weather. For safety, I recommend you consider the continuation of the mission from here."

"Absolutely not," Blue interjected. "We can't huddle underground while Earth civilization crumbles. I want to leave for the mainland at once."

"Wait a minute. Can't we just hang out here for a little while?" Amber asked. "Last night you said the landing was two days away."

"Well, now that means tomorrow," Blue said. "I must meet with the Grays to coordinate our initial contact, and then with forces from the Sirius star system who will be helping to supervise mass landings in the following days."

"How many extraterrestrial races are in on this?"

"It's an intergalactic program, and let's face it, Earth needs all the help it can get," he replied.

"This is *so* intense!" Amber exclaimed. "How are we going back? By merkaba?"

Rana stopped abruptly and turned to face them. "Blue, if you must go, for once leave her molecules alone and travel in a more conventional manner."

Blue sighed and capitulated. "If it will sedate your paranoid tendencies."

"Good. I'll order a ship prepared immediately. Now come to my private chambers and share some tea before departing." She waddled quickly down the corridor, Blue and Amber following.

"Let me get this straight," Amber whispered to him. "We're going to be conventional and go home by flying saucer?"

"You might as well get used to the interiors!" Rana trilled. "Here we are." An oval portal opened in the wall and they stepped in, followed by the Martian dogs.

Rana sent Deimos and Phobos to their throne-like beds and motioned for Blue and Amber to sit on low hassocks around a small table. Amber took a quick look around the shaman's apartment, amazed by the cosmic clutter of crystals, gems, candles, tiny bowls and boxes, and delicate glass vials of all sizes, no doubt containing powerful brews.

Before she had time to take more of an inventory, Rana said, "Shall we sit in my holographic garden?" Without waiting for an answer, she drew a symbol in the air with a pointed finger, and suddenly they were outside under a blue sky. The carpet of sand underfoot had been replaced by a violet-strewn lawn, and they were surrounded by flower beds and a high, trimmed hedge of dense foliage.

"This is the only safe way to experience the surface," Rana laughed. "I will return with the tea." She turned, walked straight into the hedge and disappeared as if popping through a backdrop.

Amber turned to Blue, who was looking amused at her astonishment. "How did she do that? Did we transport somewhere?"

"No, it's an illusory image, a hologram. But it's 3-D and pretty convincing, don't you think?"

"It's amazing! I bet people in New York City would go crazy for this!"

Rana popped back through the scenery carrying a tray with three cups. She placed it on the table, then produced a long, silver wand with a terminated crystal at each end, one clear and one pink. "This energy will strengthen and balance your auric emanations," she explained, stirring each cup with the crystalline points. "The challenges you face will require wholeness in body, mind and spirit."

Amber sipped her tea and immediately felt its power tingling through her. "I don't know, Rana, I always thought starting a marriage would be challenge enough."

"Usually, yes," Rana giggled. "But you have chosen a most unusual mate. Now the two of you have a chance to influence the destiny of an entire planet. Exciting, is it not?"

"Yeah, but that's also a scary thought, me and the planet's destiny. I've had my hands full with my own destiny so far," Amber said.

"That was the past." Blue reached over and stroked her shoulder. "We are both becoming different people now."

"Yes, that is exciting, too!" Rana agreed. "The implanted genetic codes are firing, the little strands of DNA are knitting themselves back together, and the ancient eyes of the human race are fluttering open. As for Blue, his own genetic experiment has been an obvious success. Of course, the final question is whether the mating will produce offspring." Her cheeks plumped up in a huge smile as she regarded them both.

"Uh, wait a minute, Rana," Amber began. "See, back in my world I'm considered kind of over the hill for that sort of thing...."

Loud, resonant chiming interrupted her speech. "Your escort is here," Rana announced. Instantly the garden vanished and they were back in her softly-glowing cavern. The door slid open, revealing a figure wearing helmet and jumpsuit. Blue spoke to him in Martian, then turned to embrace Rana. They looked into each other's eyes for several seconds, then Rana hurried to hug Amber.

"Remember, heed the guidance of your heart, not your tribe," she whispered in Amber's ear, "and may your decisions be motivated by love, not fear."

Amber nodded, her eyes filling with tears. This departure had a dramatic emotional quality that didn't quite befit a trip back to Phoenix. Blue took her hand, their escort spun about, and they followed him on another labyrinthine journey through the metallic maze. When they reached a large, triangular gate, it glided open and allowed them into a huge, dome-shaped hangar.

Their ship was the only craft in the mammoth enclosure. It was disc-shaped, with a round protrusion above and below, and no sign of windows, lights, or markings of any kind. To Amber it looked like a seamless silver hamburger too big for its bun.

It wasn't large, maybe thirty feet across, and was raised from the floor on tripod legs that also seemed to flow into the ship's body without a joint or connecting edge. As they walked beneath it, a soft humming became audible and grew louder until it was above their heads. The escort stopped and they were suddenly in a column of light that was so bright, Amber had to close her eyes.

When she opened them, they were inside the craft in a room with rounded walls. Everything was the same silver-gray as the outer shell and appeared molded in one piece. The only feature visible was a wide, high-backed chair, resting on a single pedestal as if it had grown from the floor like a mushroom.

"No seat belts?" Amber asked. "What happens if we suddenly go into warp-drive?"

"Not necessary. The internal environment will be artificially stabilized," Blue explained. "Unlike the depictions in your so-called science fiction, this ride will be extraordinarily smooth."

He climbed into the seat and she slid in beside him. Just like the tunnel floors and walls, the material yielded beneath her, contouring itself to her body. "Whoa! That feels kind of freaky! It's not every day that your chair tries to feel you up."

Blue put his arm around her and they sank into the organic upholstery together. "Flight time will be approximately seven and a half minutes," he informed her.

The craft began to vibrate, then rose toward the ceiling. Suddenly Amber felt the whirring twirl of their exit, but her body remained securely in place. Then all was completely still.

"Now where are we? It feels like we stopped."

"Oh, no, we're still moving," Blue said. "Want to see? I can make a section of the hull transparent."

He barked a command in Martian and the entire wall and floor in front of them dropped out of sight. Amber screamed and latched onto him with both hands.

"Darling, it's all right," he soothed. "We're still safe inside, but now we can see out."

She peeled her face from his chest and peered over her feet. "Damn, it's just that I don't like heights. And we are really up there." From what she could tell, it was at least satellite level. The blue-white swirl of ocean and clouds was far below.

"Look, that dark squiggle is Cuba," Blue pointed out. "Let's look out the side and see if we recognize the hurricane."

"Please, don't disappear more of the ship!" Amber tried to protest, but he had already given the command. Now it felt as if they were floating through space on nothing more substantial than a magic carpet.

They both looked down and back, and both fell silent when they saw the unmistakable pinwheel of clouds. It seemed to have sucked every bit of moisture in the Caribbean into its circle, forming a gigantic disc of destruction. The island of Puerto Rico was seemingly inches from its leading edge.

"Wow, it looks enormous," Amber breathed. "I'm sure glad we got the hell out of there."

They watched for a while, but even though there was no sensation of movement, the hurricane's neighborhood rotated out of sight. The cloud cover moved and they could clearly see the Gulf of Mexico passing rapidly.

"We're descending now," Blue said. "Let me know if the increased sensation of speed makes you uncomfortable."

The lower they flew, the faster the Earth flashed by, until it became a dizzying blur. "Unless you have a barf bag hidden somewhere on board, I think it's time to put the walls back up," she croaked.

Blue laughed, gave a command and turned the walls opaque again.

"Thanks. I guess space travel is an acquired taste."

"You'll get used to it," he chuckled.

"Yeah, right. You and Rana seem to think I'm going to spend a lot of time inside saucers. Are you planning an abduction?"

"Only if you won't come with me willingly," he teased.

"I don't think you have to worry too much about that," she laughed. "But what are we going to do now? Just zoom in over my subdivision and land?"

"Why not? If we make believers of a few hundred people, what difference does it make? Tomorrow, everybody will believe."

"What is it about tomorrow that's so important? Why does it have to be then?"

"Because the space shuttle is scheduled for departure late tomorrow, and I thought it might be nice to have a landing to go with their launch."

"That's perfect!" she exclaimed. "What a great idea! Every news camera in the country will be there."

"And every eye will already be turned to the sky," he added with a grin. "Government denials will mean nothing when virtually the entire population becomes witness to extraterrestrial contact."

Before Amber could ask any more questions, the room was filled with a humming noise again. "We're home," Blue said, stepping out of the chair and offering his hand. Amber grabbed it, pressed herself against him, and they were swallowed by the light beam. She opened her eyes in her own living room.

"What efficient service," she said, looking around her house in amazement. It was becoming increasingly difficult to reconcile her old life with her new one. Realities were clashing and her brain was outgrowing the things it had always believed. These rooms, and the dreams they had sheltered, seemed small and shabby compared to her recent adventures and new knowledge.

She looked at the wall clock and was shocked to see it was still only 10:30 in the morning. "Man, that's the only way to travel!" She released Blue and went to the fish tank. "You still alive, Oro?" He was, but hungry, and snapped greedily at the sprinkled flakes of food. The filter in the tank bubbled again, attesting to the restored power.

"Amber," Blue said somberly, and she turned to look at him. "I have to go."

She sighed, her shoulders slumping in resignation. "Baby, I'm really starting to hate when that happens."

"This is the last time, I promise. But until I know how the humans are going to react, it's too risky to have you close."

"What about the risk to you?" she demanded. "I've got to sit here and wonder whether my esteemed government will welcome you or try to blow you to bits? I don't trust them for a second."

"Well, trust me then."

"Yeah, big deal, you've been interacting with humans for, what? A month now? I'm telling you, we're a sleazy breed."

He walked over and collected her in his arms. "Trust me," he repeated. "Nothing can keep me from you. Their weapons are ludicrously easy to disarm, if it should come to that. And I don't think it will. I have more faith in your people than you do!"

"Just don't let that be your downfall."

He gave her a long, sensuous kiss, then released her abruptly, as if he had to force himself to do it. "As soon as contact is completed, we will be together and inseparable."

"Well, you better call in between," she warned.

"Of course. At every opportunity."

"And what am I going to tell my parents? You know they're not going to be impressed when they find out you're unavailable to meet them again."

"Tell them the truth," he suggested. "Tell them I'm out to launch." He cackled, took a step backward, and vaporized into thin air.

24

Wake-Up Call

Amber gritted her teeth and cursed in frustration. Molecularly transferring on someone in the middle of conversation was unforgivably rude! Not to mention, now she was left to explain things to the 'rents by herself. Besides, now that she was back at home, on a sunny day with no volcanoes, no hurricanes, and plenty of electricity, the situation didn't seem so dire. Couldn't he at least finish their honeymoon before running off to become America's next big news flash?

It was too early to call the homestead; she had just talked to them yesterday afternoon and it would seem awfully suspicious for her to be back in town by this morning. Instead she dialed Krystalee's number, intending to leave a message, but a sleepy voice answered the phone, "This better be good."

"Well, it must've been good if you're still in bed."

"Am-*bear*!" Krystalee shrieked. "Where the hell have you been? Your mom's been frantic!"

"Yeah, I know. I called her from Puerto Rico yesterday."

"Puerto Rico? You are wild, child! Blue take you down there for more honeymoon action?"

"Actually it was a business trip, but we managed to work in a little tropical romance. It was wonderful!"

"That's nice to hear. Must be going around."

"Oh, so it *was* good last night."

"Yeah," Krystalee said dreamily. "You know how it feels when you've been horny for a long time—"

"Which in your case is about two weeks," Amber interrupted.

"Hey, but that's two weeks of sheer hell! Anyway, this one was worth waiting for. Talk about putting an end to the drought!"

"Congratulations, I'm glad you got your rocks off. Who was it?"

"Geez, it doesn't take a psychic to figure this one out! The African-American Clark Kent, who else?"

"Damn, that was fast! You just met the cat."

"Boy, you're one to talk! How long have you known your husband? A little over a week?"

"Okay, okay, I deserved that. Just tell me what happened."

"Well, after spending a night without electricity, I figured calling him would be the best way to inform myself, and since I happened to call at around noon it seemed like meeting for lunch would be the perfect thing. Then all the restaurants were closed, so I had him come over here."

"So what was on the menu, besides you?"

Krystalee giggled. "Caesar salad, shrimp cocktail and champagne."

"That was a blatant seduction lunch."

"Hey, the shrimp were thawing out in the freezer! You wouldn't want them to go to waste, would you?"

"Perish the thought! Go on," Amber urged.

"So anyway, after we ate and talked some more about UFOs and stuff, being the open and honest kind of gal that I am, somehow the topic got around to how long it had been since I'd had sex with a man—"

"And he volunteered to help. What a humanitarian." Amber was trying to act stern but it was impossible not to laugh.

"I figured the squeaky wheel gets the grease, so I asked him if he was interested in a little uncomplicated fun," Krystalee explained. "It wasn't exactly a mercy fuck."

"Didn't say it was!"

"And there were some boundaries of decency, since he had to get back to work and everything. But by the time evening rolled around the power was back on, and he had obviously had time to think about it all afternoon. He took me to a nice restaurant, and then to ecstasy via fantasy island."

"He still there with you?"

"Nah, he left way early. You think I'd say this shit in front of him?"

"Why not? It's just uncomplicated fun, right?"

"We'll see about that. So where's Blue?"

"Off to work, too. I probably won't see him til late tomorrow."

"Listen, why don't you get your butt over here and tell me about your trip? Then I'll tell you about the one I took last night!"

"Be right over." They hung up and Amber shook her head and chuckled. Her girlfriend was smitten, no doubt about it. Maybe it really was going around. She hummed little pieces of love songs as she changed clothes and got ready to go.

Before leaving she dialed Quinn's number and left a message. If the world was really going to change forever tomorrow, she would have to hang with her homegirls tonight. On the way out the door, she tossed the last two day's newspapers inside, making a point not to unroll them and read the headlines. She wasn't quite ready for that much 3-D reality.

Krystalee greeted her at the door wearing nothing but a large T-shirt and a huge tangle of hair. "Good to see ya, darlin'," she said, giving Amber a hug. "When you disappear during disasters, I get a little nervous."

"What *is* the latest on that? I've been avoiding the paper out of sheer terror."

Krystalee closed the door and led the way to her kitchen table. "Oh, it's way fucked up," she said, trying to unsnarl her locks with her fingers. "They're still trying to dig out, last I heard. Death toll's up to like a hundred thousand. You want some OJ?" She opened the refrigerator and took out a bottle of orange juice, then set two glasses on the table.

"This is just so mind-blowing!" Amber exclaimed. "I don't understand how this could happen."

"I do. People build cities all over the damn place, and once in a while their geologic number comes up. This time it was a double blow, Mt. Rainier and Glacier Peak, practically simultaneously. The people never knew what hit 'em. Split a bagel with me?" Without waiting for an answer, she slid one into the toaster.

"A lot of people seem to think it's a sign things are accelerating, you know, toward the end-times." Amber took a sip of juice. "And all you and I can think of is rolling around with a man!"

"Oh, I feel so guilty!" Krystalee responded with a derisive laugh. "What, we should have a bad life just to show solidarity? Especially if it's the end of the world, I say make love while the sun shines." She buttered the bagel and brought it to the table.

"Thanks," Amber said and snarfed up her half, suddenly famished.

"You talk to Quinn?" Krystalee asked between bites.

"No, left a message. What's up with her?"

"Oh God, her mind's in a mess! Dab recommended some reading for her and she can't get enough of it. She's a full-bore UFO freak now."

"Yeah, me too. I rode in one this morning," Amber confessed.

"No shit!" Krystalee almost choked on a swallow of orange juice. "What was it like?"

"Super smooth, you can't even tell you're moving until they make the whole fuselage transparent. Took us seven minutes to get here from Puerto Rico."

Amber described the saucer ride in detail, then backtracked to her brief but action-packed visit to the tropics. Krystalee responded with a chronicle of her own recent romantic adventures. The two women sat tittering and sighing like two teenagers sharing date notes.

Finally Krystalee got up and took the dishes to the sink. "Damn, girl, it's almost one. The day's gettin' away from us. I gotta take a shower in case you-know-who shows up." As if on cue, the phone rang. She picked up the kitchen extension and said hello.

"Oh, hi," she said, her face relaxing. She looked over at Amber while she listened. "Yeah, I know what you mean, but she's sitting right here in my kitchen...everything's fine, calm down; she just went to Puerto Rico for a minute...well, fucking come over when you're done...yeah, I'll make sure she doesn't beam anywhere. Bye."

"Quinn?" Amber said, knowing the answer.

"No, Xena, warrior princess. She's gonna be over here, too, soon as she finishes kicking some guy's glutes."

Krystalee went to shower, and Amber decided to call her folks. For her own sake, she couldn't put it off any longer. She had to smooth everything over with them, and then she could enjoy the rest of the afternoon.

Her mother picked up after the first ring. "Amber? Where are you?"

"I'm home, Mom. Caught a flight back this morning."

"That was quick. They usually make you pay through the nose when you don't purchase your ticket in advance. This new boyfriend of yours must be rich."

Amber didn't like the tone in her mother's voice. "You don't sound too happy to hear from me," she surmised.

Her mother sighed into the receiver. "Let me read a little news item from the paper to you. 'Airplanes flying over six states were rerouted and others grounded after air traffic controllers lost almost all communications with pilots during the recent power failure.' Amber, your father called the airport and checked. There were no flights out of Phoenix to the Caribbean that night. What in the *hell* is going on?"

"Okay, you're right—you deserve an explanation."

"We deserve the truth. That's what I don't understand, you've never been shy about telling us anything and everything."

"Well, this one may be more challenging than most."

"You said you were going to come over here with him. I think tonight would be good," her mother suggested.

"Uh, he has to...work tonight."

"Amber—"

"Really! Just one more night, and then you'll see him for sure."

"Well, I hope that means you're coming for dinner."

"Sure. Maybe I'll bring Krystalee, too. She can back up my story."

"Well, we can't wait. Your father's pacing already."

Amber hung up with a promise to arrive at five o'clock, and was sitting at the kitchen table with her face in her hands when Krystalee returned, combing out her long hair. "What's up?"

"My parents' suspicions. They did some investigating and found out there was no way I could've gotten out of here Thursday night on a commercial jet. Also, they're not stoked that Blue won't be able to join them tonight, once again."

"So, what is your favorite Martian working on anyway?" Krystalee asked. "The dude doesn't seem to be paying the proper attention to his new bride."

"Oh, he's busy planning...." Amber stopped, remembering how quickly something can appear in print, "some kind of mission. Apparently they don't get any type of honeymoon leave on Mars."

"Bummer," Krystalee opined. The doorbell rang and she scurried to answer it, saying, "That must be our third musketeer now."

Amber couldn't see the foyer from where she sat, but it was obvious the person at the door was not Quinn. "Hi, baby," she heard her girlfriend croon, and then the subtle smacking sounds of an intimate greeting.

Krystalee reappeared, her cheeks flushed and a dopey smile on her face. Dab followed close behind, also grinning like the Cheshire cat. "Well, hello Mrs. Robinson," he sang when he saw Amber.

"Mr. Mitchell," she returned with a nod of her head. "Or is it now Doctor Feelgood?"

"Well, let me tell ya, sentences aren't the only structures he knows about," Krystalee testified with a lewd laugh.

"However, right now I wouldn't mind a few good phrases," he said, pulling a tiny tape recorder from his jacket pocket. "You know you're gonna give me an interview, Amber."

"Yeah, I probably will," she conceded. "But not today. Now I'd just be another kook with a UFO story. Tomorrow, well, there may be a lot more people willing to believe."

"That sounds intriguing," Dab said, "but tomorrow a more pressing news event may push you off the front page. Ever heard of Hurricane Harold?"

Amber's aura blazed. "I just saw it with my own eyes this morning. Is it going to hit Puerto Rico?"

"No, they got lucky. It already veered north. But it's on the verge of becoming a category three, and they're expecting it to strengthen as it gets out over open, warm water."

"Oh, shit! What's it aiming at now?"

"It's moving northwest, really fast, and unless it changes its heading it'll run straight into south Florida. They've already scrubbed the shuttle launch for tomorrow. Guess the scientists have to go home and batten down the hatches."

Amber's mind raced, trying to make sense of this information. If the scientists and the camera crews weren't going to be there, then Blue's landing would be postponed, too. Which meant he could rematerialize at any moment. "Damn, first the volcano and now this?" she said out loud.

"I know, it's a dangerous one-two punch for the country. Kind of like the way I'm gettin' slammed by this Texas twister." He slid his arm around Krystalee's waist.

"Louisiana," she corrected, "but who wants to get technical?"

"You two are making me sick," Amber warned with a laugh.

"Welcome to a little taste of what you've been giving the rest of us for the past week," Krystalee giggled.

"I have to go anyway," Dab announced. "We're scrambling to catch up after the power outage. When I get done, I'd like to come by. Maybe around nine?"

"That would be rather excellent." Hypnotized, Krystalee walked him to the door. Amber heard more whispering and slurping before she heard him leave.

Krystalee came dancing back into the kitchen, snapping her fingers. "Ooh, I can't wait to get me some more of that hot chocolate!"

"You're terrible. What would your mother think?"

"Are you crazy? You want to send her to an early grave?" Krystalee laughed and executed a twirl. "Man, I hope it *is* the end of the world! At least I'll go out happy."

The bell rang again and they heard the door open before either one could react. "Anyone home?" Quinn called. She marched into the kitchen, took one glimpse at Amber and Krystalee, and shoved her hands on her hips with a disgusted sneer.

"If y'all don't look like two cats who ate the canary," she accused. "And I just passed the little songbird on the street. Or what's left of him."

Quinn didn't give them a chance to jump in. "You just had to do it, didn't you?" She leveled a stare at Krystalee, who was trying not to crack up. "Just to prove you could, I guess, huge national tragedies notwithstanding."

"Hey, people need comfort during tragedies," Krystalee interjected. "Come on, I didn't put a gun to his head."

"Huh! I bet I can guess what you *did* put to his head!"

"So what? He was quite appreciative, wasn't he, Amber? What's the deal, are you pissed off because he's black?"

"Well..." Quinn hesitated.

"You *are*! You're fucking pissed 'cause he's a brother and I'm a honky! Aren't you, you racist!"

"Oh, you are so full of shit," Quinn responded. "It's just that aside from owning a dick, he really doesn't seem like your type."

"Well, why don't you yell at Amber? Her man is from a totally different species! What makes bluish skin any better than brownish?"

"Yeah, love is color-blind," Amber added.

"Oh, love, that's what you guys are calling it these days?" Quinn smirked. "A couple weeks ago you were calling it crotch-itch."

"Sometimes it's kinda hard to draw that fine line between the two," Krystalee snorted merrily.

"Speak for yourself," Amber said. "I know I'm in love, and I'm in this one for the duration."

"You mean you'll never fuck a human again?" Krystalee asked, eyes wide in feigned shock.

"No way," Amber replied. "Once you go blue, you never go back."

* * *

At five o'clock Amber pulled into her parents' driveway with a caravan behind her. She had talked both of her friends into coming with her for the spilling of the unbelievable beans, but they had each insisted on bringing their own vehicle to accommodate their later agendas. She kept expecting to see Blue at every turn, or at least receive some kind of cryptic message, but the mind-waves were frustratingly silent.

"Hello, girls!" Amber's mom enthused as she let them in the door. "This is so great to have you all here together! Come on in." She led them into the living room where they gravitated into armchairs and couches. "Hope you like margaritas. The bartender's whipping up a blenderful in the kitchen."

Amber's father came in carrying a tray of colorful margarita glasses, rims encrusted with salt and filled high with lime-colored slush. He distributed the drinks, then held his aloft. "To a rare and possibly enlightening occurrence! Amber is going to explain her latest boyfriend! It's a first!" He drank deeply, and everyone followed his lead.

"Gee, Dad, do I detect a note of sarcasm in there somewhere?" Amber asked, and they all laughed.

"Not at all, I'm truly looking forward to this," he replied impishly. "So, let's hear it. Anyone else ready?"

"Believe me, we already heard," Quinn informed him.

"So the parents really are the last to know," Mom observed. "This is so unlike you, Amber."

"Well, maybe she just didn't want you to call the funny farm," Krystalee said. "Believing this stuff will hurt your head."

"Okay, enough suspense," said Amber's father. "Let's hear the explanation! You say you went to Puerto Rico. How did you get there when the airport was practically shut down?"

All eyes were on Amber. "Well, because I didn't go by commercial airline," she stammered.

"Uh-huh. Go on." Her father took a vicious sip from his glass.

"See, Blue is a little unusual. He has powers—"

"Obviously some very strong ones because you certainly seem to be under his spell," he observed. "Could you just say this in English?"

"Jesus, Amber!" Krystalee piped up. "Just blurt it out! Just tell them he's from...."

Now Amber's father swung in Krystalee's direction. "Where? What? Who is this guy?" he pleaded.

"Mars," Krystalee squeaked. Amber moaned and slumped into her chair. "He's from Mars, a one-hundred-percent extraterrestrial, and he fell in love with your daughter."

"Oh, I see, you guys think this is all a big joke." He shook his head and took another drink. "Is this your idea of explanation?"

"No," Amber answered. "Now it sounds nuts. But the thing is, it's true. There are other intelligent life-forms in the universe."

"And she just happened to marry one," Krystalee finished.

"Marry one? I hope that part is a joke!" Amber's mother exclaimed.

"Don't worry, it's only binding under Martian law," Quinn added.

Amber's father looked at the three of them. "So you're all sticking to the same insane story. I cannot fathom why you're doing this! What could possibly be so terrible about the truth that you'd make this up? Are you doing some kind of new drug?"

"Dad, it really is the truth! If only Blue were here, he could prove it to you."

"That's the other thing," her dad said. "Where is he? All we do is hear about him. Have you girls seen him?" Quinn and Krystalee both nodded. "Maybe he has all three of you hypnotized."

"He's a Martian," Amber repeated impatiently. "Some of them survived the destruction of their planet and they've been living in underground colonies. I know it sounds incredible, but it's true! I've been in them myself! Now they're coming out, to help us keep the planet from falling apart. Blue's not here because he's going to lead the first extraterrestrial delegation to make contact with Earth."

Amber's father stood in stunned silence for several seconds, then began to laugh uproariously. "You three are really good! Really good! What are you doing, practicing lines from a play? I don't know what to think! You can't possibly expect us to believe this!"

"I didn't believe it, either, Mr. Voss," Quinn said somberly. "Until I saw the spacecraft with my own eyes."

The shocked silence was pierced by the ringing phone. "Yes?" Amber's mom said into the receiver. "Oh, hi, Violet, we're just sitting here having cocktails with Amber, Quinn and Krystalee...no, the TV's off, we're just talking...oh, really? Well, yes, I'm sure she would be...Okay, talk to you later."

Amber's mother hung up the phone. "That was Violet; she says to turn on the news," she told the attentive group. "They think they've spotted a UFO over the White House."

25

Happy Landing

Good evening, America. We are preempting our planned programming tonight to bring you a situation in progress. For further details, let's go direct to Laura Jones, our White House correspondent. Laura?"

Everyone crowded around the big TV in Amber's parents' living room. When the picture switched they could see it was already dark in Washington, D.C., two time zones away.

"Thank you, David. By all appearances we are witnessing a historic event tonight. Over an hour ago, an unidentified flying object was picked up on radar, followed as it streaked toward the nation's capitol, and it has now been hovering above 1600 Pennsylvania Avenue for approximately forty-three minutes. The craft is now easily visible with the naked eye, due to the intensity of its lights...."

The screen jumped to wobbly footage of a ring of bright lights. "This is the tape we have so far, but we should be getting better images as more sophisticated equipment is brought in. As you can see, however, it is possible to clearly see this object."

"And there have been no communications from anyone inside?" the anchorman asked.

"None that we know of, though I've just learned the president plans a press conference within the next hour. So we'll certainly learn more then. Back to you, David."

"We will be updating this story as details come in, but for now it's a waiting game. We'll be back in a moment with some opinions from experts in the fields of space travel and UFOs."

"He's just waiting for everybody to tune in," Amber said softly.

"You mean you think Blue's in there?" Krystalee squealed.

"'Fraid so. The shuttle launch was canceled, so he figured why wait? 'Course, I'm just guessing."

"What?" her father boomed. "You know something about this?"

"That's what we've been trying to tell you, Mr. V." Krystalee flung an arm out toward Amber as if presenting the queen. "Weird as it seems, the first Martian to walk the face of the Earth fell in love with your daughter. Now he's got some cockamamie idea he's gonna save the world." She turned back to the television, shaking her head. "Hell, I figured taming Amber was enough accomplishment for one lifetime."

"I just can't believe I'm hearing this," Amber's mom said. "Martians and spaceships, how could it be true?"

"Really, it makes a lot of sense," Quinn spoke up. "When you take into account the infinity of space, it would be more unbelievable if we were the only intelligent life-forms."

The next news story gripped their attention, too:

> "Hurricane Harold is rapidly becoming one of the strongest storms of the last two decades. As it churned north today, narrowly missing Puerto Rico and Hispaniola, its wind speeds soared over open water, elevating it to a category four storm. At a time when the country is still reeling over the shock of the Seattle tragedy, this deadly hurricane sets its sights on the North American continent. More from our reporter at the National Hurricane Center in Florida...."

"Damn, Amber, maybe it really is the end of the world," Krystalee gulped.

"Well, end of the world or not, we still have to eat," Mom said. "Enchiladas, anyone?"

While they feasted on cheese enchiladas, Spanish rice and another round of margaritas, the debate over extraterrestrial life raged on.

"Carl Sagan was a skeptic," Dad pointed out. "And his entire life's work was staring out into the sky. That's good enough for me."

"Yeah, but he never saw anything. You're seeing something!" Amber insisted.

"An image on a TV screen? I hardly call that proof positive. Maybe the whole thing is just a spoof, a nineties version of *War of the Worlds*."

"Those reporters looked pretty serious," Quinn said. "It's a really strange feeling to see one of these things."

"It's sort of euphoric, too," Krystalee added. "The thought of a whole world we know nothing about. It jerks you out of your navel-contemplating trance."

Back on TV, reporters were gathering to listen to a statement from a White House spokesperson. Amber's father punched up the sound.

> "To avoid any panic, the president has asked me to issue a statement, even though we do not yet have a completely clear picture of these unfolding events. He wants me to emphasize that the government is under no threat, and although military forces are on alert status, no deployments have been ordered." The man paused, waiting for the buzz of voices to die back down. "We have received a transmission from the craft, in English, and we will be releasing more information when that dialogue is completed. I repeat, there is no reason to assume aggressive intent."

"Are you saying you believe this is a UFO?" someone shouted.

"Whether the craft is Earth-made or extraterrestrial in origin is not yet known. No more questions." The man grabbed his notes and hastily departed, leaving the journalists to speculate and wait.

"Why is he drawing it out like this? Everybody in the country must be watching by now," Amber wailed. "The suspense is killing me!"

"Like anything else with the bureaucracy, there's probably a ton of red tape," Krystalee reasoned. "Imagine the paperwork for issuing a visa to a Martian!"

"How do they know it's not aggressive?" Dad demanded. "Could be something a hostile foreign power cooked up."

"Listen, I know it's hard for this to penetrate your carefully constructed belief system...." Amber began.

"But Martians do exist!" Krystalee finished. "Personally, I think it's the coolest thing. Hey, I need to call Dab at work; bet he won't be getting off early tonight."

Krystalee went to the phone, then returned to the group and related that the newsroom was in an uproar. Dab was hyper-excited; his once-ridiculed beliefs would shortly be proven true. The drama of two worlds colliding would not be lost on him. That meant he would be working late tonight, if need be all night if the craft didn't land and divulge its contents.

"Come stay at my house, then," Amber urged. "I cannot make it through watching this by myself."

"Watching what?" said her father. "The thing hasn't moved. Maybe it's some kind of holographic image."

Amber shivered. Now that he mentioned it, maybe it was, just like the projected garden that looked absolutely real.

"I never heard of an image that gets picked up on radar," Quinn observed.

"I'm glad you're all so fascinated, because I think it's getting boring." Amber's father tried clicking the channel, but almost all were broadcasting the White House standoff. "What I wouldn't give for a rerun right now."

"Dad, please! I really want to see this."

"This is embarrassing! Everybody's being totally taken in by this hoax and making the rest of us watch it!" He had no sooner finished this lament when the silver disc on the screen began to move.

Excited chatter could be heard among the press corps on the scene. "The craft is descending," the reporter announced. "There has been no word from officials, but without warning, it appears the ship is preparing to land."

With the press shining spots, the White House lit up like a birthday cake, and the blinding lights from the craft itself, there was no way to maintain it was only illusion. The disc threaded its way down, avoiding the tree branches, and glided toward an open portion of the rose garden's lawn. The lights dimmed, and an awestruck murmur swept the crowd.

"Criminetlies," Amber's mother whistled.

"No shit!" Krystalee agreed vehemently.

"This is absolutely unbelievable," the reporter said in a hushed tone, "but there is some kind of landing gear...*growing* out of the bottom of the craft." The cameras recorded it perfectly, how the material forming the hull simply flowed down and into a shape, until there were three spindly legs protruding from beneath it. Then it floated a few more feet earthward and landed with a muffled thud.

"The craft has landed!" trumpeted the reporter. Secret Service types in dark suits rushed to form a line between the ship and the press, while others surrounded the disc in a wide, respectful circle. Amber didn't like the idea that they would soon be focusing on her man.

"Oh, Lord, I've gotta get home! Darryl's mind must be splattered all over the living room!" Quinn cried. "But I can't leave now, I might miss the best part!"

The reporters on television were falling all over themselves in their excitement. No more official statements had been issued; apparently the powers-that-be had no idea how to handle this, either. "If an alien disembarks now, who will be the first human he meets, Dan Rather?" asked one journalist.

"Huh! He's already got a few humans under his belt," Krystalee answered.

"Wait! A door is opening," the reporter said, "and yes, I'm certain I see the president, coming out onto the porch and surrounded by Secret Service...He's waving and smiling! What tremendous bravery!"

"He looks scared shitless!" Amber commented.

"I don't blame him," Mom said. "Do we have any more of that tequila?"

"We're hearing a humming sound now, coming from the craft," came the reporter's voice. "Oh, God! An incredibly bright beam of light just came out of the ship's underside!"

As all cameras trained on the ship, the beam glowed briefly then winked out, leaving a lone figure standing on the scorched and smoldering grass. Telephoto lenses zoomed in to record the being's features, clearly etched in the glint of a thousand man-made lights. He was tall and bald, dressed in a tan jumpsuit with military-like insignia on the front, and as he walked out from under the craft, a crooked half-smile curled his bluish lips.

Krystalee giggled hysterically. "He looks kinda cute in that uniform."

"*Damn* cute!" Amber corrected, her heart beating madly.

"Amber, are you saying this....*this* is your new boyfriend?" her mother asked.

"No, Mom," she replied. "That's my new husband."

Amber's father started to laugh, while her mother just stared in shocked surprise. But there was no time to react any further. The Martian on the screen strode out from under his spaceship and made straight for the leader of the free world.

"I hope he can see how edgy those bodyguards are," Amber said.

"Yeah, they look like they got caught with their pants down," Quinn added.

"This can't be happening," Amber's mother stated.

The jumpsuited figure stopped short of the porch steps, but within earshot of the gathered and gawking officials.

"Looks plenty human to me," Dad said.

"That's what I thought at first, too," Quinn volunteered.

"Hush! Let's see what he says!" Amber hissed.

The cameras trained in on Blue's face, and they saw his mouth move. "We're not getting any audio, Laura," the anchorman prodded.

"Neither are we at the moment," she answered. "But there is a podium being set up, so hopefully we'll get a mike up there in a few minutes." Like roadies on speed, a group of people was scrambling around on the porch trying to hook up a wooden lectern with the presidential seal. Hordes of television technicians rushed to make sure they got plugged in, while the Secret Service men swarmed and scowled, clearly unhappy that the situation was so totally out of their control.

"The president and the, uh...pilot, spaceman, right now we really don't know what to call him, but they seem to be having a pleasant exchange. The president is smiling, offering his hand, and now the man in the jumpsuit is climbing the steps..."

"Awesome," Krystalee whispered. "I hope he brings us back some cool White House souvenirs."

Blue shook hands with the president, then spoke while the president listened. The crew clustering around the podium began gesticulating to the officials.

"I think we're ready with the audio now," said the reporter's voice. "If we can just get somebody to the microphone."

For once there was silence on television as the two tall men talked. Then the president motioned to an aide, who scurried to the microphones for a sound check.

The president strode to the podium, the expression on his face bursting with little-boy excitement. "My fellow Americans," he began, then shook his head with a gleeful laugh. "This is just so amazing and unexpected, I hardly know what to say myself."

"He can't believe he finally found a secure spot in the history books," Quinn guessed.

"If what our visitor says is true," the president continued, "and I would say his aircraft makes a pretty impressive exhibit A, we are witnessing an unprecedented event, the meeting of representatives from two different planets."

This statement unleashed an outburst of noise from the growing crowd around the White House.

"I'm sure many of you are as much in shock as I am, so with no further ado I'll turn the podium over to someone who may be able to answer our questions. Commander?" The president stepped aside and motioned for Blue to take his place.

"Commander?" Amber echoed.

Krystalee giggled, "I thought he was just a kid!"

Blue walked to the forest of microphones, looking as casual and relaxed as if he were quite used to addressing entire nations. "Citizens of planet Earth," he announced loudly, "this is a day of celebration as well as one of grave importance. Today you take your place in the galactic family. However, it is the critical condition of your world that has prompted our decision to initiate contact.

"I am an Earth-born descendant of the Martian race, known here by the human name Bradley Robinson. Except for body hair, my species is much like yours in appearance; in fact, we originated from the same seed, millennia ago. My planet was destroyed by a natural disaster; now I wish to help my adopted planet avoid the same fate." He paused briefly, but nobody made a sound.

"As many of you have noticed, the natural forces of your world have become increasingly violent. This is not only a reaction to human abuse of the Earth, it is a result of a cosmic occurrence that is affecting the entire solar system. We are moving into a huge circle of energy called the photon band, something that happens every twenty-five thousand years, and it's not all bad. Simply put, this energy is destined to usher the planet into an era of new technology and enlightenment.

"The pressure caused by the proximity of the photon band is partially responsible for the onslaught of volcanic eruptions, earthquakes and lethal storms that now seem to be in an attitude of attack. Believe me, this may prove to be the least of your problems. Much more dangerous are the stores of nuclear material that may spontaneously explode when the photon energy reaches its full potential."

"He never said anything about photon bands," Amber said, almost to herself.

"This is ridiculous!" her father burst out. "That guy is no more Martian than I am!"

"Shhh!" her mother insisted.

"...must be thinking. I don't look like the expected extraterrestrial," Blue was saying. "That's why I've come with some representatives of another species, beings that you will certainly recognize as originating somewhere else. You've seen them on your movie screens as actors in costumes, or as digital creations, but their existence has been a topic of controversy, and their motives have never been clearly understood. Let me assure you that they, too, are here to help.

"Was a crashed extraterrestrial craft recovered at Roswell, New Mexico? Have humans been abducted and studied by an alien race? Is it true that some officials have known about it and issued only denials? Residents of the Earth, a mystery that has persisted for over fifty years is about to be solved beyond a shadow of doubt."

Before anyone could react, the blinding shaft of light flashed again from the underside of the ship, and the cameras swung wildly, away from Blue's face, to record it. Then the beam winked out, leaving several silhouetted figures standing beneath the craft. The lens zoomed in on one of the faces, blurred and then snapped into sharp focus.

The screen showed a smooth and bulbous head, the eyes its overwhelming feature. They were two huge, slanted pools of solid, inky black.

26

Shift Hits the Fan

This is simply incredible! I have never seen anything like it!" the reporter stammered.

"What *are* those things?" Amber's mother screeched.

"Zeta Reticuli," Amber answered. "Also known as the Grays."

The creatures stepped from beneath the craft and began walking toward the White House. There was one tall one with long, thin limbs, and three smaller types, about four feet high. All wore jumpsuits of the same color and markings as Blue's.

Although everyone watching had seen these extraterrestrials in drawings, movies, and even greeting cards, there was no denying that these were the real thing. It evoked a visceral feeling, causing unbidden goosebumps as they strutted across the lawn, their stiff, jerky movements recalling a group of grasshoppers or praying mantis.

"It just...can't be!" Amber's father exclaimed, repeating his wife's earlier sentiment. Amber was certain she could hear the crashing of belief systems all over the country.

Even the normally loquacious reporters were stunned into silence, broken only by outbursts of disbelief. At the aliens' approach, the circle of Secret Service backed away and several reached under their jackets.

"No firearms!" the president shouted, his voice carrying clearly without amplification.

The Grays advanced, seeming not to notice the commotion they were causing. The people surrounding the president took a step backward as the odd squad marched up the steps.

"Damn, I'm glad you didn't fall in love with one of them!" Krystalee yelped.

"I heard *that*," Amber agreed.

The tall alien stopped next to Blue and the three smaller ones formed a line in front of it. "The Grays usually communicate telepathically, and they request that I act as their translator," Blue explained. He looked at the tall one for a long moment.

"First, our race greets your race," Blue recited. "We have anticipated this opportunity for a long time, and intend only for both races to benefit by this meeting. We would also like to apologize for any psychological harm done to the people we have examined and experimented with over the last five decades. However, we would like to point out that it was never our original intention to build a relationship with humans in this secretive fashion.

"The crash of a Zeta telemeter transport in 1947 was a planned mission. It seemed logical that such a spectacular discovery would lead to widespread belief in our existence, and the first step toward interaction would be taken. The reaction of the governing rulers was unanticipated; their desire to deny the incident and exploit the captured technology was in direct opposition to the purpose of our visit. Humans were deemed too primitive, limited and warlike to be safely approached as a population. We were therefore forced to conduct our research in such a way that it is often interpreted as abduction."

Blue went on without pausing for reaction. "Events on your world have reached critical mass. Your civilization will not survive much longer without our help. Our goal was to wait until human consciousness had developed sufficiently to grasp these truths, but the planet has run out of time. We join you in the hope of a positive experience during the coming transformation."

Blue glanced at the tall Gray, then turned back to the microphones. "That is all they have to say at this time. Thank you."

The crowd on the scene exploded in noisy chatter as Blue and the Grays conferred briefly with the president and his knot of aides, then disappeared with them inside the White House.

"David, I'm basically at a loss for words here," said reporter Jones. "You all just saw what I did, and I'm sure you're struggling to digest it, too. I'm shaking all over!"

"Laura, we'll all stunned here as well. Either this is the most elaborately-staged hoax I've ever seen, or the most significant event of the entire century."

For the next fifteen minutes it was journalistic chaos. Reactions were recorded and wild speculations were proposed. Camera crews swarmed around the ship, and some people even dared to touch it. The seemingly irrefutable evidence of extraterrestrial life was delivering a severe hammer blow to the national psyche.

Things were no less frenzied in the Voss living room. Her parents were in shock, and Amber and her girlfriends were only beginning to sense that life would never be the same again. Then there were some unsettling nuggets that had been dropped during Blue's speech, phrases such as "nuclear explosions," and getting whipped by the photon belt, not to mention the mind-numbing appearance of humanoid creatures that looked like they were made of gray leather.

Finally Quinn stood up and said, "Looks like the show's over; I better get over to Darryl's. If he thinks he's wiggin' now, wait til he hears I know the Martian dude."

After Quinn left, Krystalee called Dab and was not surprised to hear he'd probably be up all night. She told him she'd be at Amber's and to come over whenever he could. As soon as she hung up, the phone rang again and she snatched it up, thinking he'd forgotten something and called back.

Krystalee came into the living room, her eyes wide. "Amber, the phone's for you," she reported. "The chick says it's the White House calling."

Amber's parents exchanged startled looks. Amber broke into a grin and sprinted for the phone. "Hi, sweetheart!" she squealed into the receiver.

"Is this Amber Voss Robinson?" a woman's voice asked.

"Yes it is."

"One moment, please."

There was a series of clicks and then Blue's voice tingled into her ear. "Amber? Are you there, darling?"

"Yeah! Damn, it's good to hear your voice."

"Guess where I'm calling from. The president is just the nicest guy! How did it look? Was everyone watching?" he asked excitedly, words spilling out in a torrent.

"Are you kidding me? There was nothing else on! By the way, thanks for the warning."

"I had to abandon the Cape Canaveral site when they canceled the shuttle launch," he explained. "Then I just got sick of waiting and decided to use the cheesiest, most obvious gambit in the world, at least in the world of alien movies."

"Well, it was a very convincing special effect."

"Good! How's the fallout?"

"Pretty intense. My Mom and Dad are floored, and the media's having a field day. I bet the people who've been abducted are absolutely wallowing in vindication!"

"Wait until certain sections of the military are called to explain the cover-up. There are already some very nervous thoughts floating around over here."

"Hey, be careful what you say into these phones. Everything that happens in that place is on tape," she said.

"Then I won't be able to say what I want to you, because it would definitely be x-rated and cause your parents grave embarrassment when it came out in the press."

Amber's body shivered pleasurably. "Please say you're coming home tonight to tell me in the flesh."

"As soon as possible, but probably not before sunrise. There is much to discuss. Then I'll turn the operation over to the Grays for a few days and get back to the things that are most important to me."

"Such as?"

"Such as pampering you with anything you desire for the rest of our honeymoon."

"Now you're talking my language," Amber sighed. "I'm proud of you, baby. But come home soon, okay?"

"I will. I love you."

Amber murmured mushy declarations to him, too, then hung up with a love-struck grin.

"So that was the White House?" her father asked skeptically when she returned to the living room.

Amber nodded. "I think I'm in shock."

"I know I am," her mother added. "How could you marry someone I've never even been introduced to?"

"Don't worry, you're going to find out more than you want to know about him before these reporters are through," Dad said, turning back to the endless TV coverage.

Finally Krystalee and Amber left her parents to ponder the new universe and drove separately to Amber's house. They proceeded to raid the liquor cabinet and killed half a bottle of coffee liqueur while they sat up and talked about the evening's amazing events—along with everyone else on television. It was two in the morning when they finally unfolded the couch into Krystalee's bed and fell into an exhausted sleep.

Amber awoke the next morning with a familiar ache in her low back and a rumbling in her gut. She jumped up and ran to the bathroom, mumbling curses to herself. When she emerged again she found Krystalee already sitting up in bed reading the paper and watching CNN. "This is typical," Amber complained, flopping down beside her. "It's the end of the world as we know it and I'm on the frickin' rag!"

"Never fails," Krystalee agreed. "Just when you need it to cramp your style."

"Oh well, at least I know I'm not pregnant."

"Little Martian spawn? And you as the den mother? That's a scary thought!"

"No doubt. But Blue says he can keep me from conceiving with his mind."

Krystalee burst out laughing, but quickly stopped when a loud series of knocks erupted on the front door. The two women looked at each other in surprise.

Krystalee jumped up. "Let me get it," she whispered. "It has to be Dab. Who else would be knocking at 7:30 in the morning?"

Amber heard Krystalee open the door and say, "Oh! You're not my boyfriend!"

A deep, male voice answered, "You the Martian's wife?"

Amber's skin crawled. Something about that voice filled her with fear.

"Who wants to know?" Krystalee sassed. Amber prayed she would not be called to the door.

There was a pause, then Krystalee's voice spoke again, in a more subdued tone. "Those badges sure look real."

"Is your name Amber?" the man's voice demanded.

"No! I'm the house-sitter, that's all. You know, I feed the fish, bring in the paper and stuff. Amber's on her honeymoon, that's all I know. And hey, her husband may be a little weird, but calling him Martian is a bit of a stretch." She laughed unconvincingly.

"We heard voices inside," another man said in a sinister whine.

"Yeah, the television. In case you guys hadn't heard, the little gray men landed last night. It's all over the news."

Amber tried not to breathe, hoping they wouldn't hear her heart pounding.

"I've got ID," Krystalee offered. "Driver's license, social security number, tons of credit cards."

"We know who you are, Ms. Collins," came the reply. "This Toyota parked outside. That belongs to Ms. Voss, doesn't it?"

"Well, sure. Do you think she's going to drive on her honeymoon! Her husband is too gallant for that."

"Just how closely do you know her husband?"

"Not at all! I mean, it was a totally whirlwind romance. I barely met the guy and they were married and gone."

"Yeah, right," the tenor said. "Here's my card. Would you please pass it along when your girlfriend gets back?"

Krystalee swore up and down that she'd deliver the message. Then Amber heard her lock the screen and dead bolt the front door.

She hurried into the living room and scooted to the front window, looking out through the part in the curtains. When she'd seen the men get in their car and drive down the street, she came over and collapsed on the bed.

"How'd I do? Think they suspected?" Krystalee gasped.

"Who knows? I didn't like the sound of that at all!"

"Me neither. They were real FBI, Amber. Wonder what they wanted with *you*?"

"I don't know, but thanks for saying I wasn't here. Every instinct tells me they're not here to be my friends."

"They definitely had a very weird vibe," Krystalee testified.

"I wish Blue would get here."

"Me, too, meanwhile I'm starving and coffee's ready. Want some eggs?" Krystalee went to the kitchen and assembled a gourmet breakfast. Just as they finished there was another loud rap on the door.

"Let me go again," Krystalee said softly, and Amber nodded. When she reached the door she yelled, "Who is it?"

"Me, the roving reporter. I have a few survey questions to ask."

Amber heard her yank open the door. "So ask me," she challenged.

"Madam, is your husband at home?"

Krystalee giggled and drawled, "Why no, he'll be gone all day long." There were sounds of kissing in the hallway.

Dab and Krystalee came into the kitchen, showing definite signs of cupid's assault.

"Quite a show last night, wasn't it?" he asked. "I thought you'd be in D.C. by now."

"No, Blue wants to keep me out of this. He's coming back here sometime today."

"Yeah, I can understand why," Dab replied, untangling himself from Krystalee. "He probably figured it wasn't safe in Washington. That hurricane's heading north; already starting to affect Florida."

"The poor country's getting it on both coasts," Amber said.

"You got that right. On top of the volcano, there's another hurricane organizing in the Pacific, moving towards Baja California," Dab reported. "Get this, they're predicting it could hit southern Arizona."

"What? A hurricane here?" Krystalee exploded.

"Just when I was feeling landlocked and safe! Maybe it is the end of the world," Amber said.

"Maybe it is!" Krystalee said. "The men in black just came by." She proceeded to tell him about the men with badges.

Dab frowned. "This is not exactly a positive development. This morning the president demanded that all UFO documents be declassified and the intelligence community is having a fit. They might be willing to do lots of things to keep more information from leaking out, maybe even use Amber to silence Blue."

"But that's insane! The cat's out of the bag now and they can't turn back time and make everybody not see the aliens strolling through the rose garden," Krystalee pointed out.

"With these guys their secrets are their power, and they've been protecting them with intimidation for a long time," Dab said. "What do you think, they came here to welcome Amber to Project Bluebook?"

"Oh Lord, this is just getting too complex!" Amber complained. "I wish that man would get his butt out of the Lincoln Bedroom and come home."

"I'm actually surprised the place isn't surrounded by reporters already," Dab commented, walking to the living room windows to peer through the curtains. "Probably the locals haven't linked you to this as quick as the FBI did."

"I'm thinking we should resume our honeymoon somewhere far, far away," Amber said.

"Hey! Do the men in black travel in a white truck?" Dab asked, turning from the window to look at her.

Amber jumped up, responding in color. "Blue!"

27

Earth Irked

If the bad guys had been waiting outside, Amber would have been snatched and spirited away in a heartbeat. She flung open the front door and sprinted across the lawn without hesitation. Blue was already out of the truck and trotting toward her, still dressed in his jumpsuit.

Amber leaped into his arms and they smothered each other with kisses. "Oh, baby, you're a star!" she declared.

"Yeah? Everybody liked it?" he laughed, lowering her to the ground. "Nobody seems to be running around screaming."

"That's because they're still numb," Amber said. "Come on, let's get inside."

Dab was standing on the front stoop, watching Blue approach as if he were walking on water. "Hey, Blue. Loved the show last night."

"Good!" Blue gave him a hearty double handshake. "I thought it was kind of fun myself. But how did the press find out when I'd be arriving here?"

"I could lie and say journalist's intuition, but it was actually sheer luck that I'm here," Dab said with a side glance at Krystalee.

"Krystalee kept me company last night," Amber explained. "Actually, I think he was coming over to see *her*."

Krystalee smirked happily.

"But what incredible timing," Dab added, following them inside. "I've been wanting to ask you a gigantic favor."

"Well, they already asked me quite a few questions at the White House last night," Blue said with a weary chuckle.

"Sure, but this will be really different, an in-depth interview from the people's point of view. No government slant."

"What is your opinion of the people's reaction to the unveiling of a new reality?" Blue asked.

"I'd say most people are still in shock, and amazed that the world still looks the same this morning. We all feel a big change in the air."

"Then I haven't created a gigantic public panic, as the authorities have always feared?"

"Ha! Far from it," Dab snorted. "Politicians always treat their citizens like a bunch of mindless lemmings, but at least in this case I think the people are open to it, prepared, and a lot of us are excited as hell."

"Excellent!" Blue said. "I must admit I have been underestimating the intelligence and imagination of the American public."

"They're way more scared of the way nature is battering both coasts," Krystalee commented. "It's Mother Nature attacking, not the Martians. Like the Weather Channel is only showing disaster movies."

"Let's see what the latest is." Amber went into the living room and switched on the TV, clicking to the news network. The program in progress was a panel of people debating the stunning revelations of ET presence.

"...their ship touches down and the president runs out like a kid collecting autographs. Maybe he's too young, brought up on TV-sanitized aliens, so he assumes they are benign playmates. Is it a coincidence that they arrive during the worst natural disasters of the twentieth century? No, it's a show of force, a not-so-subtle message that we'd better adopt their radical environmental proposals or else," a gray-haired man declared.

"Are you trying to say the aliens are here to overpower us?" asked the mediator.

"Well, it doesn't look like they're here to deliver fruit baskets," the man replied. "They've dealt a severe blow to the northwest already, now we've got this windstorm chewing up the east coast, and another hurricane approaching from the south. How they're causing this, I don't know, but judging from their spacecraft, their technology appears to be superior to ours. So far."

"What do you mean by that?" asked a young woman from the other end of the table.

"I simply mean that if they wander from suggestions into threats, we may be forced to pit our technology against theirs."

"Our technology? As in, our weapons?" someone else queried.

"Well, I don't mean our all-star basketball team."

"This is crazy!" Blue exploded. "They're totally missing the point!"

"Honey, those guys get paid just to flap their lips," Amber said. "Let's check out the Weather Channel."

A new picture popped on the screen, angry red and swirling. "...forces unbelievably strong and organized. This storm has broken every record in terms of velocity, and now that it has made landfall in southern Florida, we are certain it will break damage records as well. Once again, Hurricane Harold has become a category five-plus storm, currently devastating Florida with gusts over two hundred miles an hour and heading north at almost fifty miles per hour. We have some chilling footage taken by a recovered surveillance camera at Disney World."

The film showed Epcot's signature, globe-like pavilion, surrounded by flying debris and bent-over palm trees. Then the structure shuddered, wobbled, and began to roll away like an errant silver golfball before it shattered into pieces and was scattered into the tumultuous wind.

"Wow, Mother Nature destroys the Magic Kingdom! That's way worse than aliens invading the White House!" Krystalee exclaimed.

"Incredibly, another storm of slightly less intensity, Hurricane Lennox, is threatening the United States from a southwesterly direction," the commentator continued. "Already it has caused widespread damage in Baja California and northern Mexico, and is currently threatening the southern United States. Hurricane and flood watches are in effect in Arizona and New Mexico..."

"My God, I thought we'd at least be safe from a hurricane in Arizona!" Amber cried, then changed the channel.

A man at a pulpit was screaming and gesturing with both arms. "...beginning of the end! Read Revelation, people, it's all there! Plagues will be visited upon the Earth and Babylon will fall, Amen! The rider on the white horse has descended! Everybody say...."

Amber cut him off in mid-rant. "Guess you did shake up a few people," she said.

"And many seem to be interpreting it in a manner I hadn't anticipated at all."

"Listen Blue, why don't you come on down to my office and we'll set the record straight," Dab suggested. "I will guarantee I can get your real views out to the world. The misunderstandings are already rampant."

Blue thought for a second. "All right, but Amber does not leave my side. New rule."

"You're the boss," Dab said with a grin. "Krystalee can go with me and you guys follow in your truck."

When they marched into the building that housed the newspaper's offices, everyone they passed stared in slack-jawed wonder. The biggest news event of the century had just unfolded on their monitors, and now the central figure in the drama was walking right past them, arm-and-arm with an auburn-haired woman. By the time their little parade reached Dab's cubicle they were being followed by a horde of people with cameras and notepads.

Two men rushed up and ushered them into a paneled conference room whose walls were mostly glass. The space filled rapidly, leaving the rest of the curious to crowd around the outside to watch.

Dab seated Blue and Amber next to him, then threw a tiny tape recorder out on the polished tabletop. "First interview with a Martian," he intoned into the machine, "by Dabney J. Mitchell. The paparazzi may barrage me at any time. My guest is an extremely unique personality, so let me first ask this question: Blue Robinson, who are you and why are you here?"

"I am a refugee of the planet Mars," Blue began. "My ancestors were forced to leave my world when a natural disaster rendered it unlivable. There are still underground colonies of survivors on the planet Mars, as well as Earth's moon, but in my particular case I was unable to make a choice of destination. I was just a tube of green protoplasm when I first arrived on this planet."

"Okay, wait a minute, wait a minute," Dab broke in, shaking his head. "Are you saying there are Martians still on Mars, on the moon, and on the Earth itself?"

"Yes. There's even a group of Martians in South America that live on the surface, as a so-called primitive tribe, so remote that only a few have noticed how different they are."

"Aren't you afraid you're blowing their cover?" Dab asked.

"No. Fear does not figure into the mission."

"And that would be...?" one of the other reporters asked.

"To prevent Earth from experiencing the same trauma that has fractured Mars's culture. Planetary relocation is not assimilated as easily as you might think, and we would like to prevent the necessity of a full-scale evacuation."

"You don't seem any worse for the wear," one of the older men spoke up.

"That's because I was actually born here on Earth. Any knowledge I have of other cultures is strictly cerebral," he answered.

"But Blue, you married an Earthling," Dab pointed out. "Within a week of meeting her. How did you know, given that you'd never met any before, that this was an Earthling you could spend your life with?"

"It's just a feeling, and you know it. Like the world was black-and-white before, and then when she's with you, it's full color."

"Please excuse me while I puke on my shoes," Dab choked, "but every guy says that when they first fall in love. Then later, reality sets in."

Krystalee harrumphed quietly in the background.

"Well, that's not going to happen this time," Blue replied. "Amber and I are going to create a different level of reality."

Amber smiled and squeezed his hand.

"Well, that's a lovely sentiment," Dab said. "But let's get back to something more newsworthy. Now, tell us more about this mysterious photon band."

"Mysterious is not really an accurate description of it. An Earth scientist named Halley noticed it in the early part of the eighteenth century, and in 1961 it was 'discovered' by others through the use of satellites. It is simply a cylindrical-shaped region where antielectrons, or positrons, collide with electrons, thereby destroying themselves and releasing photon energy."

"Are you sure planet Earth will intersect with this field?" Dab asked.

"If the photon band were a doughnut, our entire solar system would be about the size of a large chocolate sprinkle. We're not going to miss it. When we first enter the null zone, which is like the rind or skin of the band, there will be a three-day period of darkness. During this time, electrical appliances will cease functioning."

"That could cause a little bit of chaos," Dab allowed. "And then will the electricity come back on?"

"No. Then your world will begin switching to another power source, photon energy."

"Uh-huh. As in photon torpedoes."

"Absolutely not. In the new age people will recognize the futility of winning through destruction."

"What about the destruction the Earth is turning on itself?" a woman asked. "The Seattle tragedy, and now these killer hurricanes. What do the Martians know about that?"

"The destruction is turned toward human beings, not toward the Earth itself. The planet seeks balance, at whatever cost," Blue explained. "Extraterrestrials are not manipulating your weather, though several governments here have investigated that possibility in their weapons programs."

"That's interesting," Dab commented. "But is there anything people can do now, to prevent more of this? Or is the Earth just so pissed that it's too late?"

"Humans need to recognize that the evolution of the universe, as well as their own personal growth, is heading toward the light, toward spiritual completion. No matter how dire their situation seems, everything proceeds ultimately to reunion with Prime Creator, which is light and love itself. So-called death is only a doorway, another step in the soul's journey. Each one will experience this and know it as irrefutable truth."

"Okay, but does it have to be right this minute?" Dab asked.

"No. Something else humans must realize is the power that lies in collective consciousness. You've heard of the hundredth monkey theory?"

"Uh, not lately."

"One monkey on an island begins washing its food before eating, and soon the whole troupe is imitating the same behavior. Let's say ninety-nine monkeys are washing their fruit, then another joins in, making it a hundred. In any case, critical mass is reached, and suddenly monkeys on neighboring islands, completely isolated from the original group, start washing their food, too! Somehow they access the collective mind, and the new notion spreads.

"In the same way, people need to radiate the energy of love for each other, for Mother Earth, and for the entire cosmos. The individual thinks itself powerless, but each one who chooses love over hate, fun over the gun, gets us that much closer to a cosmic mind full of positive thoughts," Blue concluded.

"Fun over the gun? That's a good sound-bite," Dab said. "But with so much violence and wars and crimes these days, doesn't it seem pretty unlikely?"

"Not really. Negative and positive energies are simply becoming more polarized. People focus on the activities of the dark forces, but there has also been quite an increase in the forces of light. This choosing of sides, along with intensified weather and geologic events, has been predicted by many cultures as signs of the end times."

"I don't like it when you use that word," Amber interjected.

"Yeah, explain that," Dab said.

"I just mean that the accepted view of the world is changing, and will never be the same."

"Didn't that just happen last night, at approximately 9:42?"

A young man opened the conference room door with an alert. "TV news crew just pulled up to the curb. Guess somebody made a phone call."

"Oh, no they don't!" Dab exclaimed, jumping up from his chair. "How is this going to be an exclusive interview if he's plastered all over the tube? Come on, Blue."

Dab snatched up the tape recorder and grabbed Blue by the arm, hustling him out the door before anybody could protest. Amber and Krystalee hurried behind as Dab led them through a door and into a supply room. "The freight elevator's in here. We'll sneak out the back and take off in one of the vans."

"Dab, I'll have to give them a press conference sometime," Blue pointed out.

"That's fine, just do it tomorrow. Let me have my fifteen minutes of fame."

When they reached ground level Dab quickly lined up a driver and a van and they all piled into the windowless back end and sat on the floor. For the next hour and a half they drove around town while Dab served an endless supply of questions and a take-out lunch. At last Blue had enough and declared an end to the interview, but Dab managed to weasel a promise out of him to do a part two sequel in the near future.

"I'll get the truck later," Blue said, "but right now I just want to go...be alone with my wife."

"But where are we going to go? I'm afraid those cops might come back to my house," said Amber.

"What cops?" Blue asked, and they told him what had happened.

"Go over to Quinn's," suggested Krystalee. "She spends most of her time at the gym or Darryl's anyway."

Amber used the cell phone in the van to call Quinn. She was about to go meet a client but offered to leave a key hidden outside. "I swear, some of these gym rats are hard core! Not even aliens landing is gonna keep this guy away from the iron," she chuckled. "Now you know where the guest bedroom is, and the linens are in the hall closet."

"Thanks, but it's the middle of the afternoon. I doubt if we're going to sleep."

"Who said anything about sleeping? I know you better than that! Have fun and I'll see you in a couple hours."

Amber hung up, shaking her head. "Now why do you suppose she would automatically assume we'd jump straight into bed?"

Blue gave her a look that made her shiver from head to toes and drew several snickers from Krystalee.

When they pulled up in front of Quinn's house, the neighborhood seemed quiet and peaceful, almost abandoned. No strange cars or people were lurking anywhere in sight, and even at this time of year everyone had their windows closed with the air conditioning running.

They thanked Dab and said good-bye to Krystalee, then walked up to the front door. The key was in its hiding place, and Amber sighed with relief as they came in out of the sun into Quinn's cool living room.

The first thing they did was reacquaint themselves with each other's lips. "I missed you last night," Blue said. "Promise me we won't spend another night apart."

"I promise, I promise! Hey, you're the one always running off to hang out with the president or something."

"Well, from now on we're going places together," he stated.

"That sounds excellent," she agreed. "But before we get anywhere near the bed, I have to tell you something. I'm having my period."

Blue looked at her quizzically.

"Menstrual period?" she prompted. "That monthly thing Earth females go through?"

His eyes widened. "Oh! You mean the expelling of the uterine contents that coincides with the cycles of the moon?"

She nodded. "That's one way of putting it."

"That's great! That's wonderful! What an opportunity!"

"I'm happy I'm not pregnant, too, but don't go overboard."

"No, not that. I knew you couldn't get pregnant unless we both allowed it. But to experience sexual love when you are in the height of goddess power, the mixing of the red blood and the white semen, that is extremely potent!"

Amber couldn't help laughing. "People from Mars sure say the funniest things. Don't you know this is *The Curse*? You're supposed to run away screaming or send me to the menstruation hut."

"It's a blessing, not a curse," he insisted. "Now we will be truly, energetically joined, for all eternity."

"You mean like blood brothers?" She laughed and they both ascended the stairs to Quinn's loft.

28

Wild Blue Yonder

Honey, no way! Look at this white carpet," said Amber as they entered Quinn's guest room.

But Blue wasn't looking at the floor, he was mesmerized by the native art that covered the walls and decorated every surface. There were paintings, masks and carvings, many from Africa but also some from Australia, Haiti, and the indigenous tribes of North America.

"I feel the presence, the vibrations, of these ancient traditions," he announced.

"Yeah, it's a beautiful room," Amber agreed. "Notice the black-and-white color scheme. I'm not so sure we should add big blotches of red."

"The Aborigines travel the outback with practically nothing except the skins they sleep on, but their medicine woman carries a circular tube filled with the tissue passed and collected by the females during their cycles."

"Yuck," Amber commented, wrinkling her nose.

"On the contrary, the substance is quite wonderful. It's used to perform miraculous healings, like fixing a broken bone overnight."

"You mean setting a bone overnight, don't you?"

"No, I mean healing it," Blue said, sliding his arms around her. "So much knowledge has been lost since the world got civilized."

"Okay, but I don't think Quinn wants us to revive it in her bedroom. If we make love in here, it may end up looking like we were doing animal sacrifices."

"Can't we put something underneath us?" he asked.

Amber couldn't help smiling. *Ah, there's no aphrodisiac like a man's sincere desire,* she thought, feeling the prickles of budding excitement. "Okay, but we have to be careful."

"No problema," Blue answered and began to lower the bamboo blinds to shut out the sun. Amber tore her eyes from him long enough to go to the hall closet and search for appropriate bedding.

When she came back he was reclining on the bed, completely nude. He'd found two thick candles, each planted in a tribal bowl, and they cast a primeval glow on the masks and statues. The tantalizing vision of his naked body in the flickering light ratcheted Amber's heartbeat up another feverish notch.

She threw a big, purple beach towel on the bed, stacked several smaller towels on the nightstand, then sent her clothes tumbling to the floor while Blue watched hungrily. Then she crawled across purple terrycloth and slid against him with a lusty sigh.

His arms clutched her tightly while he nuzzled her face with his lips. She petted his flesh wherever she could reach, riding down the smooth curve of his butt, then sliding up his rib cage and bumping her fingertips over the tiny knob of his nipple. Her hands were like vacuum cleaners, sucking up the sensations of his skin to fuel her growing arousal.

They kissed, slowly and tenderly at first, then hotter and heavier as their pulses raced and their fingers gripped each other urgently.

"Now, let's be still and feel our energy," Blue said, leaving her mouth to rest his face in her hair.

"Well, I'll try," Amber promised. With enormous will she halted her roaming hands and lay still against him. She felt his heart slamming against her right breast and heard her own drumming loudly into her skull. Within a minute or two their combined energy fields were easily detectable as a fierce tingling that almost seemed to hum.

Soon it was impossible for her not to move, and she began rocking her pelvis softly against him and moaning from the sheer pleasure of his proximity. He sighed as she nibbled his neck, then slid her tongue down and across his collarbone.

Amber raked her lips across his chest, intending to suck those twin ornaments as if indigo nipples were going out of style. Then suddenly she jerked her head back, exclaiming, "Oh, my God!"

"What happened?" he asked, his voice tinged with alarm.

"Baby, you're...growing hair!"

They both looked down in amazement at a tiny patch of peachfuzz sprouting over his sternum, so small and fine she probably wouldn't have noticed if it hadn't tickled her nose.

"It's another sign," he said. "I'm becoming more human, and you're becoming more Martian."

"Oh, great, we really are mutating?"

"No, think of it as transforming. Like the wormy caterpillar turning into a butterfly." He pushed her gently onto her back. "Now let's seek that third energy, the new dimension we create when we join in the physical."

He drew her legs apart so he could kneel between them. Amber lay exposed in an attitude of total surrender, exquisitely aware of his caressing stare and the looming nearness of his fully swollen phallus.

"I know I've seen these advertised on TV," he said, fingering the string between her lower lips, "but I'm not sure how they work."

"Well, it's not rocket science," she giggled. "The cork absorbs the liquid, and then you yank it out and throw it away. Simple as that."

"You don't dilute it in water to put on your plants?" he asked in all seriousness.

"Not without the approval of the coven," Amber laughed. "What exactly have you been studying down in those caves?"

"It's not witchcraft, just universal truth," he countered, reaching up to comb his fingers through the hair on her pubic mound. He let his fingers skitter across her most sensitive spots while she melted and moaned. With the other hand he gave a soft tug on the string.

Amber felt the tampon slide easily out of her burgeoning wide-on. "No, don't take it out now," she protested feebly. "I'll be gushing in two minutes."

"Excellent," he replied. "That's exactly the idea." He pulled it all the way out and laid it reverently in a small tray on the nightstand as if it were a precious jewel. Then he went to the artifact-covered wall and removed a large rattle, apparently made from a gourd and decorated with leatherwork and feathers. Blue held it aloft and began to beat a rhythm into the air.

He resumed his kneeling posture on the bed, caressing Amber's anatomy with one hand while shaking the rattle with the other. Soon he added a chant, a monotonal singsong that must have been a Martian incantation. She didn't understand a word, but it was definitely having an effect.

The exotic beauty of Blue was causing sensory overload in Amber's body, mind and spirit. Either she was hallucinating, or actually seeing energy flares erupting like sunspots from the edges of her agitated aura.

"It flows," Blue announced softly, continuing to rattle out a rhythm while he bent over her. Amber flinched with desire at his touch, arching her back as his fingers parted her labia.

He sat up and smeared a dot of her blood on the back of his neck, then one behind each ear. "Now the information in your DNA will be absorbed by mine," he explained, as if this statement were completely logical.

Amber gasped, watching streaks of gold, pink and green flashed through the energy field around his head. Then she gasped again as he dipped into her juices, closed his eyes, and slid his fingers into his mouth.

Martians never cease to amaze me, Amber thought with delight. But when he started to lower his face between her legs, she reached down to grasp him under the arms and urged him on top of her.

"I need your mouth up here," she told him as he glided up her body, planting a kiss every two inches. His tongue slithered between her lips at the same time his erection slished easily inside her.

Amber moaned as the sweet rush of penetration swept through her. She locked her arms across his back, love and gratitude filling her along with his cock.

The rattle fell from his hand and tumbled to the carpet with a last, muffled shake. He used his hips to keep the rhythm going, banging the drum of her pubic bone, his blue eyes wide and wild.

Amber was almost sorry when she detected the building energy of climax. It was just too soon; she wanted to stay connected with him forever. But there was no delaying this orgasm. It zinged up and detonated, making a sound like a bursting melon in her ears and hurling her body into a meteor shower of spasms.

She lay drained and limp when it was finally over, eyes sealed shut. Her heartbeat hammered in her head, and she could feel it pounding in her chest. She wondered briefly why Blue was so still, then reasoned he must have come at the same time and be slumped on top of her. Strangely, though, she had no sensation of his weight at all. The only physical input still registering was the consistent pace of her heart, sounding each beat with a hollow thud.

Blue must have found a drum, occurred to her brain. The more she listened to it, the more she realized it must be drumbeats; she could almost sense the hands hitting the stretched skins. She struggled to open her eyes, but it was if trying to come awake from a deep dream. She tried to speak, but no sound emerged. Then she called to him telepathically, edging toward panic as nothing seemed to awaken her body.

The drumming continued, louder and nearer. Suddenly her eyelids released, and were immediately forced shut again by the brightness of the scene. She squinted, and was amazed to see that she was lying under a tree in a vast forest, a shaft of sunlight blasting her in the face.

Amber sat up slowly and surveyed her surroundings. On all sides was a tangle of green in different shades and shapes, thronging around the massive tree trunks that stretched up into the blue overhead. Exotic whistles and squawks echoed from unseen birds in the branches. *Damn, we really tore up the space-time continuum this time!*

Then she looked down at her own body, and her heart leaped into her throat. She was naked from the waist up, but there was no sign of her pert little peaks. Instead her chest was flat and carpeted with wiry fur. She lifted her hands; they were huge, square and hairy, with nails that looked more like hardened claws. Her bare feet were the hoofs of an animal used to walking on rock, calloused and thick.

Her heart keeping tempo with the drumbeats, Amber looked down at her lap. It was covered in a crude loincloth made out of something that might have been leather or some kind of bark. She picked up the edge of it with her hoary fingers and flung it back.

There, in terrifying Technicolor, rising from a dense thicket of pubic hair and lolling across her thigh like a sleepy sea monster, was her very own penis.

29

Hungry in the Jungle

Amber threw the loincloth back over herself and scrambled to her feet, attempting to scream. Instead her ears were split by a raspy bellowing, more like the sound of a wounded boar. There was no doubt left; she had become a man.

Panicked, she pushed a shock of long hair out of her face and looked around. What if Blue hadn't come through with her? What if she was caught in another dimension all by herself and would never be able to figure out how to get back?

"Don't worry, I'm with you," his voice sounded in her head, instantly soothing her.

"Thank God," she thought, "but where are you?"

A twig snapped behind her and Amber whirled around. A small, female figure stepped into the clearing, beaming an amused smile. She was clothed in similar fashion, and her long, blonde hair cascaded over her shoulders and across her bare breasts. As Amber stared she was dismayed to feel her sea monster springing to life.

"Blue?" she called telepathically. "If that's you, I think we just switched genders!"

"Apparently so," said his voice, and the girl took a few steps closer.

"We've really gone far away this time! It's got to be prehistoric, this jungle. I mean, it's huge, and look at us— we're cavepeople! What if we get eaten by a dinosaur? Or attacked by a tribe of drum-playing cannibals?"

"Come here, honey." The young woman dropped the flowers she'd been carrying as she walked to Amber and embraced her.

Amber hugged back, watching in amazement as her heavilymuscled arms clutched Blue to her broad chest. She was so much taller, he could rest his head in her chest hair.

"Don't be afraid," his voice said. "This is another message we are being given, and we must use the opportunity to find out what it means. Fear cannot be allowed to take root in our hearts. When you hear it calling, bless it and send it on its way."

Fear was quickly being replaced with another sharp emotion as Amber pressed Blue against her naked torso. "This is so weird, being on the other side. And you damn sure make a sexy woman!"

The blonde girl giggled and blushed. "Amber, of course I'm attracted to you, too, but we can't do this right now. Put that thing away."

"Hey, it does whatever it wants, don't you remember?" she said, but lowered her hand to push his hips in tight against hers.

The woman raised her face and the man bent to kiss her, their excitement growing as their hands shamelessly caressed each other's new form. The intense pangs of pleasure emanating from Amber's penis, which by now was raging against the loincloth like an angry brontosaurus, were driving everything else from her consciousness.

Blue wriggled away, laughing like high-pitched windchimes. "Come on, we can play with our vehicles later. Let's go explore and discover why we were sent here."

The woman marched into the forest, away from the sound of the drums, and there wasn't anything Amber could do except bob after her.

"What are we looking for?" she asked, trying to restrain the awkward appendage flapping in front of her as she trotted.

"I don't know, but we'll recognize it when we see it."

Blue found a narrow footpath and they followed it to the banks of a swiftly-flowing stream. They drank from the clear water, then continued to follow its downhill course. As time passed and no prehistoric creatures attacked, Amber relaxed and began to enjoy the journey. With the sun streaking through the tree tops, the energetic tingle of using strong muscles, and Blue's twitching butt filling her vision, being a caveman was starting to have its advantages. The day was warm and inviting, and these woods were fairy-tale beautiful. Amber only hoped they would stay in this serene dimension long enough to try out her new anatomy on her prehistoric partner.

Eventually the sound of the drums faded and the peace of the jungle was restored, broken only by their footfalls and the occasional call of a bird. Then they began to hear a soft rustling in the distance, its volume increasing with every step they took toward it.

"Waterfall," Blue's voice announced, and the blonde woman halted and turned with a smile. "Maybe from the cliff we'll be able to see where we are." Without waiting for an answer, she whirled and hurried in the direction of the hissing water.

Amber put her powerful thighs in gear and loped after the trotting bushwoman, determined to keep close together. The rustle became a roar, growing until it filled the ears and blotted out awareness of anything else. Then suddenly they stepped through the underbrush and out onto a wide slab of flat rock, beyond whose edge a cliff dropped steeply to the valley floor, hundreds of feet down. Beside them the stream plunged over the ledge, frothing into clouds of mist on its way to a pool far below.

It seemed as if they could see forever from this vantage point, across an endless plain that stretched from horizon to horizon. Not a single man-made structure was visible.

"Wow, this sure is beautiful! I guess that cinches it," Amber concluded. "We must be at the dawn of mankind, someplace in Africa maybe."

"With skin this color? I don't think so," Blue answered. "Where's the teeming wildlife? There's only a few birds and hardly any insects. And I'm perceiving a very unsettling vibration when I look at that strange forest over there."

Amber followed the woman's slender finger which pointed to a distant collection of tall, green spires, row upon row. There was no canopy of leaves sprouting from the tops, making it look like an entire community of dead tree trunks, covered with brush and vines.

"That does look strange. What is it?"

"I think that's what we're here to find out," Blue answered. "Let's look for a way down and keep following the water."

They hunted along the top of the cliff until they discovered a section where huge boulders had poured into the valley, leaving a series of gigantic stair steps. The wiry little female didn't hesitate to begin climbing down, lowering herself carefully from rock to rock. Amber followed, trying not to look beyond the next foothold.

A robust breeze was blowing against the face of the cliff, occasionally sending sheets of waterfall mist to slicken their path, but the limbs of the male body Amber was riding in seemed sure and confident. Blue's body was apparently used to these hikes, too; he/she was leaping and prancing on the rocks like a deer. Amber was beginning to think that Blue could inhabit the body of a poisonous snake and she would still love him to death.

As they neared the bottom, Amber lowered her caveman's foot to a stony prominence, then turned and was immediately filled with an unmistakable recognition. She had been on this rock, above this pool, many times. Well, maybe not she, but the organism housing her had definitely been here before. "Blue!" she called in her mind. "Blue, I'm getting the strongest feeling that I'm supposed to jump!"

Five rocks further down, the woman stopped and looked back up at her mate, a worried frown wrinkling her forehead. "Amber, you hate heights."

"I know I do, but this dude is completely fearless!" she marveled, looking down at the point where the waterfall churned into its basin.

Blue looked down, too, then back up at Amber, who still stood poised. Then, he suddenly leaped up, throwing a fist in the air and screeching a savage war-whoop. Apparently this was a signal to the firing nerve messages in Amber's adopted body, because it launched itself into thin air with no prompting from her brain.

Totally on autopilot, Amber couldn't even command her eyes to squeeze shut. Instead she witnessed every inch of the long plunge as her body arched, stretched out legs and arms, and dived into the pool. The water erupted in bubbles around her, then she flipped expertly around and swam to the surface.

Blue was dancing and prancing, still about fifty feet up, singing aloud in whatever native tongue these vehicles possessed. Amber howled triumphantly and waved, then ducked into the water again and headed toward shore. Scanning the pebbly bottom for a secure footing, Amber's eye was distracted by a metallic glint. She scooped up the object, then pulled her hulking frame from the water, shaking spray from her long hair and laughing with the exhilaration.

"Honey, you were magnificent!" Blue enthused, hurrying to scale down the last twenty feet. Then the woman scampered over and threw her arms around her man. "You seem to be taking Rana's no fear philosophy to heart."

"Yeah! That was fun, too." Amber pulled Blue tight and kissed the top of his blonde head. "I found something on the way out." She held out her big, calloused hand, its palm containing several small pebbles and a small disk.

Blue picked it up and scratched at it with a fingernail. "It looks like an old coin. One edge is corroded, but I think there's still some detail visible." He knelt by the edge of the pond, scratching the disk and then rinsing it in the water.

"Well, that would be excellent if we can find a date on the thing," Amber reasoned. "Then we'll have a clue of what kind of corner of the space-time continuum we're in."

"There's a man's face. Look," Blue said, turning and holding it out to her.

Amber took it and scrutinized the design. "Oh my God! That's Abraham Lincoln!" she transmitted, her mind reeling. "It's a fucking penny!"

"That's impossible," Blue maintained, taking it from her and using a sharp stone to chip the crud from its face.

"If that's what I think it is," Amber speculated, "then where are we? If this is contemporary time, where in the hell can we be that's tropical and populated by primitive tribes? It just doesn't make sense!"

"Yes it does." Blue handed her the coin, its layers of decay removed so that the date was clearly legible.

"Two-zero-zero-eight," Amber repeated. "2008? You mean we're in...the future?"

Blue looked around. "Well, it's nice to know the planet survived."

"Yeah, but what about the people! I mean, look at us! Whatever happened to technology?"

"Apparently it didn't survive."

"Blue, tell me this is just one possible reality!" Amber took the coin and stared at it, frozen with disbelief. She turned it over and over with her stained, claw-tipped fingers, trying to grasp the implications of its minutely-inscribed numerals.

"I don't know for sure," he said, shaking his head so the curtain of blonde locks shimmered and fluttered. "But it certainly adds up. If something happened to Earth—a combination of catalysts, probably— and the human population were drastically reduced, we would be surprised how fast mother nature would reclaim her turf. The strange 'forest' out there is nothing more than the shell of a city, skyscrapers turned into a trellis for the conquering vines."

"A city surrounded by jungle?" Amber asked. "Are we in South America somewhere?"

"There may have been a pole shift, or maybe global warming rearranged the weather. We might still be in Arizona, after the desert turned to rainforest."

"Friends and family all gone, just you and me," Amber said.

"It would be infinitely enough for me, but what about you? Would you be too lonely?"

Amber smiled and glided to him, gathering his little female body against her large, hirsute corpus. "You gotta be kidding, baby. Never a dull moment...." She nuzzled him into a kiss, grinding her hips against him.

Blue kissed back, reaching up to wrap his arms around the neck of his partner. Then Amber scooped the girl up and grabbed her waist, raising her and aiming lips at her swaying breasts.

The male beast took over, nuzzling and suckling in a frenzy of delight. The blonde nymph that was Blue chattered and cried while surrendering her chest to the muscular caveman's attentions.

Amber's tool was already bursting, and her post-modern body was completely obsessed with finding it a snug haven. She carried Blue to a patch of moss, lowered the quivering body to its back, and tore off the flimsy material that shrouded the female crotch.

The tingling in Amber's body and the sound of the crashing waterfall melded into one irresistible pulse as her eyes perused Blue as a girl. His female vehicle lay back on the lush, living carpet. Amber's sexual fever soared into the stratosphere.

Then something jerked her vision from Blue's displayed and waiting body to the jungle background. She blinked, trying to clear away the illusion, but it was still there. A tree, a bush and a branch with hanging leaves merged into one symmetrical mandala, creating a web-shaped circle of mesmerizing, electric green.

"Blue, look at this," Amber's mind said. She tried to turn her attention from it, but the optical trick held her locked and helpless.

The woman rose up with an expression of unmasked disappointment and turned to look into the forest. "What?" Blue said at first, and then, "Oh yes. I see it, too."

Amber looked into the green vortex, all else forgotten. It was pulling her, drawing her in. Her consciousness rushed toward the void.

"No!" Blue's voice erupted, "look away!" He grabbed Amber and attempted to push her down by her broad shoulders, but her strength was far superior. Seemingly carved in stone, she sat at attention and let herself by sucked up by the strange portal.

Her awareness shot forward, leaving all bodies behind, and careened into the web of green. Vision turned black, and there was only the sensation of rushing, hurling, soaring through time and space. Then a splash into water, and a desperate struggle for air. Amber was drowning.

A keening scream perforated her eardrums, and Amber was cannonballed into awareness, flailing and coughing to clear her lungs.

"She's awake! Praise Jesus!" said a loud voice that sounded like Quinn's.

Amber's vision snapped into focus, but what she saw left her disoriented and confused. She was lying in a bathtub, her view entirely filled by the faces of Quinn and Blue.

"She's finally warming up," Quinn reported, feeling Amber's forehead.

"Hey, don't talk about me in the third person. I'm back, I'm here," Amber sputtered.

"Thank the Creator," Blue said quickly.

"Better thank me," Quinn put in. "If I hadn't shown up when I did...well, I hate to think. You scared the shit out of me, though; thought I was looking at a murder scene."

"Huh?" Amber hacked.

"Well, look at this water," Quinn advised, standing up. "This is not from pink bath beads, dear. You two were covered with blood! How was I to know it was something so mundane as going time-traveling without your feminine protection?" She pulled Amber from the tub, wrapped her in a thick towel, and Blue took over the job of rubbing her dry.

"I'm going downstairs to fix girlfriend a cup of herb tea," Quinn said to Blue, handing Amber a Tampax. "Maybe you better take a shower." She regarded his naked, blood-streaked body, then left the bathroom and went down the stairs.

After a long, relief-laden hug, Amber left Blue in the shower and met Quinn in the kitchen.

"Here, put this on," Quinn said, handing her a long terrycloth robe.

"Thanks, Quinn. I'm sorry to put you through this."

"Are you kidding? I'm just happy you're alive!" Quinn replied. "I can't get through to you on the phone all night, and I'm leaving messages and figuring you two are just on that one-track train, and then in the morning I come home, call my friggin' head off and hear no answers, come up the stairs, and *voila*! You and your husband are all sprawled out, blood everywhere, both of you with your eyes rolled up in your heads!"

"Quinn, I'm sorry! That's horrible!"

"Well, the worst was yet to come when Blue came to but you didn't. Skin all cold like a dead reptile! We threw you in a hot tub because smacking your face had no effect. Boy, that's a big surprise."

"Wait til you hear where I was. Quinn, it seemed so real!"

Quinn brought the steaming mug of tea and a jar of honey. "Drink some of this and then we'll talk reality."

"Well, it seemed real, anyway. A world not too far in the future, when all technology is lost and the people are reduced to the level of the stone age."

"That doesn't sound like much fun," Quinn observed.

"Really it was kind of cool, all gorgeous scenery and no overcrowding," Amber said. "I think if I had Blue around, I wouldn't miss anything from this world."

"I'm glad you feel that way," he said, appearing in the doorway with a towel around his waist.

Amber put down her tea and went to hug him. "Damn, I'm sure glad we're back in our own bodies."

"I don't even want to know what you mean by that," Quinn said. "I'm going to change."

"Do you have to work?" Amber asked.

"Oh no, child, nobody's working today, except on getting ready for this storm. I have to bring in the plants and patio furniture."

"Oh God, the hurricane! I forgot about that," Amber admitted.

"Well, welcome to Earth," Quinn said as she left the kitchen. "Glad to see you back, by the way. Make yourselves at home."

Amber took Blue's hand and they sat down at the kitchen table. "She sure is a great friend."

"Yes, she is. I guess you'd really miss her if we...went away?" Blue said.

"Of course I would. What do you mean? If we went away where?"

"Well, I'm thinking about the colony in the Pleiades, specifically."

"What?" Amber asked in amazement. "You mean leave the planet?"

"The surface is turning out to be more complex than I thought; I never imagined its dangers and pitfalls." He wrapped her hand in both of his. "If I would fail to protect you from harm, I'd never be able to live with myself."

"I thought we were supposed to make decisions based on love, not fear," she reminded him.

"I am basing this on love. Without a doubt! Although, there is a humanlike element emerging in my ego that wants you selfishly, and wants our love to last."

"But what about saving planet Earth?"

"After our recent journey, there can be no doubt about this society's fate," he argued. "Your interpretation may differ from mine, but I see things pointing in one direction. The Seattle vision was a warning that came true; that leaves me no choice but to believe this vision of the future will also come to pass. Amber, I believe it is our destiny to be pioneers of a new planet."

"When you talk like this, baby, I almost believe it, too. But you don't understand my family. We're weird, we're not dysfunctional! We actually like each other."

"We can always come back for visits," he suggested.

"Yeah? As long as there's something left to visit."

"What purpose would it serve if we stay and die with everyone else? Don't you want to stay in this incarnation for a while longer?"

"A long while longer," she affirmed.

"Then remember the way you felt, standing up on that rock ledge, full of confidence and itching to show it. Secure in the knowledge that you could do it, sail off that cliff and dive into the pool."

"Yes, okay, but that's different," she replied with a laugh.

"No, it isn't. You just have to let go and trust."

Amber eyed him skeptically. "But isn't it a cop-out? To just blast out of here and leave everyone else to sort out the mess?"

"Maybe later we can help provide the assistance needed to restructure the planet and reseed life. Maybe that's the true nature of our mission."

"Yeah, and maybe I'm like the coquí frog," Amber replied. "You take me away from my home and I just might stop singing, and die," she said.

"I told you once before that you weren't from here."

"I know, but that's ridiculous. I have the birth certificate and a pile of photographs to prove it."

"I'm not talking about your body, which of course was given birth by an Earth female; I mean the spirit that animates it. Your soul is not from here. Most of the spirits who people your planet have cycled through many human incarnations, but this is your first time around.

You are a Crawl-in, a Pleiadian soul who joined a baby girl in the womb and agreed to forget she was an angel."

Amber frowned, trying to process this news. "I crawled in from the Pleiades, huh? What about you?"

He smiled. "Through my multidimensional travels, I've glimpsed many of my past lives. This is my first time in this section of the universe, too. We are kindred spirits in more ways than one."

"Pleidian soulmates?" she asked softly.

"Except that we ended up in different races, from different planets. Now we have a chance to rectify that situation." Blue squeezed her hand and leaned toward her. "Come with me to the Pleiades. Don't you feel we're being guided in that direction? If it's truly a part of our heritage, traveling there should trigger joyous recognition."

Amber pondered this for a moment, all the while hooked by his earnest blue stare. She thought of her family, her friends, and her familiar haunts. She thought of the shaky condition of the planet Earth. When her thoughts turned to Blue, she knew there was no going back to the woman she used to be.

"So when is the ship coming to pick us up?" she asked.

30

You Ascend Me

Nervous?" Quinn asked, briefly glancing away from the road to look at Amber in the Camaro's passenger seat.

"Naw. Why would traveling a few thousand light years to a star cluster in the Taurus constellation make me nervous?"

"Look, it wouldn't take much prompting for me to turn right around and take your ass home," Quinn threatened. "Insane to be driving around in the dark, with the wind coming up and this storm on the way! Why do you have to leave tonight?"

"Ask the Commander. He's the one always rushing things," Amber said.

"Well, I haven't noticed you slamming on any brakes. Where did you tell your parents you were going?"

"I tried to tell my mom the truth, but when I mentioned the Pleiades she thought I said 'the Pyrenees' and was all excited that I was going on a European vacation. I figured I'd let it slide so she wouldn't be expecting immediate phone calls and postcards."

"Uh-huh. In other words, you wimped out. And what about your dad?"

"He's a little torqued that he still hasn't met Blue in person, but I think he's secretly impressed from the TV coverage and Dab's article this morning. He laid some more words of wisdom on me, but it was real strange, not his usual cynical self. He said, 'There is nothing to fear but fear itself.' I've been hearing that a lot lately."

"Yeah, well, it's a little tough to feel that way with all these traffic lights blowing around," Quinn interjected. "It doesn't seem like a good night to fly."

"Blue says that won't effect the ship, since we'll be going through the fourth dimension."

"They don't have wind in the fourth dimension?" Quinn sputtered a laugh.

"No time or space, either," Amber reported. "It's pretty hard to imagine what they do have."

"Well, honey, it boggles my mind for sure. And what are you going to do about your house and all your things?"

Amber shrugged. "For now, I gave the key to Krystalee and took the goldfish to my parents' house. If I don't come back you guys can have whatever you want."

"Oh, great! We divide up your belongings and leave you lost in space? I don't think so," said Quinn emphatically. "Listen, if Blue doesn't bring you back, I'm personally coming up there to kick his butt, and I'm just the one to do it."

"I know that's right," Amber snickered.

"We're almost at the address he gave you, and I still say that intersection is nothing but a gigantic parking lot."

"Not any more," Amber informed her, staring through the windshield.

"Oh my God," Quinn exclaimed softly. Half a block ahead, she could see that the corner formerly consisting of a vast expanse of asphalt was now lined with stately trees.

The street was practically deserted, and for once there was plenty of parking space by the curb. They pulled over and got out of the car, the wind immediately whipping Quinn's braids and spinning Amber's hair into an auburn cloud.

"These aren't like any trees I've ever seen in Arizona," Quinn said, watching the wind strafe through the deciduous leaves. "How does he do this stuff?"

"Never mind that; how do we get in?" Amber scanned the dark facade of foliage. "Hey, I think I see a light down that way. Come on."

"That's all you're taking?" Quinn asked, eyeing Amber's tiny backpack as they hurried along the sidewalk.

"Blue says he can manifest anything we need up there, but just in case I packed my vitamins, a couple novels, and as many tampons as I could fit in." The red seaglass heart she had tucked safely in her pocket.

"Yeah, don't leave home without 'em. There may not be a convenience store on the other side of the galaxy," Quinn remarked.

They reached a gap in the trees and discovered a lighted walkway that led inside. At first Amber thought there were candles lining the path, then realized that was impossible, given the weather conditions. She stooped to investigate and discovered one of the familiar Martian bug-light globes nestled in the grass. "We're definitely at the right address," she announced.

"What about Krystalee?" Quinn asked, looking up and down the empty block.

"She'll be here. Dab wouldn't miss this for the world," Amber said. "Let's just go in a little way and check things out." The thought of being minutes away from Blue sent her pulse into a brisk trot.

Quinn agreed and they began to follow the path, the surrounding trees bending and rustling in the stiffening breeze. It was like taking a midnight stroll in a botanical garden, with flowers and plants growing in profusion on either side. They crossed a stone bridge over a gently gurgling creek, then wound through a dense stand of evergreens. Amber automatically began to look for fairies in the underbrush.

Finally they emerged onto an open meadow, a softly-curving dome of green, surrounded by dark trees on all sides. The sphere-lit path climbed up and ended at the top of the slope.

"This certainly looks like a UFO landing strip to me," Quinn said. "Your man has a definite flair for the dramatic."

"Not to mention the suspenseful. Where the hell is he?" Amber scrutinized the sky and was amazed to see blazing stars when there had only been clouds before.

"Don't leave without me!" a voice cried from the darkness. They turned to see Krystalee and Dab jogging out of the woods. She was brandishing a champagne bottle and he was lugging a huge camera bag.

"Damn, girl, you can't leave the planet without drinking your Dom!" Krystalee panted as she rushed up. "Good thing I remembered it, huh?"

"Yeah, because I sure forgot about it," Amber said. "You are truly amazing!"

"Well, you don't need food and drink; you're living on love." Krystalee pulled a stack of plastic cups from her jacket pocket. "The rest of us need good bubbly!" She handed the glasses to Quinn and attacked the cork, quickly launching it with a loud pop.

"By the way, Amber, how does Blue make a park out of a parking lot?" Dab asked as he set up a tripod.

"Maybe it's a holographic insert," Amber replied, helping Quinn hold the cups while Krystalee poured. "I saw something like it in the Martian headquarters, only on a smaller scale."

"Come on, Dab, toast time," Krystalee interrupted.

The four of them stood in the whipping wind, raising their cups of wine. "Here's to new adventures in a new world," Quinn began.

"I'll drink to that," Amber said, and they all took a sip. "Wow! This is delicious. Almost as good as Blue's kisses."

"Gives new meaning to the phrase, 'No 'pagne, no gain,'" said Krystalee, taking a hefty swig.

"Amber, you have to keep a journal up there and figure out a way to transfer it to me," Dab proposed. "No doubt there'll be a couple best-sellers' worth of information in the first week alone!"

"Yeah, you can call it, 'I Married a Martian,'" Krystalee giggled. "Oh, shit! I almost forgot! You're not gonna believe this, Amber, but your wedding stone came back in the mail today. Is that perfect timing or what?" She reached in her purse and produced the woven headpiece.

Amber took it and held it out in her hand. Already it seemed like an icon from an ancient past. She looked up to thank Krystalee, but her friend was now staring skyward.

"I think your ride's here," she said.

There was no mistaking the flaming dot, descending too fast for any human-made craft, and they all watched it as if in a trance. Then the details became visible as it approached, glowing with a silvery-white light. It was shaped like two pyramids, tips facing and intersecting each other, giving the illusion of a star with stubby prongs. When it was situated directly above the center of the meadow, it hovered briefly, completely filling the sky.

"I think you're gonna need a bigger lens," Krystalee whispered to Dab.

They all shielded their eyes, watching in shock as the enormous craft slowly descended and touched its nether tip to the ground. The entire clearing was lit up as if hosting a silvery forest fire.

Amber looked around and saw that hers were not the only tears flowing. "It's so unbelievably awesome!" she exclaimed.

"*Totally* awesome!" Krystalee concurred. "And you're getting *in* that thing?"

Amber looked at the ship, perched on the sloping lawn's zenith. Her mind grappled with the idea that her future lay inside.

Dab was snapping photographs frantically. Amber turned to Krystalee and Quinn, and suddenly she could see their energy fields, dancing with myriad colors. Quinn's halo had orange streaks erupting from her head like solar flares, and Krystalee was bathed in a mellow shimmer of pink and green.

Amber turned back to the ship, searching for a sign of Blue. Now that the moment had arrived, it was going to be very hard to leave her girlfriends, her family, her Earth.

"Well, get on up there," Quinn advised. "If he had a horn he would've honked it by now."

Amber threw her arms around her friend's muscular neck. "Damn, I'm gonna miss you."

Quinn squeezed back, crushing Amber against her. "I meant what I said; come back soon for a visit or your old man will have me to answer to."

"Deal," Amber said, wiping her eyes. She faced Krystalee, took her wrist and pressed the wedding stone and headpiece into her hand. "Sell it and become a millionaire," she suggested. "I don't think I'll need it where I'm going."

"No shit?" Krystalee's face registered joyous surprise. "Wow, thanks Amber!" They embraced, clinging together.

"Bye, Dab," Amber said, hugging him, too. "Sure was nice to meet you."

"Oh no, the pleasure is all mine," he insisted. "Give my regards to your husband."

Amber nodded, turned, then stared for several seconds at the enormous craft. She started up the path, the wind swirling around her and picking at her clothes. Halfway to the ship, she looked back at her friends, who waved and lifted their champagne. Her gaze swung back to the waiting mothership. No matter what lay beyond in the vast reaches of the galaxy, if Blue was around she would at least have plenty of good loving. She hurried toward the light.

The brilliant glow of the ship was so bright, she had to squint and protect her eyes with her hand. Then she saw him, striding out of the beaming rays like a divine apparition. But instead of dazzling raiment, he was dressed in jeans and a plain T-shirt, just like the day her tire went flat and blew up her life. Amber ran to him, thinking what amazingly wonderful scenery he made.

"Glad you could make it," he said, grinning, gathering her up and giving her a wet smack on the lips. "You look beautiful, too."

Amber's heart was full of intense and conflicting emotions. Looking up at the ship while he held her, she struggled to conquer her doubts.

"You're trembling," he said, tenderly kissing her cheek. "I know the feeling; don't forget, I've never been away from Earth, either. But it's all in perfect order. Come on, let's go inside."

He took her by the hand and led her up a glowing gangplank to the interior of the ship. From where she stood the craft seemed almost transparent, and she could see all the way out to the end of each point of the star.

Blue slipped his arm around her, and Amber felt her body and soul suffused with a deep contentment. Maybe it was coming from the light that emanated from every surface around her, maybe it was the power of Blue's proximity, but she felt as though she were sitting in the most comfortable chair in the universe, with no desire to move. All traces of fear and doubt had vanished.

She reached up for a kiss, reveling in his scent, the taste of his lips, and the sweet satisfaction of pressing his body to hers. "This could be a long trip; hope there's a bed on board."

A happy, easy laugh rumbled through him. "You wild, wonderful Earth woman!" he exclaimed, hugging her tightly. "I love the way you think. But this trip shouldn't take long. In fact, there really won't be much time involved at all."

"Don't tell me we're already there!"

"No, they're waiting for my signal. We depart when you feel ready."

"I don't get any readier than this," she declared, looking him in the eyes.

"Good," he said, then paused to telepathically contact the unseen pilots.

The craft pulsed, and she yelped in surprise. Blue laughed softly, stroking her hair. "We're on our way home," he whispered.

The ship shuddered again, levitated slowly, then streaked up in the starry sky and out into the cosmos.

About the author

Kerry Lou is an incarnated spirit currently residing in a third-dimensional earthsuit. Her intention is to assist in the planet's transformation, in whatever way Mission Control deems appropriate. This book is a facet of that ongoing assignment.